How Far
MY FIRST TWO THOUSAND YEARS

THOMAS MANN:—*Author of "The Magic Mountain"*
". . . Audacious and magnificent."

LUDWIG LEWISOHN—*Author of "Upstream," "The Island Within," etc. writes:*
"The book is in both substance and method of the highest originality; it is both fascinating and brilliant; the historic pageant is unrolled with a colorfulness and clearness that astonish me. And I am delighted too by the play of implicit wit, the quaint malice of the innuendos, the symbolical pattern sustained throughout."

DR. A. A. BRILL, *psychoanalyst.*
". . . fascinatingly interesting and instructive . . . very ingenious conception and treatment of the various psychological and philosophical themes. . . . I am particularly impressed with your ingenious way of presenting the various phases of psycho-sexuality. . . . A great work."

GERTRUDE ATHERTON, *Author of "Perch of the Devil," "Black Oxen," etc.*
"It is a remarkably interesting idea to present the pageant of the world as it unfolded before the eyes of the same man during two thousand years. Also, to keep him a young man instead of a doddering gray-beard. It is like reading a series of entrancing short stories with the added interest of logical sequence. Your erudition is amazing, and it is presented in a manner that lures one on and on, as well as inducing the pleasant belief that one is learning something really worth while. It is a big thing to have attempted, and as far as I have gone there is certainly nothing to cavil at."

BENJAMIN DE CASSERES:—
"The book is gorgeous in its epigram and cold satire. It is one of the most brilliant books of sophisticated world-wisdom ever written. It sums up the case of the intelligence against Life. Isaac Laquedem is the Ulysses of the Brain."

SALOME
THE WANDERING JEWESS

MY FIRST TWO THOUSAND
YEARS OF LOVE

GEORGE SYLVESTER VIERECK
AND PAUL ELDRIDGE

WILDSIDE PRESS

*TO
GRETCHEN
AND
SYLVETTE*

CONTENTS

I. King Herod is in High Spirits - - My Little Stepbrother is Circumcised - - I am Neglected - - Tides of the Blood and Tides of the Sea - - Slaves of the Lunar Rhythm - - I Challenge the Moon ... 17

II. Scandals at Court - - The Roman Captain Throws out his Chest - - I Disguise Myself as a Boy 24

III. I Discover the Secret Passage - - The Spear of King Herod - - Is a Boy Worth more than a Girl? - -A Royal Moralist - - Why did you Strangle My Grandmother? - - May I Kill my Little Brother? - - Was Cleopatra a Woman? - - The Sin of David - - Roman Peccadillos - - The Wife of all Husbands and the Husband of all Wives - - "Your Beard Tickles me, Grandfather" - - I Dance - - My Body is a Spiral of Fire 28

IV. My Cousin Agrippina - - Between Hammer and Anvil - - "Could I have a Baby?" - - Immemorial Pastimes - - Sportive Lads - - The Sea of Galilee - - My First Glimpse of Isaac - - The Straight Legs of Boys - - The Petulance of John - - Isaac Flaunts his Manhood - - "Would you Exchange Places with the Queen?" - - The Impudent Son of a Cobbler - - I pass under the Yoke of the Moon 37

V. My Stepfather the Fox and My Mother the Vixen - - I am Betrothed to My Cousin, Philip - - Elephants Loaded with Gifts 47

VI. My Bridal Night - - The Heritage of Herod - - I Dream of Isaac - - I am Philip's Prisoner - - The Battle of the Sexes - - Philip Dies in his Sleep - - The Dead Cannot Tattle 51

VII. I Become the Aspasia of Judea - - "If Salome were a Man!" - - My Second Husband Makes a Startling Discovery - - Between Ecstasy and Despair - - The Slave of Creation - - The Fruit of My Womb - - My Baby Dies - - God Shows no Mercy to Woman 58

VIII. My Mother's Itch for the Purple - - The Tragic Mask of Herodias - - Futile Matchmaking - - I Go into the Desert - - The Dance of Life - - I Meet Jokanaan, whom they call John the Baptist 66

IX. New Troubles and New Messiahs - - The Wiles of the Sanhedrin - - The Tetrarch Invites - - "I Am Elijah" - - The Gibes of the Baptist - - "There is neither Man nor Woman in Heaven" - - My Mother's Annoyance - - I Save the Life of Jokanaan 73

X. The Hospitality of the Tetrarch - - I Discuss Theology with the Prophet - - Vessels of Corruption - - The Cousin of Jokanaan - - The Obstinacy of Aunt Mary - - A Eunuch's Heaven - - I Woo in Vain - - The Curse of the Prophet - - "Too Vile for the Grave" - - I Meet the Ghost of Jokanaan - - I Swoon 81

XI. Past Mistress of Passion - - Storms in My Heart - - I Visit Jerusalem - - I Flirt with Pilate - - An Ancient Resentment - - I Proclaim War 91

XII. Cartaphilus, Aforetime Isaac - - The Cobbler's Boy is a Roman Captain - - I Recollect a Dream - - I Drop my Fan - - A Jew Recognizes his Own - - Cartaphilus Blanches - - I Hide My Face upon his Chest 95

XIII. The Broom of Time - - A Boyish Lover - - Woman or Witch - - Lilith, Destroyer of Men - - I Consult a Greek Leech - - Life Without End - - The Judgment of Daniel - - I Set out for the Hills as a Muleteer 102

XIV. Why not a Female Messiah? - - The Magic of Jokanaan - - I Dance Defiance - - I Hide a Large Chest of Jewels 110

XV. I am a Young Merchant -- I Hear an Ancient Prophecy -- The Princess Salome Enters Arabia -- I Learn the Secret of Herbs -- Persistent Virginity -- Royal Courtship -- A Prophecy Fulfilled   112

XVI. Arabia Totters -- The Languishing Harem -- "The King is Dead, Long Live the King" -- My Seven Arabian Husbands -- The Royal Midwife -- A Prisoner of Life -- Bark Without Compass   116

XVII. My Youngest Husband -- "Are You Afraid of Death, Salome?" -- Wife -- Mother -- Womb of the Earth -- The Knife Thrust -- Fate, My Attendant 123

XVIII. I am the Wandering Jewess -- A Pilgrim of Truth -- The Perfect Circle 130

XIX. I Meet Apollonius -- Fellow Wanderers -- Jesus and his Cousin in India -- The Miracle of the Vacuum -- Ultimate Wisdom -- Endless Chain -- The Mystery of the Baptism -- Shall Woman Conquer? -- Roads to Nirvana 132

XX. Shall I Seek Cartaphilus? -- Waters of Experience -- Into the Heart of the Hurricane 139

XXI. My Thirty-fourth Husband -- The Venus of the Triple Gate -- Dharma, Arta and Kama -- The University of Love -- And on this There is a Verse -- Unendurable Pleasure Indefinitely Prolonged -- Creative Rhythm -- This is not Love -- A "God" Honors our Temple -- Cartaphilus Blunders -- The Secret of the African Aphrodite -- Jealous -- The Keeper of the Sacred Tortoise -- I Meet Lakshmi, the Wife of Vishnu 141

XXII. Cartaphilus in Bronze -- The Cauldron of Time -- Woman the Scapegoat -- Lakshmi Shakes Her Head in Palmyra 159

XXIII. Zenobia Haggles -- Woman Rule -- "Where is the Soul, Longinus?" -- We Depart for Egypt 162

XXIV. I Discuss Immortality -- The Frontiers of Nature -- No Respite from the Moon -- The Tyranny of the Womb -- The Enemy of Woman -- World Mother 170

xxv. Cleopatra Speaks - - The Emerald Scarab - - Do the Dead Hate the Living? 179

xxvi. Aurelian Makes an Offer - - The Moon-Struck Queen - - Zenobia Pays - - Echoes of Roman Trumpets - - I Leave with Lakshmi   182

xxvii. Lakshmi Returns to Her Husband - - I Am a Monk of Buddha - - The Temple of Apollonius - - The Trail of Cartaphilus - - I Meet Zenobia in the Suburbs - - A Roman Courtesan - - A Nordic Gospel of Woman - - Ulric, Son of Alberic - - My Barbarian Husband   186

xxviii. "Why do the Young Men Look at you with Desire?" - - Time Stands Still for Me - - Last Embrace - - Hatshopsitou Sits at my Feet - - Cartaphilus is a God - - The Camel of a Thousand Humps - - I Seek a New God in Africa   194

xxix. The Temple of Ca-Ta-Pha - - The Flaming Eyes of Kotikokura - - The High Priest Snores - - I Am a Goddess   203

xxx. The Reign of the African Amazon - - The Dynasty of Woman - - A Broken Cage - - Lakshmi Breakfasts on a Young Cabbage   208

xxxi. My Matriots - - Girlish Wrestlers - - I Reverse Sex Morality - - I Choose a Male Harem - - I Battle the Moon - - Kotikokura is Lonesome - - I Deny My Sex - - I Burn My Temple - - Ca-Ta-Pha Returns - - The Revolt of the Male   213

xxxii. The Ancient Spell - - Cartaphilus the Incorrigible   221

xxxiii. We Ride into the Desert - - Kotikokura, the Missing Link - - Man and the Moon - - Predestined Mates - - Ultimate Goals - - Fantastic Fumes - - Who Am I? - - The Parting of the Ways - - Four Immortals   224

xxxiv. Christ Rises in Fulda - - Perished Loves and Perished Gods - - Idun, Goddess of Spring - - Love at First Sight - - Like a Bewildered Butterfly - - Honey or Holy Water - - "Last Night in My Dream You Gave Me Roses" - - I Make a Resolution   235

xxxv. Misgivings and Confidences - - "If I Gave You Immortality Would You Accept it?" - - I Kissed Her Eyes Filled with Tears   243

xxxvi. The Conquest of Athens - - "I Am your Shadow, Salome" - - Joan Dreams of a Triple Crown   247

xxxvii. I Bargain for the Miter - - The Papal Secretary of State - - The Eloquence of Ducats   251

xxxviii. Pope Joan - - Joan Capitulates to the Moon - - Romano Craves an Audience - - I Am the Pontiff's Procuress - - A Blushing Pontiff - - Joan Powders her Nose - - The Vatican Cackles - -The New Leprosy - - A Question of Syntax - - The Rage of the Cardinals - - A Nun Condemned - - The Judgment of Pope Joan - - Heresy or a New Gospel? - - War   258

xxxix. Drought - - I Corset His Holiness - - Non Papa Sed Mama - - The Pope has a Baby - - A Miracle of Hell - - Defeated by the Moon   281

xl. I Am the Red Knight of the Crusades - - A Sepulcher or a Cradle?   288

xli. I Meet My Lover - - Old Love and Old Magic - - The Apparition of the Nazarene - - The Wraith of Jokanaan - - "Would You Relinquish Life?" - - The Kiss of Ten Thousand Women - - The Antics of Kotikokura - - The Moon is a Frightened Bride - - The Education of Lakshmi - - Crossroads   290

xlii. I Walk Along the Seine - - I Meet a Black Cat - - The Message of the Black Spaniel - - Master Fulton Takes off his Finger - - Diana, Mistress of Hell - - Le Juif Errant qui Passe - - The Wandering Jewess - - Master Bellonius Drinks with Me - - I Buy a Soul - - The Witches' Covenant   301

xliii. Monsieur Pierre de Bourlemont Returns to Domremy - - The Poet Without a Sweetheart - - Robert in Love with My Shadow - - I Disappoint My Chief - - One Hundred and Sixty Dishes   315

XLIV. The Witches' Sabbath - - The Mask of the Goat - - The Viceroy of Hell - - Holy Duality - - Phallic Pæans - - Swollen Earth - - Hell's Sacrifice - - A Banquet of Corruption - - An Ancient Friend Returns 320

XLV. The Table Manners of Lakshmi - - I Search for a Redeemer - - Reverie 330

XLVI. Maid, Boy or Fairy? - - The Hide and Seek of Life - - "I Am Jeanne Darc, Seigneur" - - Jeanne's Freedom from the Moon - - I Plan a Campaign 335

XLVII. I Am St. Michael - - Jeanne Doffs Her Clothes - - The Real Miracle - - Gilles, Lord of Retz, Writes a Play - - Bluebeard's Library - - Bluebeard's Minion - - White Magic and Black - - Gilles de Retz Dreams a Dream - - The Boy-girl of Domremy 340

XLVIII. The Apprehensions of Lakshmi - - The Arsenal of an Immortal - - Jeanne is Wounded - - Jeanne's Tantrums - - The Moon Waxes over Jeanne - - Gilles de Retz Craves an Audience - - I Discuss White and Black Magic with Bluebeard - - Why I Never Loved Gilles - - The Martyr's Crown for Jeanne - - A Crucifix of Fire - - I Get Me to a Nunnery 350

XLIX. Festive Cordoba - - I am Burned at the Stake - - The Unrepentant Tortoise - - The Inquisition Singes the Devil's Tail - - I Destroy My Golems - - The Moon is Unconquered - - Lakshmi Yawns 363

L. Damn Queen Elizabeth! - - Slave of the Moon? - - Hunting with the Queen - - The Queen's Favorite - - Lingering Preludes - - Elizabeth is not a Woman - - Elizabeth is not a Man - - I Solve the Secret of Elizabeth 373

LI. I am Madame de la Rochouart - - I Start a Letter to Cartaphilus - - A Note from Count Leopold - - "He Loves Me, He Loves Me Not" - - Love on the Danube - - Ferdinand Sneers - - I Marry Leopold - - I Have a Rival - - Leopold's Assignation - - Metamorphoses

- - I Transform Myself into a Boy - - Eros Melts into Aphrodite - - Lakshmi's Neck Points East 383

LII. I seek the Lama, Cartaphilus - - I Enter Tibet - - Cartaphilus Worships his Navel - - The Insolence of Kotikokura - - I am a Nun of Buddha - - The Bad Taste of the Gods - - The Paralytic East and the Blatant West 402

LIII. The Court of Catherine - - Platonic Friendship - - Thirteen Lovers - - Catherine Bares Her Heart - - The Stallions of the Empress - - The Malice of the Waning Moon - - Villages of Potemkin - - Wandering Jewess and Wandering Turtle 413

LIV. I Create a New Eden - - I Dream of Homuncula - - I Am the New Mother - - My Secret Laboratory - - Mechanical Golems - - Homuncula Sleeps - - The Carrier Pigeon 438

LV. I Arrive in London - - Century-Blossoms - - My Victorian Lover - - The Metamorphosis of Kotikokura - - My Birthday Cake - - Cartaphilus Rules the British Empire - - I Have a Tiff with Dizzy - - The Mystery of Lord Beaconsfield - - I Am Received at Buckingham Palace - - Queen Victoria Is Not Amused - - I Make a Promise - - I Embark for Buenos Ayres 446

LVI. My Wedding Feast - - The Epithalamium of Nature - - Finding and Seeking - - Lakshmi Lays an Egg - - Nuptial Confidences - - I tell the Truth - - My First Two Thousand Years of Love - - Homuncula Smiles - - The Tyrant of the Skies - - The Food of Homuncula - - Homuncula, Our Daughter 466

LVII. News from Mme. Curie - - The Failure of Mrs. Eddy - - Mistresses and Kings - - Lakshmi's Elevator - - Kotikokura Rocks Himself - - The Gift of Adam - - A Fortunate Divorce - - Supersex - - "I Am I and You Are You" - - Kotikokura Growls - - The Deafness of Lakshmi - - A Thunderclap - - Homuncula Wakes - - Wild Oats and Wild Blossoms - - Cartaphilus Discovers a Fan - - The Fisherman's Ring - - "Salome, I Love You" - - The Road to Truth 478

LVIII. Vague Premonitions - - Homuncula Moves - - The Disturbance of Lakshmi - - The Jealousy of Kotikokura - - Homuncula Rises - - Earth Protests - - Paradise Lost - - Life Without End and Love Without Flaw 488

SALOME
THE WANDERING JEWESS

CHAPTER ONE

KING HEROD IS IN HIGH SPIRITS — MY LITTLE STEP-BROTHER IS CIRCUMCISED — I AM NEGLECTED — TIDES OF THE BLOOD AND TIDES OF THE SEA — SLAVES OF THE LUNAR RHYTHM — I CHALLENGE THE MOON.

My grandfather, King Herod, was in excellent spirits. He had just received permission from Rome to assassinate his sons, Aristobolus and Alexander.

His step was firm. He barely leaned upon the arm of the High Priest as he mounted the marble stairs leading to the reception hall.

The spears of the King's guard rose high above the heads of the assembled guests — court officials, priests, ambassadors, in gala costumes. Trumpets flourished. Swords flashed.

In the courtyard slaves ran, enormous platters of victuals balancing upon their heads, or tall vessels overbrimming with wines, pressed obliquely against their hips. Stewards shouted orders in Latin and Hebrew. The Captain of the Royal Guard, a young Roman, tall, handsome and vain, followed by his company, marched up and down, watching alertly for assassins, spies and uninvited guests.

I was standing, vexed, irritable, ignored, against the enormous palm-tree, whose supple branches tapped the roof of the palace. Hatiphah, my nurse, had warned me not to enter the hall. Her absence seemed interminable. I could not understand why I was neglected, why I, Princess Salome, was not allowed to partake in the merriment and festivities.

I restrained my impulse to burst into tears, a manifestation of feeling too plebeian, unworthy of a princess, even though the princess was only nine years old.

Nevertheless, I determined, whatever the consequences, to disobey instructions. I rushed up the stairs and dashed in.

My grandfather was seated upon the throne. He was dressed in his regal robe, over which flowed like two white lakes his beard, separated at the middle of the chin, and terminating in sharp points like spears. Upon his head he wore a crown the shape of a triangle, studded with precious stones. His eyes, small and keen, and his long aquiline nose gave him the appearance of an eagle about to swoop from the clouds. His hands, thin and yellow, weighted with rings, were pressed into his knees, as if crushing his prey.

The guests were silent or whispered to one another.

I made my way to the throne, and called: "Grandfather!"

Instead of welcoming me as usual with a kiss, even when he was discussing matters of state with Cæsar's ambassadors, he merely touched my cheek with his finger-tip and said: "Not now, Salome, my child."

Herod Antipas, my stepfather, Tetrarch of Galilee, glared at me, his lips trembling with rage.

"Run off," he said sharply, "go to your nurse. It is unlawful for you to be here."

I felt crushed. The guests towered over me like mountains. I was about to rush out of the room, when one of the priests entered carrying upon a small silken pillow my brother, Antipater, whom I now saw for the first time. He had been wavering between life and death since his birth, three weeks previously, and I had not been allowed to see him.

Antipater was naked. He reminded me of a plucked turkey. His face was flattened-in and almost shapeless, like the dolls of the slave-children. He cried weakly like a kitten. The violent hatred I had borne him since his birth turned to disgust.

I hid myself behind a pillar and watched.

The priests chanted and the guests repeated at intervals:

"Amen!" The High Priest walked slowly toward the throne and deposited my brother upon the knees of my grandfather. Herod scrutinized the infant. His face changed from joy to aversion.

A slave approached with a golden platter holding bandages and a knife of stone. He was followed by the Mohel, a man whose yellow beard was as entangled as the threads of wool that cats play with.

The Mohel clasped his hands together, and chanted in a voice husky with phlegm: "Boruch Atoh Adonoi Elohenu, Melech Haolom! Praised art Thou, King of the Universe, Who blessed us with Thy blessing and Who directed us to perform the rite of circumcision!"

Antipas breathed deeply, and muttered indistinctly: "Boruch Atoh Adonoi Elohenu, Melech Haolom! Praised art Thou, King of the Universe, Who blessed us with Thy blessing, and Who directed me to bring my son into the covenant of Abraham."

The Mohel tested the sharpness of the knife with a hair plucked from his beard, and addressed the audience. "Hereby I perform the act of circumcision!"

He bent over the infant.

Suddenly Antipater uttered a shriek, followed by moans.

The Mohel bandaged him, and gave him to a priest, who carried him out of the hall. A slave followed, holding aloft the platter on which lay the knife spotted with blood and the orlah.

The guests congratulated my stepfather Antipas and my grandfather, while slaves offered goblets of scented wine.

Hatiphah my nurse appeared suddenly, out of breath. She was an old woman with a thin face but a protruding stomach — the token of frequent maternity.

"Salome, where have you been?" she asked peevishly.

I did not answer. She took my hand, and pulled me gently out of the hall.

When we were out, I said: "I saw my brother."

"I told you not to go in. It's not for girls to see such things."

"I am not a girl. I am a princess!" I answered proudly.

She laughed, without emotion or reverence.

"What did they do to him?" I asked.

"Antipater was made a Jew. Thank the Lord he was strong enough at last. It was necessary to postpone the feast twice!"

"How did they make him a Jew?" I asked.

"A part of his body was sacrificed to God, that the rest might be preserved, and his power increased."

"Did they do that to me, too, when I was a baby?"

My nurse laughed. A dimple flitted vaguely across her wrinkled cheek.

"The African savages circumcise women, but we, thank the Lord, are Jews. God has given us wisdom and understanding."

We walked in silence for a while.

"But, Nurse, if they did not circumcise me, am I a Jew?"

"You are a Jewess, my dear," she sighed.

I was perturbed.

"Isn't it just as well to be a Jewess as a Jew?" I asked.

"Have you not heard the prayer of the men? Boruch Atoh Adonoi Elohenu Melech Haolom, shelow ossani ishoh! Praised art Thou, O Lord, our God, King of the Universe, Who hast not made me a woman!"

"But I shall be queen!" I said defiantly.

"Maybe, but you will still be a woman."

"What's the difference between a man and a woman?"

"God has made man in His own image. He made us out of Adam's rib. We are incomplete. They say"— and her voice dropped to a whisper—"that we really lack nothing. But whereas man's virtue is visible, ours is hidden," she sighed.

I stamped my foot.

"I am not a woman! I don't want to be a woman! I shall not be a woman!"

She laughed and looked at me sadly.

"Don't laugh! I will not be a woman!"

"There are certain things that even a queen can't do or undo, Princess. There are certain things that even queens must endure."

"What must they endure?"

"What a child! She wants to know everything. Wait until the right time. Don't shake the tree until the fruit is ripe."

"Tell me, Hatiphah," I said, cajoling.

"Is it not enough for you to learn how to read and write and dance and play the harp and speak the language of the Romans and Greek and Hebrew?"

"Tell me!"

I patted her hand, whose knuckles protruded like miniature humps of camels.

She looked at me, and smiled. "Oh, my little pest!"

"What must queens endure?"

"The proudest queen, like the lowest menial, must endure the tyranny of the Moon."

"What gives the Moon power over us?"

"I do not know. I only know this: even as the Moon rules the waters in the sea, so she rules the blood in our veins. Womankind is her slave, and, like the ocean, must obey her. The tides of our lives and the tides of the sea are as one."

She touched my chest appraisingly. "Before long you, too, will be the slave of the Moon."

The idea of slavery provoked me.

"I refuse to be any one's slave — even the Moon's."

She smiled sadly, and muttered something I could not understand.

"I challenge the Moon!" I cried. "Salome will conquer the Moon!"

I looked up. Amorphous and almost colorless, my foe, the Moon, spotted the clear sky. It seemed to me I could almost crumple her in my hand.

I shook my fist. "I shall conquer you!" I shouted.

Hatiphah laughed. "My dear, it's hard enough to conquer man, who is so near us, and is only flesh and blood, even when he's a king. How can you conquer the Moon?"

"I shall conquer her!"

Unwilling to argue any further, she said: "Perhaps."

"Is man the slave of the Moon, too?" I asked suddenly.

"Man is the child of the Earth. The Earth is a good mother."

To change the subject, she said: "Come, let's see the peacocks Herod sent as a gift to celebrate the circumcision of your new-born brother."

"No, I don't want to see them! I hate them!"

"They are marvelous birds, with legs the color of roses and eyes that glow like amethyst beads."

"I hate them!"

She smoothed my hair. "Poor little one!"

"Don't you pity me! I am a princess!"

"We all come and go the same way," she replied, undisturbed. "When I was a midwife I brought hundreds of children into the world, and I have seen hundreds of people die — even queens and kings. There is no difference."

"Was I as ugly as my brother when I was a baby?"

"You were extraordinary even then, Salome. Everybody said: 'What a lovely child!'"

Grateful, I pressed my head against her bosom.

"They say that beautiful babies grow into ugly children. I don't believe it. You grow more beautiful every day."

"Am I the most beautiful princess in the world?"

"I shouldn't wonder."

She watched me closely, scrutinizing every feature.

"Many a man shall sigh his soul out of his body for you." She laughed.

"Hatiphah, if my brother remains as ugly and as sickly as he is now, can he become king?"

"Many kings are ugly and sick. They say that once in — well, I don't know exactly where now — I'm beginning to forget things so — well, anyhow, they say that in that country, they once made a donkey their ruler. But the donkey was male!"

"Why couldn't I rule instead of my brother if I am stronger and more beautiful and cleverer than he?"

"If he lives, Princess, he will be a man!"

"Then — I shall kill him!" I shouted.

Hatiphah first caught her breath, then slowly shrugged her shoulders, and nodded thoughtfully.

"You mustn't shout such things, Salome. Every wall in a palace is a big ear, listening."

CHAPTER TWO

SCANDALS AT COURT — THE ROMAN CAPTAIN THROWS OUT HIS CHEST — I DISGUISE MYSELF AS A BOY.

I SAT on a stone bench, watching the black swans gliding noiselessly in the large pond, whose waters were replenished ceaselessly by a long thin stream gushing out of the ironic mouth of a satyr.

Behind me in the bushes, two men were whispering to each other. I listened intently, hardly breathing.

"Do you really think that Herod poisoned the High Priest?"

"There is no doubt about it. Every one knows that the chamberlain who placed the fatal cup before his master became a rich man overnight. He says he found a hidden treasure. But everybody knows what that treasure was."

"Is it true that Cæsar granted permission to Herod to kill his sons Aristobolus and Alexander?"

"Of course. The messenger arrived on the day of the circumcision. Herod is fond of snuffing out the members of his family. If Antipas escapes, he's lucky. Why do you think he invited the family here — to witness his grandson's circumcision? It's not the first grandson he has seen circumcised, with twenty wives and maybe one hundred children."

"Why then?"

"You're an unsophisticated young fool. After you've been in a palace for years like me, your eyes will be keener and your ears sharper. The old lion wants to get rid of his brood. According to the heathens did not Kronos, the father of Zeus, gobble up his own progeny? There are animals that destroy their young. Every father knows in his heart that his son is a rival. But only gods and beasts and monarchs dare to devour their offspring."

"I don't think King Herod is quite right in his head." He made a significant gesture.

"They're all mad. But Herod is dying. So they say."

"And if he kills Antipas, the Tetrarch, who will be King?"

"Who knows? Maybe his other son, Philip, the first husband of Herodias, Salome's father. But they say he's a weakling, who relinquished his wife to Antipas without saying boo!"

"I'd pay any one who would be good enough to relieve me of mine."

The men laughed.

"I hear that Antipas has given orders to return to Galilee within twenty-four hours."

"If so, he may be able to draw his head out of the jaw of the morose old lion."

"I overheard one of the Romans say that they are leaving tonight. The King won't know of it until they are miles away."

"They say the people are storming the Temple. They don't want the new High Priest."

"That may be true, too. That's the way it always begins. First the Temple, then the Palace — then the Romans will be after us."

"It'll be lucky if you and I keep our heads on our necks."

"Oh, our heads aren't so precious to be in danger of toppling. But it is always well to keep one's legs in good trim."

They left. I dared not stir for a long while. When I turned around, they had disappeared.

My head whirled. The world seemed filled with murder and menace. Was it true that my grandfather wanted to kill us? Kill me? I could not believe it, I would not! I loved my grandfather. He was the only person I really loved. He would never kill me! Besides, they said he was dying, and we were to run away the next day. Then we were not going to say good-bye to Herod. I might never see him again.

I rose. I must see my grandfather. I must ascertain if what those men said was true.

Should I ask Hatiphah to take me to him? No, I was certain she would refuse to do it. She would probably stop me. And as for my mother, ever since the birth of that ugly little brat, my brother, I had hardly seen her. She neglected me entirely. She would certainly not allow me to go.

I would go alone. I dimly remembered the secret passage to the King's private hall.

The sun set suddenly, and I felt chilly.

I walked toward the gate. In the courtyard, the slaves fell upon their faces, and the soldiers of the guard stood at attention. My pride returned, and new courage.

I approached the Captain. He saluted.

I had not until then fully realized how powerful he was. The muscles of his arms seemed on the point of breaking the metal armlets which encompassed them. His bare hairy legs were like massive pillars. He noticed my look of admiration, and threw his chest out. The breastplate rose slowly, majestically. He smiled, and his white teeth glistened.

I forgot my purpose for a while, and looking up at him, I asked: "Are all Romans as strong as you?"

"Many of them are strong, Princess."

"You must be the strongest, or Antipas would not have made you his Captain."

Unconsciously, I touched his arm. Its suppleness and hardness intrigued and delighted me. I dug my finger-tips into his flesh. My cheeks suddenly turned hot.

The Captain looked at me, his eyes half-closed and a trifle blurred.

"What makes you Romans so strong?" I asked.

He grinned. "We are not stunted."

I did not understand, but I scented in his remark a slurring reference to the ceremony that made my brother a son of Israel.

The Captain, as if reading my thought, winked.

"Are you not circumcised?" I asked innocently.

He laughed heartily.

A little irritated, I repeated my question.

"No, Princess. We Romans retain the full bounty of the gods," he answered proudly, conscious of his undiminished masculinity.

I was perplexed. Hatiphah had told me that the Jews were circumcised to give them strength. I began to suspect her omniscience.

The thickening dark recalled me to my purpose.

I took a step or two toward the gate.

The Captain stopped me.

"The Princess is not permitted to wander beyond the gate."

"Why not?" I demanded imperiously.

"By order of the Tetrarch."

"If I were a boy you would let me through," I said angrily.

"If you were a boy, you would not be Princess Salome."

His reply gave me an idea.

Half an hour later I passed him by, dressed as a page. He made no attempt to halt me, whistling unconcernedly to himself as he walked up and down the terrace.

CHAPTER THREE

I DISCOVER THE SECRET PASSAGE — THE SPEAR OF KING HEROD — IS A BOY WORTH MORE THAN A GIRL? — A ROYAL MORALIST — WHY DID YOU STRANGLE MY GRANDMOTHER? — MAY I KILL MY LITTLE BROTHER? — WAS CLEOPATRA A WOMAN? — THE SIN OF DAVID — ROMAN PECCADILLOS — THE WIFE OF ALL HUSBANDS AND THE HUSBAND OF ALL WIVES — "YOUR BEARD TICKLES ME, GRANDFATHER" — I DANCE — MY BODY IS A SPIRAL OF FIRE.

The Moon cast her reflection at my feet like a polished mirror. I remembered what my nurse had told me of her tyranny over woman. Dressed as a boy I felt that I had outwitted her. I was certain that the only real difference between man and woman resided in the dress; and I wondered why this had not been discovered sooner. I vowed that if ever I was a ruler, I would emancipate woman from her yoke by decreeing uniformity of attire for both sexes.

I walked quickly and soon left the garden behind me. Making my way through an artificial thicket of bushes, I entered the secret passage which my grandfather had shown me in a confidential mood on my first arrival. "Kings," he whispered into my ear, "must have two roads, a highway to triumph and a secret passageway to escape."

My nurse had said once, laughing, that I must be descended from the birds and the ants, so well did I remember topography, and so keen was my eye.

The underground tunnel was chilly and damp like a well,

and every now and then something crawled at my feet that made me stifle a shriek. At intervals, too, my feet stepped on piles of leaves, blown there by the winds of dead autumns, anxious to preserve something from the general bankruptcy of Time.

I was on the point of running back, but my pride and my masculine garb spurred my courage. I whistled a naughty tune which I had learned from the soldiers, and hurried on.

Suddenly, unexpectedly, my face struck against a door. I turned the knob quickly, and found myself behind a panel, my nose in the air.

I caught a glimpse of King Herod, reclining on a couch. The King detected my presence. As my head emerged he instantly hurled a spear at me, which remained transfixed in the wall behind me. Underestimating my diminutiveness in the flicker of the torch, he missed me by a thumb!

I leaped forward into the light, crying: "Grandfather! Grandfather!"

Herod stood up, looked at me intently, and burst into a nervous laughter, which sounded like neighing. His hand trembled, and his beards moved up and down rapidly.

He scrutinized me from head to foot, then opened his arms. I buried myself in his embrace.

"My little Salome! My joy, my consolation," he whimpered. "I thought it was one of my sons."

I breathed freely.

"But why are you dressed as a boy?"

"I couldn't come to see you otherwise. They didn't permit me to leave the palace."

"Fools!"

His appearance had changed considerably in the few days that had elapsed since the circumcision. His face was much paler, his eyes dimmer. The edges of his lips, protruding beyond the beard, were stained with an uncanny blue.

"Grandfather, you never told me how I look as a boy!"

He bent forward, and squinting, examined me critically.

"You make a pretty good boy," he said meditatively, "but the hips and knees betray your sex. Come here, my child, sit near me."

I seated myself. Herod patted my chest.

"Yes — for the time being you can pass as a boy," he muttered to himself. Then suddenly, frowning, and pulling at one of his beards, he asked: "When are they leaving?"

"Who, grandfather?" I asked, trembling a little.

"Antipas — my son — and your mother?"

"I don't know, grandfather!"

"They think I don't know what's going on. They think I am mad. They think I'm dying. Don't they, my child? Tell me!"

"I ——"

He interrupted me before I could utter another sound.

"I may be dying," he cackled, "but as long as there is breath in me, I am King!" He stamped his scepter angrily. "I have eyes everywhere. Let them go, whenever they please. Had I wanted their heads I would have chopped them off long ago. The fools! Your grandfather, Salome, is not an ogre. A great king must kill many people, even his own flesh and blood. The safety of the State is more important than consanguinity. A king must carry out the mandates of Justice!"

He looked at me quizzically.

"Were you afraid to come to see me, Salome?"

"No, grandfather!"

"Didn't they try to poison your mind against me?"

"I don't care what they say. I love you, grandfather!"

"My dove," he said, pressing me against his chest. "You are flesh of my flesh and blood of my blood. The rest are all strangers — traitors — ingrates — conspirators — spies." A tear rolled down his cheek into his beard. He closed his eyes and moaned.

"They are right, I'm dying," he whispered, and immediately spat, fearful of challenging Fate.

"No, grandfather! You will live forever."

"Would you like me to live forever, my treasure?"

"Yes! Yes!" I exclaimed.

"You aren't like the rest!"

His eyes brightened. "You should see the tomb I have built for myself!"

He rubbed his hands, bloodless and thin like things of wood.

"I'll show it to you to-morrow, Salome! It's more beautiful than the tombs of the Cæsars! It was finished yesterday, and it cost as much as a tetrarchy! You may go with me tomorrow, and see the golden coffin."

Exhausted, he leaned his head upon the pillow for a moment, then, too proud to show weakness, he straightened up.

"Stay with me, Salome, until I die."

"I'll stay with you always, grandfather!"

"Antipas may go unmolested, if he leaves you with me," he said, as if addressing a messenger.

He looked at me intently. "If you were really a boy!" he sighed.

"Grandfather," I said, placing my hand upon his knee, "is a boy worth more than a girl?"

"Salome, woman is weak. Being weak, she depends on treachery and wheedling. I am fond of the sex. I had ten wives, every one of them worthless." He sighed. "It was my sad duty to put five of them to death. They were strangled. One of them was your grandmother, Mariamne. She was beautiful!"

He gazed dreamily into space.

"Did you get permission from Rome to strangle your wives?"

"Permission to kill my wives, my women?" He wheezed dryly.

"Why did you strangle my grandmother?"

"That is so long ago, Salome, I don't remember the details. You may be sure that I had good reason. I am sorry for Mariamne. Perhaps she was faithful to me. But her mother, Alexandra, was a wicked woman. I had to execute both mother and daughter. Still, I always observed the proprieties. Every execution was legal. It was too bad about Mariamne," he mumbled, forgetting my presence.

A thin stream of saliva trickled down the corner of his lip. He wiped it with the hem of his royal robe, and combed his beard with his fingers.

"My son Antipas is a fool!" he exclaimed suddenly. "Herodias will be the ruin of him. He permits her to rule him!"

"Who will be King after you, grandfather?"

"Who?" he shouted. "Who? No one is fit to wear my crown! My sons will fight for it like hungry dogs for a bone. Cæsar will destroy them. I have lived in vain. I made Judea a mighty country. I raised a temple greater than Solomon's. I built bridges and theaters and amphitheaters, rivaling those of Athens and Rome. I organized a powerful army. I made the Jews feared and respected by other nations, although — the dogs say that I am not really a Jew. They have the effrontery to call me an Idumean. Alas! My women were unworthy of my seed! Their wombs delivered monsters and weaklings. I shall disinherit them all!"

"How about my little brother?"

"A worthless brat."

"Grandfather," I lifted my face imploringly, "may I kill him?"

Herod laughed, playfully slapping my thigh. "You are a true descendant of the Herods, my little lamb. But as for the young prince — we needn't anticipate Nature. He is the spawn of rottenness. He'll never live long enough to call his father by name. When they put the little worm on my lap, I felt like throwing him back at them!"

"Why can't I rule Judea, then, grandfather?" I asked jubilantly.

He looked at me, frowning and tightening his lips until they vanished entirely in his beard.

"Woman rulers bring ruin."

"But Cleopatra ——"

"She ruined Egypt."

"They say she was a great queen."

"Don't speak to me of her! Cleopatra wasn't a woman!"

I looked perplexed.

"She was neither man nor woman. Look at her lovers, Cæsar and Antony. They were great generals. I'll grant you that — but were they men? Cæsar conquered the world, but a young slave boy conquered him. Cæsar," he lowered his voice confidentially, "was the wife of every husband and the husband of every wife. His own legions made sport of him in a shameful ditty."

Herod drew a deep breath, and frowned.

"And as for Antony — why, I had to put to death your handsome granduncle, the High Priest, to save him from the concupiscence of Cæsar's boy friend!"

I asked for elucidation.

Without paying the slightest attention to my questions, Herod exclaimed: "Shameless creatures! Sodomites all! I am not a stern moralist. I forgive those that transgress for the love of woman. But I have no mercy for abnormal proclivities. No!" he panted, "give me manly men and womanly women!"

He stamped his scepter several times.

For a while I feared that he was really mad.

Some perverse imp prompted me to parade my Biblical knowledge before Herod.

"Grandfather," I said, suddenly remembering a lesson in holy lore, "was there not one member of our family who praised the love of man above the love of woman?"

Herod's face grew livid with rage.

"I hope not. My children may be assassins, adulterers, thieves and parricides. But, thank God, they are not perverts!"

"Grandfather, don't you remember King David?"

My lips rehearsed a familiar passage: "Oh, Jonathan, my brother, very pleasant hath thy love been unto me, passing the love of woman."

"Salome," Herod replied, frowning severely, "I regret to say that my historical investigations have forced me to the reluctant conclusion that my royal ancestor, King David, was guilty, in his youth at least, of grave derelictions. I attribute his own tribulations and the misfortunes of Israel to his sin. I advised my sons if they discovered that they were unduly fond of any companion of the same sex, to chop off his head at once. Both morality and sound statesmanship demand this sacrifice. It is the only way in which a king can preserve that unclouded judgment which he needs in his profession. But I beg of you, Salome, not to pursue this subject. Such matters are not fit for the lips of a pure young girl. And you are a girl, even if you are dressed as a boy."

He caressed my thighs, squeezing them with his hand.

"Be a woman, Salome," he said softly, his voice somewhat husky.

"Am I as beautiful as Cleopatra?"

Herod snarled angrily. "Cleopatra was not beautiful. She had no breasts; you will have beautiful breasts some day." He placed his gout-knotted fingers convulsively upon my bosom. "The Queen of Egypt lacked those attributes of femininity which alone make woman seductive to real men. She came to my couch naked when she stayed in my house with your unforgettable grandmother. I ordered my slaves to take her away. I did not desire her esoteric caresses. When she saw that her outlandish contraptions could not seduce me, she made trouble for me in my house and in Rome. Alas, I was always a constitutional monarch! I took the advice of my ministers and permitted that bitch to depart. If I had killed her it would have been better for Rome and for Judea!"

He stopped, and looked at me intently.

"You, my dove," he said, "you are beautiful. Your eyes shall pierce the hearts of real men, and their souls shall become entangled in the gold of your hair. They will hang to your lips as bees hang to the flowers that deliver the sweetest honey. They will cling to your body more desperately than they will cling to their lives."

He kissed me. I laughed.

"Why are you laughing?" he asked, shaken with sudden rage.

"Your beard tickles me, grandfather."

He grinned, opening his mouth wide. I recoiled, as if I had witnessed the opening of a tomb. From the shriveled colorless gums two black teeth hung precariously. I remembered the strong white teeth of the Roman Captain.

"You are a woman, Salome! You will rule kings."

"I want to rule a country like you."

"Nonsense. You will lead your husbands by the nose. They will dance attendance on you like clumsy bears."

He laughed, slapping his thighs, then exhausted, placed his head upon the pillow on which a large golden eagle flapped his wings in the unsteady light of the torch. For a long time he remained perfectly still, and I thought he had fallen asleep.

He mumbled something. I could not understand what he said, but the words Mariamne, Aristobolus, traitors, spies, assassins, parricides, occurred again and again. I pulled at my fingers nervously.

Suddenly he rose.

"Salome!" he called, as if I had been in the farthest corner of the room.

"Here I am, grandfather!"

"I am glad you came, my child. I am sad to-night. Dance for me, my love. Will you dance for me, Salome?"

"Yes, grandfather!"

He clapped his hands.

Instantly, an Ethiopian slave of colossal proportions, who could have slain the Roman Captain with one blow, appeared and fell upon his face, his palms outstretched.

"Let there be music!" Herod commanded. "Gay music! I do not want to see the musicians. Let them hide behind the screen, their faces turned to the wall."

The slave waited another moment, then rose, and walked out backward. His shadow stretched across the floor. It bent over the ceiling, and finally made a wide pool, like the reflection of a great black moon, about his enormous feet.

The music played a wild tune which throbbed in my veins like hammers. I raised my arms, turned my torso, and lifted myself upon my toes.

"No! No! Salome! Dance for me — as a woman!"

I threw off my cloak and the rest of my clothing, and stood naked in the flickering light.

Herod breathed deeply.

"Come here, my love."

I approached him. He cupped my breasts and pressed

them in his fists, until I uttered a stifled shriek. His hands ran over my thighs and legs.

"Dance! Dance!" he exclaimed at last, his voice cracked.

He placed his chin upon his scepter, which he held at an angle, and his hands around his beards, and watched me. His eyes flamed and flickered, like the last embers recovered from a heap of ashes.

The music pulsed in my blood. I was the drums. I was the cymbals. I was the harp. My body was a spiral of fire.

Herod's gloating eyes became dimmer and dimmer. The wind blew the ashes across the embers once more.

Suddenly, Herod's scepter fell clattering to the floor.

I danced on, conscious only of the rhythm that singed my body.

Slowly, softly, Herod slipped.

I stopped, breathless.

His eyes, glaring like bits of scratched marble, rolled backward. His jaw fell. I had seen the same expression on a dying animal.

Terrified, I gathered my clothes and fled, pursued by the music....

CHAPTER FOUR

MY COUSIN AGRIPPINA — BETWEEN HAMMER AND ANVIL — "COULD I HAVE A BABY?" — IMMEMORIAL PASTIMES — SPORTIVE LADS — THE SEA OF GALILEE — MY FIRST GLIMPSE OF ISAAC — THE STRAIGHT LEGS OF BOYS — THE PETULANCE OF JOHN — ISAAC FLAUNTS HIS MANHOOD — — "WOULD YOU EXCHANGE PLACES WITH THE QUEEN?" — THE IMPUDENT SON OF A COBBLER — I PASS UNDER THE YOKE OF THE MOON.

My cousin, Agrippina, sought refuge at Tiberias where Antipas constructed a palace rivaling in beauty that of Herod, who, only a few years dead, had already become a legendary figure as heroic and romantic as that of King David or King Solomon.

Her mother's paramour, a Nubian Prince, had strangled her father, and recently, weary of his mistress, directed his fiery attention to the daughter.

Caught between the anvil of her mother's jealousy and the hammer of the Nubian's passion, Agrippina fled to our court.

My mother and my stepfather, engrossed in intrigues with the Roman Court to obtain the royal crown of Judea, hardly noticed her presence, and for the time being, at least, my cousin was safe.

Agrippina and I became inseparable friends. I was her superior in music, dance and the foreign tongues, but she, only one year older, comprehended many things that bewildered me.

The Orient blossomed in her. She had black hair, heavy hips, full breasts, and eyes languorous and melancholy.

I was taller, thinner, suppler, still wavering between child and woman, but ready now, by many signs, to blossom forth.

Agrippina admired my exotic appearance — my burnished hair, my eyes which changed from gray to green tinged with violet, my straight chiseled nose, my mouth sensuous but not heavy, thinning upon occasions into a disdainful or ironic smile.

Hatiphah, my nurse, asthmatic and bored with tetrarchs, tetrarchs' wives and a wilful young princess, whom she loved but who pestered her with innumerable queries, considered it a boon to be allowed to catch her breath tranquilly in the shade of palm trees. Agrippina and I took long walks in the gardens and beyond them upon the hill which raised its scrawny neck above the Sea of Galilee.

It was very warm. We lingered in the perfumed waters of the pool, constructed after the model of the Roman Imperial baths. Two slave-women lay upon their stomachs on the upper steps of the basin, their buttocks glowing in the reflection of the sun.

We reclined upon the wide benches, holding hands.

"Are you old enough to marry, Agrippina?" I asked.

Agrippina smoothed her hair with the tips of her fingers.

"Of course," she answered with a coquettish twist of her head, which I tried to imitate. "I should have married a year ago. If the Nubian had not interfered with the messengers and matchmakers, I'd be a mother by this time."

"Could I have a baby?" I asked naïvely.

Agrippina smiled. "Not yet, Salome. You must wait until the Moon stirs your blood."

"The Moon shall never govern my blood!" I exclaimed martially.

My cousin looked at me in amused amazement. "You don't want to be an Amazon?"

"Who are the Amazons?"

"They are African women who stunt their motherhood

that they may become merciless warriors. They are horrible creatures, neither men nor women, shapeless and hipless. They have beards, and their voices are like the neighing of horses. They say they eat human flesh."

"I shall conquer the Moon, Agrippina!"

"The Moon makes us mothers, Salome," she said very seriously. "I want to be a mother, don't you?"

"I don't know," I said meditatively.

We remained silent for some time.

Agrippina caressed me gently after the immemorial fashion of girls. My blood mounted to my face. My body was in flames. My eyes closed slowly. She embraced me and kissed me, and whispered incomprehensible words.

The slaves, their faces between their palms, watched us, unperturbed, like statues.

Agrippina stood up, and sighed deeply.

"I am restless, Salome. Let us go out."

I clapped my hands, and summoned the slaves to anoint us.

We walked slowly, our arms placed around each other's waists, conversing gravely about marriage, love, and man and woman.

As we reached the top of the hill, we heard laughter and shouting. Several youths were swimming in the sea. We hid behind a bush and watched.

"Not so far out!" one of them ordered, waving his arm above his head.

They all turned around and swam swiftly to shore, their hair pasted on their necks and faces, their mouths pouting like fish suddenly cast upon the sand.

One of them, a burly fellow, whose powerful muscles heaved restlessly beneath his dark hairy skin like impatient stallions, laughed uproariously. He beat his taut stomach like a drum, as he pointed his stubby strong finger at a thin boy who screened himself bashfully in the manner of a woman caught unawares. The rest joined in taunting the boy's modesty.

"He'll be *bar mitzwah* next week, and look at him!"

"Turn around, David!" the big fellow, who seemed to be the ringleader, bellowed.

David faced the others, trembling.

"What a puny, undersized stripling!" Agrippina whispered contemptuously.

Antipater, my brother, would have been like this, had he lived, I thought, glad that the prophecy of my grandfather had come true.

Jeering him, the others indulged in anatomical comparisons and diversions in the fashion common alike to the civilized male and the savage.

Their gutter language, echoes of which I had caught in the gossip of the soldiers, assumed new and precise meanings.

The bewildering array of masculinity flustered and horrified me. I pressed against Agrippina, whose eyes were riveted upon the ringleader.

The boys boasted of women they had seen naked or had embraced, and laughed. The ringleader, disgusted, spat.

"Woman!" he sneered, his face screwed, until nothing remained of it except the heavy tip of the nose, and two tiny glittering eyes, like beads. His coarse and disgusting jests and descriptions made the others, including David, howl with laughter.

"Look at David laughing!" one of them said, mockingly. "Why, if your mother put a woman's garb on you, you'd be nothing but a girl yourself!"

"I am *not* a girl!" David shouted with an unmistakable gesture, striking his tormentor a violent blow on the nose.

"Even that puny thing," I said bitterly, "resents being called a woman, Agrippina."

A sudden pain made me catch my breath. I clenched my fists and tightened my eyes.

In the general turmoil that followed, David leaped into the sea, followed by the others.

Two lads who had been watching the rest disdainfully remained on the shore.

They were both tall and well-proportioned.

"I hate the rabble, Isaac," one of them said.

"We must seek another place for swimming, John," the other added.

John's head was tawny like a young lion's; curls encircled Isaac's head like heavy clusters of black grapes.

"I can outrun, outwalk, outdo every one of them, including that big ape," Isaac said, throwing out his chest. "Look at me, John! Feel my muscles! They are like newly tempered steel. Look at my legs, straight like those of the statues of young athletes the Tetrarch brought from Rome. Every limb articulates perfectly."

John looked at his friend admiringly.

"I wish I were as strong as you, Isaac! My arms are too soft."

Isaac touched his arm. "What you need is training and practice. You'd make an excellent wrestler. Your muscles are supple, but a trifle soft. They are like Mary's. I touched her arm while she was drawing water from the well. My hand slipped and passed across her breasts." He sighed. "Her breasts are full and hard like large apples."

John turned his face away, angrily.

"Are you jealous, John?" Isaac asked half mockingly.

John shook his head.

Isaac placed his arm around his shoulder. Then, suddenly, as if to divert the conversation and his friend's thoughts into other channels, he said: "Let's see who can throw farther."

Isaac raised a flat round stone, the shape of a discus, and hurled it with all his might. It cut the air and shone in the sun like a strange silver bird, wings clasped. It whizzed past us ominously, and missed my face by an imperceptible distance.

My heart stood still. "The fool!" I muttered.

"You've outdone the Roman discobolus at the fair of Bethlehem last week, Isaac."

Isaac threw his head back arrogantly.

"I would have tried my skill at the fair, if Jesus had not intruded with his unbearable preaching. I should not wonder if one of these days he joins some wild-eyed Messiah living on locusts."

"He is a student of the Torah, Isaac, wise beyond his years. He is only a few months older than we."

"He should devote more time to his father's trade. Better a good carpenter than a poor rabbi."

"Do you remember the parable about the trees which he recited at Bethlehem? Even the Chasidim were bewildered."

"He is an excellent plagiarist. We have enough poetasters among us!"

Isaac screwed his nose disdainfully.

John was hurt.

"Oh, I know you are fond of Jesus," Isaac said, placing a hand upon his friend's shoulder "And so am I. But he is not a comfortable companion. He does not love the Earth. He despises the joys of the body. He sneers at the most innocent of pleasures ——"

"He drinks with us, Isaac," John said apologetically.

"Drinks!" Isaac laughed ironically. "He raises his cup as if he toasted Jahveh. It isn't the juice of the grape of the Earth which he drinks, but of the vineyard of Heaven."

John was pensive.

"He prattles of eternity. I am interested in the moment as it passes. We are creatures of a single day, John. Let us not be fools! Let us pluck the flower before it withers!"

"You are right, Isaac," John sighed. "We are as fleeting as dreams," and, raising a stone, he hurled it with all his strength.

Isaac smiled and ran his hand across his friend's back.

"It was very well done. Only you must do it this way — not that — like a girl. Mary would throw it the way you did."

John was hurt.

Isaac laughed. He threw his arm around the boy's neck. His fingers were caught in John's curls like silver fish in a golden net.

"Her hair is just like yours, color and texture."

"Stop speaking about her, Isaac! I beg you."

Isaac withdrew his hand. "Very well. We'll forget her." He gently stroked John's nose with his forefinger, half patronizing, half caressing. Had I been John I would have struck his impudent mouth. But John smiled, content to be humored.

They seated themselves upon the grass.

"Your legs, at least, are certainly not like a woman's, John!" Isaac said scrutinizing his friend. "A woman's legs are never straight like yours or mine. Women are all knock-kneed."

The youths laughed, and bent their knees inward in imitation of women. I looked at my cousin. Her legs were almost deformed in their plumpness. Mine were straight like a boy's. On closer scrutiny, however, I saw here and there suggestions of that feminine imperfection which seemed so detestable to the two louts.

The youths continued to make allusions to feminine anatomy, and imitate woman's physiology with coarse gestures. Their speech gradually descended to the level of the other boys. Their words splashed in the gutter.

"Are all men so vulgar among themselves?" I asked.

Agrippina nodded vaguely, evidently not understanding what I said. Her ears were strained to catch every sound the boys uttered. Her eyes sought every angle of their anatomy.

"Our Rabbi claims that woman was made for motherhood, not for beauty," John said. "Woman without man is a pot without a cover."

Isaac laughed. "Woman was created out of man's rib. But the Lord was in a hurry to keep the Sabbath, and forgot to complete his task."

"She's an unclean animal, Isaac," John said with a gesture of disgust. "Every month there are times when it it unlawful to touch her. That's what the Rabbi said."

"Nature gave woman breasts to feed the world, but man she gave brains to rule it," Isaac said with a finality which exasperated me.

"The fool! It isn't true, Agrippina! We have brains. We are man's equal!"

Agrippina did not answer. She pressed against me, sighing.

The youths were silent for a while. They stretched out, their arms underneath their heads. Their bodies dazzled.

The hairs under Isaac's armpits were black flowers, under John's flowers of gold; and petals of black and gold dropped gently upon their laps.

"Did you see the Roman lady again?" John asked.

"Which Roman lady?"

"The one who smiled at you in your father's shop."

Isaac spoke with an affected air of disdain. "I took her sandals to her house. She paid me, then threw her arms around me and kissed me."

"Did you like it — very much?" John asked with a sigh.

"You know how quickly I respond to every delightful touch," Isaac remarked smilingly.

"It gave me a thrill, but," he added, "to tell the truth, it wasn't half as pleasurable as the kisses of the women that come to me in my dreams."

John dropped his hand softly upon his friend.

"It's a pity, Isaac, that you must ply your father's trade, with your fine body and keen mind."

Isaac raised his head.

"Never, John! I'll never break my back over the last, don't fear."

"What else can you do?"

"I'll enter the army."

"Oh, the Tetrarch's army —" John said with a deprecating air.

"The Tetrarch? Why should I serve a servant when I can serve the master? The Tetrarch is nothing. They say he had to wait nearly three years in Cæsar's antechamber before the Imperator consented to see him."

"Guttersnipes!" I muttered angrily, my pride wounded. "It isn't true, Agrippina! That's all gossip!" I said, anxious to restore our family dignity. But I knew he was right. He had voiced my own secret thoughts.

"How can you serve in Cæsar's army, Isaac?" John asked. "You forget that since our eighth day, Israel claims us for her own."

"As long as the nose isn't Israel's, we can hide the rest."

They laughed.

My pain reasserted itself. I could not catch my breath.

"Am I not worthy of a Roman Captain?" Isaac asked. "Look!"

"Even of the Imperator himself!"

"They say we Jews have greater endurance in love than the Gentiles. We are compensated for our sacrifice to Jahveh."

They slapped each other's thighs and laughed, in the immemorial fashion of boys.

"There is a woman in Jerusalem who knows the thousand secret love-ways of the Hindus! Did you hear of her, Isaac?"

"Let's visit her, John."

"Oh, she ministers only to wealthy merchants."

"We'll offer her what few wealthy merchants can offer!" Isaac said, boastfully flaunting his youth in the sun.

"Would you exchange places with a queen, Isaac?"

"Not with all the queens in all the world!" he exclaimed defiantly.

"Do you really think that woman grieves so much over her sex?"

"She should, John. Don't we thank Jahveh every morning in our prayers that we are not born women?"

"I know. But a queen — that's different. I saw Herodias, the Tetrarch's wife, the other day, reclining on the silken pillows in the litter which was carried on the shoulders of four black slaves. She did not seem particularly miserable because she wasn't a man."

"Oh, Herodias!"— he lowered his voice —"she is just a contented fat cat, and her daughter, the princess Salome, is nothing but a vain kitten."

"They say she is beautiful, Isaac."

"She will be, perhaps. She is still too scrawny and shapeless."

"Anyhow, if she invited you to her royal couch, you would not refuse, would you, Isaac?"

"A man of honor never refuses."

They laughed uproariously.

"Impudent son of a cobbler!" I exclaimed.

Agrippina placed her finger against her lips. "Sh! Salome! They'll hear you!"

The agony became violent. I wished to run back to the palace, but I was nailed to the spot. My face was in flames. My legs trembled. I moaned.

The youths remained silent. Their bodies were taut and rigid, their faces set.

I breathed heavily. The cramp bent me in two.

"Agrippina!" I moaned, grasping her arm, "Agrippina! I am poisoned! I am dying!"

My cousin started, frightened. Her hands wandered over my body. She smiled and embraced me.

"You are not dying, my dear. You are this day a woman!"

CHAPTER FIVE

MY STEPFATHER THE FOX AND MY MOTHER THE VIXEN — I AM BETROTHED TO MY COUSIN, PHILIP — ELEPHANTS LOADED WITH GIFTS.

"The fox! The fox!" The crowds grumbled and muttered as we passed by in our chariots.

Antipas whispered anxiously into my mother's ear: "Do you hear what they call me, Herodias?"

She smiled. Her eyes, which had blazed a moment ago, as she glared at the people, closed slowly until only two luminous green lines pierced her long lashes.

"Whom do geese fear most, if not the fox? Be a fox indeed, Antipas! Renard is crowned king in preference to the lion. Don't you remember the fable?"

Antipas nodded, and smiled. His long face, his lifted brows, his thin lips shivering over small yellow teeth, gave him the appearance of the cunning animal which was responsible for the nickname. His face, however, belied his nature. He was neither shrewd nor over-ambitious. He would gladly have relinquished all royal power for spicy food, strong wine, a well-chosen harem. But Herodias goaded him on, cajoled him, scolded him, excited his jealousy. Her passionate nature once seeking many goals, now concentrated upon a problematic, and at best but a shadowy, crown.

"The fox! The fox!"

"Let the geese cackle, Antipas! They have lost their keepers. Only two of the forty-seven of them still retain their heads to prove to Judea and to Rome that you alone are the real master, not the Sanhedrin or the High Priest. Let them cackle!"

"For the time being, at least, we have peace," Antipas said meditatively.

"And before long you will have the crown, my lord!" Herodias added, placing her plump, knuckleless hand, heavy with jewels, upon the protruding knee of her husband.

The procession continued. In front of us the trumpets played triumphant airs. Behind us Roman officers and Jewish dignitaries rode on horses and elephants.

For weeks I had been in turmoil, but now I grew suddenly calm, impassive. My wedding, which was to be celebrated as soon as we reached Iturea, where my future husband, Philip, ruled, became a thoroughly impersonal matter to me. I yawned, reclined, closed my eyes. I listened to the rhythmic hoofbeats of the animals, to the shouting and the grumbling of the populace, to the flourishes of the martial music. My heart was still, as if I had witnessed a mediocre performance at the theater.

At the same time, however, I realized that this calm was but a thin coating of ice over a stormy sea. I dared not press into it, for fear I should be tossed about violently, drowned. I was a princess — I must keep my royal bearing. My dignity must surround my passion, like a hard kernel protecting a precious fruit. Besides, a husband, I was told, mistrusted a consort in whom the blood coursed too hotly.

The dust rose and fell back upon the road, like the silken hem of a vast yellow toga blown by the wind. The sun stretched drowsily, unmindful of the wheels that tore through it and the hoofs that stamped upon it.

Philip was the son of my stepfather Antipas and Cleopatra of Jerusalem, and a grandson of Herod the Great. I had seen him on a few occasions at Herodium and once at Tiberias. He was still young, tall, and almost beardless. If he resembled my grandfather at all, I could not tell. I had always known Herod as very old, and his enormous white beard covered the larger part of his face. Perhaps there was something in the eyes of Philip that reminded me of my grandfather, but I could not recall the latter's eyes, except as they were when I saw them for the last time staring at the ceiling like bits of unpolished silver.

Once I spoke to Philip about Herod.

"A ruler should be more continent," he moralized angrily.

"He was a great King!" I said, indignant at choosing what he considered a weakness to characterize his whole personality. "He was the greatest king of Judea since David and Solomon, and none of his sons or grandsons were worthy of his scepter," I added.

He did not make any remark. He tried to comb his reddish beard, but only succeeded in scratching his chin. The gesture, however, reminded me of my grandfather, and I smiled to think how pathetically it had degenerated.

Philip's first two wives died soon after the marriage; the third one was in exile, ostensibly because she was barren. Rumor accused her of infidelity with a Roman officer.

Whispers had reached me for some time of Philip's desire to marry me, and I was not at all surprised when my mother informed me of the final arrangement. She warned me, however, to be sure to bear him a child.

My nurse, who was present, grumbled something about hens' eggs being unable to hatch chickens without assistance.

"Keep your mouth shut, or lose your tongue!" my mother remarked angrily. I laughed, ignorant of the meaning of the conversation. My nurse looked at me, nodding pathetically.

My heart was a cauldron of emotions. Two, however, predominated — that I soon would unravel the mystery of the things I had only known by name or by vague innuendoes, and as a Tetrarch's wife, I might become queen, and some day rule. I saw myself a new Cleopatra.

Philip allowed us a month in which to prepare my trousseau and all other necessary matters. It was a month of restless activity at Tiberias, and much sleeplessness on my part. How I should have appreciated the company of Agrippina! Alas, she had been recalled by her mother. A few weeks later she died, according to report, from an ague due to the bite of a snake. The true cause of her death I guessed too well. The hammer had struck the anvil. The Nubian had his will, and her mother her vengeance.

As we reached the gates of Iturea, my heart began to beat violently again. The ice which covered the sea of my emotions cracked, and its waves dashed against me, threatening to drown me.

Philip came to meet us, dazzling with jewels and gold, followed by his staff, and elephants loaded with gifts for us and our guests.

We alighted, and after exchanging appropriate greetings, we retired to our rooms, to rest and prepare for the ceremony and the festivities of the morrow.

CHAPTER SIX

MY BRIDAL NIGHT — THE HERITAGE OF HEROD — I DREAM OF ISAAC — I AM PHILIP'S PRISONER — THE BATTLE OF THE SEXES — PHILIP DIES IN HIS SLEEP — THE DEAD CANNOT TATTLE.

TREMBLING, his face streaked with white lines, his chin shivering like a goat's whose beard has been plucked by mischievous boys, Philip grumbled —"Just like the others! Just like the others!"

My face in flames, my body aching from the futile embrace, I moved toward the wall, trying to cool myself on the part of the bed which had not been touched.

Philip walked up and down the immense room, breathing heavily. Although he was tall and rather muscular, he reminded me of the urchin, David, who was mocked by the boys swimming in the Galilean Sea. Resenting my scrutiny, Philip screened himself.

"Immodest hussy!" he shouted.

I covered my face with my hands.

He approached the bed, and beat against it frantically.

"I suppose you'll be coveting a Roman soldier — like the others!" He waved his fist over me. "I'll slash your throat, if you do, do you hear?"

Cowering against the wall, I muttered, frightened —"I shall not, my lord! I shall not!"

He threw a cloak over his body, and clapped his hands. A slave entered and fell upon his face.

"Wine!" he ordered.

The slave brought a pitcher of wine, filled two cups and left.

Philip poured a white powder into the cups, and offered me one.

"Don't poison me, my lord!" I begged, refusing to take the cup.

"It is not poison," he said, laughing a little nervously, like the braying of a donkey. "I shall drink first."

He emptied his cup quickly. I drank mine slowly, still uncertain.

My head whirled. My body twitched. Philip stretched beside me. His eyes swam. His lips and hands pressed against me, bruised me. He muttered words of endearment. His legs were on fire. He gritted his teeth.

Exhausted, he buried his face in the pillow, and sobbed.

I placed my arm around his neck, and whispered: "What is it, my lord?"

He threw my arm off.

"It's my grandfather," he muttered in the pillow. "Cursed be his name! I suffer for his sins. May his tombstone be desecrated by swine!"

He beat his fist against the pillow, and groaned.

I crouched against the other end of the bed, and did not budge.

His groaning subsided. He turned his back to me, and soon snored heavily like a tired animal.

Disgusted, I rose silently and bent my head out of the window to cool myself. In the reflection of the moon two big cats were concluding the eternal battle of sex. I thought with a mixture of irony and disdain of man's vainglorious matinal prayer of thanks to Jahveh.

Suddenly very sleepy, I stretched out upon a couch. I dreamt the scene of David the scrawny lad and the other boys in the Sea of Galilee. But David changed to Philip, and Agrippina became Isaac, who pressed against me. I tried to push him away, but he clung to me.

"I would not take all the crowns of the world in exchange for ——"

He stopped short.

"In exchange for what?" I asked several times, but he laughed, and pointed to Philip, who, to escape the torments of the other boys, and in particular of the ringleader, jumped into the sea. The others followed.

"I shall go away, haughty Princess — but the memory of me shall always haunt you. For I am he who awakened your womanhood. You cannot escape me. All men shall assume the image of me for you. Even if you lived into all eternity, I shall be the male of your dreams. Consciously or unconsciously, you will compare all men to me, and find them wanting, to the extent that they do not resemble me."

"Go away, you cobbler's son!" I groaned, endeavoring by insult to crush the truth of his words.

"A cobbler's son is greater than a queen's daughter!" Isaac said proudly, flaunting his manhood, with the same insolent pride as of yore, and released me from his embrace.

I looked up and saw coming toward me my grandfather.

"Grandfather!" I exclaimed joyously, throwing myself into his arms. "It is you I love, not the cobbler's son!"

"You love us both, Salome. We are one."

He kissed me, his beard covering me entirely.

"No son or grandson of mine is worthy to wield my scepter, Salome!" He raised the scepter to the ceiling, then let it drop to the floor.

I awoke.

Philip was still asleep. Fearing that he might be angry because I had left the bridal bed, I returned quietly. My knees bent almost to my chin, I did not stir. I could not decide which was more detestable, his clamorous snore or his sterile caress.

For two weeks I was a prisoner in the nuptial chamber. For two weeks Philip drank wine mixed with exotic aphrodisiacs, prayed and swore and grumbled and beat the pillows and cursed his incestuous ancestors and their graves, but Nature frustrated art.

One morning he announced that he was summoned to Jerusalem by the new governor.

Pale and weak like a convalescent, I walked alone, slowly, in the gardens of the palace named after my husband, who had built it — a less pretentious structure than that of Tiberias, but beautifully situated upon the peak of a hill. All about its base were the small white houses of Iturea, with balconies almost touching one another. Surrounding the houses like a belt tightened about an enormous belly, and making breathing difficult, the walls of the fortification. To the right in the distance, the Jordan, on which from time to time a fisherman's boat rocked like a giant white duck waddling.

The crimson leaves of the trees, crisp and fragile, waved their noisy adieu to Summer, the fickle Cavalier who still lingered a moment upon the Horizon of Time.

I inhaled deeply the perfume of a thousand flowers, wide open like matrons grown careless of their appearance.

Every now and then a shadow mingled with mine for a moment and vanished. I understood the meaning of my freedom. I was watched by spies at every angle. I was a prisoner of Philip's love!

Philip returned sooner than he had planned. The governor had not yet arrived, he said. The messenger had misinterpreted the summons. I knew that his departure was a ruse to see how I would behave in his absence. He remembered, no doubt, how his other brides deported themselves under the circumstances. Pleased by my conduct, he presented me with a bracelet of green jade.

Our relations were friendly but distant. He never visited me in my rooms, where I spent most of the time reading or playing the harp. My slave-girls were homely and sullen. I was the Tetrarch's wife, nominally, but in reality, his captive.

From my mother I heard nothing. She evidently waited for the birth of her grandchild at the end of the year. The words of my nurse became clear to me. My mother had too much confidence in my charms to awaken passion and power.

What would happen at the end of the year, I began to surmise. Either Philip would announce that I had died suddenly like his first two wives, or he would exile me as a barren woman to some forsaken place whence I could never reveal the truth.

I became restless, but I was very careful not to show any symptoms of my anxiety. Whenever I saw Philip I evinced much pleasure, and manifested a profound appreciation of being his wife.

Once he accompanied me for a walk in the gardens.

"Salome," he said, "what is your idea of a good wife?"

"A good wife, my lord," I answered like a schoolgirl reciting a lesson too well learned and no longer understood, "is a faithful wife."

"That is true, Salome. And should not a wife be a mother?"

"If the Lord wills it."

"Is it not natural for a woman to yearn for children?"

"It is more natural for a woman to yearn to be a good wife."

"That is true, Salome."

He smiled, first gently, then his lips assumed an expression which I could not name, but which cut into me, sharply, like a knife — a knife slashing my throat!

He changed the conversation to other homely unimportant details of the household, to music, and a banquet which was to take place in the palace shortly in honor of Cæsarea that was just finished, and whither he intended to move his court.

My replies did not convince him of my sincerity, but confirmed his suspicions. With the keenness of a man whose mind is preoccupied with one idea, he read beneath my stereotyped remarks a violent discontent and perhaps a violent determination. Had I complained or accused, he would have trusted me more.

I realized that war between us two was declared, and that before long the final battle would be waged. Philip, as well as Herod, knew that it was not necessary to ask permission of Rome to dispose of a woman — but he feared Herodias too much to resort to murder. He was planning something subtler. Perhaps the mischief was already afoot. He would never forgive me for knowing his impotence.

I was walking at the edge of the garden, perplexed and worried. Some one pulled at my sleeve. I turned around, frightened.

"Hatiphah!"

I threw my arms around her, and wept like a little girl.

"Sh!" she warned.

She touched my stomach.

"I knew it!" she whispered, noticing its girlish contour. "Philip is not a man. My poor Salome!" She breathed quickly through her mouth. "I told Herodias — but she would not believe me."

"How did you manage to get here?" I asked.

"No matter. I was right. He shan't do with you as he did with the others. My poor child!"

"Free me, Hatiphah!"

"That's not so easy. But it shall be done. I just wanted to convince myself first."

She asked me a number of questions concerning the topography of the palace, then disappeared among the bushes, with an uncanny swiftness for a person of her age and health.

"The Tetrarch is dead! The Tetrarch is dead!"

Torches flashed, trumpets sounded, the gates were thrown open.

"The Tetrarch is dead! The Tetrarch is dead!"

Iturea flamed with lights. Soldiers, slaves, officers, rushed back and forth, shouting: "The Tetrarch is dead!"

Messengers rode madly to Jerusalem. Others came dashing into the courtyard, the nozzles and bellies of their horses bathed in foam.

I entered the room where Philip lay stretched out. The mourners gathered about his bed made room for me. He was pale and handsome. In death he resembled my grandfather weirdly. I smoothed his brow. The chill made me shiver.

I turned to the people.

My face formulated the question.

"He died in his sleep, Princess!"

Three slaves spoke at the same time, throwing themselves at my feet.

"We heard him groan, and when we entered, he was dead."

I ordered a thorough investigation to determine the cause of my husband's death.

By dawn several slaves were flogged. Leeches examined the blood and spittle of the defunct. But nothing could be discovered.

"It is the hand of God!"

I suspected what human hand had directed the Lord's hand.

I returned to Tiberias. Immediately I asked for my nurse. Herodias shrugged her shoulders. "She's been dead and buried for days now." She frowned as if trying to recollect something. "Yes, it was the next day after your husband — died — which only proves"— she added, with ironic piety —"that death makes no discrimination between the high and the low."

"What did she die of, mother?" I asked, watching her closely.

"It's easy to know why she died, being old and ill, my daughter," she answered.

"She was neither so old nor so ill when I saw her last!"

"When did you see her last?" she asked triumphantly.

"Why — here — before I left."

"Even a King can die in his sleep — though young and strong — in the bloom of life."

I turned away, my eyes filled with tears.

Herodias placed her arm around my waist.

"It's unfortunate — but the dead cannot tattle. Hatiphah died because she knew too much. Do not mourn, my daughter. You will not be a widow long."

CHAPTER SEVEN

I BECOME THE ASPASIA OF JUDEA —"IF SALOME WERE A MAN!"— MY SECOND HUSBAND MAKES A STARTLING DISCOVERY — BETWEEN ECSTASY AND DESPAIR — THE SLAVE OF CREATION — THE FRUIT OF MY WOMB — MY BABY DIES — GOD SHOWS NO MERCY TO WOMAN.

To FORGET the indignity I had suffered at the hands of Philip, I became engrossed in the study of languages and philosophy. My fame spread. I was hailed as the Aspasia of Judea. Scholars sought conversation with me and listened admiringly to my words.

"If Salome were a man," they whispered to one another, "we should have another Solomon!"

Enraged, I retorted, "Woman is man's equal! And when she finally conquers the Moon — she will be his superior!"

They smiled condescendingly, thinking my remark of lunar origin indeed. They reminded me courteously that woman was an afterthought of God.

"Man is created not of mud, but of conceit and vanity!" I protested futilely.

The gallant approaches of admirers I discouraged firmly. In their arrogance, they attributed this to my great love for my deceased husband, which, for the time being, paralyzed my passions. I became the proverbial good woman of the Bible, the model of virtue.

The stubborn insistence of Herodias, however, finally conquered me. I accepted as my second husband, Aristobolus, another son of Antipas. "He," my mother insinuated, "is like Philip only as the bull resembles the ox."

I had hardly seen my husband before our wedding day. He was a hunter of repute and a soldier of valor, always engaged in campaigns against the ubiquitous and perennial enemies of Judea. Short, stocky, a beard as heavy and as hard as iron, slightly rusty, and eyes that were motionless as beads stuck in stuffed birds' orbits, he bore no resemblance whatever either to his grandfather or to his father. Taciturn, monosyllabic, his enormous sword swinging from one side to the other, or stamping against the floor, was more eloquent than his tongue. He was my mother's choice because Antipas had designated him as his successor.

"Salome will be queen," my mother whispered.

Aristobolus appeared in the bridal chamber as he appeared upon the battlefield, resolute, frowning, teeth clenched. His muscles, as powerful as catapults, ready to take a city by assault, locked themselves about me, leaving me breathless. I was too pained, too horrified, to realize what was taking place.

His jaws unclenched, his eyes regained their luster and their immobility. Anxious, however, to achieve the full measure of his lust, he lingered awhile, muttering a few words in praise of my body, and the satisfaction it had afforded him.

He rose and drank at one gulp a jug of wine which a slave had brought in, smacking his lips in perfect contentment.

He laughed ironically. "A virgin!" he snorted. "Poor Philip! —" He never finished the sentence.

Mortified, I glared at him. He threw his cloak over his shoulders, fastened his belt around his waist, and, whistling, left the room.

I buried my face in the pillow.

At dawn Aristobolus joined his regiment, without even bidding me farewell. Assured of his masculine prowess, and far more interested in his horses than in his women, he feared no rival. Unlike his brother, he allowed me full liberty and set no spies to watch me.

From time to time he sent me a formal letter, which always began, like a dreary drum beat: "If you be in health, it is well; I am also in health, with my army," and ended with a few instructions regarding his stable and his armor.

The masculine arrogance and brutality of Aristobolus even more than the impotence and petulance of Philip convinced me that man was an ogre, a monster whom woman must meet embattled.

Everywhere I saw woman's tragedy, regardless of age or rank. Heavy shackles bound her soul and body. I read books and manuscripts in a dozen languages, trying to discover the ax which would break the fetters. I discovered nothing. All wisdom was masculine for masculine benefit. Always woman was considered the slave, the empty and meaningless vessel. Here and there in the wilderness of masculine volubility, I heard the faint whisper of a woman's voice. Her wisdom, however, was a mere echo of man's, accepting fatally, or graciously, as a divine command, her subordination.

Meanwhile a strange debility took possession of me. I was tortured with cramps and nausea. My stomach rebelled against food, and my nerves against music and reading. I felt too weary to dance. My movements became ungraceful, unrhythmical.

The learned doctor, whom I finally consulted, smiled significantly. "This is a case for midwives, not for me."

Furious that motherhood was the aftermath of a brutal and loveless embrace, in whose joy I had not participated, I drove the leeches out of the palace. They tightened their black robes about their bodies and pulled at their beards, perplexed.

"Even the hod-carrier's wife desires an heir," they moralized, mumbling.

I could not resign myself to the idea that fatherhood was so simple and motherhood so long and painful a process. Having seen a cow in the throes of creation, I shuddered to think of the day when I, Princess Salome, would undergo the same tortures and indignities. Only the birds and the fish seemed to be favored by Jahveh. I rebelled against a masculine God who prefers the sparrow and the sturgeon to woman.

Powerless to alter conditions, I watched my body become heavier until every line of its loveliness was distorted. My only consolation was that, for the time being, I had conquered the Moon.

Alas, what a sorry conquest!

I thought of the Amazons of whom Agrippina had spoken, and wondered whether they were not conscious rebels against a masculine God that mocks and spurns woman and against the sexless divinity that controls her blood.

At times, however, I felt exultant. When the travail was over I would be a mother! Mother! All the poetry and wisdom of the ages sing dithyrambs to motherhood. Mother, the golden cornucopia which carries all the generations! Motherhood, the fountainhead of existence! The mother's womb is the cradle, her breast the source of all life. She is the history of the race. She is the sea into which all waters gather.

My deformity was no longer abhorrent to me. Like the Earth, I bore the living seed which would break forth in the spring into flowers and fruit. Fauna and Flora and Athena — wisdom and beauty and abundance — all goddesses. Jupiter was only the wielder of lightning, the vain and roaring thunderer!

Like a pendulum I swung between despair and ecstasy, between anger and joy.

Unlike other mothers in Israel, I prayed that my child be a girl, whom I would teach the pride and power of woman, who would learn to wage war against the yoke of lunar and masculine tyranny, and break asunder all feminine shackles.

I could not move about any longer. I groaned at each step. My motions were like those of a clumsy animal, unaccustomed to the ground. Finally I stretched upon the bed, a vast mass of lead. From time to time, I was caught with wild pangs. It seemed as if some one beat with iron knuckles within me, and tore my entrails. Spikes pulsed in my body. Forgetting my rank and my pride I screamed and groaned and tossed about. I was no longer Salome, no longer a princess. I was woman, the primal female, the eternal slave of creation.

My women tried to console me. They had all borne children — some as many as ten and twenty. Once the birth was consummated, all pain was forgotten. And, ah, to be a mother! One woman wept bitterly. She would undergo a thousand times greater tortures if she could have a child! Barren! To be barren, what a disgrace! Better never to be born than die childless! In her desperation, she had sinned with many men, hoping that the seed would turn into fruit in her womb. In vain. Her womb was barren soil!

Aristobolus was still away. The campaign against the enemies had not ended. From time to time his sparse letters continued to arrive. Furious though I was against him, I longed to have him near. I do not know whether I wished to demonstrate to him the pain he had inflicted upon me, or hoped that by watching me he might in some mysterious way share the agony.

The torture became more and more acute. For days my body was torn and stampeded by the prisoner within me, impatient to tear the bonds that united us and made us one.

The midwives promised relief, whispered words of consolation, recounted unusual cases and clever manipulations. The doctors waited in the anteroom, should their more violent services be required.

Mingled with the piercing shriek of my agony, a new being uttered its fearful and triumphant cry of life.

"A son! A son! A son!" echoed and reëchoed jubilantly through the palace.

For the time being I was too exhausted by the loss of blood and the long travail to regret the sex of my child, or rejoice in the glory of motherhood. I was alive, that sufficed, and no longer in pain. I was alive, and some day I would walk again free from burden. I would move gracefully; I would dance. I was no longer merely the ripe and fruitful womb.

A voice, soft as a fresh stream tumbling over smooth stones, awakened me from my reverie.

"My child!" I whispered. "Let me see my child!"

I was too ill to raise my head, but with the tips of my fingers I touched a skin so delicate that I caught my breath, and withdrew my hand for fear I would tear into it. The nurse laughed.

"They are tougher than you imagine, Princess!"

The contact was sufficient for my heart to overbrim with love. I knew the rapturous meaning of motherhood.

Enveloped as in a sheet of flames, I wavered between life and death for weeks. My head pressed against my pillow like a thing of lead. My eyes were too swollen to open. It seemed to me I heard the word "death" pronounced around my bed many times. I heard wailing and lamentation, but in spite of all my efforts, I could not grasp what was going on.

The flames were quenched at last. I opened my eyes. There was silence all about me. The leech placed his hand upon my forehead.

"Judea rejoices that the Princess is well again."

I smiled. I recognized an old physician, Alexander ben Gurien. He had been a poet in his youth, and could not refrain from flowery language.

"My child, doctor," I whispered.

"Not yet, Princess. Your health is only like the sun at dawn, too delicate. When it reaches the top of the mountain——"

He could not continue his improvisation, and descended to unornamented facts.

"For a while yet, Princess, you must remain perfectly quiet. Nothing must disturb you."

I was too feeble to insist.

A week later I was strong enough to stand up.

"I want my baby!" I said.

The leech and the nurse tried in vain to dissuade me.

"If you don't bring him to me, I'll go and get him myself. I want my baby, do you hear?"

"Princess —" they pleaded.

"My baby," I ordered.

They turned their heads away.

"Give me my baby," I said desperately.

The nurse burst into tears. The leech made a few steps into the room. His demeanor betrayed what his lips refused to utter.

"My baby is dead!" I muttered.

The nurse nodded and sobbed.

I remained silent for a long time. My tongue had turned to stone.

"Where is my husband?" I asked finally. "Has he returned from the wars? Does he know that I have no baby any more?"

They did not answer.

"Answer me!" I commanded.

The leech approached me, and knelt before the bed.

"Princess, it is God's will that I be the messenger of evil news. Forgive me, Princess."

"Speak!"

"Aristobolus fell on the battlefield, Judea's hero. On the day when the evil news reached the palace, your baby died."

"Why did you not let me die? Why?" I beat his shoulders with my fists.

"It is a physician's duty to give life, not take it," he said, moving away from my reach.

"Why did you not give life to my baby, then?" I shouted.

"Your baby was doomed from birth, Princess. It is better he died. Your child was"— he whispered, bending down so that no one might overhear —"a monster."

"You lie! You lie!"

"I swear it in the name of our Lord, Princess."

I laughed hysterically. My peals of laughter rang through the palace, reverberating through its columned halls.

The leech rose, frightened.

"He was the son of Aristobolus, not mine. He was bound to his body, not mine. That's why they died the same day."

Alexander made a gesture of helplessness.

"It is well, leech. Make me whole, leech."

"Yes, Princess. You shall be as whole as a new-born child."

"Stop speaking of new-born children!"

"Yes, Princess."

"Make me whole. I want to live. I want to break the shackles of the Moon. I want to destroy the male God who shows no mercy to woman!"

The leech, startled, looked at the nurse significantly, then stretched out his hands toward me. "I implore you, Princess, do not be overwrought."

"It is well, leech," I smiled drearily. "Do not fear. I shall be quiet. I shall obey your instructions."

I stretched out, and closed my eyes.

CHAPTER EIGHT

MY MOTHER'S ITCH FOR THE PURPLE — THE TRAGIC MASK OF HERODIAS — FUTILE MATCHMAKING — I GO INTO THE DESERT — THE DANCE OF LIFE — I MEET JOKANAAN, WHOM THEY CALL JOHN THE BAPTIST.

DESPITE the machinations of my mother and the vast sums sent to Rome, the Emperor refused to proclaim Antipas king.

Nevertheless, Herodias transformed our court at Tiberias into a palace more luxurious and more magnificent than that of a real monarch. She styled herself "Augusta," and addressed Antipas as "Rex."

She strutted about gaudier and more vain than a peacock, never realizing that the onerous taxes imposed upon the nation were bringing Judea to the verge of bankruptcy and rebellion. Blinded by the glow of the future, she saw nothing of the night gathering about her. Deafened by the roar of an imaginary triumph, she could not hear the steady grumbling of the approaching storm.

Judea, which at one time seemed enormous to me, assumed its true contours — an insignificant stretch of land crowded with haughty and conceited priests and rulers and nearly as haughty and conceited a populace. A dung-hill upon the peaks of which ridiculous cocks crowed hoarsely their vainglorious pæans to the impassive sun, and at the base of which cockerels shrieked their apostrophes of envy.

At the university of Tiberias, now nearly as famous as that of Jerusalem, arguments deafened wisdom, and truth was overridden by personal interest.

The teachers and students who saw the sorry pass learning had come to, wrung their hands and muttered desperately the dictum of the wisest of our kings: "Vanitas vanitatum et omnia vanitas." Others, more optimistic, caught glimpses of a brighter day through the almost opaque curtain of night. Others, still a little furtively and under breath, repeated the words of the new prophets, who preached of the end of the world, and the coming of the Messiah.

My mother spoke to me of a new suitor — an Arabian Prince, her second cousin. Herod's line was tainted and diseased. Her own family, however, she insisted, was potent and vigorous. It was destined to revive the glory of Arabia, once the envy and the awe of the world.

"What Arabia needs," she said, "is a Princess like you, Salome. Your sons will conquer the East and the West. Rome cannot last forever. Her emperors are degenerates. Tiberius fears to make Antipas king. He fears the Jews."

I smiled.

She continued. "The trouble with the Jews is that they are not united. If they had a king, they would rally as in the times of David and Solomon, and throw off the Roman yoke."

"The Jews will never unite," I said unemotionally. "Each Jew considers himself the equal of a king and as sacred as the Messiah."

"Even so, my dear. Since the Jews are bound to remain slaves, let Arabia blossom again, Salome! Let it awaken from its slumber! Arabia is the source of all knowledge, all power. The source is not dry."

"I am not concerned with Arabia or with her rulers," I said with a tone of finality, which, I hoped, would end the conversation.

She placed her arm around my waist.

"I know what it means to lose a son, Salome. I, too, am a woman."

Her simple words startled me. I had never thought of Herodias in terms of woman. She was either my mother or the scheming wife of the Tetrarch — a she-fox, a vixen. As I watched her face, I saw something pathetic suddenly cross it, like the shadow of a weary animal. I began to suspect that her intrigues, her vain pomp, her clamorous efforts for honors, her vices and her adulteries, were but a refuge from the tragic reality of womanhood.

"It is not only the loss of my child," I said, "but ———"

She interrupted me. "I know the inadequacies and brutalities of husbands. Every woman, from the slave-girl to the queen, passes through the same disillusionment ———"

We looked at each other in painful silence.

"But what can woman do?" she sighed, helpless, suddenly grown old.

"She can rebel!" I exclaimed. "She can break the chains! Mother of the race, she shall be its ruler."

"Because she is the mother of the race, she cannot be its ruler."

"She shall conquer the Moon!" I said defiantly, thinking to astound her with the startling idea.

"Salome is still a child. Every woman, my dear, begins by challenging and ends by worshiping the Moon. What is a woman when no longer under the dominance of the Moon?"

She looked at me, her eyes nearly closed, her lower lip drooping.

"Antipas still hopes for a male heir. I am obliged to feign lunar visitations. Alas, the tides have receded for all time!"...

I looked at her disdainfully.

"I know. You think I am a she-fox. Maybe I am. What else can a woman be? A she-fox, or a worm trodden underfoot! A woman's glory is motherhood or a potential motherhood. When the tree no longer bears fruit — the woodman swings his ax."

"It is better for the woodman to swing his ax than to be nothing but a tree bearing fruit for others!"

She smiled indulgently.

"Think of what I told you, Salome. You hold the destiny of our family in the palm of your hand. You are the granddaughter of King Herod of Judea and the granddaughter of King Aretas of Arabia!"

I remained silent.

"I must go to cheer up Antipas. He is worried about those noisy Messiahs — particularly about a fellow by the name of Jokanaan, who is dirtying the waters of the Jordan by dipping into it all those who consider him Elijah risen from the dead, to purify the souls of men and announce the end of the world."

She laughed ironically.

"Antipas is a child, like all men. I humor him and read fables to him."

She clapped her hands. Two slave-girls appeared, and dropped upon their faces, exclaiming "Augusta! Augusta!"

"See if the paint on my face and lips is cracking," Herodias commanded.

The girls rushed to the table, brought several jars of salve, and retouched my mother's features with uncanny deftness. They arranged the train of her robe, and fastened the coronet upon her head.

Herodias made a sign to them to retire.

She breathed deeply, smiled, and asked me: "Do I look like a queen, Salome?"

"Yes," I said flatly.

She graciously bowed, and swept regally out of the room.

Weary of my mother's obstinate pleadings that I marry the Arabian Prince, weary of the hair-splitting argumentations of the scholars whom I invited to discuss with me, weary of my own futile rebellion, I decided to go into the desert to find myself.

Dressed as a merchant's daughter, I left the palace at dawn. I was accompanied by Aquila, a young Idumean woman, homely, but faithful as a dog, and Hariman, a Persian, middle-aged and powerful like a gorilla. Both were of a taciturn nature, and accustomed to my vagaries.

I rode on a camel and Aquila and Hariman on donkeys, while a camel laden with provisions of the simplest kind, completed the cortège.

Soon the houses disappeared, then the trees, the mountains, the grass. Nothing remained save a dazzling sky and the glittering sand which undulated from time to time like the rhythmic breathing of a giant animal sleeping on its back. From time to time, too, a small caravan passed us by. The people looked at us, at first suspiciously, then wonderingly.

The fifth day we reached the Dead Sea. Heavy as lead and a gangrenous black, its waves stroked wearily the salt-encrusted shore. I halted, and watched it for a long while. No fish lived within it. No birds sought food on its surface. No boat ever rocked upon it.

The Moon, monarch of the waters of the Earth, had relinquished her domination over it — and it was dead! Was the Dead Sea an admonition and a moral lesson to Woman who dared rebel against the goddess of the night? Was death the penalty of rebellion?

"What is a woman when no longer under the dominance of the Moon?" I heard my mother say. Was my attitude toward Man and the Moon merely the silly arrogance of youth? Would I, like the rest, accept the yoke and the insult, when the flaming passion of youth sank to the pale glow of maturity?

We wandered about, turning now to the right, now to the left, as my fancy or humor dictated. From time to time we came across small oases with clear streams of water and fig and date trees.

I was surrounded by utter silence, and in this utter silence, my soul regained its voice. Forgotten were my husband, my child, the court, the scholars — everything.

I cast off my clothing, and in complete abandon I danced. In the vast reflection of the Moon I danced — the rapturous dance of life!

"There he is! There he is! Princess!" my companions shouted, pointing their forefingers to the horizon.

"Who?" I asked, irritated that I was interrupted.

"The Prophet, the new Messiah!"

"What Messiah?"

"Jokanaan. They call him John the Baptist. Some say he is the Prophet Elijah."

I gazed in the direction their fingers pointed, and saw

over the rim of the reflection of the Moon, a tall man, naked, except for a leather girdle about his loins. His long curls encircled his neck like restless snakes, and his reddish beard, terminating in a point, sparkled like new gold. I could not distinguish his face. It seemed like another luminous moon.

I threw my robe over me quickly and asked, my heart trembling: "Who is he, did you say?"

"Why, the Baptist — Jokanaan — the new Messiah. Were you not seeking him in the desert?"

"I seek no one and nothing except my soul," I said more to myself than in reply to their question.

Jokanaan approached, surrounded by many men, women and children.

"Who are they? Who are those people?"

"They are his followers, Princess. They say that he has baptized half of Judea and Galilee."

I trembled with an emotion I could not name.

Slowly the procession approached. We stood apart.

The Baptist turned to the people.

"Repent ye; for the Kingdom of Heaven is at hand. For I am he that was spoken of through Elijah the Prophet, saying:

"'The voice of one crying in the wilderness,
Make ye ready the way of the Lord,
Make his paths straight!'"

"We repent, Rabbi! We repent!" all exclaimed.

"Not thus must ye repent — not with mere words! Repent ye with your hearts! Repent ye with your souls!"

"We repent with our hearts, Elijah! We repent with our souls!"

"Come ye then, and be washed of your sins!"

"Baptize us in the Jordan, Jokanaan!"

The Baptist glared at a few Pharisees and Sadducees who were standing apart, whispering among themselves.

"Ye offsprings of vipers!" the Prophet admonished them furiously. "Who warned you to flee from the wrath to come? Bring forth, therefore, fruits worthy of repentance; and think not to say within yourselves: 'We have Abraham to our father!' For I say unto you, that even now the ax lieth at the root of the trees; every tree, therefore, that bringeth not forth good fruit is hewn down, and cast into the fire."

"Baptize us! Baptize us, Elijah!" the others begged.

Jokanaan turned to me. His eyes burned two black holes in my white robe. For a long time he continued to gaze at me, muttering words I could not understand.

My blood beat in my temples like fists.

"I am the voice crying in the wilderness!" he exclaimed suddenly, raising his arm. "Make ye ready for the way of the Lord!"

He turned his back on me, and continued his way toward the Jordan, followed by the people, who uttered from time to time, "Baptize us, Elijah! Baptize us, Jokanaan!"

The procession was a black spot that shivered awhile on the horizon, then disappeared.

"Let us return!" I said.

CHAPTER NINE

NEW TROUBLES AND NEW MESSIAHS — THE WILES OF THE SANHEDRIN — THE TETRARCH INVITES — "I AM ELIJAH" — THE GIBES OF THE BAPTIST — "THERE IS NEITHER MAN NOR WOMAN IN HEAVEN" — MY MOTHER'S ANNOYANCE — I SAVE THE LIFE OF JOKANAAN.

I RETURNED to Tiberias, in my heart a new peace and a new disturbance.

Messengers from Pilate, the Roman Governor at Jerusalem, brought letters of complaint and threats unless the commotion in Judea was quelled. The swords of our soldiers were unsheathed. The multitudes vociferated at the gates of the palace. Antipas deliberated with the newly appointed Sanhedrin and the High Priest. Herodias strutted about, consoling my stepfather and invoking the gods of Arabia against the Prophets and the Messiahs. The scholars moaned and prayed to Jahveh to postpone the end of the world.

In my heart was the peace of the desert and the tumult of two eyes.

The Sanhedrin insisted upon the death of Jokanaan and his disciple, Jesus of Nazareth. My mother added her voice to theirs. The Tetrarch, however, was obstinate. Neither the pleadings of Herodias, nor the priests' endless expositions, argumentations and quotations from the Talmud, convinced Antipas. He found neither man guilty. Jesus, he thought, was of no consequence. His execution would be sheer murder. The Baptist had too great a following to be trifled with, and there might be a grain of truth in what he preached. Besides, Rome, never favorable to him, was watching for an opportunity to quarrel. And not only Rome, he murmured to himself, but the priests.

"If Rome quarrels with you, Antipas," the spokesman of the Sanhedrin smiled suavely, "you will easily prove to Rome that the son of King Herod the Great is mightier than Tiberius. You are the son of a king. He is the spawn of a commoner."

"Yes! Yes!" the others added, nodding to one another.

"You will gain not only the crown of Judea, but the independence of our people."

Herodias, inflamed by their words, declaimed against Rome, and expostulated on Rome's fear of the Jews.

"True! Augusta! True!" the members of the Sanhedrin exclaimed, rubbing their hands and pulling their beards.

Antipas, angry, stamped his scepter, the shadowy symbol of a possible future glory. "If I am the son of Herod, then I shall act like my sire! Jokanaan shall not die by my order!"

The elders shrugged their shoulders and made gestures and sounds of despair. My mother breathed haughtily.

I whispered: "Antipas, why not send for the Baptist? Let him tell us what he desires to do. Perhaps we can dissuade him from causing any further disturbance."

"Well said, Salome! You are blood of my blood. Let it be as my daughter says! Let Jokanaan be brought here," he announced, adding a little uncertainly, "as our guest."

The elders grumbled, nodded significantly, pathetically, uttered sighs of self-pity, but seeing that Antipas was obdurate, agreed to convene again when the Baptist would be brought to Court — as a guest.

My mother walked up and down the hall, waving an enormous fan of ostrich feathers, the gift of a prince of Cathay, who sought love, and found death, in Judea.

Antipas took my hand in his, and looked into my eyes, as if he had seen me for the first time. His lips trembled and his eyes became blurred. He suddenly resembled my grandfather, Herod. I drew my breath.

Herodias approached us, frowning, then smiling over-tenderly, she placed her arm around her husband's shoulder, and said, softly: "You are right, my lord. It is well that Jokanaan be brought to our Court."

"It was your daughter, not I, who thought of it."

"It is you who ordered it, however."

"Your daughter is the cleverest woman in Judea," Antipas blurted, and fearing the sudden stare of my mother, continued laughing a little, "she is the worthy whelp of the she-fox."

My mother laughed, and struck his shoulder lightly with her fan.

Antipas ran his hand over my arm, pressing his fingers into it.

"You are weary, Antipas," my mother said solicitously. "Come, I shall read you a fable, which will amuse you greatly."

He was reluctant to rise.

She whispered something into his ear, which I could not hear. He breathed deeply and accepted her arm.

Antipas sat upon the throne, his father's crown upon his head. On his right my mother. On his left, I occupied the seat of his chief counselor.

The Sanhedrin were seated, lined against the walls. Their eyes scrutinized my mother and me, and their hands as they combed and played with their beards, were an eloquent satire.

The sun, pouring through the open window, set ablaze the gold and jewels that encrusted the walls and the pillars.

The Tetrarch made a sign with his hand. Two soldiers left the hall, walking backward, and returned a moment later, Jokanaan between them.

A garment of camel's hair clothed the Baptist's upper body, and his loins were covered with a girdle of leather. He looked about the room, undaunted by its magnificence or the people who were in it. His eyes finally rested upon me. He turned his head away proudly or indignantly, I could not tell. Did he recognize me as a princess? Did that gesture of turning his face away signify that he despised me or that he would not allow my presence to determine his attitude toward the gathering?

"Are you Jokanaan of Hebron?" Antipas asked in a friendly manner.

"I am Elijah! I am the voice in the wilderness!"

"What sign has the Lord given you to prove that you are Elijah?" one of the elders asked.

"They who are not blind see it."

"The Lord makes His signs more evident," the elder answered.

"Blinder than he who has lost his eyes is he who closes them tightly and refuses to see the light of day," Jokanaan answered haughtily.

"Elijah died and was borne by the angels to heaven. If you are Elijah, tell us something about Heaven," they asked, hoping to entrap him in heresy.

The Sanhedrin stretched their necks forward, their lips hidden in their beards.

"There is neither man nor woman in my Father's house, neither marriage nor giving in marriage," the Baptist said at last.

"What! Neither man nor woman?" one asked, biting the tip of his beard. "Then who is there? Is it the fowls of the air or the fish of the river, perhaps?"

There was general snickering.

Seeing that the discussion would turn into endless metaphysical argumentations, Antipas waved his hand to the Sanhedrin for silence.

Turning to the Baptist, he said: "Jokanaan — Elijah — why do you disturb the peace of my people?"

"I come to bring peace!"

"That is well, Elijah. We all wish for peace."

"Peace does not dwell in the bosom of iniquity. I come to bring peace at the point of the sword."

"That is not well, Elijah. The swords of the Romans are already too numerous. A Jew should not direct his sword against his brethren."

The Baptist frowned.

Antipas placed his hand over mine with senile lasciviousness.

Jokanaan saw the Tetrarch's gesture.

"A Jew should direct his sword wherever the evil is!" Jokanaan's eyes, like two swords indeed, stabbed the hand of Antipas, who removed it quickly from mine.

"Are not our rabbis and our elders chosen by God to crush evil?"

The elders, pleased, nodded to one another and to Antipas.

The Baptist raised his hand above his head, and exclaimed:

"Think not that by saying, 'We are rabbis and we are elders,' the tree of iniquity shall blossom into fruit worthy of the Lord!"

"Blasphemer!" several of the elders exclaimed.

"Bring forth fruit worthy of the Lord! The Kingdom of God is at hand, and the roots shall not hide any more beneath the soft cover of the earth. They shall not say, 'We are the roots of the tree of Life,' when they are the roots of the tree of Death!"

"Antipas, do you suffer this vile-tongued man to insult us?" the elders asked threateningly.

"What do you mean by the roots of the trees of Life and Death, Jokanaan?" my stepfather asked, secretly pleased at Jokanaan's arraignment.

"I am the ax that lieth at the root of the tree!" Jokanaan answered, dodging the question.

"Who is the tree of Death?" Antipas insisted.

"The roots of the tree of evil are they that despoil the poor, that preach falsely, that take the name of the Lord in vain, that worship secretly strange and vile gods, that place false crowns upon their heads, that wallow in lust and walk in adultery and incest!"

My mother sprang from her seat and faced Antipas.

"Will you allow this wicked tongue to wag insults at me?"

The elders made no comment. The Baptist had changed the direction of his poisoned arrows. They were no longer the target. What Jokanaan said about the Tetrarch and his family was exactly what they had whispered to one another, and never dared utter aloud. The Baptist had become for the moment their spokesman.

Antipas lost the calm he had affected. His face blanched and lengthened. His upper lip quivered. His eyes bulged.

"Govern your tongue, Jokanaan," he commanded, raising his scepter in the air.

"Foxes and she-foxes!" the Baptist pursued, unheeding the warning. "Your lair has been discovered! The hunter of God is tightening his bow, and his arrow never misses the mark."

Antipas rose.

"Vipers and sons and daughters of vipers!" Jokanaan continued. "Hearken to the voice of warning! The Kingdom of Heaven is at hand."

The trial of Jokanaan had become the trial of Antipas and Herodias.

The elders looked at one another furtively. The Baptist's hand stiffened in the air, two fingers pressed together. The soldiers at the door were motionless statues. It seemed as if the Court had been enchanted and put to sleep.

Suddenly the elders began to whisper to one another, moving their bodies from side to side as in prayer. The soldiers coughed. Through my brain pealed like a bell —"There is neither man nor woman in my Father's House."

Herodias shrieked, her voice sharper than many needles. "This man shall not live, my lord! This man shall not live."

From the street voices filtered into the hall. "Elijah! Elijah! Baptize us!"

Antipas listened attentively. He struck the floor with his scepter.

"Jokanaan, you blaspheme against the elders and utter vile accusations against the descendants of David and Solomon. You should die, but"— he raised and lowered the scepter silently —"I have mercy on you."

"I crave only the Lord's mercy," John the Baptist said proudly, his curls beating gently against his pale cheeks.

From the street the voices came more distinctly.

"Elijah! Elijah! Baptize us! Come forth to baptize us!"

"And ye," Jokanaan moved his forefinger slowly in a semicircle, until it pointed to every one present, "ye wallowers in the cesspool of vice, ye strutters on the muck-heap of the universe, pray to the Lord that He may have mercy on you! His hunter has his arrows ready and his heels raised. Your wicked hearts shall be pierced and your carcasses crumbled in the dust!"

"Who is the hunter whose ways you know so intimately, you venom-mouthed son of a she-dog?" one of the elders asked, rising angrily.

"He is at the gate even now," John answered quietly.

"Is he the wine-bibber of Nazareth, whose cheap magic ensnares the people? Is it he, the friend of harlots and publicans?"

The Baptist smiled ironically.

"Who is it?" the elder shouted.

"He is the Chosen One of God! He is the Messiah who warns the iniquitous. His mouth is filled with the words of the Lord!"

"If it be you," Herodias flared, "then the arrow shall rebound on the hunter." Turning to Antipas, she pleaded, "Let him not live, Antipas! Pluck his vile tongue from his mouth!"

"The tongue has already uttered the truth, daughter of shame, wife of adultery and incest!"

"Tear his head from his neck, Antipas!" my mother screamed.

Antipas opened his mouth ready to utter the irrevocable sentence.

I bent my face until my lips touched the Tetrarch's ear.

"Do not slay him yet, Antipas," I whispered. "Listen to the people outside. His death may precipitate a rebellion. Cast him into prison. He may recant. He may moderate his words."

Antipas looked at me. His eyes caressed my breasts.

"Whatever you say, Salome, shall be done! You are my good counselor."

"So be it! Jokanaan, your life has been spared for the time being."

John looked at me. His lips moved, but he said nothing.

The elders bit the points of their beards, and raised their eyebrows. Herodias glared at me, and reseated herself.

Antipas made a motion to the soldiers.

"Let this man be cast into the prison of Maccharus," he commanded.

The soldiers approached the Baptist, grasping him by the arm, and turned him about swiftly.

CHAPTER TEN

THE HOSPITALITY OF THE TETRARCH — I DISCUSS THEOLOGY WITH THE PROPHET — VESSELS OF CORRUPTION — THE COUSIN OF JOKANAAN — THE OBSTINACY OF AUNT MARY — A EUNUCH'S HEAVEN — I WOO IN VAIN — THE CURSE OF THE PROPHET —"TOO VILE FOR THE GRAVE"— I MEET THE GHOST OF JOKANAAN — I SWOON.

The Fortress of Maccharus had long been abandoned as a means of defense against enemies. The outer walls lay crumbled, hills of débris. The others, although pierced by Roman javelins, were still impenetrable. My grandfather, Herod the Great, had turned the fortress into a jail. Many had been its occupants — generals and rulers and priests whom the King wished forgotten rather than executed.

The chief cell was a well in the center of the courtyard, which legend called "the well of life," because its waters, before it miraculously turned dry, had cured many diseases. History called it "the well of death," for he who was thrown into it rarely saw the light of day again. It was connected by a subterranean passage with the rest of the fortress, now occupied by the jailer Rahab, an Abyssinian giant, and his family — a thin Jewish woman and two children, one black-skinned, one white, with large swollen stomachs and tiny faces.

My mother had destined Jokanaan for the "well." But I ordered the jail-keeper to give the Baptist a room in the fortress and treat him with the greatest deference. He was to be allowed the freedom of the courtyard, and to receive or send messages to his friends.

He was my guest, I explained, and not in the true sense a prisoner. A cynical smile crept over the jail-keeper's face. He was accustomed to the strange whims of the Herod family.

The Baptist was standing on the parapet, his head lifted, his eyes closed, motionless, breathless.

Rahab was about to call him. I stopped him.

"Do not disturb him. He is a holy man," I whispered. "I shall wait until he ends his meditations."

Rahab grinned, showing enormous white teeth like an elephant's tusks.

"He stands that way for hours, Princess. At first I thought he had died standing."

John opened his eyes, and looked at me. His eyes bored themselves slowly into my face, until I could not endure it any longer.

"Bring him down!" I ordered.

Rahab, wishing to parade his agility, did not climb the steps, but, like a monkey, swung himself to the top, holding by two branches of a tree which had grown into the wall.

John descended the steps slowly, and approached me. I made a sign to Rahab to leave us alone.

"Jokanaan," I said, "I wish to speak with you."

"Speak!"

His tone annoyed me, but I was determined to keep my temper.

"Jokanaan, do you remember that we met once in the desert? I was dressed as a merchant's daughter."

"I remember."

"Did you recognize me when you saw me in the palace?"

"I recognized you."

"I saved your life, Jokanaan!" I said, expecting a look of gratitude.

"God alone gives and takes life."

"Nevertheless, if I had not persuaded Antipas to cast you into prison, where you are harassed by no one, you would certainly be dead now."

"Man must die to be born a second time."

"Why should man be born again, Jokanaan? Is not one life sufficient? Why repeat the pang of birth and the agony of death?"

"Woman gives birth through sin and her offspring is corruption. The second birth is the birth of the soul."

"Without the first birth there can be no second birth, Jokanaan. Without woman the soul cannot be born. Why speak disdainfully of her agony? Why call her tragedy sin, and her motherhood corruption? Without woman the children of the Earth would perish."

The Baptist raised his arm above his head, and spoke as to a great multitude.

"I say unto you that God is able of these stones to raise up children unto Abraham!"

"Then why does not God do so, and relieve woman of her pain?"

"Woman is the vessel of corruption. She suffers for her iniquity."

"Why has God poured iniquity into the vessel?"

"Vain and arrogant woman!" he exclaimed, pointing his forefinger at me, "question not the infinite wisdom of Elohim!"

"Are you not vain and arrogant yourself, Jokanaan?" I answered suavely. "How have you fathomed the infinite wisdom of Elohim? Are you man or superman?"

His face, white from the long fasts and vigils, flushed. His lips trembled.

"You are Lilith, the betrayer of man! Your logic is the logic of the serpent! Avaunt!"

I smiled. "Jokanaan, why do you fear woman? Why do you tremble before her logic? Why do you fear me, Jokanaan?" I teased him, approaching him, and touching his arms, thin and sunburnt.

He withdrew with a shudder.

"Your disciple, Jesus of Nazareth," I pursued, "does not hate or fear woman. I hear he forgave a harlot and promised her a place at his right in Heaven."

"My poor cousin, Jesus"— John's lips tightened into a

condescending smile —"takes me too literally. He does not grasp fully the meaning underneath my words. His mother's influence saps his manhood. My Aunt Mary is an obstinate woman. She has persuaded Jesus that God must have a mother." Jokanaan grinned.

"Is not the male born of the female in all Nature?" I asked.

Jokanaan's eyes flashed like torches.

"If God has a mother — why not a grandmother? Why not a great-grandmother? Why not a mother-in-law? Permit one false preposterous notion, and soon the God of the Universe is reduced to the level of a pagan idol! If Jesus wants to count among the prophets of Israel, he must cut loose from his mother's apron strings."

"I heard from a messenger at the Court that Jesus shamed his mother, saying angrily, 'What have I to do with thee, woman?'"

Jokanaan smiled drearily. "For once he rebelled against her constant interferences. It is she who makes him perform his parlor tricks."

"Parlor tricks? Jesus performs miracles, Jokanaan! He heals the sick and raises the dead."

Jokanaan's eyes relaxed their sinister look. "Yes — and changes water into wine!" he added disdainfully. "Miracles? What are miracles? Every Hindu fakir performs miracles for the amusement of children."

"Did not Elizabeth, your mother, Jokanaan, perform a miracle?"

"Yes," he said bitterly. "She was fleeing with me — her first-born — to escape the wrath of your grandfather, Herod, who ordered the slaughter of the innocents."

The Baptist stopped a moment, as if to allow the flame of the hatred he bore my family to blaze within him.

"His hounds were on our heels, when we reached a mountain. She prayed, 'Mount of God, receive a mother with her child,' and the mountain opened and received us. It was the will of the Lord. If she did a miracle, it was not to startle the rabble."

To avoid further reference to our family, I said quickly: "Jokanaan, your cousin Jesus has many converts."

"Publicans and harlots," he retorted. I detected a note of jealousy in his voice. "He wins them with easy and vain promises. I speak of another conversion."

"Of what conversion, Jokanaan?"

The Baptist looked at me for a long time. He deemed it below his dignity to offer an answer.

"What conversion?" I repeated pleadingly.

"I speak of the conversion of the spirit through the mystery of baptism," he condescended to reply.

"Baptize me, Jokanaan!" I exclaimed.

"Your spirit is too arrogant, woman. You have inherited the cunning of the fox. I will not baptize you!"

"Why do you insult me, Jokanaan? Why do you mock my intelligence? Scholars and philosophers call me the wisest woman of Judea."

"Woman's wisdom is drivel from the venomous fangs of the snake," he said, tightening his lips in disgust.

Why did not the acrid words of this man stir my anger and my pride? Why did I continue humble before him?

"There is neither man nor woman in Heaven, you said. Prepare me for Heaven, Rabbi."

"The tongue of the cloven gender is subtler than the cloven tongue of the adder. Her words are like an evil wind which bends the flames of the torch, distorting the shapes of things. In Heaven woman cannot corrupt man. Her wiles avail her not!"

"A Heaven of eunuchs!" I taunted.

Jokanaan answered unperturbed. "Even on Earth they who love God truly relieve themselves of the burden which estranges them from Him."

"Do you not love God truly, Jokanaan? Yet you have not severed your manhood for the Kingdom of Heaven's sake."

"The bird which sings the sweetest presses his breast against the thorn. The fir rises swiftly and straight athwart against the sky; the trunk of the olive tree, which endureth forever, bends and twists in agony."

He turned from me, taking several steps into the yard. He stopped near the shadow of the "well," which fell upon his feet.

I followed him.

"Jokanaan," I said gently, "I love your soul. I love the words that pour from your mouth. Baptize me, and let us both go and preach the love of God and His Heaven of Love."

"Get thee behind me, Satan!" he said, covering his face with his hands.

"Why do you call me Satan, Jokanaan? Do I not repent? Do I not wish to follow the path of God!"

"God rejects the spawn of Hell!" He stretched his arm until the tip of his forefinger touched my breast.

I shivered, and moved nearer. He shook his hand as if he had touched an unclean thing.

"Jokanaan, do not repel me. Let Princess Salome, the proud granddaughter of King Herod, atone for the sins of her sire. Baptize me!"

"Not the whole Jordan, not all the seas of the Earth, can cleanse you of your sins!"

"I have not sinned, Jokanaan."

"Unto the fourth, yea and unto the fortieth, generation, are you damned, blossom of the cesspool, flower of vice!"

"Jokanaan, for your sake I have danced before Antipas and his drunken companions. For your sake I let his lips bite into mine. For your sake I have mocked and scorned the words of my mother."

He looked at me, frowning, trying to grasp my meaning.

"Jokanaan, I come from the feast of Antipas, that I may save you. I have danced for Antipas and given him my lips that I may obtain that which I desire. He offered me half of his kingdom and jewels that glow like the sun at noon, but I refused them, and would accept nothing, save you I saved your life to be your slave!"

"I need no slaves! I have come to preach against slaves and against masters. God is my Master. I am His slave!"

"Let me be His slave also. Let me be a slave with you, Jokanaan. I despise the brutality of man. I hate the slavery of woman. Let me go with you, Jokanaan. Let us preach the freedom of man and woman. Let us preach the Kingdom of Heaven, where there is neither man nor woman, where each is judged according to his deserts!"

The Baptist turned his face.

"My words have persuaded rabbis and scholars. My body has dazed Kings and Tetrarchs. Why do you scorn me, Jokanaan?"

He did not stir.

"I am beautiful, Jokanaan! My dance enraptures the hearts of men! I shall dance for you, Jokanaan!"

I threw my robe to the ground, and danced. John never turned his head. But I knew that he watched my shadow upon the parapet. I moved so that he could see the profile of my breast. From time to time, I whispered —"Jokanaan, I love you! Jokanaan, I love you!"

Suddenly a violent pain made my body quake. My head turned. My face flushed. I stopped.

"Jokanaan," I whispered feebly, pathetically, bending over myself.

He turned around as if to speak. He looked at me intently. His mouth assumed an expression of intense disgust. His nostrils quivered. He covered his eyes with his elbow.

"Vessel of uncleanliness!" he muttered.

The Moon, Goddess of Mockery, cast her scarlet shadow over me. Relentless Monarch, she extorted her tribute.

I closed my eyes in shame and degradation. I was not Salome, Princess, scion of kings. I was not the symbol of beauty and passion. I was a slave of the lunar rhythm.

I opened my eyes. Jokanaan's face remained frozen in disgust. His nostrils continued to quiver. He turned his head slowly, and stretched forward to ward me off.

My loins were lacerated as with knives. I burnt with fever. Mortified beyond endurance, I threw my cloak over me and exclaimed, pointing my finger at Jokanaan: "I gave you the choice between love and death! You have chosen! You shall die!"

He turned toward me. "So be it! I shall die, but you must live!"

I looked at him, taken aback.

"Fool! I am mistress of my body! If I choose I can seek the embrace of Death!"

"You must live!" he repeated. "The bowels of the Earth shall refuse to hold you. The tomb shall vomit forth your corruption. You are too vile for the grave!"

His eyes, like two daggers, ripped my body. I tottered. Things swam as upon the surface of a sea.

"You shall die!" I muttered.

Like an echo beating against the mountainside, he repeated: "I shall die, but you must live! You are too vile for the grave."

Like an animal pursued, already hearing the hoofbeats of the horses and the howling of the hounds, I dashed away.

I rushed into the banquet hall. The guests were stretched upon couches or rolled upon the floor, linked in amorous postures.

Antipas, his crown toppling to one side, his face scarlet from wine, made a vague motion with his arm, and hiccoughed. "Salome, come here! Come here, my love. Give me your lips! Give me your lips."

My mother, like a goddess of sobriety, approached me.

"Salome! Give Jokanaan to me!" she pleaded. "The good of the state demands it! It is not my vanity, Salome! He will ruin us! He must die!"

"So be it! Take him! He is yours!" I said.

"So be it," said Antipas, gurgling drunkenly.

Astounded at my sudden resolution, and fearing a change of mind, my mother summoned one of the soldiers, and whispered something into his ear.

"Salome," Antipas insisted, "come to me! Give me your lips!"

I approached my stepfather. He tried to embrace me, but he could not move his arms, paralyzed by the wine.

"Your lips, Salome!" he muttered.

"Wine!" I ordered.

"Wine!" he repeated my order. "Wine for Salome!"

A slave filled a large cup. Through the open window, the

blood-stained Moon fell into the wine and mingled with it.

"Drink, Salome!" Antipas said kindly. "Drink!"

I drank three cups. The taste of the wine was the taste of blood. My head felt light. I laughed, Antipas laughed also.

"Laugh, Salome, laugh!"

He placed his wet lips upon mine. I withdrew.

"Do you not wish to share the throne with me, Salome? Dance for me again, Salome! You shall have my whole kingdom for a dance! My kingdom!" he stammered, his crown slipping to the floor.

My mother watched us, smiling indulgently. Jokanaan was worth the momentary loss of her husband's affection.

"Dance, Salome, dance!" Antipas hiccoughed.

Several guests repeated: "Dance, Salome, dance!"

I rose, unsteady.

Suddenly the door opened, and upon the threshold Jokanaan appeared. He was naked. His head was encircled by a flame, and his body glowed like a cataract of diamonds. He pointed his forefinger at me, and said something, which I could not hear, but the meaning of which I understood perfectly.

"Jokanaan!" I exclaimed, rushing forward.

The door closed. Jokanaan disappeared.

"Jokanaan!"

Antipas laughed —"Jokanaan!"

The other guests joined him in his laughter. "Jokanaan!"

I rushed out of the room.

"Jokanaan!"

As I reached the middle of the garden Rahab, like a tall black tower, broke the reflection of the Moon.

"Here is the Prophet, Princess, as you commanded," he grinned, holding in front of him a deep silver platter upon which the head of Jokanaan balanced gently like a grotesque boat in a pool of rubies.

"I severed his head with one blow of the sword, Princess," he boasted.

A mad wind howled. The Moon cracked into a thousand spears piercing my body. The stars fell upon me like a rain of fire.

The blood-spattered lips of Jokanaan opened, and thundered: "I shall die, but you are too vile for the grave!"

His eyes stared out of their orbits into mine, until mine turned into stone.

I shielded my face and screamed — a sharp cry like a wounded beast.

"Too vile for the grave!"

It was the hiss of a giant serpent. The wind carried it away, whirled it about, struck it against every tree and every wall, until the whole universe reverberated: "Too vile for the grave! Too vile for the grave! Too vile for the grave!"

My heart stopped beating.

I swooned.

CHAPTER ELEVEN

PAST MISTRESS OF PASSION — STORMS IN MY HEART — I VISIT JERUSALEM — I FLIRT WITH PILATE — AN ANCIENT RESENTMENT — I PROCLAIM WAR.

Herodias regained her confidence once more, and once more began her indefatigable intrigues to obtain the crown. She proved to Antipas that she had been right about slaying Jokanaan. The Baptist's followers, contrary to my stepfather's belief, made no attempt to rebel. After a mild demonstration, followed by futile grumbling, they sank into apathy. The Jordan continued its eternal rhythm, no longer carrying off into the sea the sins of mankind; no longer anointing man for the Kingdom of Heaven.

John's cousin and disciple, Jesus of Nazareth, fared no better. His followers, ignorant fishermen and harlots turned saints, went about repeating his sermons, speaking of his resurrection, warning man of his second advent. He would come as a reaper, dividing the chaff from the wheat.

The priests laughed in their sleeves. The merchants continued to drive hard bargains. The workers gained their meager bread by the sweat of their brows. Woman groaned under the weight of motherhood. Peace reigned upon Earth.

There was no peace in my heart. In my breast there was a cyclone and a thunderstorm, and a sentence that at intervals struck like a blow.

To forget, I turned Tiberias into a perennial banquet hall. My life was an orgy. My dancing and my amours became a byword, even as in the past my scholarship and my wisdom.

I was famed as the past-mistress of passion, the woman of occult delights, the scarlet rose of evil.

Poets composed dithyrambs to my beauty, and princes of many nations offered their lives and their treasures for a dance.

The tumult of passion, however, did not completely drown the tumult in my memory, and often in the midst of an embrace, I felt two eyes stab me, and heard a voice hurled at me like a javelin. An involuntary shriek would escape my lips, which my lover, in his conceit, attributed to unendurable rapture.

The Messiahs and prophets were dead, and largely forgotten, but the dove of peace was a short-lived bird. The Roman eagle screeched. Pilate, the Procurator of Judea, never friendly to Antipas, weary of the latter's political scheming and his endless skirmishes with the Sanhedrin and the High Priest, threatened to unloose the anger of Rome.

To avert an imminent conflict, whose consequences were not difficult to foresee, Antipas persuaded me to act as his emissary in Jerusalem. Curious to make my acquaintance, Pilate invited me as his guest.

I entered Jerusalem, not as the stepdaughter of the Tetrarch of Galilee on a plea for peace, but as Princess Salome, granddaughter of King Herod, already called the Great, even by the Romans. Ten elephants, twenty dromedaries and a regiment of picked soldiers accompanied me. I was the conquering Queen on a triumphant march.

Pilate received me with much dignity, but underneath the lacquer of formality I sensed the tremor of passion. Whatever I should desire, Pilate would concede, I was certain of it. Procla, the Procurator's wife, on the other hand, manifested much enthusiasm and pleasure, which hid, but not too well, her jealousy and her disdain. I was a king's granddaughter, but she was the daughter and granddaughter of emperors! More important still, she was a Roman matron.

Procla was pretty, but duty and respectability had begun

to harden somewhat her lips, and carve a frown between her eyebrows.

I was a dangerous visitor, and she was determined to watch me. She did not mind or protest against the Governor's amours. She evinced no jealousy of Roman matrons, Jewish virgins, or Attic slave boys. That was part of the code, a thing both proper and natural. But she would not allow her husband to indulge even in a vague flirtation with me.

She was always present at our conferences, and always reminded Pilate that his duties were very onerous, that his work could not be postponed.

Pilate and I exchanged glances, silently agreeing that Procla was a charming and delightful child whom we would not hurt.

"Princess," he said, "I know an excellent companion for you, during your visit — which I hope will be long."

Procla listened intently.

"My favorite Captain of the Guard, Cartaphilus — a man of the world and a philosopher. Am I not right, Procla?"

Procla became enthusiastic in her praises of the Captain. Her cheeks flushed. According to her he was the handsomest of the Jews and the most gallant, and certainly an excellent companion.

Pilate smiled. "Procla is half in love with him herself. I should banish him. I think I will."

Procla protested, a little too seriously.

Pilate burst into laughter.

"Do you see, Princess?"

I smiled.

"I shall appoint him as your royal bodyguard, Princess!"

"A Jew?" I asked nonchalantly.

"He was. He is a Roman now — more Roman than a Senator." He laughed a little.

"He has the charm of the Jew and the culture of the Roman!" Procla remarked.

"Besides, he is worthy of his name," Pilate whispered, winking — "Cartaphilus — the Much-Beloved."

Although intrigued, I accepted rather superciliously. Who was this Jewish Captain, more Roman than a Roman, a philosopher and gallant?

"To-morrow Cartaphilus will report!"

Procla reminded Pilate that a messenger from Cæsar was waiting for him in his study. The Governor smiled, placed his arm around her waist, a little too thin, I thought, for amorous pleasures, and promised to attend to the matter at once.

I was restless. The hours were leaden-footed. Why should I be so anxious to meet an insignificant Captain of the Guard, highly praised by the jealous wife of a Roman Governor? I had known princes, tetrarchs, high priests, heroes, philosophers, kings.

In what way could he be different? What was man but the compound of vanity, awkwardness, conceit? Intelligence, genius, rank were but the thin veneer hiding or romanticizing the brute, alert for his prey. An enormous foundation clumsily conceived to uphold the organ of generation!

Woman had accepted her slavery merely because she was more harmoniously constructed, because as a tribute to modesty and beauty her sex was concealed within her. In her ignorance and humility, she imagined she had been created incomplete by a divinity whose ideal was an unruly organ, imperfectly constructed!

I awaited the arrival of the Captain, planning to make him my scapegoat, the scapegoat of all womankind. Militant, a goddess of vengeance, I proclaimed war against Cartaphilus — and the Moon!

CHAPTER TWELVE

CARTAPHILUS, AFORETIME ISAAC — THE COBBLER'S BOY IS A ROMAN CAPTAIN — I RECOLLECT A DREAM — I DROP MY FAN — A JEW RECOGNIZES HIS OWN — CARTAPHILUS BLANCHES — I HIDE MY FACE UPON HIS CHEST.

I ENTERED the hall reserved for me in the Palace of the Procurator. The Captain, in full regalia, anointed and perfumed like a bridegroom, saluted me obsequiously. His anxiety to impress me was obvious.

"I am Cartaphilus, Captain of the Guard," he said pompously, as if proclaiming himself Monarch of the Earth.

I looked at him startled. There could be no doubt. Cartaphilus was Isaac, the insolent youth I had seen bathing in the sea, displaying his nakedness. He was the cobbler's son who had mocked woman and ridiculed my mother and me.

Like a whirlwind the entire scene reënacted itself before me. I saw once again the boys swim to shore. The ringleader, with the body of a powerful ape, mocked little David. Isaac and his friend disported their masculine prowess. Agrippina pressed against me nervously. Isaac threw the discus in the air and nearly grazed my cheek. The youths stretched out upon the shore. Isaac's clear limbs and the three black flowers under his arms and upon his lap, glistened in the sun.

I heard Isaac say, "Women are all knock-kneed. Woman without a man is an empty vessel, a pot without a cover.

95

Nature gave woman breasts to feed the world, but man she gave brains to rule it!"

I heard myself say: "The fool! It isn't true!"

His friend said: "They say Salome is beautiful!"

"She is scrawny and shapeless."

"Anyhow, if she invited you to her royal couch, you would not refuse, would you, Isaac?"

"A man of honor never refuses!"

My face flushed. I felt once again the pang that initiated me into womanhood.

"Cobbler," I was about to shout, "back to your last!"

No, that would be too trivial, a reprisal too cheap, a vengeance too inconsequential for a princess, for Salome! I would torment him, slowly, delicately, like a cat playing with a mouse. I would taunt him while he tortured his brain to know the reason of it. The Much-Beloved would know the meaning of scorn!

I walked slowly, deliberately to the throne. He approached me and helped me seat myself, then stood at attention.

I played lazily with the pendant of my necklace, a piece of jade, the shape of a tortoise, which Cleopatra had given to my grandmother Mariamne.

Meanwhile, furtively I watched Isaac. Reluctant, unwilling, I was forced to acknowledge to myself that he was handsome, even handsomer than when I had seen him for the first time. His face had acquired the dignity and confidence of his new rank and his new citizenship. Only about his mouth there lurked a smile of servility, which now and then changed into superciliousness, accentuating rather than obliterating the humbleness of his origin.

His body retained its suppleness, and I smiled to think that I knew exactly how perfectly each member articulated, as he boasted to his boy friend. What was the boy friend's name? I thought of many Jewish and Roman names, but none seemed to fit. Suddenly I murmured "John!" I shivered. It was a name I sedulously avoided. My face clouded. My hand dropped upon my lap.

I was about to ask him —"Isaac, is your friend also a

Captain in the Roman Army? Do you still entertain your romantic affection for him? Do you still excite his jealousy and then yield to his humor? And what about the young girl whom you loved so much — Mary — Mary of Magdala, whose breasts you once touched while she drew water out of the well? Is she perchance your wife or your mistress?"

Cartaphilus waited for a word of approval. He watched me, his eyes wandering over my body with the insouciance of a man who knows how to appraise feminine pulchritude. His impertinence enraged me. What right had this cobbler's son, masquerading as a Roman Captain, to covet me, to remove my clothing, denuding me of my rank? I was only a woman to him, and he a man, and therefore my superior, my master!

Nevertheless his presence pleased me, like that of a lover once cherished, then forgotten, and long after discovered once more.

Suddenly I recalled the dream I had in the bridal chamber of my first husband, Tetrarch Philip.

"I shall go," Cartaphilus said, when I scorned his caresses, "but you cannot escape me. All men shall assume the image of me. For I am the first who awakened your womanhood."

Was it true? Would the memory of this man haunt me forever? Would I always desire him. even in the embraces of the others?

Exasperated by the tender twitchings of my heart, I became obdurate in my disdain.

"Captain," I said without looking up, as if I addressed a menial, "are the roads in good condition for chariots?"

Cartaphilus was taken aback. I watched him with the corner of my eye. I knew that Pilate had whispered delightful promises in his ear, and that scandalous rumors concerning me and my amours must have reached him.

Piqued, he answered like a school-boy reciting a lesson. "The roads are in good condition, Princess."

"It is my wish to drive through the city to-day."

"As the Princess desires," he said.

I looked out of the window. The sun splashed its gold on the deeper gold of my hair. The Captain's eyes were riveted upon me. I had never been so conscious of my beauty. No sword, I realized, was half so sharp. "Alas," I thought, "the sword so soon gets dull. There is no whetstone powerful enough to resharpen it."

"In an hour I shall be ready!" I said.

"It is well, Princess. In an hour."

I walked slowly out of the hall, moving my body voluptuously in the manner of an Egyptian dancer.

When I reached the door leading to the rest of my suite, I dropped my fan, and turned around.

Cartaphilus, his teeth clenched, his eyes languid with passion, was unable to stir. I waited, yawning lightly. He approached, raised the fan, and pressed it into my hand, striking my thumb with restrained fury.

We rode for a long time in silence. I could almost hear the Captain's thoughts. They were an anguished plea for my attention and a violent tirade against my haughtiness. Why had I singled him out for my revenge? Why did I take seriously a youth's boastfulness and mockery of woman? His low birth was of little importance. Only the pariahs ridicule those who succeed in rising above their caste. Was not the Roman Emperor himself the son of a common officer? Did not the blood of the denizens of the desert flow in the veins of my grandfather Herod the Great?

Why had I not chosen for vengeance the High Priest whose beard was like a sheaf of hay burnt by the sun, or the Roman Senator whose eyes were crossed by two golden streaks, or Hermocrates the Greek poet, or Justus the builder of bridges and temples, or any of my variegated paramours?

Why Isaac, Cartaphilus, the Much-Beloved? What strange emotion attracted me to him, repelled me, made me desire and renounce him? Was it hate, was it love? Was it something nameless that plunged into the abyss of instincts, something that had its birth in the primordial wilderness of my being?

Why could I not be to him the royal visitor, affable, and gracious, even if I disdained his masculine advances? Why did I not treat him as the messenger of Pilate, the Captain of the Guard?

Procla had spoken of his brilliant mind. She called him a poet and a scholar.

I asked him his opinion of a new philosopher who had created a stir in Rome. He spoke with eloquence, quoting Latin and Greek, illuminating his arguments with aphorisms. His voice was well modulated and harmonious, but beneath it, like an undercurrent, I detected the same youthful conceit that irritated me when he first flaunted his masculinity in the sun.

Cartaphilus was still Isaac, would remain Isaac always, however heavy and dazzling the veneer of his accomplishments. He would always be the cobbler's son, proud of the biological accident that differentiates the male from the female.

My ancient anger flamed within me once more. I could not be polite to him. He was the symbol of man!

The Captain, mistaking my apparent interest in his conversation, subtly introduced the subject of love as exemplified in the poetry of Ovid and the songs of Solomon. Gradually abandoning generalities, his words began to balance delicately upon the golden fence which separates the permissible from the forbidden. In another moment, he would have apostrophized my beauty and my incomparable charm. His words were grazing his lips. This was the moment for me to strike against the vulnerable spot of his soul, which he concealed all too carefully — the humbleness of his origin. Cruel, perhaps, and unsportsmanlike, I aimed the arrow to the very heart.

Playing with my pendant, I asked casually: "What is the Roman population of Jerusalem, Captain?"

He caught his breath and frowned. His hand twitched. I had annihilated at one blow his long and well-planned siege.

"Princess," he answered irritably and changing instantly his voice to one of unconcern, "I have not consulted the archives."

"Should not the vanquished know accurately the strength of the enemy?"

"Rome is not the enemy of Judea," he answered proudly, conveying the idea that he was one of the conquerors.

"But should not a Jew remember his forefathers who never brooked the yoke of the invader?"

He looked at me, trying to discover whether I guessed the truth of his origin.

"You may deceive the Gentiles, Isaac," I said to myself, "but a Jew always recognizes his own. However straight the nose, however perfect the tongue, whatever the uniform or the name, a Jew cannot hide his identity from a Jew. The soul, too, bears the scar of his circumcision."

His eyes clouded. His back bent. He sighed. Suddenly, however, his lips lengthened and tightened into a defiant smile.

"That, too, Isaac! Defiance and irony, arrogance and humility!"

Our charioteer pulled the reins suddenly, swearing at the top of his voice. The horses raised their hoofs high in the air like circus animals trained to walk on their hind-legs. We were nearly thrown out. Our bodies touched for a moment.

The street was blocked by a multitude of people, harangued by an emaciated man, whose eyes had vanished almost completely within their orbits, and whose beard danced about his face like a mad goat's.

"Make way there!" the charioteer shouted. "Make way, or I'll drive the horses over you!"

The man continued to speak. The crowd never budged.

"Hearken ye!" the man expostulated. "Hearken ye! He has risen from the dead! He is now seated at the right hand of the Father!"

"Make way!" Seeing himself unheeded, the charioteer urged his horses forward. The animals snorted, foamed, but refused to move.

"He was crucified and buried, and the third day He rose from the grave, and He was raised to Heaven!"

"True! True!" some exclaimed.

"He died that you may live! Believe in Him, and you shall know no death!"

"I believe! I believe!"

"He was the Son of God who sent Him to Earth that He preach His Holy Word. Hearken ye to it, men of Judea, or ye shall suffer His vengeance on the Day of Judgment!"

"Make way! Make way, ye sons of she-dogs!"

The charioteer cracked his whip. Some one screamed in pain.

The preacher pursued:

"Do not tarry like the Accursed One, who must wander over the face of the Earth, as a beast pursued, who shall never know the meaning of peace and home!"

A sudden wind howled about the chariot and rocked it. Cartaphilus jumped from his seat. His face was white. His eyes glowed with an unnatural glow, as if a sea of fire had poured its flames within them. He stretched his arms forward, his fists clenched. What malediction was shaping itself on his trembling lips? Against what divinity would he utter—anathema maranatha!

His words were strangled in the wind.

Breathless, exhausted, he fell back into the carriage. In mortal terror he pressed his hands against his face. His knees trembled against mine. His teeth were clenched.

I cowered. Something in Cartaphilus roused memories I wished concealed forever. The wind became articulate. I pressed my hands against my ears. My chest heaved as if I had climbed mountains.

Over the heads of the multitude rose the head of Jokanaan, blood streaming like the rays of a setting sun.

The eyes of Cartaphilus met my eyes. What strange cord bound our gaze? What terrible fate united us?

"Cartaphilus!" I whispered.

"Salome!" he muttered.

The mouth of Jokanaan opened, and once again he hurled at me his eternal invective. "I shall die — but you are too vile for the grave!"

I uttered a shriek, and buried my head upon the chest of Cartaphilus.

CHAPTER THIRTEEN

THE BROOM OF TIME — A BOYISH LOVER — WOMAN OR WITCH — LILITH, DESTROYER OF MEN — I CONSULT A GREEK LEECH — LIFE WITHOUT END — THE JUDGMENT OF DANIEL — I SET OUT FOR THE HILLS AS A MULETEER.

TIME, the mighty Broom, had swept the Earth of two generations of men. Herodias and her husband were dead in exile in Vienna. Pilate, according to rumor, had committed suicide in Rome. Procla was ashes. Three procurators had supplanted one another in Jerusalem. The old temples were crumbling. New temples rose to new divinities. Prophets and Messiahs preached and threatened, and were gone. History changed, gods changed, geography changed. I alone remained unaltered. For me the grains of sand no longer coursed through the hourglass of Time.

My paramours were dust within their coffins or too old and too weary to remember passion — but my blood still raced with undiminished lust through my veins, and the Moon, inexorable Tyrant, demanded her tribute as punctiliously as of yore.

How had I escaped the inevitable? Was I really young, or was it only my skin that retained its youth, my skin and my passion? How long would I continue this way? "Too vile for the grave!" rang in my ears. What did it mean? Was I destined never to grow old, never to die, until the twilight of Time? Never to die! The idea loomed colossal. I trembled, I knew not whether with joy or with fear!

To stop the wagging of tongues and the envious looks of

acquaintances, who were skeptical of the power of cosmetics to keep indefinitely a skin as fresh and as young as mine, I retired to the outskirts of the Capital. As the widow of a merchant of Smyrna, I led a simple and solitary life.

I returned from my walk in the woods earlier than usual. About to open the door, I heard Hagar, one of my maids, exclaim: "She is a witch, Daniel! She is a vampire!"

My hand remained on the knob. I listened.

"You are a jealous fool, Hagar!" Daniel admonished.

"I am jealous because I love you. But I am not a fool. I swear by God, she has bewitched you. She is a vampire devouring your soul, Daniel!"

Daniel laughed.

"She has devoured the souls of many men. She drinks their blood — that's how she remains young. She'll drink your blood, Daniel!"

Daniel continued to laugh.

"Don't laugh!"

"You want to make me believe that Salome is an old woman?"

"She must be a hundred years old. I know it. Everybody knows it."

"Did you ever see the bodies of old women, Hagar? Did you ever touch their skin — like scales of fish, that make you shudder? Did you ever see their breasts, shriveled like old crab-apples, which rot under trees? The skin of Salome is whiter than milk. Her lips are dipped in fresh honey. Her breasts —"

"Stop!" Hagar cried. "Her skin is the devil's! Satan gave her youth in exchange for her soul. Her lips are red with the blood of her lovers!"

"Don't be absurd. It's you who are bewitched by false gossip!"

"Daniel, I am your friend. People are beginning to suspect that you, too, have sold your soul to the devil. You are wearing your heart out for a witch. She saps your youth to restore her own. She drinks your vitality to rejuvenate hers."

Daniel laughed. But his laughter was hollow.

"Everybody knows that she is an old witch. You are the

only one who won't see the truth. You are young. You belong to me. Youth belongs to youth. Why, she was a grown-up princess in the time of her grandfather Herod the Great. You've studied the Talmud. You ought to know how long ago that is."

Daniel laughed. He pinched her breast gently. "That's not in the Talmud, little wench!"

"Wherever it is. It's a long time ago. Isn't it?"

"It is."

"Her mother was Herodias and her father Herod Antipas. Who remembers them? Do you? Do I? My grandmother used to tell me terrible stories about them. They were godless assassins in league with demons. Salome is a she-devil who seduces and murders her lovers."

"Nonsense, you little fool," he shouted, his voice husky and unconvincing. "You speak not of Salome, but of Lilith. Lilith is the destroyer of men."

"Then she is Lilith. She destroys men. She has had a thousand lovers. My grandmother, who knew her when she was a child, remembers how she slew two of her husbands. In the mikvah the women speak of nothing else but her now. Before long they will go to the Rabbi and accuse her of witchcraft."

"They are ugly hens cackling!" Daniel exclaimed, angrily.

"They've been too patient with her, Daniel. She should have been driven into the desert long ago."

"You women are all jealous of her beauty."

"She is not beautiful as a woman should be beautiful. There is something in her eyes which is not of the Earth. Her eyes dazzle with the glow of hell fire."

Tenderly, she placed her arms around his neck.

"Stay away from her, my love. Do not risk your life. They will stone you, Daniel, together with this bawd of a witch!"

"She loves me, and I love her. I don't see any harm in it. If she wants to, I'll marry her."

"Oh!" Hagar shrieked. "Will you barter your stalwart manhood to her and the devil, like a male prostitute? Marriage with her means eternal shame and eternal damnation!"

I walked quickly away, fearing that Daniel might open the door at any moment and find me there listening.

I had heard enough.

The time had come for immediate action.

I hired a litter and rushed to Araxemis, the most famous of the Greek leeches in Jerusalem.

Araxemis paid no attention to me. I was certain he knew that I was in the room, but he pretended to be totally oblivious of his environment. He pondered over a phial, muttering strange sounds to impress me.

"Doctor," I said at last, fearing that his comedy would last indefinitely.

He turned about with a start, his beard jumping in the air, his forehead a mass of wrinkles.

"I am sorry to disturb you," I said.

Without waiting for his effusive greeting to end, I recounted the history of my case, omitting only my name and my rank.

He squinted his eyes, until nothing could be seen of them, save two shining dots.

"There seems to be a new malady among the Jews." He cackled with senile humor. "Have the gods infected them with their own affliction — eternal youth?"

"What do you mean, Doctor?"

"Only the other day a man consulted me about the same matter. He was thirty years by every sinew of his body, but he claimed to be more than twice as old."

"Who was it?" I asked anxiously.

"That I cannot disclose, madam, without violating my vow of secrecy to Æsculapius."

He tested my nerves, my muscles, examined my blood, my saliva, the organs within which life perpetuates itself. He used a dozen strange instruments. He consulted manuscripts, charts, and uttered words of incantation.

"Madam," he said at last, "you are at most thirty. I swear it by Jupiter and Æsculapius."

An idea whirled about me like a hurricane. I would be the Mother of the World! Endless generations of children and grandchildren and great-grandchildren and great-great-grandchildren nestled upon my eternally youthful lap and continued their journey through time and space. I was the creator of poets and kings and heroes. I was the root of Life. I was the womb of a magnificent humanity, half gods, half men, long-lived and mighty like oaks.

"Leech! Leech!" I asked, "can I be a mother? Can I bear fruit?"

The leech examined the hidden world where life germinates.

He shook his head.

"The seed of no loins shall have the power to stir new life within you."

Did I constantly renew myself? Was that the meaning of my youth? Was I root and flower as well?

Were the words of the leech truth? Was he a charlatan trying to flatter my vanity? I was shaken with a strange turbulence. Too impatient to ride I ran home.

Daniel awaited me. His eyes were bloodshot. His face was haggard and drawn, as after a long debauch. The words of Hagar had eaten into his soul.

I wished to silence the fever of my mind in the passion of my body.

"Have you been waiting long, Daniel?" I asked, smiling.

"Yes," he answered metallically.

"Your patience shall be rewarded!"

I looked at him intently. I had never realized how closely he resembled Isaac of yore, who now was Cartaphilus. The same lips, the same eyes, the same hair, the same proud bearing in his nakedness! Or was it an illusion? Was it true that I loved Cartaphilus vicariously in every man?

What had become of the Captain? We had not met since our strange experience in Jerusalem. Why did he blanch when the itinerant preacher babbled of some one doomed to live forever? Was he the man who had visited the leech on a mission similar to mine?

"Why do you look at me like that, Salome?" Daniel asked, trembling.

"I thought of a friend you resemble, dear — of a friend — who died — long ago."

"Long ago?" he asked, scrutinizing me.

"I must be careful of my dates," I thought.

"At — least — a hundred years, Daniel," I answered laughingly.

His face paled.

Suddenly conscious of my youth my breast stiffened with desire, kindled perhaps by the memory of the impudent boy whom Daniel so strangely resembled.

"Daniel," I said, "love me fiercely, as if death stood watching at the foot of our couch."

I threw his cloak upon the floor and tightly encircled his limbs.

"Will you love me always, Daniel?" I asked, as thousands of generations of maidens have asked.

Something in my touch must have aroused his misgivings. The torch of passion flickered, and went out.

He did not answer. He looked into my eyes.

"What do you see within them, Daniel?"

"I am afraid of you, Salome," the boy whimpered.

I bent my fingers, and stretched my neck forward like a bird of prey seeking to capture and devour its victim. He recoiled.

"Beware of Salome!" I waved my forefinger warningly. "Lovers die in her embrace!"

Daniel tightened his eyes, and caught his breath. Seeing that he took my words seriously, I burst into laughter.

He regained confidence somewhat.

"My foolish little lover!"

I caressed him with my hands.

Desperately, like one who wishes to forget something that torments him, Daniel pressed against me, dug his teeth into my body. The torch of passion remained unlit.

"What ails my strong lover today?" I asked, mocking gently.

He did not answer. His face had turned ashen.

"Does my beauty no longer bewitch you, Daniel? Has my kiss lost its savor?"

He jumped off the couch. He pasted his forefingers to his middle fingers and the thumbs tip to tip, holding his hands in front of him like a superstitious rustic warding off evil.

"Vampire! Sorceress!"

I smiled. "Even greater lovers than you sometimes dally before the altar of Venus without an offering."

"Hagar is right! It is true! You are a witch!"

"As old as Eve," I said playfully.

"Death himself spurns you, accursed vampire," he cried, reiterating the curse of Jokanaan. "You are vile, too vile for the grave!"

He covered his face with his hands, trembling. He buried himself in the angle of the wall, and sobbed.

I watched the convulsions of his angular, boyish body.

"My foolish little lover," I said tenderly, "why do you hearken to the stupid chatter of jealous women? Come to me, Daniel. Do not fear me."

The sobbing subsided. Resolutely, Daniel walked to where his clothes were spread on a divan.

I stretched out my arms, and closed my eyes. "Come!" I whispered.

Suddenly he uttered a piercing shriek.

"Daniel," I cried, jumping off the couch.

Daniel fell to the floor, the hilt of a dagger shivering over his heart, from which blood spouted like a stream.

I bent over him, and pulled out the dagger. His eyes rolled upward. His chin dropped.

"Daniel, my poor child!"

My face turned to stone. I had seen many people die. But the death of this boy unnerved me. It seemed a symbol, a warning, a prophecy of something I could not define.

I wept quietly for a long time.

Footsteps in the courtyard awakened me to my situation. It was unsafe to linger any longer. I covered the body with the cloak, and bolted the door.

Summoning Hagar, I bade her go to the city and make several purchases. In a like manner I disposed of my other servants.

An hour later I emerged as a young muleteer dressed in

the cast-off clothing of a lad in my service. Loading two of my donkeys with the jewels of my husbands and the treasures saved from the ruins of the House of Herod, I set out for the hills.

CHAPTER FOURTEEN

WHY NOT A FEMALE MESSIAH? — THE MAGIC OF JOKANAAN — I DANCE DEFIANCE — I HIDE A LARGE CHEST OF JEWELS.

I REACHED the desert. I had enough provisions to last me for days. I remembered that at intervals of some leagues, there were always oases with water and fruit trees. I could live in the desert for months or years, even. I could become the Witch of the Desert, or pose as a new Messiah.

There had never been a woman Messiah. Would not a woman Messiah be more persuasive than a man? A Messiah of which god? A Messiah preaching what — the end of the world, the freedom of Palestine, the resurrection of the saintly dead or heaven on earth?

No, I was not in the mood for Messianic glory or martyrdom.

Martyrdom?

I shivered.

What awaited me, if I should really never die? What tortures, what ailments were in store for me? I remembered the Greek to whom the gods gave eternal life without eternal youth. Perhaps I too should grow old. Jokanaan said that the grave would reject me. But he never said that pain, perhaps endless pain, would not be mine. He did not mean to bless me. His words were the most blasting curse he could pluck out of the angry depths of his being.

The enormity of the situation overwhelmed me. The desert became my soul — a desert destined never to blossom, perhaps never to wither — a vast sea of sand undulating forever! That's what Jokanaan meant! What had given him the right to cast such a spell over me, over Nature? Was he a god? Had his eyes and mouth such power over life's destiny?

A profound hatred, such I had never experienced, racked me. I clenched my fists and shouted: "I curse you, Jokanaan!"

"Too vile for the grave!" thundered the desert.

My animals galloped away madly, braying as if wild creatures pursued them.

I straightened up. I threw my masculine rags off my body. Naked, proud, I cried to the winds of the desert: "So be it, Jokanaan! Too vile for the grave! But undaunted of Life!"

Seized by the passion of a wild rhythm, I danced. Not before Herod, not before Antipas, not even before Jokanaan, had I danced with such abandon. There was pride and defiance, and joy, and passion, and fierce courage! I flung my arms to the sun. "I dance to you, Eternal Source of Life, I, Salome, Eternal Woman!"

Near the Dead Sea there were several caves never frequented save by mad prophets and animals at bay. In one of these I hid a large chest of jewels, which included the crowns of Antipas and my mother, the gifts of my first husband, a bracelet worn by King David which my grandfather had bequeathed to me, to spite his male heirs, fistfuls of rubies, amethysts, diamonds and pearls, rings, earrings and brooches.

I covered the place with sand and rocks. My knowledge of mathematics and astronomy would help me determine for all time the spot where I could replenish my wealth. My other chest which I took along contained a fortune sufficient to buy a city. Besides, was not a woman's beauty, imperishable as the planets, an inexhaustible treasure?

I was unafraid of the future.

I remembered my mother's advice to marry into the royal house of Arabia, and revive the glory of our ancestors. The prince she had selected for me was doubtlessly long gathered among his fathers, but other members of the dynasty could not be lacking. I would carry out at last my mother's wishes.

CHAPTER FIFTEEN

I AM A YOUNG MERCHANT — I HEAR AN ANCIENT PROPHECY — THE PRINCESS SALOME ENTERS ARABIA — I LEARN THE SECRET OF HERBS — PERSISTENT VIRGINITY — ROYAL COURTSHIP — A PROPHECY FULFILLED.

I ENTERED Arabia for the first time as Saloman ben Duvid, a young camel merchant from Damascus, who had recently inherited a large sum of money. At once I was surrounded by a flock of very solicitous and affable men hoping to pluck the fledgling. The plucking, however, was not as easy as they had anticipated, and the fledgling, to their surprise, had solid wings and a hard beak.

"Alas," they bemoaned, "the new generation is born with the gray beard of wisdom. The tree bears fruit before it sprouts leaves. The chick is shrewder than the hen."

Outwitted in the matter of camels, the merchants endeavored to recoup their loss by proposing to me maidens of such rare beauty and impeccable purity that even Hussein, King of Araby, would covet.

"Is Hussein's harem very large?" I asked.

They winked to one another, and pulled at their beards.

"The King — may his name be blessed — does not consider his three hundred and seventy-five wives sufficient for the strength of his loins. He sold six of his favorite steeds to buy three new wives."

"That," one merchant exclaimed, indignantly, "is even as you say. What a desecration of the Law! When a man pays more for a woman than for a horse, the country is on the brink of ruin!" Seeing, however, that his remark might tend to discourage me, he added quickly, "Now, for a young gentleman like yourself — Saloman — that is another matter altogether. You need a harem to exercise your mettle and beget children to perpetuate your seed. They will inherit your incomparable wisdom and prudence — and the great wealth which a young man of such unusual perspicacity will certainly amass."

"You should be like the Great King whose name you bear," another added, "for although you are not a king, you may be —" He fumbled for an appropriate compliment.

I interrupted —"I may be a queen."

They laughed, slapping each other's backs and thighs.

"A queen's pleasure!"

"Indeed, our Saloman seems well provisioned for it!" he remarked, eyeing my sturdy thighs with a salacious smirk.

"Has Hussein many descendants?" I asked.

"Alas, his seed dies in the wombs of our women."

"That is according to the prophecy!"

"What prophecy?" I asked.

"The prophecy of the Princess from the other side of the desert, whose virgin womb and none other, the King will fructify. Her descendants, they say, will rule over Araby. They say that when that happens our country will once more be the greatest and most powerful in the world. So they say," he sighed.

"Since Hussein has no heir, who will rule over Arabia, should the Princess from far away never come?" I asked.

"His Majesty — may he prosper forever — has nine brothers!"

"Must the Princess from beyond the desert be a virgin?" I asked.

"Our King will not couch with a woman who has been defiled even by another man's eyes."

"Man," I thought, "even as the Moon, demands a woman's tribute of blood."

I laughed. "How foolish man is! What is virginity but an impediment to his pleasure!"

They shook their shoulders merrily.

"And has not the Great King said that three things leave no trace — a snake crawling over a rock, a bird in flight, and the way of a man with a maid?"

"O wiser than the wisest of Kings!"

"O Solomon of Damascus!"

"What will our friend become when his beard is as long as ours?" they asked one another, clicking their tongues against their palates.

While the merchants were gathering incomparable virgins for my prospective harem, I disappeared.

Six months later, Princess Salome, granddaughter of Salome, daughter of Herodias, daughter of Aretas, King of Arabia, followed by a retinue as imposing as that of a conquering monarch, knocked at the gates of the capital.

Mecca became a cauldron of joy. Astrologers and soothsayers and oracles proclaimed from the temples and the market-places the glad tidings that the day for the fulfillment of the great prophecy had come. Araby was about to blossom once again.

The Moon was streaked with blood. The Planets arranged themselves in a perfect circle. Stars fell across the desert. The Earth trembled. Animals uttered proverbs.

But all this did not occur without the help of my secret messengers, who for months had bribed the astrologers of the King.

His Majesty, Hussein ben Hedjaz, sent ambassadors with priceless gifts and tongues heavily laden with the honey of eloquence and the perfume of poetry to recount his great love, and his yearning that I rule over his heart and his dominions.

Reluctant at first, as became a young bride, I accepted the will of the gods and the hand of the Potentate.

I summoned to my aid the magic of potent herbs. Juno-like I was a virgin again. I entered, Symbol of Purity and Modesty, into the chamber reserved for the royal bride.

For three days I was a prisoner, achieving the final purification by prayers and baths. The fourth day, Hussein, in full regal glory, entered, almost suffocating me with incense and perfumes.

Passion had destroyed what the years had left. His chin was hardly hidden by his sparse beard, which looked as if birds had pecked at it. His long, hooked nose, pinched and sharp, rose triumphant over his face. His lips were enormous and shapeless like those of a camel.

I kissed his shoulder, as became a timid wife. He lifted my veil gently. When he beheld my face, he caught his breath.

"More dazzling art thou, O Queen, than the sunshine on swords in battles, more gorgeous than the full Moon over the desert," he recited, quoting the lines of the official poetaster.

"More desirable art thou, O King, than the cool fresh stream of the oasis," I answered.

"Thy voice is the voice of the nightingale, O my Bride!"

"Thy arms are mighty like the wings of eagles, O my Husband!"

"Thy breasts are hillocks of pleasure!"

"Thy limbs are pillars of the Honor of God."

"Thy skin, O My Bride, is whiter than milk and sweeter than fresh honey."

"More welcome is thy fame, O King, than rain to the parched flowers!"

"Purer art thou than the new-born lamb."

"Stronger art thou than the flood that breaks the dykes of stone!"

"More delicious is the caress of thy hand than the thought of paradise!"

Weary at last of the immemorial platitudes of Oriental courtship, Hussein enfolded me in his arms, and gently laid me on the nuptial couch.

CHAPTER SIXTEEN

ARABIA TOTTERS — THE LANGUISHING HAREM —"THE KING IS DEAD, LONG LIVE THE KING"— MY SEVEN ARABIAN HUSBANDS — THE ROYAL MIDWIFE — A PRISONER OF LIFE — BARK WITHOUT COMPASS.

ARABIA was tottering like a chair balancing itself on one leg. The news that the great prophecy had been fulfilled was a mighty hand that planted it once more firmly upon the ground. The army recovered its morale and repulsed the Persians whose pointed spears were already peering over the fortifications. The temples, the market-places, the universities blossomed once again, as if a sudden spring had cracked the heavy ice of winter.

Hussein forgot his vanity, and his ministers their envy. I was not alone the Chief Counselor, but the real ruler. My wisdom, since it could not be attributed to age or sex, was attributed to the gods.

Only the harem, neglected, forgotten, like an attic crowded with things once valuable, grumbled and gossiped and plotted. Slowly, their words pierced through the walls, and like an evil scent spread through the capital.

"The prophecy has not been fulfilled," they whispered, then argued, then shouted.

"The prophecy promised heirs!"

"Heirs who into all eternity would rule over Arabia and conquer the world Where are the heirs?"

"It is two years now since she has lain in his couch — and yet her womb is barren!"

"Salome is like the desert whence she comes!"
"She is not the Princess of the prophecy!"
"She is a witch!"
"She will bring misfortune to our land!"
"The King has neither ears nor eyes nor passion for his other wives!"
"Is it not written in the Law that a man, be he a commoner or a monarch, must visit each of his women at regular intervals?"
"For two years we are untended and unwatered like despised weeds!"

Nevertheless, Hussein allowed his harem to languish. His concubines, once the pride of all Araby, were constrained at last, to seek consolation in the dreary embraces of eunuchs or in the vulgar arms of camel drivers and foreigners dressed as women. Those who forbore to sin with men transplanted to the soil of Arabia the secret rites of Lesbos.

Hussein became sullen. He sacrificed rams and bulls and male elephants to all the divinities of generations and creation, consulted astrologers, soothsayers, oracles, aged hags who culled strange herbs when the horns of the crescent moon were tipped with stars; epileptics who muttered wild prophecies in vain. My womb was not soil for his seed.

Just as some generations previously, my first husband Philip, Tetrarch of Iturea, had planned my death to avenge his impotence, so now Hussein was determined to wreak vengeance upon me for his sterility. Life, however, had since become infinitely more precious to me. I could not trifle with danger. Suspicious of my attendants, I watched their hands for concealed weapons. A slave tasted my food before I touched it. I dared not smell a flower. A shadow in motion frightened me.

I realized the necessity of increasing my prudence and my knowledge until they became proportionate to my longevity. A great treasure could not be carried in one's hands, absent-mindedly through the crowded thoroughfares of life.

I decided to learn whatever magic, whatever lore, whatever incantations, whatever skill, medical or religious, were hidden in every land.

The King had been gone for several days. He was on his final errand for secret enchantments, to a miracle-worker living in a cave. The seed of a lion, king of beasts, swallowed at night in the shape of a pill was to fortify the seed of Hussein, King of men.

It was time to flee. Already disguises were in my coffers. My jewels were concealed beyond the reach of imagination or hand. My animals pawed the ground impatiently. I had bribed attendants and eunuchs The gates would open silently at my touch

I was pondering over the last details of my disappearance, when the door to my room opened and Aliman, the brother of Hussein, entered smiling, a small casket of jewels in his hands. I covered my face quickly with my veil, and uttered a meek cry of modesty.

Aliman approached me, pulled the veil gently off, and presented me with the casket.

"Salome, my wife," he said succinctly.

"Where is the King?" I asked, perturbed.

"I am the King!" he answered, his eyes blacker than his brother's and larger, blazing with pride.

"Where is Hussein, your brother, my lord?"

"Hussein, may his soul rest in peace, is with our ancestors, with your great-great-grandfather the mighty King Aretas."

Aliman waited a moment, twirled his beard, a little thicker than that of his brother, revealing only a glimpse of his fat chin.

"Salome," he said gently, smiling, his teeth broad and flat, like spades, "you are making secret preparations to leave Arabia."

I made a gesture of disavowal.

He laughed.

"The sword is mightier than the purse," he said. "The only way to insure secrecy is to remove the head. Even the removal of the tongue is not sufficient. For the hand learns something of the eloquence of her noisier sister."

It was good advice to remember.

"The wife who flees the harem, even if she be a queen, dies in the powerful grip of the eunuch's fist, which winds itself around her delicate and beautiful throat. Salome knows the Law."

Was he making love to me? Was he threatening me with death?

"But Salome is more than wife, more than queen. She is the prophecy of the gods. And Hussein — may his soul rest in peace — had not the might to fulfill the prophecy."

"The mouth of my husband is filled with the words of the Lord!" I said.

"And his loins with the seed of prophecy," he added significantly.

Then, with the usual formula, he praised my beauty. His words were the words Hussein had spoken, and my answers were the echo of my old responses.

I devoted the three days of purification which preceded the consummation of my marriage with Aliman to my pristine reintegration. Herbs and lotions transformed me into a maid once more.

Aliman flaunted his masculine prowess like the standard of a triumphant army. He trumpeted abroad the reason for the unfulfillment of the prophecy. The murder of his brother Hussein ben Hedjaz lay lightly upon his conscience and the tongues of the people. The Lord had meant Aliman and not his brother to consummate the divine command.

Jesting about his brother's incapacity, Aliman pranced about like a young stallion.

"My brother Hussein — may his soul rest in peace — and blossom at the right hand of Abraham — stormed fortresses and cities and put to the sword thousands of enemies, for he was a great warrior, but the citadel of love was mightier than rock and mortar, and the arrow faltered and missed its aim."

I assumed a modesty a trifle inconsonant with my experience. Delighted by the evidence of my innocence, Aliman showered me with gifts and praises. He compared me to all the beautiful and pure phenomena of nature, to the fauna and flora, to the gazelle and the nightingale and the swan — pillaging in my honor all the poets of Araby.

I was no longer the true power of the kingdom. The priests seized once more the reins. The throne became the footstool of the altar. Little of what occurred in the country pierced the walls of the harem. I was merely the symbol of Arabia's future glory, the holy vessel holding the ichor of the gods. But the cup that held the destiny of the present was snatched out of my hands.

Aliman sold or gave away the wives of his predecessors. Not a few were dispatched to a more peaceful and less transitory world. The minimum number that regal dignity compelled Aliman to retain were huddled together in a few rooms of the palace, while I occupied the rest of the gynæceum.

The King dedicated exclusively to my use and to the army of eunuchs the inner garden, the pools, the vast hall, where once his brother's wives had displayed and disported their beauty like peacocks.

Flight was out of the question. Rebellion was both useless and dangerous. I pretended a great beatitude and spent my time studying the secrets of herbs and the mysteries of religion.

At the end of some months, Nephtoah, royal midwife-in-chief, paid me a visit. She was a mountain of flesh. A reddish beard encircled her chin and upper lip like a vegetation in early spring. Her voice was deeper than my husband's. I remembered my poor cousin Agrippina, and her description of the Amazons, and I wondered if Nephtoah had dedicated herself to the goddess who conquers the Moon.

My surmise was quickly refuted.

"I bore eighteen children, Queen," she said, "and my four husbands — may their souls rest in peace — were but camel merchants and usurers — not kings."

Nephtoah examined my body minutely and promised me a progeny as numerous as the sands of the seas and the stars of heaven — but with propitious mates. She gave me intricate and abstruse instructions, which I promised to follow, and promptly forgot.

Aliman disappeared one day, even as Hussein, and his brother Bazluth announced himself as the King of Araby and my lawful husband. Like his predecessor he believed he discovered the true cause of my barrenness, and, like him, he found, alas, that he was not the chosen one to fulfill the divine destiny.

Impatient to rule the kingdom, and snatch from fate the greater crown, the royal brothers, urged by the priests, one by one came, conquered and disappeared. With each my virginity blossomed again like a flower in spring.

Gradually their faces and their names merged into one another, and I no longer knew who it was that uttered the shout of triumph or who was summoned to the peaceful bosom of Abraham.

I had already mastered whatever Arabian science and philosophy I considered necessary, and a great restlessness overcame me. I longed to flee to a country where woman was neither a slave nor a goddess, where man dared not dispose of her as he listed.

Where was that country? Did it exist only in my imagination? Should I have to create it with my own hands and brain? How could I escape?

I had finally succeeded in acquiring a small bodyguard of faithful attendants. In the patio that wound itself about the periphery of the harem, I was protected. But one step beyond this magic circle, there lurked great and unforeseen dangers.

From distant rumors that reached me I knew that the people were beginning to rebel against the crumbling dynasty of Aretas. A revolution would not spare me.

What could happen to me? What had I to fear, if I was truly destined to live on indefinitely, if Jokanaan had the power to dictate over life and death? Could I walk through flames and emerge whole? Would the fists of assassins drop paralyzed? Would the sword break against my chest?

But if death should truly be impotent against me, was I

immune from mutilation? Illness, except for a cold, or a headache, the partial tribute of the Moon, had not molested me for generations. But was I destined to remain untouched forever? Was there no vulnerable spot? Was the armor of life tightly drawn about every atom of me?

What horoscope could foretell my destiny? If my fate was written in the stars, what Pythagoras could read its numbers, what Hermes interpret them?

A prisoner of life, I was destined to solitude and silence.

No human being needed greater courage. No mariner had ever sailed a more perilous sea. What compass should guide me? What winds should my bark obey?

CHAPTER SEVENTEEN

MY YOUNGEST HUSBAND —"ARE YOU AFRAID OF DEATH, SALOME?"— WIFE — MOTHER — WOMB OF THE EARTH — THE KNIFE THRUST — FATE MY ATTENDANT.

ONAM, the youngest of the princes of the House of Aretas, approached me, and like the others presented me with a casket of jewels, and called me his wife. He stammered his love like a school-boy who has not learned his lesson properly. Bored, and accustomed to the vagaries of masculine love-making, I waited patiently for the dénouement.

Onam resembled none of his brothers. He was thin, tall, blue-eyed, and his voice had a vague tremolo, as if he were frightened always, and sought refuge. He knelt at my feet, and covered my hands with kisses, and now and then with tears. Once I drew him gently toward me. He closed his eyes, and buried his face in my lap like a sick child.

I caressed his head. My body tingled with love — a love that I had not experienced since I had touched for the first and last time the soft face of my baby. The passion which men had aroused in me, their kisses, their embraces, receded, disappeared. I was a mother again. In motherhood I found the consummation of joy.

"Salome," Onam said, "you are not a woman. You are a goddess."

He looked at me intently.

"You are from the North. You come from the land of my mother."

"Do you remember your mother, my lord?"

"I remember nothing else. I was a child when she died, but her image is carved in my heart. No other woman can find room there. None save Salome, and Salome is a goddess."

"How did your mother look?"

"She had eyes like yours, and hair like yours, and a mouth like yours, and her lap was as soothing as your lap."

We remained silent for some time.

"Did you know my mother, Salome?"

"How could I know your mother, my lord, since she died long before I came here?"

He smiled sadly. "Salome, you have been since the beginning of time. You have been everywhere, always. And everywhere, and always shall you continue to be."

Had my secret been discovered? Had rumors floated about? Or was it merely this lad's way of making love, of evoking the image of his dead mother?

"Salome, why did my brothers kill one another? Why did they make me king? I loved my brothers. They did not hate each other. Only Aliman was ambitious. The cabal of priests and officers forced them to kill one another. They always pacify the wrath of the people with ancient prophecies and new kings. I do not wish to be king. I should like to travel to the North, the land of goddesses with golden hair and eyes which dazzle like seas when the sun lies upon them. I should like to wander upon the peaks of the tall mountains where the snow burns like white fire. I should like to converse with the spirits of life and death."

He stopped, and looked at me sadly.

"You do not make sport of me, Salome?"

I kissed his hair, and pressed his face between my palms. "My son!" grazed my lips, but never reached his ears.

"I know that people call me the 'Mad King,' as they used to call me the 'Mad Prince.' My brothers — may their souls rest in peace — mocked me, too. When they spoke of woman, I used to turn my face. I could not endure their attitude. They lorded over their harems like pompous cocks over their barnyards. They taunted me, calling me eunuch and catamite."

I caressed him, and whispered words of love.

"I knew they were wrong about woman, for I remembered my mother. She was as gentle and pure as the dawn, and her voice was music. Just like yours, Salome. Tell me a story of long ago."

When I finished one story, he begged me for another, and a third. He pressed his mouth against my knee, and closed his eyes. Now and then he asked me to repeat an incident or a name.

The shadow of the couch mingled with the shadow of the columns, and the shadows of the walls fell softly upon each other like feathers of giant black birds. The trumpets announced the approach of night, and warned evildoers.

"Let us go into the garden, Salome," Onam said. "I am restless this evening."

There was a strange glow in his eyes, whose color had changed from blue to gray. Two red spots burned upon his cheekbones like the torches of fever, and his arm, as it encircled my waist, trembled.

"My lord, are you ill?" I asked anxiously.

He looked at me quizzically.

"Is it true, Salome, that the souls of those we once loved are united with ours after death, becoming one, and that this union gives birth to gods?" he asked, dodging my question.

"Why speak of death, Onam?"

"Are you afraid of death, Salome?"

"Did you not say that I was a goddess, that I have been since the beginning of time, and that I shall continue to the end of time? Why should I fear death?"

"True, Salome. The gods have nothing to fear but life."

I shuddered.

Had he read my thoughts? Did he possess the weird clairvoyance of children, of madmen and saints?

The clouds, thin and ragged, allowed from time to time the sight of the Moon, as thin and ragged as themselves. The garden was heavy with perfumes like a prostitute in the market-place eager to attract the attention of men. At intervals, a dove, awakened by our footsteps, flapped its wings, rose a few yards from the ground, and alighted again.

We walked in silence for some time. Every now and then Onam looked about him, and pressed my hand.

"My brothers considered me a coward, Salome, because I hated war and wept when a slave was flogged. But I do not fear death. They were afraid to die. They surrounded themselves with an army of spies; they trembled at the sight of a drawn scimitar, even that of a friend; they dared not sleep profoundly. But I seek surcease from life. I want to bury myself in the uttermost depths, to emerge from this labyrinth of creation — to reach the final goal — Nirvana — I long for the womb of the Earth."

"Do not speak of death, my lord, I beg you. Let us both flee to the North, Onam! I love you, Onam. I am as a virgin to you, who has never known the love of man."

"You will always be a virgin, Salome. No man will ever know you. You are, even as your name indicates in Hebrew, Perfect."

"Flee with me, Onam. We can elude the cabal. I have discovered a secret passageway which leads to safety. If I had not loved you, I should have fled already."

"I know."

"You know, my lord?"

"In your eyes there are mountains and deserts and seas. In your voice there is the breath of the free wind. Your arms are wings outstretched."

What strange power had this lad to read my mind and soul? If only I could, like Jokanaan, pronounce upon him the curse or blessing of endless life. If I could keep him at my side throughout my long peregrination!

He smiled sadly. "No, Salome," he said, as if I had uttered the words. "You must go alone. Men are a burden to the gods."

"You must not think of me as a goddess, Onam. I am your wife and your mother. Come with me."

He continued. "As for me, it was written that I would be the king of Arabia. And it is also written that I must die in Arabia."

There was an unearthly look in his face. He spoke as a man who gazes into the past and into the future, but sees not the present.

"You must go away, Salome. You will travel through space and through time. A thousand lovers will kneel at your feet. Poets in all lands and in all centuries shall sing of your beauty and wisdom. Wherever you will be, priests will offer praises and sacrifices in their temples, and prophets utter benedictions."

His eyes, his uplifted arm, his thin heaving chest, reminded me of Jokanaan — a Jokanaan reversing himself — a Jokanaan who, loving woman in the image of his mother, blessed me. Would this youth's words have the power to counteract the original curse? Was this hour as momentous as that in which the blood-stained lips of the prophet pronounced my doom?

"Who are you, Onam?" I asked, trembling. "Who speaks through you, my lord?"

"I am he who recognizes Salome. I am he who understands the true meaning of the prophecy. I am he through whom Time speaks."

He stopped a moment, then laughed sadly. "I am Onam, the mad king of Arabia."

"Do not say that, my lord. You will be the greatest king of Araby. Your name shall be glorified forever."

"Only when Salome thinks of me."

Was he a prophet indeed? Was he but a madman uttering words that crossed his brain? Was he quoting at random from some book he had read?

"How can Salome ever forget you, my lord?"

He bent and kissed the hem of my robe.

We continued to walk.

He stopped and looked upward.

"I see Arabia crumbling into dust. I see my people wandering about the deserts of the world, companions of the melancholy camel and the bleating sheep. I see their bones whiten and mingle with the dust and the sand."

He breathed deeply. "I see the Prophet born in the desert. I hear his word thundering and its echo battering against the mountains of the earth and ruffling the faces of the seas. Arabia blossoms again. The long drought is over. Behold, she is the Queen of the Nations! The prophecy is fulfilled!"

He tottered. I grasped him in my arms and pressed him against my chest.

He opened his eyes and looked around, shivering.

Here and there the torch of a watchman blinked like the eye of an animal awakened from sleep.

We walked slowly, in silence.

Suddenly I realized that we had entered the outer garden, beyond the magic circle of safety, watched over by my spies.

"Let us return, my lord," I said anxiously.

He looked at me, as if I were standing at a great distance.

"Let us return, my lord," I repeated. "We are unattended."

"Our fate always attends us," he said sadly.

I heard cautious steps behind a bush and the rustling of leaves. A nondescript shadow wavered a few feet away.

"Come! Come!" I cried, frightened.

I tried to pull Onam along, when the bushes opened and three colossal men, with drawn knives, emerged.

"My lord!" I shrieked.

Onam threw his arms about me, and kissed me passionately for the first time. "Farewell, Salome!"

Before he could utter another word three knives thrust themselves into his heart. His arms unclasped themselves from my neck, and in another moment his limp body disappeared in the bushes.

I remained standing — a statue of stone. When I recovered from the stupor, I shouted — "Onam! Onam! Onam!"

In the distance several dogs barked wildly. Watchmen called out the time, and warned malefactors.

Helpless and miserable, I burst into sobs, but the primordial instinct of self-preservation, redoubled in me with the years, prompted me to retrace my steps quickly.

The gates were flung open. My eunuchs and my guards had vanished. The palace was a desert, except for some women who ran up and down, bewildered, muttering prayers and imprecations.

All my elaborate preparations for escape had been unnecessary. I was able to leave the palace unattended.

"Our fate always attends us."

CHAPTER EIGHTEEN

I AM THE WANDERING JEWESS — A PILGRIM OF TRUTH —
THE PERFECT CIRCLE.

I WANDERED about, now as woman, now as man, young, old, poor, rich, as the occasion demanded. At last weary, dejected, I retired to an ancient castle, long deserted, upon a hill on the outskirts of Ispahan.

Since I pretended neither riches nor poverty, I excited neither the cupidity nor the distrust of the authorities, and my simple, studious ways interested before long the scholars and philosophers of the country. My home became a university, where each master endeavored to convert the others, a Babel of knowledge and opinion, while the Tower of Truth lay crumbling.

"What is the meaning of life and death?" I asked desperately of each one, and each one expounded and explained, and quarreled and quoted and contradicted. I always remained empty-handed.

"Is there no place on Earth," I asked, "where one may discover the truth?"

Upon this they all agreed. "Greece!" they exclaimed.

"Greece is the seat of all knowledge, even as Arabia was before Aretas and his descendants, wicked and sensuous and superstitious, destroyed its universities and brought the country to ruin."

"Is Arabia in great plight?"

"Do you not know," they asked, surprised, "that the last of their kings, a mad youth, was murdered a generation ago? Arabia is razed to the ground. Arabia is no more. Her people are nomads, like their progenitors."

The first part of Onam's prophecy, then, was fulfilled. Would the second one come true? Would Araby again rule the world? Was Onam a prophet indeed? Or was he a madman? Was it in madness only that man discovered truth?

The philosopher continued to extol the wisdom of Greece.

"Who among us equals Apollonius?" they asked.

"If he still lives," some one added.

"Who is Apollonius?" I asked.

"Is it possible you have not heard of him?"

"He is a man — but also a god!"

The praises of him tripped upon one another.

"He knows everything."

"He has fathomed the earth and scaled the skies!"

"He has discovered new laws of mathematics."

"The soul of Pythagoras dwells in him."

"Where can I find Apollonius?" I asked.

"It is said that he who seeks him is sure to find him — everywhere — anywhere."

"Some one has called him the Perfect Circle."

A week later I set out to discover the wise man who excited no jealousy among the wise.

CHAPTER NINETEEN

I MEET APOLLONIUS — FELLOW WANDERERS — JESUS AND HIS COUSIN IN INDIA — THE MIRACLE OF THE VACUUM — ULTIMATE WISDOM — ENDLESS CHAIN — THE MYSTERY OF THE BAPTISM — SHALL WOMAN CONQUER? — ROADS TO NIRVANA.

MY SLAVES remained at a distance, while slowly, almost on tiptoes, I approached Apollonius. The Master was sitting upon a rock facing a lake which was as smooth as a mirror. The mountains rose about him in an immense semicircle.

His head bent over his tall staff, the branch of a cherry tree, over which meandered a gold snake, Apollonius was motionless as a statue carved in snow. His hair, his beard, his toga, made a symphony of white.

I, who had seen and loved and spurned monarchs — I, who occupied thrones, I, Salome, proud granddaughter of proud Herod the Great, trembled in the presence of this aged man.

Slowly Apollonius raised his head. He looked at me for a long time. His eyes, large and black, penetrated me, but unlike those of Jokanaan their glow soothed and caressed like the hand of a friend.

I was no longer uneasy, no longer afraid.

"I have been waiting for you, Salome," he said.

Astonished at his greeting, I asked: "Master, how did you know that I was seeking you?"

He smiled. His face was like the dawn which squats upon the window-sill, bringing new dreams to the sleeper.

"Your arrival, Salome, is the final term that completes the equation."

He motioned to me to sit opposite him on a rock, and offered me wine and sweets.

"When I left Cartaphilus and his young friend Damis — they thought I went on a last pilgrimage to meet Death. In truth a man should not wait until Death like a highwayman waylays him, but should go to the gate, and bid him welcome."

"Cartaphilus?" I whispered, bewildered.

"It was to welcome you, my daughter, that I left my friends upon the threshold of my dwelling."

"Master!" I said, my eyes clouded from gratitude, "I am not a gracious guest. I have made you tarry too long."

"You are punctilious, Salome, for this is the hour appointed by destiny for your visit."

"Master, did you mention Cartaphilus? Cartaphilus — ?"

Apollonius nodded.

"Cartaphilus!" I exclaimed joyously.

"Jesus cursed him with the same immortality with which Jokanaan afflicted you."

"Master, where is Cartaphilus, and what does he know of my fate?"

"He spoke to me of your beauty and of your cruelty. He does not yet know the fate that links you together."

"It is true, Master. I was cruel to him for to me he was the symbol of masculine conceit."

"Also," Apollonius added, "the symbol of love."

"It was he who first made me aware that I was a woman."

A cloud as large as a fist rolled over the sky like a ball of snow and melted into the blue.

"Master, am I immortal?" I asked timidly.

"The mind of man cannot conceive immortality or infinity. Immortality is but mortality arrested indefinitely. Infinity is space beyond the horizon."

"How did Jesus work his miracle on Cartaphilus?" I asked.

"The same force which stretched the thread of your life stretched his."

"How, Master?"

"A ray of the Moon may capture a wave in mid-ocean and hold it motionless, while all the tides roll on and on, seeking the shores."

"Forever, Master?"

Apollonius smiled. "Forever, Salome, is a long word."

"Were Jesus and John divine that they had the power to transfix the rhythm of our lives at the mysterious point where time merges with eternity?"

"They did not have to be gods for that, my daughter," Apollonius said. "It is one of the tricks known even to the lesser magicians of Tibet."

"Tibet? Was Jokanaan in India?" I asked, astonished.

"Both Jokanaan and his young cousin Jesus owed their recondite knowledge to the lore taught beyond the Himalayas. They never disclosed the secret to their disciples. The Master should remain an enigma to his followers."

"Can any one acquire this power over death and life?" I asked, a strange hope in my heart, that I might choose companions on the road without end.

Apollonius bent forward and placed upon my hand his own, long and sensitive, on which two rubies shimmered like restless eyes.

"To him who masters time all is possible. But the life you give may not be a boon. Companionship without end may turn the blossom of love into a festering sore. Ask not power until you acquire wisdom. Once you acquire wisdom," he smiled wistfully, "you may no longer desire power."

He pursued, his words coming full-fledged out of his spirit. "There is a greater miracle than the miracle of eternal life, Salome."

"Which one, Master?"

"The Miracle of the Vacuum."

"I do not understand, Master."

"In emptiness only is there truth. Do the four walls and the ceiling constitute the house, or the emptiness they create? Is the jar the clay or the gold that surrounds it, or the emptiness which these frontiers describe, that wine or other precious object may find room within? What is the

Earth: the mountains, the seas which circumscribe it, or the vacuum they form, that man and animals and plants may live and breathe? Emptiness is all powerful, for in emptiness only is existence possible. He who makes of himself a vacuum, has discovered the greatest miracle of all, for he creates Nirvana in himself. Salome, create Nirvana in yourself. That is the ultimate wisdom."

He stopped and with his staff made the sign of infinity upon the ground.

A thousand questions tripped upon my tongue, but none shaped themselves into words.

Apollonius continued gently. "Knowledge is but the ore within which burns the imperishable gold, Truth. Greater than knowledge is wisdom, and greater than action is contemplation. Through contemplation we conquer ourselves and the world. Both Jokanaan and Jesus died too soon to grasp the ultimate significance. The roots penetrated deeply, but the flower had only begun to bud."

I was perturbed. Had I danced for the head of one who might have been to the Jews what Apollonius was to the Greeks? Was I guilty of an irremediable and unforgivable offense against the World Spirit?

Apollonius, reading my thoughts, shook his head.

"Compose yourself, Salome. Men and events are links in an endless, immutable and unbreakable chain."

"Master," I asked, "is life a boon? Does Cartaphilus yearn for death?"

"Death is above us, and below us, and at every point of the infinite circumference. They who wish may pluck it, like a flower. We die because we choose to die. Death is self-inflicted. Life is a passion. The flames of all passions finally turn to ashes, and we seek rest. Cartaphilus loves life, but he fears it."

"I do not fear life, Master!" I exclaimed triumphantly.

"I know. Woman has greater courage. She fashions life, and knows its meaning more truly. Man never grasps at reality. He dwells in the dream of his own creation. Reality frightens him."

I played with the bracelets encircling my arm, watching

the while the luminous face, the perfect serenity, the utter calm of the Master.

"Our Messiahs, Master, preach love. But their hearts stifle with hatred. Our teachers speak of peace, but their eyes are poison-tipped arrows. Our priests pray to an all-merciful God, but they trample their brethren under heel. I have never felt either peace or love or mercy until I beheld you and heard your voice."

Apollonius placed both hands upon the top of his staff, and his chin upon his palms.

"Peace is born out of the thunder of war and love out of the turmoil of hate — but man lives hardly long enough to witness the birth pangs."

"Our race is famed for longevity, Master. Many of our priests are centenarians."

Apollonius smiled.

"There are rocks thousands of years old. Have they grown into mountains? The rose blossoms in a day, and dies overnight, and yet it has time to scatter its exquisite perfume and color the earth with its scarlet. What is time? To the fly the life of man is endless. What is space? To the snail the courtyard of a pariah is a great dominion. But what is a city to the eagle?"

As he uttered the words, a great eagle darted past us and like a boat with sails outspread cleaved the air. He reached the peak of the mountain opposite us, where he alighted, his argent whiteness mingling with the whiteness of the snow.

Apollonius pointed his staff to the bird.

"Thus time merges with infinity and life with death."

Like one who does not wish to disturb the sleep of a friend, the sun moved, slowly, silently, on the tips of his golden rays, and disappeared.

"Master, Jokanaan refused to baptize me. Shall I forever remain unredeemed?"

Apollonius did not answer at once. He breathed deeply. His tall body stood erect. How old was he? As old as the mountains that surrounded us, as young as the waters that replenished forever the lake over which our shadows fell. wavering lightly.

"The body must be purged that the soul may blossom," he said, gazing into the distance. "Every muscle, every nerve must be drained of its sap, that the source may be limpid and unpolluted. Plunge deeply into the waters of experience, Salome!"

He turned his look toward me.

"There is no redemption save the redemption by passion. Fear not its flames. They consume the dross and leave the gold. Let the storm of your senses rage unhindered. Out of the chaos of the blood, the soul is born."

"Is the soul of man superior to the soul of woman, Master?"

"The soul knows neither male nor female, Salome."

"Jokanaan said that in Heaven there is neither man nor woman. Yet he rejected me."

"He mistook the symbol for the reality, the shadow for the object."

The peak of the mountain burst into flames. Suddenly, like the monarch of a triumphant army, the Moon appeared emerging from a sea of blood, which inundated the snow.

I rose.

"Shall woman overcome her nature, Master? Will she ever conquer?" I asked pointing my forefinger to the Moon.

"Perhaps," Apollonius answered unemotionally.

"I will it! I shall conquer! Woman shall be baptized in the Jordan of herself! She shall emerge man's equal! Her soul shall partake of Heaven! I challenge the Power which shackles her to her womb!"

The eyes of Apollonius were the reflection of the lake. There was neither scorn nor incredulity about his lips. His brow was a white flame of thought.

"Cartaphilus seeks perfection. Salome seeks freedom," he spoke as in a trance. "Freedom and perfection are two lines running parallel across the face of the Universe. The Universe is curved, and the parallel lines meet and mingle — before infinity — perhaps. Cartaphilus is the slave of the Earth. Salome is the slave of the Moon. But the Moon and the Earth are the slaves of the mind of man. They are flaming steeds harnessed to his thoughts, galloping through endless time and measureless space to Nirvana."

His face was a radiant torch in the bosom of Night.

"All roads lead to Nirvana," he pursued. "Some roads are straight; some are circular; some are zigzag like the path of lightning; some meander languidly like a brook; some rush like a hurricane."

"I shall be the hurricane and the lightning, Master!"

He nodded imperceptibly.

I waved to one of my slaves. He approached. I whispered something to him. He left and returned with an alabaster flask filled with spikenard. I broke the neck of the flask, and poured the contents upon the head of the Master. With the tips of my fingers I smoothed his hair and beard. The perfume filled the air like incense. The Universe was a Temple.

He rose.

"The cycle is completed," Apollonius said. "We must part, Salome."

We looked at each other. Our eyes did not bear the sad look of separation, but the joyous gleam of discovery.

We walked in silence for some time. Our shadows mingled even as our souls.

He stopped.

"Farewell, Salome."

He kissed my forehead.

I kissed his hand.

"Farewell, Apollonius."

The Moon, purged in her own flames, glowed a resplendent silver. Apollonius broke its reflection, and luminous, like a morning Sun, climbed over the crest of the mountains.

CHAPTER TWENTY

SHALL I SEEK CARTAPHILUS? — WATERS OF EXPERIENCE — INTO THE HEART OF THE HURRICANE.

How had Apollonius achieved Nirvana in one brief life? Had he, conscious, perhaps, of the countless incarnations which preceded his last one, built tier upon tier upon his previous lives, until the tower finally climbed to heaven? Or could he press the centuries into years, and squeeze their essence, like a bowl of precious wine, from multitudinous clusters of grapes? Did generations gallop in his veins even as the years were held in rein to a standstill in mine?

The numberless paths open to me bewildered me. Whither should I go? How achieve my emancipation? Apollonius said that all roads led to Nirvana. Was there no short-cut, no unbrambled passage?

But no! I must first immerse myself deep in the wells of experience. If I could only find Cartaphilus! Perhaps together — No! Cartaphilus was to find himself by a separate road, parallel to mine, but not united to it — except in infinity, where perfection and freedom merge.

Still, would it not be better if we two wandered together, eternal and inseparable companions? Nature herself proclaimed us mates forever. Why seek beyond love? Was not love the zenith of all things? What mattered it if the Moon controlled my destiny or the Earth his? Together we could mock at our slavery. Together we could fashion an oasis in the vast desert of life. Out of the wastes beautiful roses would grow, and intoxicate us with their perfume.

Something within me turned upon my idea like a tigress in rage. It clawed at it, tore it to shreds.

"Never! Never!" I exclaimed. "Have I received the gift of life merely to spend it in serene security, cultivating a little garden, watching a million generations of roses bloom and die? Then, Jokanaan, may you indeed mock me! And Cartaphilus, may you indeed retain forever your preposterous air of masculine superiority!"

I drew a deep breath.

"I refuse to escape from the storm of life into an imperceptible breeze! I shall walk into the heart of the hurricane, and conquer it! Salome shall wage the greatest of battles — the battle of life against death, of freedom against slavery, of woman against man!"

Like a sea life surged within me, and I danced to the tumultuous music of the Eternal Tempest!

CHAPTER TWENTY-ONE

MY THIRTY-FOURTH HUSBAND — THE VENUS OF THE TRIPLE GATE — DHARMA, ARTA AND KAMA — THE UNIVERSITY OF LOVE — AND ON THIS THERE IS A VERSE — UNENDURABLE PLEASURE INDEFINITELY PROLONGED — CREATIVE RHYTHM — THIS IS NOT LOVE — A "GOD" HONORS OUR TEMPLE — CARTAPHILUS BLUNDERS — THE SECRET OF THE AFRICAN APHRODITE — JEALOUS — THE KEEPER OF THE SACRED TORTOISE — I MEET LAKSHMI, THE WIFE OF VISHNU.

The ancient schools of Babylon and Greece had long fallen into ruins. Only here and there an obstinate philosopher wandered about them, like a disconsolate ghost. His words were the vague echoes of the masters, long silent. But India — India the unchangeable — still offered wisdom and knowledge.

For a few generations I learned from the Brahmins and Buddhists and friars of a dozen minor sects the divers mysteries which they taught — levitation and hypnotism, and the secret powers of herbs and minerals. I learned how to stop breathing, how to fast for weeks, how to walk unscathed over burning coals, how to heal scars.

My thirty-fourth husband, a yogi, promised to initiate me into the supreme mystery of yogi love, but before he could fulfill his promise he died, piously contemplating his navel.

The ancient school of Venus of the Triple Gate, long neglected, reopened at last, endowed by the King of Ahira, who sent his wives there for instruction. The Princess Babhravya, whose reputation for purity and knowledge extended throughout the empire, presided over its destiny. Aphrodite had many devotees and many priests, but the school of the Princess Babhravya was the high seat of amorous love, the University of Love, the sole institution which could grant the degree of Magister Amoris.

The Temple of Venus of the Triple Gate was situated in a valley of the Deccan, known only to the initiates. The worship in the Temple was open to all comers during the month of Nargashirsha, the moonlight festival of the month of Kartika and the spring festival of Chaitra, but the school was jealously reserved for students of the princely caste, who were required to pass rigid physical, mental and spiritual entrance examinations.

A diploma from the school of Venus of the Triple Gate was valued more highly than rare jewels. Women graduates were sought for royal harems, while men proficient in the theory and practice of the thousand varieties of love studied in the school became the favorites of queens and princes.

But greater far than the terrestrial rewards were the heavenly ones. For he who achieved perfection in the lore of the Triple Gate leaped at one bound over numerous rungs of the ladder of Incarnation.

A notable thesis, several hundred pages long, written with golden letters upon imperishable parchment, was the requirement for the title of Magister Amoris. Rare indeed were the fortunate ones to obtain this distinction. The incomparable Gonardya and Gonikaputra and the immortal Vatsyayana took greater pride in this achievement than in all the honors showered upon them by hierarchs and potentates. Princess Babhravya, the latest head of the institution, was the only woman of her generation whose deep erudition merited the diploma.

It sufficed, however, to receive a letter of recommendation and the praises of the teacher, for any practical purpose. Students rarely contemplated going beyond this.

I passed the entrance examination with honors, and began at once the work on my thesis: "Unendurable Pleasure Indefinitely Prolonged."

Princess Babhravya considered me her favorite pupil, and her successor, should the gods see fit to call her to Nirvana before me.

It was the month of Kartika. The moon was full. The worshipers thronged to the Temple. Our Mistress recapitulated the major topics of our studies.

After making the sign of the Triple Gate, and praying in silence for an hour that the spirit of the Goddess descend upon us, Princess Babhravya commenced:

"In the beginning the Lord of Being created man and woman and in one hundred thousand chapters laid down rules for regulating their lives with regard to Dharma, Arta, and Kama."

She emphasized every syllable. After every two or three words she breathed deeply, lifting herself, and pressing her fists against her knees. Her long spinster face, emaciated by fasts, meditations and study, flushed a trifle under the stress of her enthusiasm in imparting knowledge.

"But more chapters did the Lord of Being devote to Kama than to the other two combined — for in Kama have Arta and Dharma the roots. Kama is the beginning of life, the middle of life, and the end of life. Through Kama we are reborn, live, and pass at last into Nirvana!"

The students, seated in a semicircle on the cushions, upon which the symbols of Kama were embroidered in gold and silver threads, bowed acquiescence, and manifested their great admiration for the incomparable wisdom of the Past Mistress of the College of Love.

In the four corners of the hall, the threads of incense rose steadily from the golden bowls studded with jewels, and midway from the ceiling, curved, and scattered like petals of a delicate flower.

Babhravya continued, her voice rising and falling regularly, like a chant, her arms stretched forward, her thin chest heaving.

"Man is divided into three classes and thirty-two subclasses, according to the proportions of the male, and woman likewise is divided into three classes and thirty-two subclasses, according to the proportions of the female. There are three equal unions, therefore, between persons of corresponding dimensions. And there are six major unequal unions between persons of unequal dimensions. But the minor unequal unions are so numerous that even our great master, Vatsyayana, erred in the calculation.

"And on this subject there is a verse, as follows: 'Just as there are an unlimited number of shades in every color of the rainbow, which blend and mingle and are unrecognizable by the naked eye, so are there unlimited nuances in the man and the woman, which blend, and bring about the great Kama, which is the source and meaning of life!'"

The Mistress rose, and upon a large ebony tablet supported on an easel of ivory, she drew the diagrams and formulæ which explained her theory. When she had finished, she read the numbers slowly, and asked the students to repeat them at the top of their voices.

"Men," she continued, "are divided into hare, bull and horse, which equal the Mrigi, Vadawa and Hastini, or the deer, mare and elephant in woman. But unequal are the hare and the mare, the hare and the elephant, the hare and the deer and the horse and the mare. And of the thousand other inequalities we shall treat in a later lesson."

The Mistress looked at me.

I bowed three times, and said: "As to the quality of unions, this is the formula: 'High unions are better than low unions, according to the incomparable master Vatsyayana. But from the difference in the ways of working follows the difference in the consciousness of pleasure, for a man thinks, "This woman is united with me," and a woman thinks, "I am united with this man." But this objection is groundless, according to Nandi Keshevaro. There is no difference in the pleasure they feel. But on this again the masters disagree. For we find that sometimes two things are done at the same time, as for instance the fighting of rams, both the rams receiving the shock at the same time on their heads. But sometimes we find that two things achieving the same goal are not done at the same time, as for instance two horses racing. They reach the same goal, but one arrives a few moments sooner than the other.'"

I stopped a moment to refresh my memory.

"On this subject there is a verse, as follows: 'Men and women being of the same nature feel the same kind of pleasure.'

"And this is in accordance with the Ratirahasya or the Secrets of Love, the Panchasakya or the Five Arrows, the Smara Pradipa or the Light of Love, the Ratimanjara or the Garland of Love, the Rasmanjara or the Sprout of Love, and the Anunga Runga or the Stage of Love, also called Kamaledhiplava or a Boat in the Ocean of Love."

The Mistress smiled beatifically, her long teeth sparkling.

"O Princess Sa-lo-ma, deeply have you drunk from the well of Kama, and our throats feel the coolness of the sweet waters!"

The other pupils rose and bowed to me.

A pupil erased the tablet, and the Mistress of the Venus of the Triple Gate wrote upon it the formula of the embraces.

"I beg of you to recite the names after me," she said, breathing deeply, "for knowledge comes with constant repetition, as the great master Gautama says. And he also says that they who only see remember with their eyes only. They who only hear remember with their ears only. But they who see and hear and recite also, they remember with the three gates which lead to perfect knowledge, even as the three gates of our Temple lead to perfection of Kama."

We rose and bowed.

"The five major embraces are —" The head mistress pointed to the tablet.

We repeated: "The five major embraces are —"

She pursued:

"First — Jataveshtitaka — or the Twining of the Creeper.

"Second — Vriskshadirudhaka — or the Climbing of the Tree.

"Third — Tila-Tandulska — or the Mixture of Sesamum Seed with Rice.

"Fourth — Kshiraniraka — or the Mixture of Milk and Water.

"Fifth — Anparishtaka — or the Gate of the Eunuch."

Six times we repeated the words in unison to the rhythm of the golden staff struck against the tablet.

"Many are the minor embraces, but the chief among them are: the sounding or pressing of the nails, known as the half-moon, the circle, the line, the tiger's claw, the peacock's foot, the jump of the hare, the leaf of the blue lotus, the token of remembrance."

A Brahman, whose white beard was as delicate as a spider-web at dawn hanging from two branches, rose. The Mistress bowed, and with pedantic severity asked him to recite.

"The following are the different kinds of biting: the hidden bite — the swollen bite — the point — the line of points — the coral and the jewel — the line of jewels — the broken cloud — the biting of the boar.

"And on this subject there is a verse, as follows:

"When a man bites a woman forcibly, she should angrily do the same to him with double force. Thus a point should be returned with a line of points, and a line of points with a broken cloud."

He bowed three times, his beard swinging in the air like a mass of feathers from a torn pillow.

The sun which had lacquered the hall with an impeccable silver had long retreated, and hung now over the window-sill like a tablet of gold upon which the trellised shadow of the incense wrote the epitaph of day.

The chimes of the Temple rang softly as in a dream. The Mistress stopped her lecture, and bade us bow our heads in prayer to the Lord of Creation, Father of Dharma, Arta and Kama.

The chimes rang louder and louder, became more and more impetuous, until the Temple shook in a tempest of abandoned music.

The three gates were thrown open. The worshipers approached from the nine roads which converged to the Temple like the rays of a star.

The school was situated in the west wing of the Temple, and opened into it by a secret glass door, invisible from the

Temple, but through which everything that took place within the cubicles of pleasure could be seen.

We seated ourselves in a semicircle according to our rank and proficiency, while the Mistress occupied the center. As the sole candidate for the Master's degree, I sat at her right.

The walls and the ceiling of the Temple were covered with mirrors, and the floor with a polished stone which caught the images like a mirror. Everything reflected itself in an infinite perspective. For was it not written by the incomparable master, Vatsyayana, that Kama is tiny like an eye, but mountains and seas and skies find ample room within it?

The High Priest bent over the altar and chanted from the Rig-Veda:

"I laud thee, Agni, the Purohita, the great High Priest of God, minister of the sacrifice.

"The herald, lavisher of wealth!

"Worthy is Agni to be praised ——

"He shall bring hitherward the gods ——"

The worshipers knelt reverently before the Goddess whose Triple Gates were masses of rubies and whose triple rows of breasts were fists of gold, and the triple arms and legs were silver serpents.

"I laud thee, Agni, the Purohita," the people repeated, and the invisible choir sang:

"Worthy is Agni to be praised ——

"He shall bring hitherward the gods ——"

The priest continued:

"Come hither with thy long-maned steeds, Indra.

"Come hither to this song of praise!

"With worship we glorify thee, Agni, who art like a long-tailed steed,

"Imperial lord of sacred rites!

"As cows low to their calves in stalls, so with our song we glorify thee, Indra!"

The choir repeated: "As cows low to their calves in stalls, so with our song we glorify thee, Indra!"

The people followed: "As cows low to their calves in stalls, so with our song we glorify thee, Indra!"

The High Priest turned from the altar, and facing the Goddess of the Triple Gate, chanted:

"I laud thee, Supreme Deity, who art Agni, the god of fire, and Indra, the thunder-wielder, and Narasansa, the desire of men! I laud thee, Goddess, whose gates are each perfect, each leading to Nirvana, which opens into the heart of the setting sun!"

Two friars brought a goat whose legs were tied to a golden pole and whose beard and horns swept the ground. His bellowing made a strange cacophony in the solemn chant.

The monks placed the animal upon the altar. The worshipers rose and turned three times around the Goddess of the Triple Gate.

The High Priest raised his long knife and held it horizontally over the throat of the beast. The gesture repeated itself in the mirrors like an endless succession of lightning.

"Accept, O Goddess, our sacrifice!" he exclaimed.

"Accept, O Goddess, our sacrifice!" thundered through the Temple.

The priest moved his muscular arm swiftly from left to right. The blood gushed and fell into the golden bowl held by the friars. A thousand goats dropped their heads upon a thousand altars, and seas of blood rained across the universe.

The priest dipped his hand in the blood and made over the heads of the worshipers the symbol of the Triple Gate. The worshipers repeated the symbol waving their arms, and in the mirrors an infinite forest shook in the throes of a mighty storm.

The priest walked slowly, with measured step, to the Goddess and anointed with the blood of the sacrifice the Triple Gates. The rubies melted and dripped to the floor.

"O Sarasvati, O mighty flood of Blood.

"Illuminate every thought!"

The choir changed to a mad music of fifes and tabors and bells. The friars filled the cups with soma and the blood of the sacrifice.

The priest raised his goblet.

"Come hither with thy long-maned steeds, O Indra.

"Come hither, O Agni, with thy tongues of fire.
"Come hither, Thou Goddess with thy gates of Rubies,
"We call you when the juice is shed!
"Come to this song of praise, to the libation poured for you:
"Drink of it like stags athirst.
"Drink of the soma, drink the moon-plant, for your delight!"

The priests drank.

The friars passed the cups to the worshipers.

Intoxicated with the soma and the incense which rose thickly from the gods that lined the walls, and the music and the blood that poured from the Goddess of the Triple Gates, the worshipers laughed and groaned and shouted, and waved their arms, frantically, and dropped to the floor in passionate embraces.

Calm, unmoved, our Mistress called our attention to the details of Kama translated into practice. Pedantically she criticized the false movements of the hare and the bull. She resented to see the bunglers mutilate the perfect formulæ of the text-books. The slightest deviation from the standard was desecration in her eyes.

"Look at the barbarism of these people! Behold the dire consequences of ignorance!" she said sadly, her long face lengthening. "Of what avail is practice without theory? A house built on sand, crumbling in the wind, a flower plucked from its stem withering in the hand."

Now and then, however, we discovered motions in perfect accord with the precepts of erotic theology.

"Excellent!"

"The small plus middling is perfect!"

"Watch the Jataveshtitaka!"

"Yes, but look, by a blunder of the woman, it has degenerated into Kshiraniraka!"

"What a pity! One more turn to the left would make a perfect equation!"

The rites of Kama reduplicated themselves in the libidinous mirrors, above, below and in all cardinal points of the compass, as if the whole Universe, earth and heaven and hell, were concentrating upon the creative rhythm. But despite the sanctification of religion and the pedantic prattle of the Spinster and the students, candidates for the harems or Nirvana, this tumultuous sea of carnality filled me with nausea.

"This is not love!" I said indignantly, turning my face away, "this is not love!"

The Mistress nodded.

"Alas," she answered, "love is based upon the strict principles, whose roots are in numbers and geometric symbols! When the eternal formulæ are followed with unerring punctilio love comes into being!"

"And the soul?" I asked. "What of the soul!"

"The soul?" she repeated, looking at me quizzically. "The soul enters Nirvana, purified and perfect."

Was this what Apollonius meant by the baptism? Was this the chaos out of which souls were born? Had the sight purified me? Was I free at last to strike the first blow against woman's slavery? Had I discovered the true path to Nirvana?

The Mistress rose suddenly, and pointing to a group of worshipers, exclaimed —"Look, my friends, look!"

We all rose, and craned our necks in the direction indicated by her forefinger.

The Mistress raised her eyes upward: "I thank thee, O Lord of Creation, Father of Dharma, Arta and Kama, for allowing my eyes to behold the profoundest of thy mysteries."

The pupils accustomed to repeating the words of their teachers, mumbled thanksgivings.

"Is it a man or a god, honoring our Temple? Has She of the Triple Gate sent us her messenger to teach us the way? O Princess, Sa-lo-ma," she said, pulling my sleeve, "Look! Take notes! This is invaluable for your thesis."

Priestesses of joy, ecstatic, delirious, danced about the Goddess. The music turned into a voluptuous tempest. The priest and the monks improvised prayers and benedictions, and cut the air ceaselessly with the sign of the Goddess.

My eyes were riveted upon the man who was the focus

of attention. Was it possible? Could it be he? Did he indulge in these preposterous acrobatics? Was it thus he sought perfection in the embrace of priestesses of joy?

A turn of his head convinced me. It was he! Arrogance was written on his face and in his very limbs even in the spasm of love!

It was Cartaphilus, Isaac aforetime, my companion in eternity!

Disdain, disgust, anger flooded me. My hands twitched, yearning to encircle his defiantly virile throat!

"He is a god!" the Mistress whispered breathlessly.

"A god!" the others repeated.

A god indeed! I was about to shout: "Miserable cobbler, back to your last!"

My face flushed. What ailed me? Had I forgotten the slow march of the centuries? Could I nevermore erase from my memory the picture of the youth, handsome and vain, bathing in the lake near my stepfather's palace in Judea? Generations of men had been born and died. The palace was erased from the face of the Earth like an inscription upon the bark of a tree which has been thrown into the flames. Nothing remained of all its hectic history save some names and some legends. But in spite of this I still saw the scene enacted as if it had happened yesterday. In my ears still rang the taunts and the boasts of the cobbler's son, Isaac. His mockery of my family exasperated me still.

Why had he come here?

Had he wandered from Temple of Love to Temple of Love, gathering admirers? Aphrodite, Istar, Venus of the Triple Gate, had he worshiped everywhere, and everywhere been worshiped by the rabble and the priests and the priestesses?

I came here to learn the mysteries of the senses — theoretically. He dared to put them into practice! I was still a woman, still yoked by fastidious inhibitions. He was a man, experimenting freely, unhindered! He was still my superior by dint of his sex!

My thoughts galloped in my mind like mad runaway horses, and my emotions pressed into my heart like hedges of bayonets.

"Wonderful! Magnificent! Perfect!"

The worshipers forgot the Eternal Goddess and worshiped at the shrine of the new god.

Why was I so unreasonable? Why did I not join in the general admiration? Who, more than I, should take pride in my compatriot, companion of my strange fate? What obligation did he have toward me? Had I not mocked and scorned him? Had he not the right to seek in the embraces of the multitudes what I had refused him?

Logic was a futile armor against the fury of my emotions.

I was jealous.

Salome, jealous!

I was as a young bride who catches her lover in the arms of her maid. For a moment this knowledge thrilled me.

I was still young, still human!

But I could not endure the evident relish Cartaphilus took in his performance! He did not seek the meaning of love, as I sought. He did not seek liberation and baptism. He took delight in his senses!

"He is not a god!" I exclaimed. "He is not perfect!"

The Mistress looked at me.

"You are right. He spoiled the equation of Vatsyayana and modified the formula of Suvarnanabha. Look," she continued, "what text-book sanctions this unorthodox Chinese variation?"

"He has distorted the arithmetic of unendurable pleasure indefinitely prolonged," I said.

The Mistress sighed.

She reseated herself, and the other pupils followed her example.

"He has mixed the accents," the Spinster muttered bitterly.

"He has corrupted the Arithmetic, the Rhetoric, the very Grammar of Love!" I exclaimed.

"It is true, O Princess Sa-lo-ma! Your eye is sharper than the eye of the eagle, and your understanding deeper than the sea. Your thesis shall be sacred among the books of the Temple."

Determined to demolish Cartaphilus, I pursued. "He is

grossly ignorant of the mystery of the African Aphrodite. Without it, no one can achieve unendurable pleasure indefinitely prolonged."

"True, he is not a god," the Mistress bewailed. "And the day of glory has not yet risen. The gods do not come to their own temples. They visit us only in our dreams, and the dreams vanish with the silver tip of Dawn's slipper."

"What," asked one of the younger pupils, "is the secret of the African Aphrodite?"

"Even," the Mistress remarked, "as a great prince possesses among his groups of retainers those who obey him instantly, those who obey him but sullenly, and those who rebel against his command, until he learns to subdue them, so the human body has three sets of muscles, some completely subordinate to our will, some half voluntary, and some which refuse to obey.

"The secret of the African Aphrodite is to achieve complete control over all three groups. He who has not mastered these servitors cannot achieve the perfect rhythm of unendurable pleasure indefinitely prolonged."

The Mistress spoke meditatively, her eyes half-shut.

"Have many mastered this secret?"

"Few men have mastered all steps in the intricate formula of unendurable pleasure indefinitely prolonged. The last man to master all the mysteries was Conardya. His mind was the monarch of his senses. But Conardya lived a thousand years. His body flourished like the eternal trees upon the peaks of Himalaya. Alas, the gods no longer bless man with the longevity requisite for perfection. The soul forgets at each incarnation much that it has learned in the last."

Cartaphilus rose.

The priest, less critical than we, placed a golden chaplet upon his head, and sang a litany from the Rig-Veda. The worshipers, astonished by his proficiency, danced around him as they had danced about the Goddess herself. The friars filled the cups with wine mixed with the sacrificial blood and offered them to the people. The choir intoned a triumphal air. Cartaphilus, radiant, haughty, like a monarch returned from conquest, accepted the vulgar adulation of the crowd.

I could not bear the sight. I rushed out of the room into the garden encircling the Temple. I felt indeed baptized, purified! What Jokanaan refused to perform, Cartaphilus accomplished unwittingly.

At last I understood Apollonius.

I longed to breathe the free air, to flee forever from the bondage of my body.

Woman's weakness and her ignorance made possible this intolerable display of carnality. If woman were free, if woman equaled man, love would have its roots in the senses, but its blossom in the soul.

I inhaled deeply the perfume of the eucalyptus and the sandalwood wafted from the trees upon the hill by the breeze which cooled my face and like a child's hand gently ruffled my hair.

Loneliness overwhelmed me. I yearned to speak, to utter my thoughts, my indignation, my anger. To whom could I confide my secret? Apollonius — if only I could sit at his feet again! If still alive — he was, alas! beyond human reach. Onam, my Arab husband, with his exquisite sensibility, and his look that transcended the earth — he would understand, he would console me! But Onam was dust of the dust! Cartaphilus, to whom I did not need to explain anything, whose life was akin to mine — no! No! Let the little priestesses listen to his words! Let his ears be filled with the applause of the vulgar!

The doors of the Temple opened wide. The High Priest, a small image of the Venus of the Triple Gate raised high above his head, descended followed by the chanting friars. Behind them Cartaphilus, crowned, walked with the pride which distinguished him in the house of Pilate. Worshipers, priestesses, and choirs followed. They crossed the garden, breaking the reflection of the Moon, and climbed upon the hill that faced the Temple.

Princess Babhravya, Mistress of the School of the Goddess of the Triple Gate, followed by her pupils, entered the garden. I hid behind a tree.

She discussed the Grammar and Rhetoric of Kama which are inferior to its Arithmetic, but which are essential to the achievement of perfection.

"There are sixteen regular conjugations and twenty-two declensions, but the irregular conjugations and declensions are sixty-four in number, which are further subdivided into fourteen classes."

"On this subject there is a verse, as follows," one of the pupils added. "The word is bound to the number as the sea is bound to the shore."

The Mistress thanked the pupil for his information.

Once more she continued her pedantic prattle. Her voice sounded like the beak of a woodpecker drumming against the bark of a tree.

"Stop your senseless chatter, Spinster!" I muttered to myself, exasperated beyond endurance.

The school walked slowly past me, directing its footsteps toward the hill, where the hero was fêted and crowned amid a pandemonium of bonfires and acclamations.

Suddenly something struck my ankle. I turned around, startled. The neck of a giant tortoise moved in the soft grass, rhythmically, like a pendulum. Its carapace shone like mother-of-pearl, changing colors. In the center was carved Vishnu, the God of the Universe.

The touch of a living being was grateful. I yearned for companionship. But the hand of a man would have made me shudder, and woman seemed slimy like a snake in rut.

I bent and caressed the head of the tortoise crested like a fantastic coronet. Tame as a kitten or a dog, the tortoise accepted my caresses joyously.

"Who are you?" I said, feeling the need of speech. "What strange history lies encrusted in your gorgeous plastron? At any rate, you have been spared the scholastic vagaries of priestesses of the Goddess of the Triple Gate, and the coarse exhibitions of Roman Captains."

I ran my hand across the carapace, cool and smooth as the surface of waters.

"Lakshmi! Lakshmi! Lakshmi!" a voice called. An old man, whose beard and hair almost hid his face, limped toward me.

He bowed several times, and looked at me strangely.

"I am the Keeper of the Sacred Tortoise, Princess," he said. "This is the first time in fifty years that Lakshmi has accepted the caress of a human hand. My father and his sire told me that she never made friends with any human being."

"How old is Lakshmi, then?" I asked, caressing her head.

"How old is Lakshmi, Princess?" he repeated my question, hopping from his lame foot to the whole one and back again several times, evidently in an amazement greater than any he had ever experienced.

"Yes — how old is Lakshmi?" I asked quietly.

"Lakshmi, Princess, is the wife of Vishnu, Creator of all Things. Lakshmi was born before the world was born, and will live until every living being, including the tiniest maggot evolving in the bowels of the crushed worm, enters Nirvana."

The Keeper brushed his hair from his eyes and pulled at his beard as one pulls the leash of recalcitrant animals.

"Behold, Princess, Vishnu himself carved his image upon Lakshmi's back, with his hundred hands, each hand carving one line.

"Look!" he exclaimed triumphantly. "Look, Princess, see how it glows in the dark! It's the eye of Vishnu watching over the earth! During the day the eye goes up into the sky and enters the forehead of the sun — but at night it watches from the back of Lakshmi."

The phosphorescent eye of Vishnu glistened between the horny fingers of the old man.

"Often I wake in the middle of the night, thinking it is already day, but it's only the eye of Vishnu watching. Lakshmi once left the sacred Temple and wandered about the Earth for centuries, visiting every city, to see that the laws of her spouse were obeyed. One stormy day, when the clouds were so heavy that people used torches to find their way, the eye of Vishnu blazed like a great flame, and the descendant of the keeper who had lost her, recognized her, and brought her back to the Temple, where she has been since. Lakshmi is never lost, Princess."

The tortoise placed her head in my palms and squinted her flaming eyes obliquely like two elongated red rubies.

The Keeper spoke on: "If every drop of blood were drained from the body of Lakshmi, her heart would still beat on forever. Lakshmi can swim in the sea as well as she can walk upon land. She can go without food for years."

He sighed.

"Indeed she has not eaten for weeks now. The people forget Lakshmi and her keeper. They let us starve. The world will soon come to an end, Princess. The world will soon come to an end!" he repeated mournfully.

"Think of it, Princess, Lakshmi who brings love and fidelity upon Earth, who protects the home of man, who twirls the sea that it may give forth the riches that lie at the bottom of the world, Lakshmi, symbol of perfect womanhood — Lakshmi and her keeper must starve!"

He covered his face with his hands and sobbed.

"Lakshmi, Lakshmi," he called bitterly, "come to our hovel, where the eye of Vishnu is the only sunlight that ever penetrates it, where the water we drink is yellow with mud, and the food we eat is the crumb that the servants of the rich forget to sweep away."

Lakshmi, heedless of him, continued to peck at my ankle.

The Keeper knelt before me.

"O daughter of Vishnu!" he exclaimed, "for only his daughter has the power to enchant Lakshmi."

"My good man," I said, "let me be Lakshmi's keeper."

He jumped up.

"No, no, Princess, that cannot be!" He made a gesture as if to lift the tortoise, which doubtless weighed more than he.

I took a few steps. The tortoise followed me, her head balancing in the air.

"You see, that Lakshmi considers me already her keeper. I shall provide for her as you cannot.

"Let me have her, and neither of you will starve. I shall

treat her as the wife of Vishnu deserves, and I shall honor her keeper."

I pulled off my finger a ring with several large jewels, and placed it in his cupped hand.

He fell on his face, kissed the hem of my robe, and crawling a little, kissed the carapace of Lakshmi.

"It is the will of Vishnu, Lakshmi. Farewell."

Tightening both fists over the ring, the Keeper dashed away, skipping like a young child.

"Lakshmi," I said, "you shall be my companion from now on, and if it is true that you live on forever, then you shall be my companion forever."

The tortoise licked my hands. Then satisfied she withdrew her head and legs.

"Like you I shall withdraw within the shell of my knowledge and experience and my great secret. Only you shall hear from my lips what I think or feel, for unlike man you do not mock, and unlike woman you do not betray. Prisoners of life both of us, Lakshmi, we shall travel across time and space, until we achieve perfect freedom. Then you can return to Vishnu upon Mount Mandara, where the gods dwell."

I slowly departed from the Temple, Lakshmi following.

CHAPTER TWENTY-TWO

CARTAPHILUS IN BRONZE — THE CAULDRON OF TIME — WOMAN THE SCAPEGOAT — LAKSHMI SHAKES HER HEAD IN PALMYRA.

WEARY of being cradled between the enormous humps of my camel, I ordered the driver to stop. I descended, and walked leisurely along the "Path of the Immortals" which bisected the capital from the eastern to the western gates. It was bordered by enormous palm trees and no less enormous statues in honor and memory of victorious soldiers and successful merchants, for the people of Palmyra revered strength and glorified wealth, typical of a nation ruled by a woman.

I read the inscriptions upon the pedestals to familiarize myself with the history and ideals of the country. Suddenly I came across the following: "To the memory of Cartaphilus, Prince of India, Citizen of Rome, Merchant of Palmyra. He organized the silk industry of Palmyra which rivals that of Cathay, and built temples and bridges. He lost his life at sea. May the gods honor him!"

I burst into laughter. The statue of Cartaphilus dead at sea, amused me hugely. The Temple of the Venus of the Triple Gate, the Mistress of the school, the thesis on unendurable pleasure indefinitely prolonged, had all become dim shadows in my memory. The Mistress had long ago delivered her last lecture, the pupils had honored harems and delighted monarchs, and were certainly on the shortest road to Nirvana. The little priestesses had turned their final erotic somersault, and the worms had consumed the remnant of their sweetness. The anger and resentment I bore Cartaphilus changed to the vague indignation a mother bears a disobedient child.

Lakshmi tapped my ankle with her mouth, which resembled the imperial beaks of eagles.

"Time, Lakshmi, is a shrewd witch, in whose cauldron all things mingle and melt and turn to thin streams of smoke and vapor and pinches of gray and black ashes, to stir the melancholy meditations of immortals such as you and I and Cartaphilus!"

Lakshmi continued her caress.

"Ah, but you do not know Cartaphilus, Lakshmi? Well, he is the son of a Jewish cobbler, vain and arrogant, who dared mock Princess Salome, granddaughter of Herod the Great, who ridiculed the royal family and scoffed at woman! Princess Salome, however, returned his mockery and scoffing, which he tries to forget by making merry with little priestesses! This is Cartaphilus."

I patted Lakshmi's head.

"I hate Cartaphilus! No, that is not true. I love Cartaphilus. It was his beautiful body that stirred my womanhood into life, and always I seek his lips and his arms in the lips and arms of my husbands and lovers. But he must not know it. He must always think that I hate him, that I despise his caresses, until I shall emerge free and triumphant. Then — then only — shall we consummate our love."

The tortoise threw her head back, and opened her mouth wide as if she intended to swallow the universe.

"You do not understand, although you belong to my sex and are the wife of Vishnu. You do not understand the tragedy of woman. The gods have chosen her as the scapegoat of the world. Oh, the indignity and the pain and the ugliness of it all, Lakshmi! And because of it, man has tyrannized over woman, and made her his slave and the butt of his ridicule."

I raised my fist. "But Salome shall bring another era into the world! She will break the shackles of the Moon and tear asunder the chains of man!"

The tortoise turned slowly, raising one leg in the air.

"It is possible, Lakshmi! Look at the magnificent Queen of this country! Zenobia — a name that strikes terror in the hearts of Roman generals and Egyptian monarchs! Zenobia! Salome will inspire her and aid her until the Earth belongs to her, and mankind kneels to do her homage. Then Salome will begin her greater and subtler war!"

The tortoise had made a complete revolution and faced me once more.

"Lakshmi, wife of Vishnu, supporter of the Earth, tell me, shall I succeed?"

Lakshmi looked up at me with her sleepy eyes. Her scrawny neck moved slowly from right to left like a tongue in derision.

"What! Is this your answer?"

She continued to shake her neck.

"Do you not know, Lakshmi, what happens to oracles that predict evil? They are slain! I shall slay you, and give your carcass to my slaves! They say the flesh of tortoises is sweeter than the flesh of lambs. The flesh of Lakshmi must be more precious than manna and nectar! But you do not fear death, Lakshmi, do you? You are like Salome! Well, no matter! War is declared! I have unsheathed my sword, and shall never return it to its scabbard until the victory is mine! But let us go back to our patient camels and impatient slaves!"

My steward helped me mount into my pavilion upon the great back of the camel, then two slaves hoisted Lakshmi. I placed the tips of my slippers upon her carapace, and ordered the caravan to continue its journey.

CHAPTER TWENTY-THREE

ZENOBIA HAGGLES — WOMAN RULE —"WHERE IS THE SOUL, LONGINUS?"— WE DEPART FOR EGYPT.

The Queen sat upon her throne of red gold encrusted with jewels. She wore a coronet from which hung loops of diamonds and emeralds. Her throat was encircled by a triple necklace of pearls. The train of her brocaded robe wound about her feet, rising like a hillock of silver and gold. Her sword, sheathed in black velvet, was studded with pearls.

The pillars of the hall were imbedded with mirrors and mother-of-pearl. The rugs surrounding the walls glimmered with jewels of all colors. The chairs were of solid gold.

In this ocean of wealth, Zenobia haggled with her stewards over every item of the household expense, as an old Jewish fisherwoman haggles with prospective buyers. From time to time she addressed me —"See how they try to cheat me, Princess! They believe they can deceive me, just because I am a woman!"

An officer entered, and knelt.

"Rise and speak!" the Queen commanded.

"Another town has fallen to her Majesty!"

"Did you hear that, Princess? The Roman eagle is shedding its feathers." And turning to the officer, "Order double pay for all my soldiers."

The officer made a motion to leave.

"Stay!" the Queen ordered.

"Double pay would demoralize them, would it not, Princess?"

Without waiting for my opinion, she pursued:

"They will expect double pay for every victory. That will not do. Give them a banquet, Officer, and promise them a maid each. Are there enough women in the conquered town?"

"I believe so, Augusta!"

The officer turned to go.

"Wait!" Zenobia commanded.

"Women weaken men. Do not promise them maids, Officer."

"No, Augusta!"

"What reward shall we offer them, Princess?"

And once again without waiting for my reply, Zenobia continued: "Officer, tell them that Zenobia, Queen of the East, and before long, by the help of the gods, Empress of the World, is proud of her army! Tell them that she rejoices in their bravery and strength! Let them eat and drink their fill before marching to further conquests! Tell them that medals shall be struck for each with my effigy upon them! Go!"

The officer left.

The Queen laughed.

"Men are children. They must have toys."

"Yes, Augusta, men are children, and, like children, cruel and tyrannical."

Zenobia did not listen. She fixed her sleeve with the tips of her fingers.

"Since my chief tailor died I have never been able to replace him. My slaves are not artists. What magnificent robes you have, Salome! Sit near me," she continued, pointing to the armchair to her right.

I approached. She watched me intently.

"How beautiful you are, Salome! The blood of monarchs courses through your limbs, and your breasts have the pride and coolness of virginity. But your eyes — your eyes have seen — what have they seen?"

Drawing my face to her, she looked into my eyes for a long time, squinting her own.

"What have they seen, Salome? Tell me!"

"They have seen the tragedy of woman, Augusta."

"Do not call me 'Augusta,' Salome. When we are alone, I am not the Queen, but your friend."

"Zenobia, my friend, I have seen the tragedy of woman. And now I see her redemption. Now I see, as I look at Zenobia, the march across the desert, and the conquest of the holy city."

Zenobia misunderstood me.

She stamped her sword. "I shall conquer Rome, Salome! I shall sit upon the Imperial throne! What Cleopatra could not achieve, I shall!"

"Rome is but the antechamber of the Empire, Zenobia. With you begins a new dynasty!"

"My sons, Salome, shall own the Earth!"

"The dynasty I speak of, Zenobia, is greater than the dynasty of monarchs."

"What dynasty, Salome?"

"The dynasty of Woman!"

She brushed away the loop of pearls and diamonds which cast thin shadows over her face.

"I am not a woman, Salome, nor was Cleopatra — I am a Ruler."

I suddenly remembered the words of Herod, my grandfather. He, too, claimed that Cleopatra was not a woman. The denial of womanhood was the vilest insult he could fling against Cleopatra's memory. Zenobia spoke of it as her greatest glory. Her pride in her royal rank and her renunciation of womanhood stirred my anger.

"The time will come, Zenobia," I said, "when it will be a greater glory to be a woman than a queen!"

Her eyes, black as shadows of forests at midnight, blazed.

"Salome!" she thundered, "Queens are divine, descendants of gods!"

"From the womb of woman gods are born, Zenobia. Woman is the giver of life! Woman is the breast which feeds the universe! Woman is the eternal seed from which blossom all things!"

"Woman is weak, Salome," Zenobia said sadly. "She cannot be a soldier. What woman has equaled Cæsar or Alexander? And in commerce — who has seen a woman comparable to Cartaphilus, the Hindu Prince?"

"Cartaphilus!" I exclaimed, exasperated.

"Man has not allowed woman to develop her brain and her courage, Zenobia. He has kept her in slavery. He has made her the vessel of his pleasure and the lap of his progeny. A toy and a scapegoat he has made of her. But woman shall awaken from her lethargy. She shall demand freedom. No longer shall she be the shadow of man!

"Within her lie infinite possibilities. The Earth shall flourish into another Eden when she becomes Mistress of it. The cruelty, the injustice, the bestiality which the rule of man has brought upon earth shall disappear. Man shall become what Nature has intended him to be, the inferior of woman!

"As in the world of bees, he will be merely the pursuer of the Queen, to be slain when her womb is quickened. In the beginning woman was the Mistress of the Earth. She relinquished her power. But the time will come when she will reign once more, queen and goddess!"

The Queen placed her sword across her knees, and sighed.

I pursued, my arm in the air, like a Messiah.

"Zenobia, be the hammer that breaks the chains which bind woman to her slavery. Strike the blow which will resound through all space and all time! Zenobia — the very name is a clarion call!"

The Queen breathed deeply, and closed her eyes slowly.

"Zenobia, Empress and Liberator! Zenobia, Queen of Women, Mistress of the Earth!"

She opened her eyes, and clenched her fists.

"Salome, your words stir my blood like the gallop of my first victorious horsemen! I shall conquer Aurelian, and bring him to Palmyra chained to the back of my chariot! I shall raze Rome to the ground. Palmyra shall become the capital of the world!"

She placed her sword upon the floor, rose and embraced me. She motioned me to sit at her feet, and placed my hands upon her lap, covering them with her own.

We were silent for some time. I planned a new attack, a

new way of identifying the conquest of Rome with the liberation of woman, for I realized that Rome was infinitely nearer to the Queen's heart than her sex.

Zenobia caressed my hands and arms, pressing into them from time to time.

"Salome, who are you? Tell me. Who are you?"

And without awaiting a reply, she said: "Salome, I am Cleopatra. The soul of Cleopatra lives within me. Do I look like her?"

"Cleopatra was the bud. Zenobia is the blossomed flower. Cleopatra's beauty stirred the blood of men, Zenobia's the blood of men and women."

"How shall I free woman?" she asked suddenly.

I had not yet thought of a practical means. I forgot that I could not expect Zenobia to live for centuries, to experiment, to sow the seed, and wait.

Longinus, philosopher and physician, who could come and go at pleasure in the Queen's palace, entered jubilantly, waving a manuscript in his hand.

"Augusta, Augusta," he said out of breath, "your soldiers have brought me another manuscript, from one of the looted temples."

Zenobia laughed.

"He considers the finding of a manuscript a greater victory than the conquest of a city," she whispered in my ear.

Longinus was tall and heavy, but his face was delicate and pale, and his eyes gentle as a deer's. He wore two long side beards, yellow like hay, in the manner of the Assyrians. His satin toga shimmered like a black sea.

Longinus rubbed his hands in glee.

"Longinus," Zenobia asked, "how does the soul travel into a new body?"

"There are mysteries we cannot fathom, Augusta!"

"What is the soul?" she asked.

"Alas, Augusta, I cannot answer. All the philosophers and poets speak of the soul, but no one defines it."

"What is the body, Longinus?"

"The body, your Majesty, is as subtle as the soul. I do not know what the body is."

"Have you ever heard the like, Salome? The greatest philosopher and physician knows neither what the soul is nor what the body is. Then what do you know, Longinus?"

"In truth, Augusta, I know nothing."

Zenobia laughed heartily.

"Did you hear that? Did you hear that, Salome?"

I nodded, my mind preoccupied with a plan which I was formulating for the liberation of woman.

"I only know certain manifestations of the body and the soul, and even of those I am not absolutely certain."

"What bodies have souls, Longinus? Do you know that, at least?"

"Every body has a soul."

Zenobia laughed.

"Even the bodies of my slaves?"

"Yes, Augusta."

"Why are they slaves, then, Longinus?"

"The vicissitudes of the body are purely accidental."

"My slaves have souls!" She laughed again. "Did you hear that, Salome?" Suddenly her brow clouded, and her full lips pouted.

"That is not true, Longinus!"

"As the Queen commands," he answered suavely.

Zenobia smiled. "You are a wary old fox, Longinus. Your head is precious to you."

"Neither life nor death is so precious that man need fear the loss of the one or the embrace of the other."

Zenobia was disarmed.

"I shall remember what you said, when I order your not over-precious head to be removed from your equally unimportant neck, Longinus."

She extended her hand which he kissed.

"But really, Longinus, does each man possess a soul?"

"Each man and each woman!"

"Did you hear that, Salome? Each woman too! Thanks for that, Longinus. And how is the soul manifested?"

"In the breath, your Majesty. Remove a man's breath — does he live? But as long as he lives, has he not breath regardless of his station in life?"

Zenobia closed her eyes half-way, and smiled ironically. She asked the philosopher to retire, and promised to send an army expressly to unearth more manuscripts.

When he left, she clapped her hands. An officer appeared.

"Officer, strangle three of my slaves. Do not sacrifice the strong ones. We need them. Or rather, take three girls. Place a feather in each mouth, before you close it. Tie a bit of parchment on each feather, with the following words — 'Longinus, tell me whither my soul has departed that it cannot ruffle even so tiny a feather.' Then send the heads to Longinus as a gift from his Queen."

The officer left.

Zenobia arranged the train of her robe.

"Salome," she said calmly, "I shall free woman from her bondage as soon as I have conquered Rome. I will issue an edict to make woman mar's equal. I shall free all female slaves. I shall choose my ministers among women as among men. I shall open schools for women. No man will be allowed more than one wife to whom on the penalty of death he must be faithful. I shall proclaim as many goddesses as gods in the temples. No woman will be allowed to bear more than six children. Any man who cohabits with a woman who has borne six children shall be beheaded, unless the woman has passed beyond motherhood. I shall raise statues to beautiful and clever women."

I looked at her astounded. What a strange mind! While she was speaking of one thing and another, she evolved a practical program, so comprehensive and excellent! How many brains did she possess?

"But first I must conquer the Romans! I must sit upon the throne of the world! And that cannot be until ——"

She bent and whispered into my ear —"until I have conquered Cleopatra. The shade of Cleopatra stands between me and victory!"

Which Zenobia spoke now? Where had Zenobia, the practiced monarch, disappeared?

"Cleopatra is dust of the dust, Zenobia. How can she forestall you?"

"Cleopatra is alive, Salome! She is alive! I see her in my dreams mocking me!"

"What are dreams, Zenobia, that you should take them seriously?"

The Queen did not listen.

She pursued: "She hates me because I am more beautiful than she, because I am stronger, because my army has defeated the armies of the Emperor. I must conquer Cleopatra before I conquer the World!"

I waited, thinking that she would turn to another idea more amenable to logical discussion. But she persisted: "I shall go to Egypt, Salome," she said, stamping her sword. Her face hardened until she looked like a warrior recently returned from battle.

"I shall open her tomb, and burn her body, that she may no longer torture me in my dreams. I am stronger than she! I shall conquer her!"

"Zenobia," I said cautiously, seeing her mood, "this is not the time to go to Egypt. The Roman soldiers are on the verge of defeat. Remain in your capital to encourage the army, and direct the destiny of the nation."

She glared at me.

"Who is Queen, Salome, you or I?"

I was tempted to say that if she was queen once, I had been queen several times, and of more ancient and greater lands than hers. But I restrained my wounded vanity, and spoke calmly.

"I do not contradict the Queen. I speak to my friend."

She embraced me. "Forgive me, Salome." Her hands lingered upon my arms and chest. "It was the Queen that spoke, not the friend. Now it is the friend again."

We remained silent for some time.

Zenobia spoke mainly to herself, stamping her sword meditatively. "Within three days we go to Egypt!"

She stood up. "So be it!" And turning to me, she said, "You and Longinus shall accompany me."

Like a somnambulist, she descended from her throne, and walked out of the hall.

169

CHAPTER TWENTY-FOUR

I DISCUSS IMMORTALITY — THE FRONTIERS OF NATURE — NO RESPITE FROM THE MOON — THE TYRANNY OF THE WOMB — THE ENEMY OF WOMAN — WORLD MOTHER.

For weeks a hundred slaves, under the direction of priests and scholars, broke the walls of the pyramid which enclosed the remains of the Queen, whose love Herod, my grandfather, had spurned.

Meanwhile, Longinus and I spent many hours discussing philosophy. There was something of Apollonius in his voice and manner which endeared him to me. He was of the earth, not of the Heavens.

The morning was as delicate and frail as the body of a young bird. The breeze blew gently like a perfumed mouth whispering the name of a beloved mate.

Longinus and I were walking slowly among the pyramids whose shadows stretched out and united in the distance like sheaves of Titans' spears.

"The soul," Longinus said, placing his hands in his wide, brocaded sleeves, "is the desperate hope of man that he may live forever — a hope and a delusion."

"Does not the soul live on after the death of the body?"

"The soul does not exist!" He bent his head toward my ear and whispered. "The pyramids harbor skin and bones which would be more useful to Earth's fertility. But man yearns to be immortal, even to the extent of preserving his dust."

"Is immortality so cherishable?"

"The desire for immortality is in the nature of things, Princess. A stone thrown into the air yearns to fly on forever, and struggles against the wind that hinders its speed and against the Earth which pulls it back to its bosom. The wheel once turned would continue its dizzy career to the end of time. The voice breaks into echoes that it may not vanish and become part of the silent air. The petals of flowers battle against the cold hands of winter. Nothing willingly relinquishes its form and condition. Man is like the stone and the wheel and the voice and the flower. His ingenuity and fear, however, have created a shadow which lives on forever — his soul."

"Longinus, what would happen if mankind in general accepted your view?"

He smiled sadly, raising one eyebrow.

"Mankind will never accept my view, Salome. Truth frightens man. In the débris of his thoughts he plants forever new illusions, which he nurtures and cherishes more than the light of his eyes."

Longinus looked in the distance, beyond the pyramids, beyond the white houses and the ruins, which once were palaces, beyond the sea. His eyes, like the eyes of Apollonius, sought the last of the horizons.

"But if some day man should dare relinquish his illusions and his fears, and accept truth — if some day he accepts the Earth in lieu of Heaven, and the present instead of the past, which is a handful of ashes, and the future, which is an armful of clouds — then — then —" He sighed. "Alas, man lives so little — and Truth is leaden-footed."

Joy flooded my heart. I was about to shout: "I shall live long enough! I shall see Truth upon Earth!"

Lakshmi approached from the distance, her carapace dazzling in the sunlight.

Longinus pointed his forefinger at her.

"How many generations of men will this creature outlive? Certainly if no one is tempted by her meat, Zenobia and Longinus —" He looked at me quizzically, then continued: "And Salome, alas, will long be dust, while Lakshmi will still crawl her silent way among the pyramids of silent monarchs, and still spawn her eggs in the sand, that her precious race may continue to teach man that he is not the favorite son of the gods."

"Cannot the human body achieve immortality also?"

"Immortality escapes the mind of man, which can judge the passing of time only by the shape and position of the Moon."

"Apollonius claims that man can live as long as he desires."

"Apollonius was a great thinker — perhaps the greatest — but he allowed meditation to usurp investigation. Besides, he spoke in parables. He identified man with the universe and death with Nirvana."

"But has there never been an individual, man or woman, who lived indefinitely — as long as he desired to continue to exist?"

Longinus smiled, and rubbed his hands slowly, thoughtfully.

"Everything is possible, Princess, but it is more rational to deal with probabilities. Experience teaches us that each species of animals and plants has a more or less determined span of life. The fly, however fortunate, cannot equal the longevity of the dog, or the dog that of the elephant, or the elephant that of this creature with the symbol of Vishnu upon her back, pecking at your dainty ankles, Salome."

I laughed, and bent to caress the head of Lakshmi.

"Lakshmi," I thought, "you and I know better. You and I know that one can go far beyond the frontiers prescribed by Nature, and that the impossible may be the truth. Apollonius, sitting silently like a statue carved in snow, discovered what Longinus, incomparable physician, shall never discover in all his researches. You and I shall always consider the possible the root from which all things blossom."

Longinus smiled, a little ironically, at my caresses.

"Longinus," I said, "why do you think that woman is merely a child playing with toys?"

Longinus looked at me, a little taken aback.

"Have I said that, Salome?"

"You have just thought it."

He laughed. "It is true. I cannot hide my thoughts from Salome. That I discovered long ago."

"Do you not think that woman will equal man some day, Longinus?"

He shook his head.

"Why not?"

"Nature willed it so, Princess."

"Not Nature, but man!" I exclaimed, angrily.

"Man only follows the example of Nature. The weak are always enslaved by the strong. But it was Nature which set the example. Has not Hippocrates, Father of Medicine, said that the entire life of woman is but a constant, never ceasing disease?"

"Cannot woman alter it, Longinus? Can she not conquer the Moon?"

"There have been women who escaped the tyranny of the Moon either because of some natural disturbance in their constitution or by forceful means. But were those creatures really women?"

"Perhaps they were superior to both men and women — a third sex, whom people despised because they did not understand."

"To overcome Nature is to destroy oneself. They who destroy sex destroy life. Look at the eunuch! Is he superior to man? Is the ox superior to the bull, or the horse that drags dully his load superior to the stallion? Why does the bird sing? The lily — why does it clothe itself in its white robe like a royal bride? Extricate sex, and you eliminate beauty and joy and song — and life itself!"

"Must woman always pay a penalty for her sex, Longinus?"

"Woman's life is a disharmony, a cacophony from the cradle to the grave. Neither crown of jewels nor crown of beauty can do more than mitigate her tragedy. Her sex life begins in pain and ends in torment. Man may learn to pity her, but never to understand her, for there is as much stability in her as in the tides of the sea or the winds which change forever their direction."

The irritable reply which shaped itself upon my tongue

would have convinced him more than ever that he was right in his judgment. I waited. He pursued, posturing a little, as if talking to disciples. For a moment I was reminded of the Mistress of the Temple of Venus of the Triple Gate, but his face was so flooded with intelligence and kindliness, that I repented my thought.

"At the very portal of love," Longinus pursued, "woman pays a toll of blood. While man thrills with voluptuous delight, woman's share is agony. He must inflict a wound upon her before she may reciprocate his caress."

I felt a shadow cross my face.

"Man can not assume paternity without a spasm of joy. But the seed may be sown while the womb remains insensible to pleasure."

My memory was a knife cutting into me.

"Even before mating," Longinus continued, his hand caressing the smooth surface of a pyramid, "woman's body mobilizes all its resources to prepare the soil for the new life which may spring from man's loins into her. Every month irresistible forces fashion within her a mysterious organ, like an orange-colored moon, which dominates ovulation, sending a summons which may not be gainsaid to her breasts and her womb.

"Every organ of her body is affected. Her voice loses its pitch. Her stomach is rebellious, her nerves twitch, her muscles lose their elasticity. Often the people she cherished, she now despises. Words of love change to mockery. The hand that caressed seeks to strike. The blood deserting her brain nurtures those parts where life is cradled."

"Does not the blood of the male also rush away from his brain at the call of sex, Longinus?"

"Yes, but when passion is stilled, it flows back. It does not linger for days in the same place, until it overbrims the organ and must perforce seek egress. If the normal channel is obstructed, it finds other exits. There are women who pay their tribute to the Moon through their nostrils. And how futile it may all be!"

Longinus looked at me pathetically, as if I were the symbol of womanhood. "For unless impregnation occurs, all the fuss and fury within her body is in vain. Nature, cheated, expels the barren egg. The orange-colored moon shrivels and vanishes, but like a merciless creditor, it returns month after month to the womb of the woman, superimposing upon her individual rhythm the rhythm of the race."

He stopped for a long while, but like a Prophet of Pain, he resumed: "And when woman's body bears fruit, the orange-colored moon at last disappears, but another equally mysterious and implacable organ dominates the humors of her body until the new life greets the Earth. Like its predecessor, it holds the womb in thrall, and prevents it from asserting its own rhythm by the expulsion of the unborn one.

"A relentless parasite, the fœtus feeds upon her, and draws like a many-rooted canker the life of its mother. Not until the child is ready to be born, is the spell that paralyzed the womb broken, and the offspring is torn from its mooring."

"Why are the gods so cruel to woman, Longinus?" I asked bitterly. "Why cannot woman give birth as the birds, painlessly?"

"As the birds?" Longinus smiled sadly. "The mother bird endures a travail comparable to that of woman. Besides, a harsh voice, an unexpected tremor of the nest and the tender egg within her cracks and she dies in agony. Motherhood is a fierce warfare, a battlefield of blood and torture. The enemy of woman, Salome, is her own body."

"Why," I asked, "must maternity lacerate our bodies? Why cannot your science, Longinus, discover a balm for us?"

He answered sadly: "Woman must pay the penalty for man's intellect. The head must be large enough to house the infant's brain. It cannot force its way through the narrow channel without havoc and bloodshed. If it be true that man's brain will continue to increase, the woman of the future will suffer unsupportable agonies."

"Why is the receptacle wherein woman bears the child so ill-adapted to carry its genetic burden? Why has Nature or God been so ill an architect?"

"If the pelvis were larger mankind would not be able to stand upright and lord it over creation. Its weight would compel man to crawl on his belly and walk on all fours, like the beasts of the earth. Since the female of the species carries her burden standing upright, the child would be jeopardized by every movement, if it were not bound to the mother with a thousand cords of nerves and blood. The animal needs no such anchorage. No device can save the human mother from suffering.

"What I am telling you, Salome," he lowered his voice to a whisper, "is the secret lore of Æsculapius. I am aggrieved that my pledge forbids its revelation save to the cognoscenti. For if man but knew the heavy atonement Nature exacts from your sex, in fecundity and in barrenness alike, he would be kinder to woman."

"If he knew," I answered angrily, "it would only intensify his abominable conceit."

"Perhaps that is the reason, Salome, that Æsculapius in his wisdom prohibited the promulgation of the secret."

As if anxious to break the bond of mutism enforced by the Father of Medicine, Longinus pursued:

"Even after the child is born, woman's subservience to her biological functions continues. She gives her milk as she gave her blood. Nurtured by white blood and red, the little vampire prospers. Her heart, her brain, every nerve in her system responds to the slightest demand of her babe. The umbilical cord between mother and child is never completely severed. It remains a mystical tie from which the child may emancipate itself, but which is as a chain wound forever around the heart of the mother."

"How fortunate for woman that she does not live forever, and procreate forever!"

Longinus smiled kindly.

"Even in this woman is handicapped. Nature deposits in every female child about seventy thousand eggs. Of these six or seven thousand only survive by the time she is mature enough for the marriage couch. If you lived seven thousand years, you could give birth to an army of seven thousand children—but no more."

"Every male, on the contrary, carries within himself enough of the essence of life to impregnate, in one embrace, every nubile female in the world. He may, until the shriveling hand of age is upon him, embrace a woman every day. Nature sets no limits upon his potential paternity. Woman pays humanity's debt in vitality and blood. Man may pluck with impunity the flowers of pleasure. If he wearies of pleasure, he may stay unimpeded by the demand of the blood in the garden of wisdom."

"Woman is man's superior," I retorted, "if she carries the burden of humanity."

"In the race with man," Longinus answered, and his voice had the pride of his sex, "woman is like a runner who carries a heavy chain about his feet. She lives not for herself, but for the species."

"Even," I asked, "after she ceases to pay her toll to the Moon?"

"Then," Longinus answered, "she withers like a flower gone to seed."

"Man has modified Nature, changed her appearance, discovered many of her secrets — is it not possible, Longinus, is it not possible that some day woman may too learn to dominate the Moon and create without peril and without torment?"

The Physician shook his head, but said nothing.

"We shall master Nature, Longinus! We shall rule the Moon and determine the period of motherhood!" I exclaimed, annoyed by his skepticism.

"I shall awaken her from her sleep! I shall shout in her ear until she hears me: 'Hearken, Mother of the World! Reach forth! Reach beyond yourself! Awaken to your possibilities!' She will hear me at last! She will understand! Then shall we have not merely one queen like Zenobia, but the universal Royalty of Womanhood!"

Longinus continued his silence.

"Longinus," I said pleadingly, "if I lived a thousand years, ten thousand, could I meet with success in the end?"

He looked at me intently. Did he suddenly guess the secret of my existence? If I told him, would he believe me?

Would he accept the reality of a miracle? Would he think me mad?

"Perhaps," he said, condescendingly and a trifle bored, as one speaks to a petulant child.

A blare of trumpets announced the discovery of Cleopatra's sarcophagus and the arrival of Queen Zenobia.

CHAPTER TWENTY-FIVE

CLEOPATRA SPEAKS — THE EMERALD SCARAB — DO THE DEAD HATE THE LIVING?

WHEN the last coffin came into view, Zenobia ordered it opened, and forbade the slaves to cast a single glance, on penalty of being blinded. Their work finished, they turned their faces and walked backward to the mouth of the tomb, where they kept watch.

Only Longinus and I remained with the Queen.

Twenty-eight days had elapsed since our departure from Palmyra. Again Zenobia's face was flushed and a hysterical quiver altered her voice.

The mummy's face was intact. A diadem, studded with enormous jewels, dazzling like many-colored suns, encircled her forehead. In her hands she held a golden scepter, crowned by a snake whose eyes were two rubies. Her golden gown, molding tightly every part of her body, was embroidered with fantastic animals whose heads and tails were masses of precious stones. An emerald scarab — so perfectly fashioned it seemed alive — crept half-way out of her mouth. The cloth which covered her ears and portions of her cheeks did not entirely conceal a smile, haughty and cynical.

There was a startling resemblance between the shriveled mummy and the living queen.

"I see myself as in a mirror," Zenobia whispered hoarsely. Her face was rigid, her brow knit. What did she experience — anger, fear, surprise?

Longinus and I did not stir. Zenobia's eyes were riveted upon the dead queen. My own thoughts wandered back to my grandfather, King Herod, and my grandmother, Mariamne, Cleopatra's friend. I heard Herod rage against this woman who was not a woman. I heard him inveigh against Mariamne's machinations. His beard tickled me. I laughed. Had centuries elapsed in truth? Had I merely slept and dreamed? No, I had been awake, I had lived! I was alive! A sudden pain reminded me that I was still under the yoke of the Moon!

Zenobia waved her arms, screaming, "I hate her! I hate her!"

We were startled, but dared not speak.

"The dead woman mocks me! Look at her mouth! How she grins!"

It seemed, indeed, as if Cleopatra's lips had moved.

"See how she scoffs! She tells me that I shall be some day as she is now! I hate her!"

A few rays of the sun that sieved between the bodies of the slaves at the door fell upon the lids of the mummy.

"Look at her eyes!" Zenobia shrieked. "She hates me! She hates me, Salome!"

Turning to me, she asked pathetically, "Why does she hate me so, Salome?" Then addressing Longinus, she continued: "Do the dead always hate the living, Longinus?"

Neither of us answered.

"Are they jealous of us?"

We continued our silence.

"I do not fear her, Salome! I am the living Queen!" she said proudly. "She is but the reflection of me! She is the skin I cast off!" Zenobia laughed ironically.

"I wonder if the spot which the snake pierced is still visible," she added, curiosity besetting her like a demon. She placed her hand upon the bandages swathing the dead woman.

"Zenobia!" I warned.

She glared at me.

"Zenobia!" I repeated my warning.

Longinus, his eyes half-shut in meditation, stroked his beard with his finger-tips.

"Who dares interfere between me and my double?" Zenobia shouted, her eyes aflame.

She rent the cloth from Cleopatra's breast.

Suddenly the eyes of the mummy moved. The scarab crawled out of her mouth slowly, and opened wide its jaws. A voice, rasping, like the slow sharpening of a knife upon an unsmoothed whetstone, shouted: "Be thou accursed! Be thou accursed! Be thou accursed!"

It was a strange contraption, no doubt, that the priests had invented to protect the royal dead, but the effect was ghastly. I tried in vain to explain to her that it was not Cleopatra who spoke, but a magical device.

Covering her face with her hands, she rushed to the door. We followed her.

From the mouth of the tomb, Zenobia hurled back: "You lie! You lie!"

Once more the scarab uttered, "Be thou accursed!"

Zenobia shrieked and, pushing the watchers aside, ran out.

"Burn her! Burn her!" she ordered her slaves.

Longinus made a gesture of protest. But Zenobia, trembling with ire and fear, repeated her command.

Three slaves with torches entered the tomb. Shortly after, a thick smoke belched forth, crawled on the ground like overfed black snakes, clambered upon the pyramids, broke in the air like flocks of birds of prey.

"I have conquered Cleopatra! I have conquered myself!" Zenobia exclaimed from time to time.

She watched until the smoke was as thin and pale as the breath of a person in winter, then, pressing my arm, she said: "Let us return to Palmyra! Now I shall defeat Aurelian! Her shadow will no longer stand between me and my goal! The Eternal City shall vanish in the smoke even as the Eternal Queen! Zenobia alone is immortal!"

CHAPTER TWENTY-SIX

AURELIAN MAKES AN OFFER — THE MOON-STRUCK QUEEN — ZENOBIA PAYS — ECHOES OF ROMAN TRUMPETS — I LEAVE WITH LAKSHMI.

During Zenobia's absence in Egypt, the Romans had defeated the bulk of her armies, and it was by sheer good fortune that we were able to reach the capital.

Unwilling to remind her of the fact that I had warned her against the disastrous expedition, I was determined, nevertheless, to help her drive the enemy into the desert. I supplied her with money and stirred in her a valor which astounded the Romans.

Zenobia was herself once more. She gave her commands with amazing wisdom and precision. I counseled her to organize several regiments of young women who were not only of great value as nurses and cooks, but excellent archers.

The men could no longer speak with disdain of the courage and prowess of my sex. I was more than ever convinced that training alone differentiated man from woman.

For months the Roman siege proved futile. Spies reported that the Emperor wrote to Rome that the campaign against a woman was less ridiculous and ignoble than he had expected. But Mars, who had always been on his side, would finally grant him victory. Had he prayed to Luna, the Moon Goddess, his triumph might have come sooner.

The nations subject to Zenobia one by one joined the standard of Aurelian. It was clear that, despite the greatest fortitude and sacrifice, Palmyra would soon fall into the hands of the invaders, unless Zenobia saved the situation by a supreme stroke of strategy. I suggested a new alliance. She consented, but again confused by the Moon at the critical moment, spurned the offers of the ambassadors and put her ablest general to the sword. When his lieutenants protested furiously, she stripped them of their rank, and drove them with lashes into the lines of the enemy.

Seeing all my hopes for a woman ruler of the Empire crumble because my enemy the Moon was the ally of Rome, I determined to save Zenobia from an ignoble end.

Without the Queen's knowledge, I persuaded Longinus to visit the Emperor's camp and procure advantageous terms as the price of surrender. Longinus presented Aurelian with a manuscript of Apollonius, and so delighted him by his wisdom and knowledge that the Emperor offered to allow Zenobia a splendid retreat with royal honors. Palmyra was to escape with a ransom that would leave her the greatest city between Rome and the East.

Zenobia, still under the lunar spell, rejected indignantly the extremely generous proposal, and commanded the death of Longinus.

"Zenobia," I protested, "the world will never forgive you this unkindly and ungrateful deed!"

Zenobia forgot her royal rank. Shouting and ranting like a common washerwoman, she threatened to quarter me if I uttered another word!

When Zabdas, the new general-in-chief of our armies, favored for his conquest of Egypt, added his protest to mine, she beheaded him and ordered his body thrown to the dogs.

Suddenly, in the throes of agony, she threw herself upon the couch, and drove us out of the palace. I knew it was not the great Queen who uttered the fatal decrees, but an unfortunate woman paying the eternal penalty of her sex. It was not Aurelian who conquered Palmyra, but the Tyrant who subjugated the waves of the sea and the lifeblood of women.

The next morning the cadaverous head of Zabdas,

perched upon a spear, faced his army. Longinus smilingly drank a goblet of hemlock.

The soldiers refused to fight any longer, and the priests cursed their ruler. The populace rose in rebellion.

The echoes of the triumphant trumpets of the Romans resounded through the palace walls.

I entered the Great Hall. Zenobia, unattended, was sitting upon her throne loaded with jewels.

"Zenobia," I said, "the time has come. Let it not be said that a woman cannot die as gloriously as she has lived. Let a queen die as a queen. One mouthful of this"— I offered her a poison I had distilled myself —"and you will not hear the footfall of Roman boots in your palace. One mouthful and the world shall remember forever the glory of Zenobia in victory and defeat."

"It is she who prompts you," she answered petulantly.

"Who?"

"Cleopatra! It is she who prompts you to kill me! She wants me to share her fate to avenge the destruction of her bandaged shell!"

"It is not she who prompts me to do this, but womanhood! Let the world know that woman is equal to the bravest of men!"

"Go away!" she screamed, dashing the cup out of my hand.

"Lakshmi, you cannot sacrifice your carapace, nor I my skin to a trifling incident of history. Zenobia, Palmyra, Cleopatra — what are they but dust blown together in various shapes? The wind blows again. The dust is scattered.

"No matter!

"We seek that which no storm can destroy. The world has known great queens. But the great woman has not yet appeared! Our will shall create her! We shall herald her advent until she finally hears us and obeys our mandate!

"We must not lose hope, Lakshmi!"

Lakshmi chewed a tender cabbage-leaf, her large body resting upon her legs, her tail raised in the air.

"Come, Lakshmi, this is not precisely the moment for a banquet."

I pulled the cabbage out of her mouth.

"Our faithful allies — Time and Space — are clamoring for us. Come!"

The wall to the north had not yet been surrounded by the Roman armies. A handful of gold opened a gate for me and Lakshmi and our dromedaries heavy-laden with supplies.

As we reached the peak of a hill at nightfall, I noticed to the south a blazing light.

"Palmyra will soon be ashes — but for one night it is transformed into a constellation. Here is a cabbage-leaf, my friend."

Lakshmi chewed. I turned away, and wept.

CHAPTER TWENTY-SEVEN

LAKSHMI RETURNS TO HER HUSBAND — I AM A MONK OF BUDDHA — THE TEMPLE OF APOLLONIUS — THE TRAIL OF CARTAPHILUS — I MEET ZENOBIA IN THE SUBURBS — A ROMAN COURTESAN — A NORDIC GOSPEL OF WOMAN — ULRIC, SON OF ALBERIC — MY BARBARIAN HUSBAND.

"Lakshmi! Lakshmi! Lakshmi!"

My slaves searched every corner of Ispahan. The name of Lakshmi reverberated through the city like an invocation to a divinity or a tribute to a triumphant Shah. "Lakshmi! Lakshmi!" In vain!

The wife of Vishnu had left me to embrace her lawful and immortal husband. Or perhaps she had ascended to Mount Mandara where gods and devils twirl the seas for inestimable blessings. Or perhaps — oh, I knew quite well what had happened! Cartaphilus, enraged at a trick I had played upon him and his grotesque companion, Kotikokura, had carried her off!

I missed her greatly, particularly this day, when I felt the need of some one to whom I could relate, without fear of being betrayed, the discomfiture of the Much-Beloved and the fright of Kotikokura, whose powerful arms lay paralyzed in the arms of a shadow.

I laughed aloud. My slaves looked at me furtively, grinning. What sweet revenge! He who boasted full command of the mysteries of the East, who had traveled through India and Cathay and Arabia and Africa, who had been the disciple of Apollonius, could not fathom the magic of a few mirrors!

He who nearly consummated unendurable pleasure indefinitely prolonged, and was acclaimed divine in the Temple of the Venus of the Triple Gate, stood agape, aghast, before the phantom orgy of dancing shadows cast by torches upon glass!

"Oh, why are you not here, Lakshmi, that I might tell you how I tormented Cartaphilus with jealousy by borrowing for a night his fantastic companion in preference to himself.

"Why are you not here that I might imitate the look of Kotikokura and his shriek at the sight of the shadowy vampire? Will the Great Lover still despise Salome, and think woman incapable of thought or of courage? Will he — oh, Lakshmi — When he said —'Salome, I love you!' my heart leaped like a kangaroo that hears the footsteps of hunters! My lips were flames that yearned to devour his!

"But it cannot be, Lakshmi — not yet — not for centuries perhaps. I cannot come to my lover as his inferior, as a weak creature of whom he must tire in a few generations! I can only be his equal, his love, his immortal companion!"

As a Buddhist monk, I wandered about the country endeavoring to raise woman from the mire into which she had sunken. But Persia was in no mood to listen to my revolutionary ideas. The women accused me of sacrilege and immorality. Only immediate flight saved me from their clamorous fury.

The old world was dead. Deserts are reputed to blossom again when the Earth, tilting, changes the course of the seas. Perhaps Time, too, tilts, and old civilizations are flooded with youth once more. But I was too restless to wait. My blood galloped in me. Let the dead bury the dead!

I wended my way to the youth of the world, the conqueror of the Earth — to Rome!

Ashes, dust, ruins, everywhere — a vast cemetery. Only Tyana, the birthplace of Apollonius, was still intact. The

Roman army did not destroy the spot over which the spirit of the Master hovered like a white dove.

The Temple dedicated to Apollonius, of unveined marble, gleamed like a cupola of snow upon the Hill of the Palms. I entered. It was empty save for a statue of the Master, so perfectly conceived, it almost breathed.

Overjoyed at the sight of the luminous face, I exclaimed: "Hail, Apollonius, God of Wisdom! Blessed be thy name forever!"

I broke a vase of perfume and anointed the cold head of the statue. I placed a gold laurel upon the marble brow.

The caretaker, almost as ancient as the philosopher himself, approached me, and smiling, said:

"I thank you, madam, in the name of the Immortal One!"

"Do many worshipers come to the shrine, my friend?" I asked.

He sighed. "Alas, madam, the last in many years was the Emperor Aurelian, on his way to Palmyra. He ordered his army to march in reverence around the Temple, and under the penalty of death forbade them to touch any person or object within the frontiers of the town."

He rubbed his forehead.

"No, I am wrong. I am getting old, and my memory is weakening. A year ago a Hindu Prince spent a whole day in the Temple. When he left, he placed this gold tablet at the feet of the Master. I cannot read it. It is in a strange tongue."

I bent and read in Sanskrit:

"To the immortal in spirit from the immortal in flesh — homage and love, Cartaphilus."

I knelt and kissed the feet of Apollonius. My lips slipped and touched the name of my lover.

"Who will take care of the Temple when you are gone, my friend?" I asked.

"The Master will provide."

I felt a little ashamed.

"It is true. The Master will provide," I said.

I begged him to accept gold and jewels.

"I need nothing, madam! I cultivate my own little patch

of ground. My goat gives me milk to drink. The words of the Master sustain my spirit."

His humble pride delighted me. We spoke of Apollonius. Some of the things I told him reminded him of Cartaphilus. Cartaphilus, I thought, you precede me always. But by coming a trifle later, I know your whereabouts, while you — seek me in vain!

The sun set, and the Temple of Apollonius was a goblet of flames.

The caretaker bent his head in prayer.

I walked silently away.

Was Aurelian, the Imperator, clement or ironic? Zenobia was taken captive to Rome. She followed the imperial chariot in fetters of gold. Two slaves supported the dazzling chain which encircled her regal neck. But the procession over and the acclaim of the people lost amid the dust raised by the hoofs of the horses and elephants and dromedaries, Aurelian presented the Queen of the East with a villa at Tibur, about twenty miles away from the Capital and with a husband, Corelianus, a former senator, middle-aged, bald, stout and taciturn.

Soon after my arrival in the Capital of the World, I drove to the home of the former Queen.

The villa nestled in a valley like in the hollow of a cupped hand. A vineyard to the right, olive trees to the left, and rose bushes in front almost smothered the view.

Zenobia sat upon the veranda weaving on the distaff. I wished to approach unseen, but a large mastiff chained to his kennel barked more noisily than the cackling of the seven geese which saved the Eternal City from destruction.

Where was the Monarch of the East? I watched in vain for the flaming eyes, the imperious gesture. The very contours of her face had changed. Her nose had become stubbier, her cheeks slightly puffed, her chin lay will-less in a tiny cradle of flesh.

She chattered interminably about her household and her grandchild, more interested in the price of olives than in the destiny of the world.

"Do get married, Salome," she advised me solicitously. "And have children and grandchildren!"

Were her words a rebuke or a consolation? Did the duck disdain the wings of the eagle? Was Earth's solidity more desirable than the empyrean? Was I offering woman that which her nature refused or was incapable of assimilating? Did a crown upon a woman's head weigh more heavily than progeny in her womb?

I was walking along the shore of the Tiber, aflame with the setting sun, meditating on the words of the former gorgeous Queen of the East, now the contented suburbanite. What had caused the sorry metamorphosis? Had the Moon, which formerly demanded of Zenobia so painful a toll, compensated her for her suffering with a largesse of intelligence and power and magnificence?

I suddenly became conscious of the presence of a tall man, whose long fair locks moved in the breeze. His large blue eyes looked at me pleadingly, caressingly, timidly. It was not the look of Cartaphilus. It was not the look of Onam. It was not the look of any man I had ever known. There was pride and gentleness and desire and reverence in his look.

He was dressed in the manner of the Barbarians, plainly, but with distinction, and his bearing had neither the haughtiness of the Roman nor the subtleness of the Oriental. The absolute assurance of his power needed neither pomp nor fawning. His spirit seemed to flow evenly like the river, and the flame of his eyes was like the flame of the sunset in the cool embrace of the Tiber.

For a long time we looked at each other in silence.

A courtesan reclining on a couch carried by Negroes passed us by. She dazzled with jewels and in her hand she held a silver mirror. She was bare to the knees and her breasts were uncovered. Two slaves fanned her, while a swarm of flutists played a lascivious air. Three dwarfs, grotesquely dressed, brought up the rear.

The Barbarian watched the procession until it disappeared. An ironic smile played about his lips. But his eyes were sad.

"Woman is the soul of a nation," he said. "Rome is dying not because her Emperors are assassinated or her Senate is corrupt. She is dying because her women have lost their virtue."

There was neither the voluptuousness of the Oriental in his voice nor the bombast of the Latin.

"Is this the fate of all old nations?" he asked suddenly.

"Rome is young!"

"Rome is decrepit and rotten!" he exclaimed. "Rome is like yonder log lying on the shore. The water has eaten into it until it is good neither for building nor for fire."

"Is there any new country?" I asked desperately. "Is there a place where corruption has not set in, where the worm does not gnaw at the foundation?"

The young man pointed his forefinger to the North.

"Beyond the mountains, across the Rhine — there the new tree is blossoming."

He looked longingly in that direction, then sighing, said: "They call us Barbarians because we despise their effeminate pleasures, because we abhor luxury, because our music stirs our souls, not our bodies, because we demand purity of man and woman before and after marriage, that our children may inherit strong bodies, untainted, because we revere woman and consider motherhood divine."

He stopped awhile, then, defiant, continued:

"Let them call us Barbarians, let them mock us — what matters it? The future is ours!"

He sneered. "Rome is the Mistress of the World! So be it — the mistress — the courtesan — and like the mistress and the courtesan — corrupt and short-lived and loathsome!"

The crescent moon, like a vast eyebrow, frowned over the Capitol.

A Captain crossed the street and stopped in front of me. I shivered, startled. I thought it was Cartaphilus. The same uniform, the same bearing, the same haughtiness.

I turned my face. The Captain shrugged his shoulders, and walked on.

The Barbarian breathed heavily.

"Had he spoken one word to you, I would have crushed him!"

"Is it worth while to risk your own life for a woman you see for the first time?"

"The honor of a woman is a sacred thing. Besides, this is not the first time I have seen you, madam."

"I have been in Rome only a week."

"True, and for a week I have followed you, as your shadow. I waited at your gate for a whole night. I drove with you to Tibur and back. I do not know how I mustered up courage to address you now. Forgive me."

He made a motion to go away.

"Do not go."

There was a sincerity in his words that thrilled me. Not thus did Cartaphilus make love to me, nor any of my husbands. They came as conquerors, not as equals.

This man belonged to another world.

"Come with me," he pleaded. "Come to my country! Be my wife and the mother of my children. Come away from corruption and vice. Come where men and women are free!"

"Do your men propose marriage at the first encounters, without even knowing the antecedents of their beloved?" I asked, smiling.

"I know who you are."

"Who?"

"You are Freya, goddess of love. And I am Ulric, the son of the chieftain Alberic. Come with me!"

My cheeks suddenly burned. I was like a virgin in the presence of her first lover. To hide my embarrassment, I turned away, and watched the Tiber. The recent drought had depleted its waters, and it dragged wearily on to the sea like an aged and rheumatic beast.

I thought of Cartaphilus, of Herod, of my mother — strange I had not thought of her for centuries — of my nurse, of Agrippina — Suddenly the Tiber turned red with the blood of the head of Jokanaan. I uttered a stifled cry and hid my face in my hands.

"Your modesty," Ulric said, "is a torch that sets my heart aflame. I cannot live without you. If you do not come with me," he unsheathed a dagger, "I'll die at your feet."

I uncovered my eyes and blinked in amazement. I had entirely forgotten the existence of my suitor.

"Ulric," I said, "your words delight and honor me — but —"

"But — what?"

I did not answer.

"You love some one else?"

There was sadness in his face. I dared not hurt him.

I shook my head.

"You disdain the hand of a Barbarian!"

"No, Ulric."

"Then why will you not come with me? When my father dies, I shall be the chieftain, and you will be queen!"

"Queen?" I waved my hand wearily.

"Do you fear my people?"

"No, Ulric, I fear myself. Salome brings sorrow to her suitors."

"Who is Salome?"

"I am Salome."

"You are Freya!" he said irrevocably.

"Freya, too, brings sorrow to man."

"That is merely a legend."

"It is the truth!"

He looked at me for a while, then said:

"I fear neither happiness nor sorrow."

Was Zenobia right? Was the ultimate desire of woman — a good husband — and children? I was weary of the long peregrination, of the search for freedom. I yearned for a home and love. I yearned to be merely a woman.

"So be it, Ulric! Take me to your country!"

"My wife!" he exclaimed, pressing my hand to his lips.

CHAPTER TWENTY-EIGHT

"WHY DO THE YOUNG MEN LOOK AT YOU WITH DESIRE?"
—TIME STANDS STILL FOR ME—LAST EMBRACE—HATSHOP-
SITOU SITS AT MY FEET—CARTAPHILUS IS A GOD—THE
CAMEL OF A THOUSAND HUMPS—I SEEK A NEW GOD IN
AFRICA.

The years flowed tranquilly on like the Rhine which shone in the distance. The past was a dream dimly remembered. The future the vague tinkling of sheep in the pastures.

I walked slowly between the two rows of poplar trees whose tops waved like plumes on the helmets of a conquering army.

Time does not exist, I thought. Time is an illusion.

On a rock which had the shape of a cradle, Ulric sat watching my approach. I waved my hand and hurried my steps.

"Is my husband sad?" I asked, seating myself next to him.

He did not answer for some time.

I patted his head.

"This is the third time it happened," he said bitterly.

"What, my love?"

"For three days I tried to bend the bow without success. The young officers in the field nudged one another. I dare not try it again."

"That is nothing. You are tired, or perhaps you are not well," I said solicitously.

"I am old, Freya."

I laughed. "Old? Why, time is an illusion, Ulric. I have been thinking about it only awhile ago. Time does not exist."

"Time does not exist?" he repeated ironically. "Was my hair white and thin when I spoke to you of my love on the bank of the Tiber? Did my hand shiver as it does now?"

He breathed heavily.

"When you approached, my eyes were too dim to recognize you. If time does not exist, who changed me into an old man?"

"You are not old, my love," I said, smoothing his face.

Strange, I had hardly noticed the disintegration of my husband's superb physique. It had come gradually, imperceptibly.

"Time does not exist," he laughed bitterly. "Why then do the young men dare to look at you with desire, Freya?"

"Who looks at me with desire?"

"Aleman and Alaric and Gustav — all of them. They are not afraid of me. I can no longer challenge them to combat — I, Ulric, who once broke the back of a bear. You remember, Freya, do you not?"

"Of course, Ulric, I remember. You were the handsomest and the strongest of men."

He laughed, an old man's laugh, that sounded like a great number of "e's" strung upon a chain.

Suddenly he grew furious.

"I heard them whisper to one another —'He's old enough to be her grandfather!' They even said that I was incapable of being your husband."

"You know better, Ulric," I laughed.

His face lighted up for a moment. He looked at me intently.

"There isn't one wrinkle in your face, not one gray hair upon your head, not one tooth is missing from your mouth. You are as beautiful as when I first beheld you."

"Does not my lord desire a young and beautiful wife?"

"No!" he said emphatically. "It is not natural for old age to share the bed of youth. Why do you not grow old with me?" he asked pathetically. "I am the laughing stock of the young. I dare not leave you alone for a moment. My arms cannot hold you firmly, and my lips are cold."

"I love you," I said, placing my arms around his neck. But I realized with a pang at the heart that I lied.

"You love me as a child loves its father. I know it. I cannot satisfy the passion of your youth. The contact of my body makes you quiver with disgust."

I made a gesture of denial. He wound his hands about my throat and pressed until I coughed.

"If you as much as glance at another man, I'll kill you! Do you hear?"

"Ulric," I said gently, "have I not been a faithful wife to you?"

"Yes."

"Have I not shown you tenderness and admiration?"

"Yes."

"Does Freya need the love of impertinent youths?"

"Forgive me, Freya, I am mad with jealousy. I am old and you are so beautiful. Why have you not become an old hag — ugly and undesirable like the other women? Why has not your fire turned to ashes as mine has turned? I can no longer love you, as a man loves a woman, Freya, and the memory of your embrace is a perennial torture."

He stopped for a moment, then continued:

"Do you remember what you said when I asked you to be my wife in Rome?"

"I said that I loved you, and I love you."

"You said that Salome brings sorrow to her lover."

"Who is Salome?" I asked.

"That's what I asked then. And you told me it was you. I said you were Freya, goddess of love. And you said that Freya, too, brings sorrow to her lovers. I answered that I feared neither the joy nor the sorrow of love. I was a fool, Freya. The sorrow of love is like a thousand swords piercing the heart at once."

"Ulric, my master, my love," I said, caressing his head. He pushed my hands off.

"Don't pity me! Don't humor me if you cannot love me!"

"I love you."

I laughed suddenly. He looked at me.

"You think I am not old, Ulric? You think my face is unwrinkled and I have no gray hair?"

"You are as young as when I first kissed your lips."

"That is because I wanted to please you. From now on, since my lord will not have it so, you will see wrinkles on my face and gray hair on my head."

He looked at me, squinting his eyes.

"Are you a witch?"

I laughed. "Are only witches anxious to please their husbands? I shall no longer use the herbs to color my hair or the unguent to smooth my face. I shall be old, for your sake!"

His lips tightened and bent into his mouth.

"Time does exist, dear — for all of us. But the Earth is kindly, and one may pluck from her heart balsams to erase for a while the traces of the claws of the merciless Tigress. I thought I pleased you. But I was wrong. Let Freya, goddess of love, be an old hag!"

"No!" he exclaimed. "Freya must be young and beautiful always."

He took my head in his hands and looked at me intently.

"How beautiful is Freya! How soft is the touch of her skin! How luscious is her mouth! Her eyes are heavy with love like ripe grapes. Her hair is the setting sun slumbering over the cool crystal waters of a pool. Her breath is the breeze that has ravished the first perfumes of the violet and the rosemary. Her breasts are fistfuls of snow on which rosebuds blossom. Freya is youth. Freya is love. Time dares not touch her. He skulks past her like a wolf at noon."

He closed his eyes, and remained silent for a long time.

"Freya, is there no balsam which restores the strength of arm and the power of limb? Give me my youth, Freya, for one day, for one hour! For one hour, Freya!"

I embraced him. "Come with me, Ulric, and I shall give you once more the strength and the joy of youth! The blood of my heart shall gallop through your veins, and the flame of my lips shall set yours afire. Come with me!"

Ulric uttered a cry of triumph.

"I am young, Freya! You have given me youth! I love you, Freya!"

Suddenly he caught his breath, and pressed his hands against his heart.

"Freya!" he whispered. "Freya, I love—" His words gurgled in his throat, and his head fell upon my arms. His eyes rolled slowly upward, staring at the ceiling. His hands were cupped as if they still held my breasts within them. There was utter peace on his face.

Immediately after Ulric's death my house swarmed with suitors — strong men who clinked their swords, vain men who strutted about, their chests swollen like those of pigeons, bashful ones who looked at me with half-closed eyes, sighing, eloquent ones whose thunderous voices shook the walls, young men who swore I was their first love, middle-aged ones who vowed I would be their last. Husbandless I could not remain. Woman's freedom and equality among the Barbarians existed only in the idealistic vision of Ulric. The others merely rendered lip-service to the remnants of an older faith — the rule of the Mystic Mothers, long overthrown in reality.

The day for my choice arrived.

Seated upon the throne which once belonged to an Emperor, and dressed as an Arabian Queen, dazzling with the jewels of the House of Herod, I called my suitors, one by one. I praised their prowess and flattered them according to their special vanity. They formed a semicircle about the throne, awaiting my decision with the eagerness of hounds pulling at their leashes, impatient for the call of the hunting horn.

My eyes rested now upon one, now upon another. They glared at the favorite of a moment with a murderous frown.

"I have planted a rosebush upon the tomb of my husband. When the first rose blossoms, I shall name his successor," I said finally, and rising, walked slowly out of the hall.

Never was a man's tomb tended with more delicate care. Never was a rosebush cherished more lovingly. Night and day the men watched, their swords drawn. Witches and doctors were consulted, and rare fertilizers blessed by priests were brought in sacks and wheelbarrows. The sun and the rain were invoked with more impassioned prayers than those of the Rig-Vedas.

"A bud! A rosebud! A bud!"

The triumphant shout reverberated through the cemetery one early dawn. The army, the priesthood, the populace, all forgot Rome and the destiny of the new race, and shouted ceaselessly, "A rosebud! A rosebud!"

I suddenly realized that for nearly the entire span of a lifetime I had dwelt in the stupor of love and conjugal felicity. The full Moon had risen hundreds of times, but I had forgotten my challenge. I had forgotten my mission of liberating woman from the bondage of man and nature. In a week's time I should have to decide upon a new love — and spend one more life in the rôle of wifehood.

Never!

My body itched for change, my mind for battle.

Among the Barbarians it was futile to attempt reforms. In one generation Roman civilization had corrupted the character of the women beyond recognition. They dressed luxuriantly, paraded in the chariots captured from the enemies, hired hetæræ from beyond the Alps to instruct them in coquetry. They preferred a broken and ridiculous Latin to their own simple and powerful tongue.

It would be easier to influence a race which had reached its maximum of corruption than one which had just tasted its joys.

It was time to leave. But where should I go? Once more I was compassless in the center of all the roads that led to Nirvana.

I sat disconsolate, watching the clouds. Behind me, like a shadow, stood Hatshopsitou. She was African, black-skinned, tall, broad-shouldered and muscular. Captured by the Romans and sold in the market-place as a slave, she had killed her master and joined the Barbarian army. She took part in a dozen battles, but finally, weary of camp life, she wandered for months alone from tribe to tribe. One day, starved and naked, she stumbled at my feet and begged to be my slave. I persuaded Ulric to retain her. He acquiesced, although he despised her color.

During Ulric's life, Hatshopsitou was taciturn and diffident, but since his death she became solicitous as a dog and talkative as a magpie.

"Come here, Hatshopsitou. Sit at my feet."

She wound her powerful body around my feet like a giant cobra.

"In a few days the rose will blossom, Mistress," she sighed.

"Whom shall I marry, Hatshopsitou? Shall I marry the chieftain who can uproot a tree? Shall I marry the timid scholar who places a violet upon my window sill every dawn? Shall I marry the general who vowed he would bring the Roman Emperor bound to my feet? Shall I marry the merchant who owns fifty boats? Whom shall I marry?"

She looked up at me, her heavy lips shivering.

"Whom? Hatshopsitou?"

She kissed the hem of my robe.

"No man is worthy of my Mistress, neither chieftain, nor king, nor emperor. No one save god Ca-Ta-Pha —"

"Who is Ca-Ta-Pha? Of what nation is he god?"

"Ca-Ta-Pha is everywhere. He is up. He is down. He is in Heaven. He is upon Earth. He has made the Stars and the Moon. His face is more dazzling than the Sun. His masculine prowess outlasts a thousand goats. He descended from Heaven to Earth to bless my country. He came with his wife and son."

"Who is his wife?" I asked anxiously.

"The Camel of a Thousand Humps."

"And his son?"

"The Parrot on whose Beak Shine a Thousand Stars."

"Ca-Ta-Pha," I meditated. The name sounded both ludicrous and familiar.

"Ca-Ta-Pha," I repeated.

"Ca-Ta-Pha," she said after me, making strange, suggestive signs with her hand over her body, which I understood were the symbol of the god and the wife and the son.

"Ca-Ta-Pha has also a nephew whose mother is Lak-Shak-Mi, the Tortoise who carries the Moon upon her back."

"Lakshmi!" I exclaimed, delighted. There was no doubt — God Ca-Ta-Pha was my beloved — Cartaphilus!

"Kotikokura?" I asked, astounded.

She nodded.

Was that strange creature about whom there was still the scent of primeval forests also immortal? Had Cartaphilus learned the art of Jesus and Jokanaan and called forth eternal life in the body of his bizarre companion? Mortal, Kotikokura would have been mingled with the dust for generations.

"Are Ca-Ta-Pha and his nephew and Lak-Shak-Mi still in your country?"

"Ca-Ta-Pha is in Heaven. But the High Priest and his Mother and the Holy Parrot are in the Temple. Nobody dares to gaze at them during the day. He who looks, dies on the spot."

Cartaphilus, I thought, you have learned that fear is a god's most efficacious weapon!

"Mistress, come to us! Be the wife of Ca-Ta-Pha!"

Her words startled me. The wife of Cartaphilus!

"Ca-Ta-Pha predicted that some day his wife would come to us from the North, and then our country would prosper beyond any other. He said she would have hair like the setting sun and her body would be a cataract of milk."

She looked at me in adoration, her small black eyes turned upward.

"Ca-Ta-Pha said she is eternally young, and her name is Sa-La-Ma! You are the wife of Ca-Ta-Pha, Mistress!"

"How do you know that my name is Sa-La-Ma?"

"I heard Ulric call you once Sa-La-Ma!"

"Would not the Camel of a Thousand Humps devour me if I become the wife of Ca-Ta-Pha?"

Hatshopsitou raised herself and whispered in my ear: "Ca-Ta-Pha slaughtered her because she was unfaithful!"

"Unfaithful?" I asked, scandalized. "And with whom?"

She looked around, and whispered: "They say with his nephew, the High Priest!"

I laughed heartily.

Hatshopsitou shivered.

"Do not fear, Hatshopsitou! Sa-La-Ma will protect you!"

She embraced my legs, and hid her face between my knees.

"Come to us, Mistress! Ca-Ta-Pha promised to descend to Earth once more when Sa-La-Ma comes."

"Did he also promise them a son with her — another parrot or tortoise?"

"She will give birth to a new world, he said."

"Cartaphilus loves me! Cartaphilus loves me!" rang in my mind like golden bells.

I rose.

"So be it! Hatshopsitou, be my guide! Lead me to the country of Ca-Ta-Pha!"

Hatshopsitou uttered a shriek of delight, and danced about me, her knees raised to her chin, until her mouth frothed.

CHAPTER TWENTY-NINE

THE TEMPLE OF CA-TA-PHA — THE FLAMING EYES OF KOTIKOKURA — THE HIGH PRIEST SNORES — I AM A GODDESS.

Hatshopsitou ran ahead of my dromedary shouting at the top of her powerful lungs: "Sa-La-Ma! Sa-La-Ma! Sa-La-Ma!"

Men, women, children, dashed out of the houses, screaming —"Sa-La-Ma! Sa-La-Ma! Sa-La-Ma!"

Drums, kettles, kitchen utensils — mouths, palms, buttocks — the tribe of god Ca-Ta-Pha turned into a black ocean churned by a hurricane!

"Sa-La-Ma! Sa-La-Ma! Sa-La-Ma!"

A hundred hands grasped at my tent. I was raised and carried aloft like a banner.

"Sa-La-Ma! Sa-La-Ma! Sa-La-Ma!"

The town lay in a valley scooped out of the side of the mountain as with a broken shovel. The houses were rounded at the top like mushrooms, and out of the tall priapic chimneys threads of smoke rose piercing the white light of the full Moon like long black fingers.

Rocked upon the backs of the carriers as upon a drunken camel, I finally reached the temple of god Ca-Ta-Pha, a wooden structure formed like an immense pumpkin.

A forest of black fists knocked at the gate, shouting: "Sa-La-Ma! Sa-La-Ma! Open! Open! Sa-La-Ma has come! Sa-La-Ma has come!"

The gate opened slowly, and Kotikokura appeared dressed

in a white silk robe painted with strange animals. Around his waist was a wide belt studded with emeralds. Tilted upon his woolly head a heavy tiara balanced itself punctiliously like a pitcher of precious ointment. On his open palm a parrot perched, screeching: "Ca-Ta-Pha! Ca-Ta-Pha!"

The people fell upon their faces. Their buttocks formed a black moon.

Kotikokura glared at me.

"Sa-La-Ma! Sa-La-Ma!" my carriers shouted, depositing me upon solid ground.

"Sa-La-Ma! Sa-La-Ma!" the others repeated.

Lakshmi, her carapace glittering with Vishnu and jewels, the shape of a Moon, which Cartaphilus must have studded in my honor, appeared upon the threshold. Seeing me after a lapse of a century she rose like a miniature bull, and waddled toward me like a tugboat in a gale.

The people waved their arms frantically. The tortoise pecked at my ankles.

The people rose as if flames had been applied suddenly to their skins, and roared like a cage of mad animals.

"Sa-La-Ma! Sa-La-Ma! Sa-La-Ma!"

The parrot, unaccustomed to the new word, bent his head to one side and listened attentively. But unable to repeat it, he screeched, "Ca-Ta-Pha!"

The natives, however, did not hear him, and shouted more lustily, "Sa-La-Ma! Sa-La-Ma!"

The eyes of Kotikokura were flaming coals trying to scorch me. His nostrils opened wide. His lips stretched and his powerful teeth flashed ominously. He raised his enormous arms whose heavy coat of hair betrayed his aboriginal descent. His chest inflated like a bellow. He uttered one terrific roar. The natives caught their breaths. Their backs bristled, and their fists pressed against their bellies.

I did not budge.

Slowly I stretched my arms forward. My finger-tips, like swords, pierced the eyes of the High Priest. He tried to turn his head away, but could not. He wanted to pounce upon me like a tiger. I moved my fingers. His entire face was flooded with light. He recoiled. Reciting a Hindu incantation I riveted my eyes upon his, which moved swiftly back and forth like frightened mice caught in a trap.

The parrot lighted upon my head and screeched: "Ca-Ta-Pha!" Kotikokura, frantic at the bird's impiety, grasped it in his hands, wrung its neck and hurled it against a tree, smashing its body. The people screamed.

Startled at his own sacrilege, he gasped. His jaw dropped. His arms fell lifeless to his sides. I continued my incantation, and whispered, "Sleep! Sleep!"

Kotikokura's eyelids grew heavy.

"Sleep! Sleep!"

His eyes were blurred.

"Sleep! Sleep!"

His body weakened.

He dropped slowly upon the threshold.

"Sleep!"

He stretched out. The tiara rolled to one side and hung upon his ear like a cluster of grapes.

The High Priest of god Ca-Ta-Pha snored.

The people rose and rushed upon Kotikokura.

I raised my arm.

"Let no one touch him!" I commanded.

The natives recoiled. "Kotikokura is inviolate! He who touches him or in any way molests him shall be torn to bits upon earth and burned forever in hell!"

The people crouched and huddled against one another in utter awe. I walked among them like a white river flowing among black rocks. Lakshmi followed at my heels.

Suddenly Hatshopsitou rose and shouted a command. The natives started to their feet. She repeated the command, and began running. The others followed, shouting —"Sa-La-Ma! Sa-La-Ma! Sa-La-Ma!"

I remained alone with Lakshmi. I patted her head which moved like a bell jubilantly rung on a holy day.

"Lakshmi, you have witnessed the fall of god Ca-Ta-Pha! The High Priest himself killed his son that carried upon his head a thousand stars. Poor stars! They were crushed against the tree and drowned in the blood of the martyr."

I laughed. "But I forget, Lakshmi, according to these

people you are the mother — out of wedlock to be sure — of the High Priest who is snoring upon the threshold of his own temple! Well, no matter. We shall treat him kindly. Your maternal instinct shall not be lacerated. Vishnu has had his revenge! You have been unfaithful to your lawful husband with a minor divinity! But where is Ca-Ta-Pha, your paramour, Lakshmi?"

The tortoise tapped my ankle.

"He will return, Lakshmi. If not for the love of you, for the love of Sa-La-Ma."

In the distance flames were rising.

"Lakshmi, what is the meaning of this? Is it anger against the impotence of their former god, or the desire to honor their new divinity — Sa-La-Ma?"

Lakshmi walked around me as if drawing a magic circle against evil.

The people rushed back, headed by Hatshopsitou, carrying a bloody knife.

"Sa-La-Ma! Sal-La-Ma! Sa-La-Ma!"

She approached, and fell at my feet.

"The King who opposed the divine rule of Salome is dead!" she exclaimed.

"His body shall not be devoured by the holy worms!"

"His soul shall not go to Heaven!"

"Flames have devoured his body!"

"Sa-La-Ma," Hatshopsitou said calmly, "the palace is ready!"

"So be it, Hatshopsitou, take me to the palace."

"To the palace! To the palace! To the palace!"

Upon open palms, outstretched, I was carried in solemn step, while behind me Lakshmi wriggled upon three heads. Around us kettles, drums, buttocks — made an infernal noise.

Kotikokura snored.

The temple of god Ca-Ta-Pha was falling into ruins. Kotikokura sat mournfully upon the threshold, his priestly vestments fading in the sun. The tiara, muddy and tarnished, lay at his feet. One plume of the dead parrot shivered in his hair. From time to time he muttered —"Ca-Ta-Pha — Ca-Ta-Pha."

Only one worshiper continued to frequent the house of the former god — a very aged man to whom Cartaphilus had given the sun in safe-keeping — a Roman gold coin which he had pasted on his bald pate that it might illumine the world.

Meanwhile the people raised the Temple to the Queen and Goddess Sa-La-Ma upon the peak of the hill which dominated the desert.

CHAPTER THIRTY

THE REIGN OF THE AFRICAN AMAZON — THE DYNASTY OF WOMAN — A BROKEN CAGE — LAKSHMI BREAKFASTS ON A YOUNG CABBAGE.

"Hatshopsitou!"

Hatshopsitou fell upon her face.

"Rise!"

She rose and stood at attention.

"Hatshopsitou, henceforth you are the General-in-Chief of my army."

"Sa-La-Ma! Your Majesty!" She made an obeisance again; I raised her.

"It is not sufficient to be something, Hatshopsitou; one must be appropriately attired. Whom do you think the soldiers obey — their leader or his uniform?"

Hatshopsitou smiled, her heavy, yellow lips thrust forward.

"This uniform belonged to a Prince. Do it honor, Hatshopsitou."

She kissed my knees.

I clapped my hands. Two slaves appeared to dress the new General-in-Chief.

"Now, let me see, Hatshopsitou. Walk across the room. Stand at attention. Raise your sword. Command your army to go forward. Command it to halt. Slay your enemy. Excellent! Excellent! You are haughtier than a Roman Captain I once knew and much less ridiculous than his High

Priest — I mean — his adjutant. Excellent! And now to business, General!"

"Yes, Your Majesty!"

"And first about my palace. I do not complain against it. I have dwelt in more spacious and more luxurious quarters, but ——"

"Order a new palace, Your Majesty! Our people ——"

"No, no! First we must do something worthy of a new palace. I accept the palace as it is. You have seen, however, how easily kings are despatched and their souls prevented from going to Heaven."

"Yes, Your Majesty."

"Of course, I am not merely a Queen. I am a goddess."

"Yes!"

"But you have seen how quickly even gods are forsaken, and their sons hurled and crushed against trees."

She nodded.

"A prudent ruler, so my grandfather, Herod the Great, once told me, must have two roads — a highway to triumph, and a secret passageway to escape. He prospered much and lived long."

"Yes."

"Choose twenty strong men, to build a secret passageway which will lead from the palace into the desert. See that they never leave the place nor have converse with any one whomsoever. When they finish the work you will give them wine to drink — a wine that will instantly sever their bodies from their souls, which will fly directly to Heaven. Their bodies you will then take to the desert and consign to the purifying tongues of the flames."

"Yes, Your Majesty."

"Meanwhile, if any one inquires after them, you tell them that Sa-La-Ma has sent them on a sacred pilgrimage."

"Sa-La-Ma has sent them on a sacred pilgrimage," she repeated.

"Do we really rob them of anything valuable, Hatshopsitou, if in exchange for their miserable bodies, whose existence is as precarious as the worm's that crawls on the leaf which has dropped to the ground, we offer them — Heaven?"

"No, Sa-La-Ma."

"As for yourself, your body is as precious to me as your soul, and I need not ask any vow of secrecy, for you are both my general and my friend."

Her eyes dimmed as she bent to kiss my knees.

"Hatshopsitou, you once told me that when Sa-La-Ma comes to your country and becomes the wife of Ca-Ta-Pha, she will give birth to a new world."

"That is the sacred truth."

I bent my head, and whispered: "Ca-Ta-Pha has made me his wife ——"

Hatshopsitou looked at me, startled.

"In my sleep," I pursued. "And in my dream I have conceived a new world."

"Yes, Sa-La-Ma."

"A new world is about to be born."

Her mouth opened in bewilderment.

"This birth is different from other births. It is a birth of ideas. The travail is much longer, and the result — no one knows. It may really be a new world — or a pinch of ashes. No matter, Hatshopsitou, I am the mother, and mothers must welcome their offspring."

The General nodded.

"People claim that woman is inferior to man because it was the will of the gods that she be inferior. It is not true. Woman is inferior because man keeps her in ignorance and servitude."

"Yes, my Queen!"

"I shall prove to the world, Hatshopsitou, that woman is the equal — nay, the superior — of man, that she is the fountain of all life and truth."

Hatshopsitou began to dance, raising her knees, but suddenly remembering her uniform, she desisted.

"We are the creatures of our clothes, are we not, General?"

She grinned.

"And of our training."

"Yes, Your Majesty!"

"This is what I shall prove, Hatshopsitou. Henceforth in the country of Queen and Goddess Sa-La-Ma woman shall rule and man obey!"

"Woman shall rule and man obey!" the General-in-Chief repeated, stamping her sword.

"Woman shall be soldier and priest and master!"

"Soldier and priest and master."

"She shall conquer man first, and then she shall learn to break the bondage of the Moon."

"Yes, Your Majesty."

"And Sa-La-Ma shall at last become the wife of Ca-Ta-Pha forever."

"Lak-Shak-Mi! Lak-Shak-Mi! Lak-Shak-Mi!" some one shouted, desperately.

"What's the meaning of this?" I asked.

The General-in-Chief drew her sword, and rushed to the door. She nearly tumbled over Lakshmi, who waddled into the hall at top speed followed by her keeper, whose enormous ebony face was gray with fear.

"What's the meaning of this, Khon-su?"

The keeper fell upon her palms.

"Sa-La-Ma! Sa-La-Ma!"

"Speak!"

"Lak-Shak-Mi broke her golden cage. She desecrated the altar, and ran out of the Temple."

"Lak-Shak-Mi does not desecrate, fool!"

"Sa-La-Ma! Sa-La-Ma!" Khon-su muttered.

"And Lak-Shak-Mi does not run out of the Temple."

"Sa-La-Ma! Sa-La-Ma!"

"Lak-Shak-Mi anoints the altar and comes to pay her devotion to Sa-La-Ma!"

"Go, Khon-su, bathe seven times in the lake, and rub seven times your tongue with sand that the impious words may be cleansed forever."

"Sa-La-Ma," she muttered gratefully, and stumbled out.

"Replace your sword in the scabbard, General. Use it sparingly, but well.

"And now — to work — gather your twenty men, General!"

Hatshopsitou saluted in the Roman fashion, and left.

I caressed Lakshmi's head.

"Lakshmi, you are the symbol of woman's revolt. You have grown weary of your cage although it is golden, and prefer the highroad to the Temple, where man both worships and enslaves you. Woman has been goddess and queen, symbol of beauty and of joy; she has been demon and slave, symbol of ugliness and abomination — always the cage, golden or iron; always the temple, the altar, or the corner where impure spirits lurk. But never, Lakshmi, has woman been woman! I am giving a second birth to woman, Lakshmi! Let her desecrate the altar and break the cage, and breathe the free air! Lakshmi, you are a good omen! You shall have for breakfast the heart of a young cabbage!"

CHAPTER THIRTY-ONE

MY MATRIOTS — GIRLISH WRESTLERS — I REVERSE SEX MORALITY — I CHOOSE A MALE HAREM — I BATTLE THE MOON — KOTIKOKURA IS LONESOME — I DENY MY SEX — I BURN MY TEMPLE — CA-TA-PHA RETURNS — THE REVOLT OF THE MALE.

LIKE Moses I concentrated upon the new generation. The girls I dressed in masculine attire. They were taught to wield arms, hunt, wrestle, and suffer physical pain unflinchingly like the Spartan youths, to disdain toys and games and consider housekeeping below their dignity.

The boys were dressed in feminine garb. They were instructed in coquetry and modesty. Their toys were limited to dolls. As soon as practicable, they were taught to cook, to sew, to weave, and take care of infants. They were not allowed to associate with the girls. Boisterousness was severely reprimanded. Their chief occupation was to appear as pretty as possible, and after puberty to wait for a woman to ask for their hand in marriage. Male infidelity was a capital offense. Woman was permitted unlimited sexual latitude.

Only the feminine sex was allowed to enter the Temple, and every morning its members chanted the praise of Sa-La-Ma that they were not born men. The boys prayed outside, and bewailed the fate that Ca-Ta-Pha had not made them women.

I chose my assistants and advisers among women exclusively. All property was in the hands of women. Motherhood was sacred. Fatherhood was a mere accident impolite to mention save in connection with certain religious sacrifices and ceremonies.

In order to bring home to the male the responsibility of paternity — to make him realize the agony which the female pays for his pleasure and his progeny, whenever one of my women gave birth to a child, the father was compelled to lie in a hammock for a week.

He was subjected to painful processes of purification and to severe fasts. Throughout this period the mother nursed the child, but the father was required to take care of it in every other particular. Before he was permitted to arise from this metaphysical child-bed, his wife lacerated his skin with a whip of thorns; then men of the tribe rubbed his wounds with the juice of the pepper plant until his body from head to toe was a bloody paste. He was not pronounced fit to be a father unless he acquitted himself with honor and bore his ordeal without a whimper. Thus a new and mystical union was established between father and offspring.

However, the scales were still in favor of the male so long as woman alone was compelled to pay toll to the Moon. To even the balance between the sexes, destroyed by some malignant male divinity, I decreed that one day every month when the Moon blossomed like a full-blown flower with petals of silver, every male of the tribe beyond the age of puberty must submit to a severe blood-letting administered with due religious ceremonies by the chief Medicine Woman. For three days thereafter he was taboo from the rest of the tribe. No one was permitted to approach him, not even for the purpose of bringing him food.

The men recognized the justice of bearing the pangs of childbirth with their wives, because they saw in the child a symbolic reward of their suffering, but they fiercely resented the compulsion to share, every lunar month, woman's barren sacrifice to the moon.

The older generation dared not rebel, for the sword of Hatshopsitou was sharp and relentless and my magic inspired awe. Those who grumbled were sent on long and divine errands from which they never returned.

Before long the new order of things was accepted naturally, and the people of Sa-La-Ma were content and prosperous. Under the leadership of Hatshopsitou, aided by tricks I had learned in many lands, my army defeated all the neighboring tribes, and peace reigned.

My royal dignity necessitated a well-chosen harem. I did not require a royal consort, because my groom was none other than god Ca-Ta-Pha, who was awaited with anxiety and impatience. He had left Heaven on the night I arrived, but every one knew that Heaven was far away, and that gods were too dignified to run, even to meet their brides.

Besides my harem of men, I chose a harem of women, on whom I tried various experiments to discover an efficient weapon against the Moon — herbs, minerals, baths, magnetism. My success proved ephemeral always and impracticable. I was not discouraged, confident that sooner or later I would conquer the pallid Goddess.

Meanwhile, the old generation died and the new one became old. Hatshopsitou was buried with her sword and uniform. A year later, I canonized her, the first saint of the new religion. My male harems, guarded by feminine eunuchs, and my female harem, guarded by castrated males, were replenished several times. The man to whom Cartaphilus had entrusted the sun had long relinquished the burden of illuminating the world, and the gold coin made into a ring dangled from the ear of the former High Priest.

Only Kotikokura and Lakshmi remained of the past. The latter tapped at my ankle; the former sat on the threshold of the Temple, which was overgrown with giant weeds.

On several occasions I bade him come to the palace. He always refused. His lonesomeness pained me. His fidelity piqued and annoyed me. Finally, one day I stopped at the Temple of Ca-Ta-Pha, determined to win him over.

"Kotikokura, who are you?" I asked.

He did not answer.

"What strange power, natural or supernatural, made you immortal?"

His eyes darted to and fro.

"Are you the god of the jungle?"

His heavy nostrils shivered.

"What man has such arms, such legs, Kotikokura?"

Pleased by my compliment, he thrust out his powerful chest.

"And such a chest!" I added in mock admiration. "Who, what are you?"

"Kotikokura," he grumbled.

"Where did Cartaphilus find you?"

He made no reply.

"Tell me, Kotikokura," I insisted.

"Ca-Ta-Pha — God," he said, making the sign of his religion.

"Sa-La-Ma is also god."

He shook his head vigorously.

"What, you doubt my divinity?"

He nodded.

"I shall have you burnt on a spit for your blasphemy."

He looked at me, his eyes darting like drunken grasshoppers.

"Do you not fear Sa-La-Ma?"

He shook his head.

"Whom do you fear?"

"Ca-Ta-Pha — God."

"You worship him?"

He nodded.

"Yet he has abandoned you."

"Ca-Ta-Pha — God!"

"Where is he now?"

"Ca-Ta-Pha — God."

I laughed ironically.

"What sort of a god is he? Look at his Temple — a mass of ruins! Spiders and rats and snakes are his only worshipers. See, the Temple of Sa-La-Ma shines like a jewel upon the hill, and it is always crowded."

"Ca-Ta-Pha — God!"

"You lie!" I exclaimed, exasperated. "He is not god. There are no more men gods. Sa-La-Ma is the only God."

"Ca-Ta-Pha — God!" he reiterated like an incantation.

"The rule of man is over!" I said angrily. "Man boasted that he was master of the Earth from all creation. It's a lie! You see it. In two generations, you have noticed what an ignoble creature he has become — merely by dressing him as a woman and relegating him to feminine occupations!"

"Ca-Ta-Pha — God!" he muttered.

"Look at man, Master of the Universe!" I laughed ironically. "He has become weaker and smaller than woman. He cannot wield a spear. He does not know how to aim an arrow at a bird. His voice is shrill and lacks confidence. He has forgotten the meaning of frankness and courage. He is in terror of his wife's shadow."

Kotikokura looked at me in utter disdain, his nose shivering like a dog's.

"Sa-La-Ma is the only god, and Woman is the Master!" I exclaimed, stamping my scepter.

"Salome — woman," he said quietly, contemptuously.

There was something in this strange being's word "woman" that made me shrink. He uttered the word as if he scented her very uncleanliness, as if he laid open her carcass to the scorching sun. I could hear Jokanaan exclaim, "Woman is the vessel of iniquity!" but his words were mild and unconvincing. "Woman," as this creature pronounced the word, was of the earth — earthy. It reeked with the primal disgust of the male for the female. It was irrevocable and eternal.

Infuriated, I raised my scepter.

"Fool! Salome is not a woman! She is —" I stopped short. My arm dropped. I was miserable. I had accused woman more ignominiously than he — for I denied her!

"What is Salome," I asked myself, "if not woman?" A goddess? Sa-La-Ma is ridiculous! She strikes awe in the hearts of these poor black creatures without culture, without history — bewildered animals. What has she accomplished? She has brutalized man, and changed woman into a virago! All that was beastly in man she has transferred to woman. All that was mean and petty in woman she has infiltrated into man!

I laughed bitterly. "Jahveh, scorn the work of your competitor!"

I turned slowly away, and walked back to the palace.

I fell, despondent, into a chair. Lakshmi tapped my ankle. I pushed her away with my foot.

"Go away, ugly creature! You, too, are female!" The tortoise unaccustomed to such treatment, described several circles, as if to discover why I had subjected her to the indignity.

The sun was setting. Its last rays, like a queen's robe, trailed on the floor.

I rose, "So be it!"

I clapped my hands.

A slave entered.

"Summon the General!"

A tall, thin, angular woman, breastless and hipless, stood at attention.

"General!"

"Your Majesty!"

"Summon all the people to the Temple!"

"Yes, Your Majesty!"

"Let each officer of the royal guard be provided with a lighted torch!"

"Yes, Your Majesty!"

"Go!"

At my approach, the people fell upon their faces, muttering, "Sa-La-Ma! Sa-La-Ma!"

"Hearken!"

"We hearken!"

"Sa-La-Ma! Sa-La-Ma!"

"Henceforth Sa-La-Ma is no longer your goddess!"

They wailed and beat their chests.

"Sa-La-Ma is our God always," the High Priestess exclaimed.

"Silence!"

"Sa-La-Ma! Sa-La-Ma!"

"Hearken to what I say! Forget that Sa-La-Ma has ever been with you!"

"Woe is us! Woe is us!" the High Priestess moaned.

The others repeated: "Woe is us! Woe is us!"

"Such is the will of Sa-La-Ma! General, set fire to the Temple of Sa-La-Ma!"

The Priestesses rushed forward.

"Sa-La-Ma! Sa-La-Ma!" they implored.

"Stand aside, women!"

"Woe is us! Woe is us!"

The General hesitated.

"Obey orders! Set fire to the Temple! Let it burn until nothing is left of it save ashes and smoke!"

The General and her staff applied the torches.

The people groaned and moaned and shrieked. They beat their chests and one another's backs and buttocks. They rolled on the ground. They ran back and forth. The Priestesses chanted strange prayers which still lingered in the memory of their race. They invoked weird names of primordial gods.

Kotikokura stood upon the tottering roof of the Temple of Ca-Ta-Pha, his arms akimbo, watching, unimpassioned. From time to time he grinned.

Did he guess that it was he who had vanquished the goddess Sa-La-Ma?

Crawling through the crowd, Lakshmi made her way toward me. The people crouched at her approach, muttering, "Lak-Shak-Mi! Lak-Shak-Mi!"

Suddenly Kotikokura threw his arms in the air and shouted frantically, pointing to the desert: "Ca-Ta-Pha! Ca-Ta-Pha! Ca-Ta-Pha!"

The people rose screaming — "Ca-Ta-Pha! Ca-Ta-Pha! Ca-Ta-Pha!"

Kotikokura jumped off the roof like a tiger, and began running toward the desert, shouting and waving his arms.

As if driven forward by a hurricane, the people jumped up and ran madly in the direction indicated by Kotikokura.

In a few moments, every one disappeared.

The flames were devouring my Temple. The wood crackled

like fantastic musical instruments. The sparks danced a mad dance. The smoke curled about the ruins like the gigantic arms of black divinities. Lakshmi tapped my ankle convulsively.

The Temple collapsed.

In the distance I could distinguish Cartaphilus riding upon a huge camel.

"Ca-Ta-Pha! Ca-Ta-Pha! Ca-Ta-Pha!"

In my heart there was a greater tumult.

The smoke rose like titanic trees, breaking in the air. The flames were weary tongues of sated beasts licking the last remnants of their victims.

No matter, Cartaphilus, I thought, your Temple crumbled, and mine is devoured by flames. The day of the gods is over. The day of man — and woman — is dawning, perhaps.

The Moon broke through the cloud like a gossip-monger who opens slowly her window to watch her neighbors unaware of her presence.

"Come, Lakshmi, let us go back to the palace, and await the arrival of Cartaphilus!"

CHAPTER THIRTY-TWO

THE ANCIENT SPELL — CARTAPHILUS THE INCORRIGIBLE.

I SAT upon my throne dressed in my royal robes, Lakshmi reposing at my feet.

Cartaphilus entered and saluted. His look indicated that I had not changed since our first meeting in Jerusalem at the court of Pilate. Nor had he changed. There was the same haughtiness, the same irony, the same masculine confidence. But instead of being irritated now, I was delighted. It was so long since I had seen a man!

"Salome, I come to save you from serious discomfiture."

"I am grateful to you, Cartaphilus."

"The men have risen in rebellion against the feminine reign."

"I know."

"We must not remain here another moment."

"Do not worry, Cartaphilus. The granddaughter of Herod the Great plans for a possible defeat in the midst of glory. You and I, who have seen dynasties rise and fall like the tides of the seas, know too well how soon the wind of popularity may change. I have a secret exit which leads directly into the desert. Three camels are at our disposal."

"Salome is incomparable."

He kissed my hands, grazing them a little with the edges of his teeth.

Kotikokura, in a corner of the hall, pulled at his fingers nervously, shifting from one foot to the other, like a restless bear.

"Has he been a source of displeasure to you, Salome?"
"He has been faithful to you!"
"He is as a brother to me."
"No brother loves half so well."
"Kotikokura," Cartaphilus called.
Kotikokura approached.
"Kneel before Salome. She is your mistress."
Kotikokura hesitated.
"Do you disobey Ca-Ta-Pha?" Cartaphilus demanded.
He knelt.
"Salome is not your mistress, Kotikokura, but your friend," I said, extending my hand. He kissed it, making a noise like the striking of cymbals.
Cartaphilus laughed heartily.
"Cartaphilus is a boy always," I said.
"The happiest boy in the world in the presence of Salome."
"Ca-Ta-Pha! Ca-Ta-Pha! Ca-Ta-Pha!" a parrot's voice screeched madly outside.
"What is this?" I asked, taken back. "Have you the power to resurrect dead birds, Cartaphilus, even when nothing is left of them save a feather stuck coquettishly in the hair of a High Priest?"
Cartaphilus stroked the head of Kotikokura, and laughed.
"That's my second son, Salome. Suspecting that the first one might have gone the way of all parrots, I thought it advisable to conceive another. Gods must be prudent, and ingenious, as you have discovered for yourself, Salome."
I laughed. "Gods generally have only one son. Ca-Ta-Pha is unusually prolific."
"Ca-Ta-Pha — God," Kotikokura added.
"And Salome?" I asked.
"Salome — woman," Kotikokura said, petulantly. But the word "woman" had a totally different significance this time. There was voluptuousness and desire and tenderness in the sound. Woman was the Earth whose womb bore all things.
"The sorceress! The sorceress! Kill her! Kill her!" the people roared.
"It is time to leave, Salome," Cartaphilus said anxiously.

"Ca-Ta-Pha! Ca-Ta-Pha!" the parrot screeched.

"Ca-Ta-Pha! Ca-Ta-Pha!" the mob repeated.

"Ca-Ta-Pha — God," Kotikokura whispered, like an "Amen."

I rose, and offered my arm to Cartaphilus, who pressed it, and whispered —"I love you, Salome."

I pretended not to hear.

"Take your wife," Cartaphilus said to Kotikokura, pointing to Lakshmi.

"I thought she was his mother," I said.

Cartaphilus smiled. "Among immortals incest is a matter of no consequence."

"Besides," I added, "how otherwise can blue blood remain blue?"

"I love you," Cartaphilus whispered again.

I pressed his arm.

CHAPTER THIRTY-THREE

WE RIDE INTO THE DESERT — KOTIKOKURA, THE MISSING LINK — MAN AND THE MOON — PREDESTINED MATES — ULTIMATE GOALS — FANTASTIC FUMES — WHO AM I? — THE PARTING OF THE WAYS — FOUR IMMORTALS.

THE desert undulated like an immense cradle of an infant divinity rocked by a sleepy nurse. Kotikokura and Lakshmi rode upon one camel, Cartaphilus and I upon another. The third was laden with provisions.

"Who is Kotikokura, Cartaphilus?" I asked.

"I do not know. He has kept his origin a secret even from me."

"Is he a man — or a simian?"

"He is perhaps the link that binds our ancestors to us. But he is becoming more and more human."

"Yes, I noticed that."

"During my absence he has made great progress — if it is progress to become man," he smiled ironically. "At any rate, his gait has less of the swing of apes in trees. His speech is more articulate, his skin less hairy and one shade whiter. If he lives long enough, he may become the symbol of Caucasian perfection," he laughed.

"Is he immortal — as immortal — as we?"

"Time will tell whether my blood has lasting power."

"Your blood?"

"It is to my blood that I attribute Kotikokura's longevity or immortality. When I came to Africa for the first time and became god Ca-Ta-Pha, the natives, infuriated, were about to tear Kotikokura to pieces, for what crime I have never been able to discover. I saved him and took him along. In the desert I fell asleep. Suddenly I felt a sharp sting. A snake bit me. Instantly my arm began to swell. I thought my fate had been sealed. Jesus had forgotten to include in his anathema the descendant of the creature whose subtle hiss precipitated the collapse of human felicity."

Kotikokura in the distance laughed. The echo of his laughter rolled across the shoreless sea of sand.

"I do not know whether I welcomed or regretted the apparent termination of my immortality."

"Regretted?" I interrupted, smiling.

"Perhaps. I had little time to weigh the benefits and the losses, for Kotikokura sucked at the wound like a giant leech. My arm resumed its normal size. I was saved. I watched Kotikokura anxiously. I expected him to drop dead instantly, as Damis and other friends into whose veins I essayed to inject my immortality."

"Our blood is poison to others. I, too, have discovered that," I sighed.

"Kotikokura did not die. Centuries have passed — he is still blooming."

"Perhaps the venom of the snake counteracted the poison of your blood, Cartaphilus."

"The idea struck me immediately. A great hope swelled my heart. I would immortalize whomsoever I loved. I sprinkled a few drops of the blood mixed with the snake's venom upon the parrot's food. The bird swallowed a few seeds. Instantly, as if struck by the blow of a hammer, he rolled upon his back, rigid as his artificial brethren in birdstuffers' shops. Of course," Cartaphilus said after a silence, "Kotikokura may have derived from some other power the gift of deathless youth. Kotikokura means 'the rebel' in one of the dialects of the African tribes. Who knows what Messiah he enraged, what divinity he mocked? Who knows what aboriginal Jesus or Jokanaan arrested in him the double rhythm of Nature — life — death?"

We rode in silence for some time.

"Did you really believe that a nation in which man was the slave and woman the master could progress?" Cartaphilus asked suddenly, his tone a trifle sarcastic.

"Why not?" I answered irritably.

"Man's rule is ordained by Nature."

"Cartaphilus," I exclaimed, "you are incorrigible! Centuries have been unable to eradicate your masculine vanity!"

"Nor my prowess," he added smartly.

I ignored his remark, and continued: "Woman was the first ruler. She was mother and queen."

"That may be. The nearer man approaches the animal, the greater the power and significance of woman. The reason you were able so quickly to change the rôles of the sexes among these people is because they are only a few steps beyond their cousins, the apes. A civilized community would rebel ferociously, especially the women."

"That is true, Cartaphilus," I said sadly. "But the day will come when woman will be once again the ruler — when she conquers the Moon."

"The Moon?" he asked, looking at me quizzically.

"When the Moon no longer draws the blood from her brain into the organs of procreation. Slave of the frozen goddess, she gives birth to innumerable buds never destined to blossom. Her body endures every lunar month the agony of childbirth without child."

"Can you change the course of Nature?"

"How can you doubt that Nature's course may be changed? What makes it possible for us to ride together through the desert, when for centuries we should have been less than the sand the hoofs of our camels are treading upon, if Nature could not be arrested, altered, mastered? Nature is a wild and refractory stallion, but the brain of man can lasso him and mount him and drive him wherever it pleases!"

"We shall see," he said, an ironic smile playing about his lips.

"We shall see!" I repeated challengingly.

The rocking of the camel made me drowsy. I yawned. Cartaphilus smiled.

"Is the Queen sleepy?" Cartaphilus asked.

"A little. Even Salome must yield to the Wielder of Dreams."

"Kotikokura!" Cartaphilus called.

Kotikokura appeared instantly, as if he had flown through the air.

"The Queen is weary, Kotikokura. Raise the tent that she may rest — and sleep — and forget the presence of Cartaphilus."

"To try to forget is a greater compliment, Cartaphilus, than to try to remember."

"A thousand centuries would not suffice to forget Salome, while each hour was crowded with her memory."

"Even when the little Priestesses of the Temple of the Triple Gate ministered to the joys of Cartaphilus?"

He looked at me, astonished.

"Even when he almost achieved the miracle of unendurable pleasure indefinitely prolonged?"

"Have I become history already, Salome?" he asked, forgetting his surprise in his vanity.

"History? What is history, Cartaphilus? Does gossip please you so? I was a witness at your coronation. I was the chief adept in the Temple of Venus of the Triple Gate."

Cartaphilus frowned.

"Did you expect me to wait, my hands in my lap, until Cartaphilus, the Much-Beloved, came to propose marriage to me? Must I not find my soul, even as you, in the great baptism of the senses? Have you forgotten the words of Apollonius, Cartaphilus? Have you forgotten the tablet which you placed at the feet of his statue in the Temple of Tyana?"

"Salome has honored me too much by following in my steps!"

"Conceit and vanity!" I exclaimed. "Followed you? Did I have to follow you? Could I not guess where you were?"

"How?"

"Do you still believe it is impossible for woman to

reason? Will you never understand that woman's brain may work as subtly — or even more so than man's?"

"It is difficult to overcome an idea held for hundreds of generations, Salome — an idea transmitted to us with the milk of our mothers."

"Well, that shall be my mission — to combat this idea! To combat the male and his arrogance!"

"I shall not fight you, Salome!"

"Yes, always, whether you will it or not! Man and woman are the eternal antagonists. Even the love they bear each other is a battle. Every gesture of their embrace is war. But man's victory is short-lived, and the booty is woman's!" I said triumphantly.

Kotikokura motioned to us that the tent was ready. A little farther off, he raised another for himself and Lakshmi.

We sat, our legs underneath us, upon a leopard's skin. I filled two small ivory pipes, and offered Cartaphilus one. The air was pervaded with a delicate incense.

"Not all the papyrus in the world, not all the silk, not all the marble, could hold half of the dialogues between Salome and myself that reverberated in my brain in the hundreds of years and lands," Cartaphilus said, watching the smoke curl out of his pipe.

"I have no doubt that always Cartaphilus emerged triumphant," I smiled.

"Generally," he admitted, laughing a little. "If you only knew how I loved you, hated you, how often you were demon, how often angel; how often my sword pierced your heart, how often my breath revived you. No priest drunken with his god ever invoked hymns more passionate than I; no prophet, scorning his generation, uttered such maledictions!"

He stopped, and taking my hand, placed it against his cheek.

"But now — now, as I hold your hand smoother, softer than the throat of a young pigeon, now I remember nothing — save three words, 'I love you!'"

He puffed at his pipe.

"To have lived centuries, Salome, and yet be unable to say more than an adolescent in the presence of his first inamorata!"

"Centuries? What are centuries, Cartaphilus? We who have lived them know that the more things change the more they remain unaltered. How can it be otherwise — since the brain cannot break the bondage of the skull, and the heart beats against the chest with the same eternal rhythm? What is different since I was Princess Salome and you Captain of the Royal Guard? Countries have changed their contours, and kings and gods their names; languages have broken into dialects or are no longer remembered at all; the roofs of houses have altered their forms, and the dress of woman its shapes. But still spring follows winter, the sun scorches, the rain floods; still people are born, live awhile and die; still the flower quivers under the fluttering wing of the bee and the butterfly; still the old rhythm of turgescence and detumescence reiterates itself; still the wild beast of the forest seeks his mate and kills his rival; still 'I love you' is the formula of passion."

"And still Salome is the mirage, the Fata Morgana that Cartaphilus pursues beyond the desert and the horizon."

I made believe I did not hear him.

"Ah, if man lived for centuries, perhaps then—! But, no, man as he is constituted must remain forever the slave of the elements. If we could only create a new being, Cartaphilus, a being fashioned for joy and for wisdom!"

"If you and I, Salome, could have offspring ——"

"No — even if the life force which gives us our strange longevity demanding sterility in return, could be mastered, it would be dangerous to bring forth progeny. Our children might be Titans, gods, monsters of thought and passion, who, finding the earth ridiculous and insufficient, would crush it and hurl it against infinity!"

The Moon turned slowly in a wide circle over our heads. The stars massed themselves in great clusters. The smoke of our pipes curled about our faces.

"Why were you so cruel to me, Salome, when you were Princess of Judea?"

"Do you still remember that?"

"The venom still poisons my heart."

"I was not cruel, Cartaphilus. I merely resented your air of invincible masculinity. Besides, it was my vengeance."

"Vengeance?"

"Some years previously, a haughty youth bathing in the Sea of Galilee behind our palace vaunted his masculinity before his friend John, and ridiculed woman, especially Salome. He said she was scrawny, homely, undesirable. He mocked her mother and her family."

"I used to bathe in the river behind your palace with my friend John — that is true. He became a Christian saint and dabbled with letters. John is the author of one of the gospels, and of the Apocalypse, a collection of predictions and maledictions too exotic for my comprehension. He was the 'beloved disciple' of the Nazarene. But once"—Cartaphilus blushed charmingly —"he loved me."

"Mary also appeared in your amorous day dreams."

"I loved both John and Mary. They deserted me to join Jesus. Ever since, I have been seeking the Double Blossom of passion, John and Mary in one. But how did you happen to overhear my conversation with John?"

"I was hiding in the bushes with my cousin Agrippina."

"You did not turn away with maidenly modesty but watched us," Cartaphilus remarked with mock indignation, to hide his own confusion.

"You strutted about like a peacock in all the glory of turgescent youth."

Cartaphilus smiled.

"I looked. Then something strange overwhelmed me, and I became a woman. When Cartaphilus, Captain of the Royal Guard, appeared in the palace of Pilate, I recognized at once the youth whose image had buried itself in my mind like a thorn, like a flower. He had remained as handsome, as vain, as haughty. I hated him and I loved him as of yore."

"Did you love me, Salome?" he asked, looking into my eyes.

"I loved you, and for that reason I would not give myself to you — and for that reason I shall not give myself to you, until your mockery of woman shall no longer hold the semblance of truth."

"Salome! Salome!"

I refilled the pipes.

"Centuries have obliterated the silly words of my youth. Come with me. Be with me forever, Salome!"

"Let us not grow sentimental, Cartaphilus. We are no longer — precisely — children," I laughed.

"Salome, are we not logical companions, the predestined mates, bound by one race and one fate — forever?"

"We are two parallel lines drawn very closely to each other, so very closely that no third line, however thin, can intrude between them."

"Will the two parallel lines ever meet?"

"Yes — in infinity."

"Never — before?"

"Perhaps."

Our silence was long and uninterrupted, then gradually we began to speak of our lives and experiences. We recalled Apollonius and Longinus and Zenobia and Pilate and Marcus Aurelius. We laughed and sighed over multitudinous incidents. We crowded the history of Arabia and Judea and Persia and Palmyra and China and Rome into small fistfuls of events.

"In Persia, Salome, you have become the mother of Zoroaster who was born of a virgin. In Arabia you are Princess Scheherazade who embroiders a thousand and one nights. Among the Barbarians you are the divinity of love. In China and India you are the theme of poets, philosophers and philologists. You are the vision of perfection appearing each century in the gardens of the Emperor. You are the symbol of immortality. You are the golden tortoise supporting the world."

"And you, Cartaphilus — you are god, and devil, and Antichrist, Prophet of good and of evil, Priapus, Pan, Bacchus, and Mammon! History? We are much more, Cartaphilus! We are legend!"

"Together, what a marvelous legend we should make, Salome!"

"Together we might become the symbol of conjugal felicity, and — monotony!"

"When we have crossed the desert, shall my solitary wanderings begin anew, Salome?"

I laughed heartily.

"Solitary, Cartaphilus — with the vastest harems? Solitary — in the courts of emperors and kings, and in the arms of empresses and of queens?"

"Solitary, if Salome be not with me!"

"You forget your search for perfection, Cartaphilus!"

"Salome is perfection."

"Not until she has achieved freedom!"

His pipe fell out of his hand. His words came slowly and vaguely.

"Give me your lips — Salome," he whispered.

"Not yet, Cartaphilus."

"A thousand women — a thousand years of love — can they compare with your lips, Salome?"

He stretched out.

"Your lips — Salome "

I dropped my pipe.

He closed his eyes. "Your — lips — Salome!"

I pressed my lips upon his, and stretched out next to him.

"Mary — Mary Magdalen — your lips —"

"Salome," I whispered, taunting.

"John —"

"Salome!"

"I — love — you —"

"Whom do you love?"

"I — love — you."

"Who am I?"

"You are — she — who has returned — from the uttermost rim of Time — before the soul split asunder — into male and female — you — are — she —"

"My lover."

The stars were a rainfall of silver and gold. The smoke of our pipes wound itself around our naked limbs. . . .

"Lakshmi! Lakshmi! Lakshmi!" Kotikokura ran in all directions at the same time.

"What has happened, Kotikokura?" I asked.

"Lakshmi! Lakshmi!" he muttered, searching the sand.

"Do not worry, Kotikokura," I consoled him, when all our efforts at finding the tortoise proved futile. "She has probably returned to be the High Priestess of Sa-La-Ma. The Parrot who carries a thousand Stars upon his Beak will be the High Priest of Ca-Ta-Pha. Thus at last the two divinities shall merge into one, and the prophecy is fulfilled."

"Ca-Ta-Pha — God," Kotikokura grumbled.

Cartaphilus, his brows knit, was thinking in silence.

I placed my hand upon his shoulder.

"Are not all things relative, Cartaphilus? Dream and waking — memory and forgetfulness — possession and desire?"

"Were you mine, Salome?"

I smiled.

"I had a vision of incomparable beauty — was it merely a dream?"

"Look, Cartaphilus, I see houses in the distance. We must part."

"Tell me!" he insisted.

"Even the patient camels are becoming restless, Cartaphilus. Their long knotted legs yearn for locomotion. Come!"

"Salome, tell me!" he begged.

"Vision — reality — who shall undo the subtle weaving? Come!"

We reached the gate of the town.

"Come with me, Salome," Cartaphilus insisted. "Let us both fight the Nazarene and his religion of superstition and slavery."

I smiled. "Fight religion? We gods should be more class-conscious!"

"The world has become uninhabitable. Logic and reason and truth are banished, and fanaticisim is rampant."

"Cartaphilus is a child playing games."

"I must crush the Nazarene!"

"Shall Ca-Ta-Pha replace him — or Sa-La-Ma?"
"Ca-Ta-Pha — God," Kotikokura said with finality.
"You at least have one true worshiper, Cartaphilus. Who knows if the Nazarene is as fortunate?"
"The religion of the Nazarene must perish!"
"And the Moon must be conquered!"
We looked at each other in silence for a long time.
"Farewell, Cartaphilus."
He embraced me.
"It was not a dream!" he exclaimed.
"Perhaps."
"Farewell, Kotikokura."
He kissed my hand.
"Farewell!"

CHAPTER THIRTY-FOUR

CHRIST RISES IN FULDA — PERISHED LOVES AND PERISHED GODS — IDUN, GODDESS OF SPRING — LOVE AT FIRST SIGHT — LIKE A BEWILDERED BUTTERFLY — HONEY OR HOLY WATER — "LAST NIGHT IN MY DREAM YOU GAVE ME ROSES" — I MAKE A RESOLUTION.

THE city of Fulda was a cocoon nestling in the mist of the Dawn. The Sun, the silver Cock, appeared, triumphant, upon the peak of the hill, announcing the rebirth of Day. The threads of the mist tore, and the city emerged.

The streets were already crowded with merchants arranging their wares — masks and toys and eggs painted in all conceivable colors, and spice breads the shape of rabbits, sweets in cornucopias, trinkets, shawls, headgear, embroidered sandals and bodices, amulets and crosses, and dolls of wood and ivory representing Jesus, the Virgin Mary, Joseph and the minor saints.

In the vacant lots mummers rehearsed their parts. Astrologers dressed in flowing togas painted with the signs of the zodiac and flowing beards, false or natural, turned the wheels of fortune, mumbling incomprehensible sounds.

Over the doors of inns and wineshops hung garlands of evergreens and vines. On the walls were painted barrels mounted by Bacchus, hunters returning from the chase, dancers, whose legs were never destined to touch solid earth again, corpulent friars feasting at long tables in imitation of The Last Supper.

"Christ has risen! Christ has risen!" the passers-by called to one another.

The streets became crowded with pedestrians, riders on horseback and mules, carts drawn by oxen with gilded horns and flowing ribbons. Men masked as wild animals or dressed as women, flushed and merry from the new wine, sang, howled, roared, blew horns, rattled toys.

A giant friar, standing on the back of a mule, like an acrobat, waved his arms wildly, exhorting the people:

"Miserable men, putting counterfeit and monstrous faces over the features God gave you! What reasonable man turns himself into the appearance of a beast? How vile to be born men and be clothed in women's garments! Slaves to gluttony and sin! Impious generation! You are not Christians! You are barbarians and heathens! The baptism has washed your bodies but not your souls! Your souls still belong to the devils of your ancestors! You mumble the prayer of our Lord Jesus, but in your hearts you worship idols of wood and stone! Tear off your masks and your women's garments and spend this day in which our Lord has risen in prayer and fasting, as becomes Christians, or else you shall broil in Hell forever and ever, Amen!"

For a while there was silence. Some crossed themselves; others muttered prayers.

The monk seated himself upon the mule, and urged the animal forward. A little farther off, he repeated his exhortation.

The merry-makers wriggled their thumbs upon the tips of their noses, and made wry faces, muttering —"Kill-joy! Scarecrow! Dog in the manger! Wet blanket!"

"You'd think the Church is as pure as a babe!"

"Pure! Hahaha!"

"And the Pope? They say he's the sire of a whole regiment of papal bastards!"

"He makes his own soldiers!"

"Hahahahaha! Heheheh!"

"The Pope! Which pope? Why, there are as many as three popes at one time. If you've got enough ducats you can buy the Fisherman's Ring!"

"Sh! There!" they nudged one another. "There's a monk listening," they whispered to one another, pointing to me, dressed in the habiliments of the Church.

"Christ has risen, brother!" some one addressed me, obsequiously.

"Christ has risen," I answered.

I walked along the shore of the river. The noise of the revelers gradually died in the distance, and only the chimes of the convent upon the hill, which rang gayly and unceasingly like the chatter of birds, reminded me that it was Easter and that Jesus had risen from the dead to save mankind.

This was the spot where I had been Ulric's wife, where the valiant Barbarians prepared for war against Rome, where chieftains and poets and mighty soldiers waited for the first rose to blossom out of the body of my husband that they might marry Freya, goddess of love and beauty. Nothing, nothing remained — not even a name, not even a ruin. A new race, a new religion, a new language. Only the river flowed on as before.

"Do you still remember, O Waters, the castle whose shadow lay within you? Do you remember the boat in which Ulric, handsomest and strongest of men, looked in rapture at Freya, his beloved? Do you remember the altar the Druids erected here when the giant trees had not yet been felled to make the wineshops in the town? Do you remember the bullocks sacrificed to Odin the All-Father, and Bori the fashioner of the world? Do you remember the other gods — Vidar and Forseti, and Bragi and Ymir — all mighty and young, lovers of the Earth?"

I raised my eyes. My heart stopped beating. Who was this? Was it Idun, goddess of Spring, dancing upon the shore? I approached on tiptoes afraid that the apparition would disappear.

The dancer stopped, caught her breath and smiled.

"Who are you?" I asked.

"I am Joan — Joan d'Anglois, frater," she answered simply.

"No, you are Idun, goddess of Spring. This is your birthday, not the resurgence of Christ!"

Her blue eyes twinkled like forget-me-nots with the dew at daybreak.

"Let me place a laurel upon your head, Idun!"

She seated herself. I made a wreath of roses and placed it upon her brow.

She smiled, and asked roguishly:

"Does the wreath become me better than the veil, frater?"

"The veil?"

"To-morrow I shall be a nun," she said a little sadly.

"A nun!" I exclaimed indignantly.

"Why not? You are a monk! And yet I think the myrtle becomes you better perhaps than the cowl!"

Her utter naturalness disarmed me. Was this a young girl, a woman, a goddess indeed? Did she penetrate my disguise? Did she guess who I was?

"Perhaps," I said, and seated myself next to her.

"Who are you, frater?"

"I am Simonedes. I come from Greece."

"From Greece?" she repeated thoughtfully. "I come from over the seas, Simonedes, from the North."

"Idun comes from the North naturally."

"Alas, I am not Idun, but Joan. I come from the land of the Angles." She stopped a moment. "Greece — Athens — the land of wisdom and beauty and knowledge! Oh, would I had been born there!"

"Come with me there, Joan! Come to Greece, the land of Apollonius!"

She did not answer. She looked at me intently.

"You are not a friar, Simonedes."

"What am I then?" I asked, fearing, yet hoping, that she would say —"You are Salome."

"You are a Prince, a King, disguised as a monk."

I laughed.

"Monks are ignorant and boorish. You speak the pure and perfect Latin which only the ancient Cæsars knew. You shudder at the idea of my becoming a nun. You are not a friar, and I suspect that you are not even an honest Christian!"

"Not a Christian?"

"You are a pagan — a pagan god — stranded in a Christian country. This is not the first time I see you, Simonedes."

"When did you see me before?"

"Last night I saw you in my dream. It was just like this. I was dancing near the river. Then you came, and placed a wreath upon my head, and called me Idun, goddess of Spring."

I placed my hand upon hers.

"Your hand is softer than the kiss of the waves, Simonedes."

"Your hand is a petal of a lily fallen on the lap of a woman dreaming of her lover."

"Your voice, Simonedes, is the tinkling of the bell of a sheep in the middle of the night."

"Your voice is the echo of a dream dissolving at dawn."

She stood up suddenly. "Simonedes, I am afraid," she said with a strange catch in her voice.

I rose. "Why are you afraid, Joan?"

She hid her face, and it seemed as if the sun was eclipsed.

"Why are you afraid, Joan?" I asked again, placing my arm about her waist, supple as a willow.

"I am afraid of the boldness of my words, Simonedes. But this is a dream — this is the dream I had, and these are the words you and I uttered."

"This is more beautiful than a dream, Joan. And your words are the young buds on trees in spring."

"I must go now, Simonedes, before the dream is shattered, before the Mother Superior sends some one to search for me."

"You shall never leave me. You are my child, my daughter — my ——"

She laughed. Her laughter was the rippling of a stream.

"Your child — your daughter — Simonedes! That is what you said in the dream, and I laughed, and woke up."

"Be whatever you wish — but you shall never go away, Joan!"

"I am so happy my dream came true, Simonedes. I shall never forget it even when I am a nun!"

"Our meeting was fated when the first spring began. You saw me in your dream, Joan, but centuries before you were born your image was rooted in my heart. This morning the flower has blossomed."

I caught her in my arms. "Let not sloth or fear divide you from your destiny. Have courage! Fulfill your dream! Come with me!"

Like a bewildered butterfly between two chalices, Joan wavered between honey and holy water.

"You shall never go back to the convent, Joan, even if I must hold you by force!"

"If you were a friar, Simonedes, would you not tell me that I am sinful and godless? Would you not order me to fast for a year and pray to the Virgin to forgive my transgression? Would you not yourself confess to the Bishop that on Easter Day you tempted a bride of Jesus with pagan enticements to desert her betrothed? I may be the Devil come to tempt you, in the shape of a woman!" The strange catch in her voice delighted me like a caress.

"He who rejects loveliness yields to the Devil, Joan," I said over-seriously.

"You believe neither in God nor in the Devil, Simonedes," she said sadly, but without condemning.

"I have seen the birth and death of too many gods and too many devils, Joan, to believe in them."

She looked at me, somewhat startled.

"Do not fear me, Joan!"

"I do not fear you, Simonedes. In the garden of the convent, a rose bush grows, planted, according to legend, by Freya, goddess of love and beauty. When a man offers a maiden a flower plucked from this bush, she becomes his bride forever. Last night in my dream you gave me a rose. This morning there was a flower missing on the bush."

"All truths become legends, and all legends truth, Joan. You are mine forever."

She placed her arms about me, and her lips pressed into mine. Then she turned away, her eyes glistening with tears.

"I shall keep the rose you offered me in the dream in my heart, and the garland you placed upon my head, I shall treasure beyond all things. In my lonely dreams I shall be not Christ's, Simonedes. In Heaven or in Hell, we shall be wed and be inseparable forever, but on Earth we must part."

I clasped her in my arms.

"No, no! You shall not go away! Come with me! We shall be inseparable on Earth — for there is neither Heaven nor Hell, and when life passes, all passes. Beyond this truth, there is no truth. Come!"

She was silent for a long while, deliberating.

"What would it profit me to go, Simonedes? What can a woman do? The women in Athens, I am sure, are treated with disdain and mockery as the women everywhere. I shun the world where woman is but a slave and a tool. If I become a nun, I shall be spared at least the humiliation and indignity that man imposes upon my sex."

"Joan! Joan!" I exclaimed, my heart over-brimming. "You are another Salome!"

"Who is Salome?"

Salome is the superwoman, the rebel, the unyielding sister of Lucifer; she who conquers the arrogance of man and the governance of the Moon!"

"I am no superwoman. I am humble and weak!"

"I shall make you strong and proud."

She shook her head.

"Discard your feminine habiliments! Come with me as a man, Joan!"

"As a man!" she exclaimed jubilantly.

"The time will come, Joan, when a woman shall not utter a cry of joy when told that she is a man. The time will come when man will pay to woman in the world the homage he pays to the Holy Virgin in the church! Perhaps you and I will help to usher in the new era. Come with me!"

"How can I dissemble my sex, Simonedes?"

"Other women have temporarily divested themselves of

their femininity. This very day you are my brother, John...."

"John d'Anglois! I shall have to remember my name. It will be difficult at first."

"You will soon get accustomed to seeming what you are not. You will emulate the chameleon changing colors according to necessity. Life is legend and make-believe."

"And will you remain a friar?" she asked, smiling.

"I shall be whatever the exigencies of the moment demand. Today it is easy to get clothing to suit us without arousing suspicions. They will take us for masqueraders."

The chimes of the Convent of Fulda, which had ceased for some time, began ringing again. Joan cast another glance in the direction of the convent, a shadow dark and threatening.

"Christ has risen!" she whispered, crossing herself.

A moment later, taking my hand, she said: "Take me away."

CHAPTER THIRTY-FIVE

MISGIVINGS AND CONFIDENCES—"IF I GAVE YOU IMMORTALITY WOULD YOU ACCEPT IT?"—I KISSED HER EYES FILLED WITH TEARS.

THE sapphire of the Mediterranean turned silver in the glow of the moon. The boat glided smoothly along like a sea-gull in search of prey. The voyagers, mostly Venetian merchants, were asleep in their bunks. Joan and I walked up and down the deck in silence, interrupted at long intervals only by sailors reconnoitering or reporting the time and the weather to their superiors.

"Do you regret that you followed me, Joan?"

"I am happy!" She pressed her head against my shoulder. "Let us sit down," she whispered.

We squatted in a corner of the prow. Joan took my hand in hers.

"People are not at all surprised that you are my brother, Joan. Many even say that we resemble each other."

"That is not true, Simonedes. You are infinitely more beautiful than I."

She looked intently at me.

"Your face, Simonedes, is radiant like the moon. Your hair is the sun setting over the hilltops. Your eyes are deep wells in which swim gold and silver fishes. Your cheeks are two roses. Your brow is marble. When you pass by the people stop breathless and look back, their hearts filled with yearning and dreams. Oh, I love you, Simonedes, as no one ever loved — a brother or a betrothed."

"And I love you, Joan, as I never believed I could love a human being — save one."

"Save one? What a fortunate woman! Would I were she!"

"Not a woman, Joan — a man!"

"A man!"

Her firmly curved mouth shivered a little, and her eyelids drooped.

"You are not jealous of — a man — are you, Joan?" I asked.

"I am not jealous. I love whatever and whomever you love, Simonedes.

"Simonedes —" she said after a brief pause.

"Yes, Joan ——"

"You have no faith in me. You do not love me. You wish to experiment with me, to prove to the world that woman's brain is equal to man's. That is why you take me to Athens. But you do not love me, Simonedes!"

"Why do you say that, Joan?"

"Simonedes, why don't you tell what you are? Will you not confide in me? Do you believe that being a woman I cannot keep a secret? Besides," she said proudly, "I am really a man from now on!"

I caressed her face.

"Is it not enough for you to know that I am Simonedes?"

"In my dream you were not Simonedes! You were ——"

"What was I?"

"I cannot tell you — I do not really know. You were a vision of beauty — a divinity. Tell me who you are, I pray you! I yearn to become part of your life, to enter your soul, to be the breath you breathe!"

She placed her arm around my neck, and kissed me as if to draw my soul out of my lips.

"Am I not your bride?"

"Yes, Joan — my bride."

"Your — wife?" she asked hesitatingly.

I did not answer.

"Oh, I know I am unworthy to be anything but your slave. I am your slave, Simonedes."

Should I entrust this child with my secret? What had I

to fear? I could always laugh it off as a childish fairy-tale. I could seal her lips with a kiss or with a spell benumb her memory. I could disappear from her presence, or cause her to disappear.

A yearning, mingled with vanity, prodded me to tell of my marvelous life. I took her head into my hands and looked into her eyes. They were more candid than a babe's. No, she would never betray me! Besides, if she was to accomplish what I proposed, it was better if she knew the truth. I could not conceal my sex from her indefinitely. She would not be content to be merely my betrothed. And in the strange dream she had, perhaps she already guessed who I was. Yes, I would tell her as much of my fate as her mind could endure. I would leave out incidents which might prove dangerous, if by chance she should prattle. No one save Lakshmi should ever hear the full truth — Lakshmi, and perhaps Cartaphilus, my equal!

"I love you," Joan murmured, like the chirping of a bird. "Tell me———"

The moon had gradually vanished like the petal of a giant dahlia that's slowly swept away. The mysterious silence which like a bridge unites Day to Night, descended upon the sea.

"Have I told you a legend, Joan, or the truth?"

"The truth."

"Do you fear me now?"

"I love you!"

"Was I Salome in your dream, Joan?"

"You were Freya, goddess of beauty and love."

"And who were you in the dream?"

"I was your mate."

She looked at me, her eyes half closed.

"You were a woman, and I was a woman...?"

"I did not think of your sex in my dream. When I awoke I was abashed, and tried to forget, but you came, and I recognized you at once."

She pressed her lips upon mine.

"I shall love you always, Salome. And I love Cartaphilus." She smiled. "And I am so fond of Kotikokura and Lakshmi!

They are so funny and dear!" She laughed like a child, the catch in her voice mingling with her laughter. "Shall I ever see them, Salome?"

"Perhaps."

She shivered.

"Are you chilly, my dear?"

"My soul is chilly. I thought of the day when I shall be old, like Ulric, and you will remain young forever."

"If I could give you immortality, would you accept it, Joan?"

"No!" she answered emphatically. "I wish to live awhile, and die. One must be strong beyond my strength to face immortality. I could not live if the world I knew grew old and died."

I drew her tightly to my breast.

"I wish to live as a dream in your life, Salome — a beautiful dream, that lasts one night — and is gone."

"My darling! My child ——"

"Then when Cartaphilus finally makes you his mate, you will whisper while you are in his embrace that once upon a time Joan adored you, and relinquished Heaven that she might be your love — for a day."

I kissed her eyes filled with tears.

The sun was a delicate red line drawn across the horizon....

Joan slept, her head upon my lap.

CHAPTER THIRTY-SIX

THE CONQUEST OF ATHENS —"I AM YOUR SHADOW, SALOME" —JOAN DREAMS OF A TRIPLE CROWN.

JOAN, her arm in the air, her last sentence still reverberating in the great hall of the university, smiled to me across the heads of the multitudes.

The scholars who had listened in silence for hours rose and applauded vociferously. Xenocrates, most illustrious of philosophers and head of the university, motioned to the people to reseat themselves. He cleared his throat several times, and rising and falling incessantly upon his heels as a means of emphasis, he addressed the audience in embroidered Greek.

Never, he said, since the golden days of Athens, never since Socrates, never since Apollonius, the divine Tyanian, had such wisdom been uttered couched in such perfect language. The night of ignorance which engulfed the world for centuries had suddenly been dissipated. Once more the Earth dazzled in the Sun. Most fitting, too, that Athens, the alpha of wisdom, should also be the omega. Could they not see how the Parthenon upon the hill in the distance had recovered its pristine beauty? Could they not hear the golden strings of the lyre of Homer mingle with the honeyed sounds of his verses?

Reminded abruptly, however, by the large cross which beat against his chest that the gods of the Blind Poet had been ostracized by the Church, he coughed, and altered the rhythm of his discourse. His voice became staccato and his fist beat the air. A greater wisdom was the wisdom of Johannes the Youth of the North — the wisdom of the Crucified One, which had descended upon him like a dove. His words were not the vain words, however beautiful, of heathens and pagans, but the sacred and divine ones whose pure and eternal source was — the Cross!

Xenocrates, interrupted by the outburst of the people, cleared his throat, blinked, breathed deeply, but could not recapture the trend of his thoughts. He motioned to a slave, who brought him a golden wreath which he placed upon the head of Joan. The people rushed forward to the pulpit, and raised the victor upon their shoulders.

I waited until the people wearied of carrying her, shouting their congratulations.

Joan embraced me. My face was wet with her tears.

"Come, brother," I said, for there were still a few laggards who watched us, "come home. You are tired. You must rest."

Stretched upon the couch, under a bower of roses, Joan placed her head upon my bosom.

"Salome, am I still desirable? Are my kisses still perfumed with the perfume of youth? The people no longer call you the elder brother, Salome. They look at both of us and are undecided. Some take you for the younger. If I live long enough — they will take me for your father."

"Joan, you are beautiful, and your kisses delight me."

"If I become old, and my face is wrinkled, and my lips lose their fragrance, will you pierce my heart in my sleep?"

"You must not speak of such things, Joan!"

"Promise me, Salome! Promise that if I am enamored of life, although life becomes ugliness, you will not allow me to live!"

"Old age is not ugliness. Apollonius was perhaps a century old when I saw him, and yet he was fairer than young Adonis."

"A man, Salome, may become handsomer with age — a woman ——"

"Do you still think of yourself as a woman, Joan? For

years now you have been the handsome and brilliant youth of the North," I said, smiling, caressing her.

"Clothes do not change one's sex, Salome. I wish I could proclaim from the house-tops 'I am a woman!'"

"Had you accepted the burden of our sex, Joan, do you think the people would acclaim you the prince of scholars? Would Xenocrates, famed for wisdom and knowledge, place the golden laurel upon your lovely head? Some day we may reveal the truth, not yet, not now."

"Is my scholarship mine? Is my wisdom mine? I am your shadow, Salome. My words are merely the echo of yours." And embracing me, she continued, the indefinable, heart-rending catch in her voice. "Do not take amiss what I say, Salome! I wish to be your shadow and your echo!"

I smoothed her hair and played with her ears, tiny and translucent like shells of pearl.

"If you lived to be five hundred years, Joan, and if your face were merely parchment on which Time had carved his hieroglyphics, I would still love you, and still think of you as Idun, goddess of Spring, who danced on the shore of the river Fulda, and whose beautiful head I crowned with a wreath of roses."

The rays of the sun filtering through the bower, danced upon us.

"I love you! I love you!" she whispered.

She slept.

I made a wreath of roses and placed it upon her head.

She opened her eyes and smiled.

"I suppose I only slept a few minutes, Salome!"

I nodded.

"Strange, how many things I dreamt! Our whole life together."

She took the wreath and pressed it against her lips.

"It must have been the flowers that gave birth to the dream. I dreamt I was on the boat again, and you told me the story of your life. I dreamt we traveled once more through India and Persia, and Arabia. I dreamt we worshiped in the Temple of Apollonius at Tyana, and you read for me the tablet that Cartaphilus laid at the feet of the master. My whole life flitted past me in the dream."

Joan sat up. "And then just before I woke up, I dreamt that I was sitting upon a golden throne, and you placed a crown upon my head," she laughed, a catch in her throat, "three crowns!"

"Often our dreams foreshadow truth, Joan."

She looked at me quizzically.

"The time has come, my dear, when you must reap the reward of your scholarship and wisdom."

"I want to be with you here — always, Salome. That is the reward I desire. I love you."

"Nothing is greater than love, Joan, but Life is a tyrant clamoring for her toll."

"What do you wish me to do?" she asked anxiously.

I patted her cheeks.

"We are going to Rome, Joan. And you — you study the words of the Fathers of the Church."

She pouted her lips a little, then placed her head upon my shoulder with the utter confidence of a child.

CHAPTER THIRTY-SEVEN

I BARGAIN FOR THE MITER—THE PAPAL SECRETARY OF STATE—THE ELOQUENCE OF DUCATS.

I DECIDED to make Joan the ruler of the world. She should wear the triple crown of the Popes.

We walked arm in arm on the embankment of the Tiber, conversing about many things.

"Cartaphilus is wrong to fight religion, Joan. If he succeeded, and Logic ruled life, man would soon turn Logic to God, and the lemmata, the data, the enthymemes, the sorites and the dilemmas into devils and saints. He would worship or fear them as fervently, as falsely, as tenaciously, as illogically, as he does Jahveh and Jesus and Mary and Joseph and Allah and Mohammed. He would raise a cathedral in honor of Saint Epagoge, a monastery to Holy Postulate, and a convent to Virgin Premise. There would be quite as many friars and nuns and rabbis and sheiks and bishops, and a Pope, just as now, and superstition and hatred and bloodshed would not diminish. Indeed it is Logic which makes of religion a thing of ugliness and cruelty. What Jesus said had its origin in the heart, not the brain. If his followers obeyed him without attempting to rationalize his words the world would be a gentler place to live in. Alas, the theologians discovered Logic!"

"Yes, Salome," she said sadly.

"My experience as a god taught me to avoid religious disputes. A tortoise or a parrot, a camel or a burning bush — man accepts anything, provided his awe is stirred. We are in a Christian world, let us accept Jesus then, and with Jesus as a premise — let us build a newer and better world. Let us not steer against the current, but slowly, imperceptibly let us change its course."

Joan pressed my hand. "I am happy you say that, Salome. For deep in my heart I have never relinquished the Bridegroom of my childhood."

"You were destined to serve him — if not as bride — at least as brother. I have already arranged matters. Next week you and I will be ordained — priests."

Joan's superb oratory, her profound scholarship and her innate predisposition for theology added to her unimpeachable private life, in an age when the ignorance and corruption of the clergy were proverbial, made her before long the most famous of the ecclesiastics of Rome.

In imitation of Jesus, Joan visited the poor and the unfortunate. Upon many occasions by her touch and prayers, aided by the simple remedies and therapeutic suggestions I had taught her to use, she healed the sick and brought relief to the suffering. The people called her a saint and the Holy See offered her a diocese.

Meanwhile secretly, like a mole, I meandered my way through courts and cathedrals, filling fists with gold and jewels to achieve my aim.

The bells of St. Peter's rang uninterruptedly. The Church was filled to the brim. Those who found no room within were kneeling and praying in the streets. Cardinals, bishops, friars, physicians, officers, scurried in and out of the Vatican, whispering to one another. Messengers on horseback galloped, their animals frothing at the mouths.

The people implored for news. Wild rumors were circulated, to be immediately disproved by others. Pope Leo the Fourth was dying, that, at least, was a fact. Whether he was poisoned as some claimed, or bewitched, as others asserted, or devoured by leprosy or the canker, nobody could assure with convincing finality. At any rate, for twenty-four hours now the struggle between Life and Death continued valiantly. The soul of the Pope could not tear itself away from its mortal habitation, nor could it remain there in comfort, and neither the masses of the cardinals nor the prayers of the people proved efficacious to restore his health or terminate his agony.

Restless, wandering about the Capital, I entered an inn to refresh myself.

The people were drinking and talking about the miraculous cures of Monsignor Johannes. One of the men was incredulous.

"It's all sham, I tell you!"

"Sham? And Marius who was blind all his lifetime, and now sees better than a new-born babe?"

"Sham!"

"And what about Bonifacio — the old fellow, you know — who couldn't lift a leg for twenty years or more — after the bowlder fell on his back. Isn't he walking as straight as you?"

"Sham!" the man persisted, emptying a large jug at one gulp.

"You knew Francisco, didn't you?" one asked the innkeeper, who deposited jugs in front of us.

"Whom?" the innkeeper asked.

"Francisco — the fellow with the palsy?"

"Yes. His hands shook so he couldn't hold a feather."

"Well, you ought to see him now. He can swing an ax better than any of us."

"Sham!"

One of the men rose, furious.

"Shut up!" he shouted.

"Sham!" the man said, turning his head away.

"Well, is it a sham that my sister, Angelica, barren for a dozen years, has now a belly as round as a barrel?"

The skeptic laughed.

"What the devil are you laughing about?"

"Who filled the barrel?"

"What do you mean?"

The other made an attempt to rise, but found his seat more comfortable.

"What do you mean?" the man repeated.

The other grinned and made an obscene gesture.

The man drew out a knife from his belt and planted it in the other's throat.

Suddenly the bells of St. Peter's began to ring, measured, muffled strokes like the iron hoof-beats of horses pulling a hearse.

The people shouted —"The Pope is dead! The Pope is dead!" They rushed out of the wineshop leaving the skeptical victim to swim in his blood, while the assassin escaped.

My heart beat against my chest like an iron hammer. Had the moment for which I waited for years, really arrived? Was I to triumph at last? Was woman through Joan to achieve the temporal and spiritual rule of the civilized world?

I pushed my way through the multitudes and climbed the hill until I reached the gate of the palace. An officer with drawn sword stopped me. I mentioned a word. He stood at attention and stepped aside. I crossed several corridors, always accosted by officers, whom I always placated by the passwords required.

Finally I reached the secret office of Cardinal Marianus, Secretary of State to the Pope. I rapped at the door three times, then twice, then three times again. The door opened by itself. I took three or four steps to the right. Another door opened. I entered into a large hall, whose golden ceiling shed a gentle light like the setting of the sun. The walls were frescoed with scenes depicting the life of Jesus. At the immense marble table in the center of the room, covered with manuscripts and scrolls, the Cardinal sat, pen in hand. At my approach, he rose, bowed and made the sign of the cross over me.

Everything about him was circular, his belly, his face, his eyes, his chin imbedded in a cushion of fat, his nostrils, his nails turned over the tips of his fingers, his hands which he always bent into fists. He wore a robe of red velvet over which shook, as he breathed through his open round mouth. a diamond cross in a circle of gold.

The Cardinal could read Greek and speak correct Latin,

— accomplishments rather rare among the clergy. He had one passion — gold. It was rumored that he spent his spare time in a secret vault where he kept sacks of gold. His jaundiced face was attributed to this habit.

"The Lord is punctual, Padre," the Cardinal said, squinting. "Sanctissimus Leo Papa IV obdormievit in Domino."

We crossed ourselves.

"The ways of the Lord are inscrutable," he added, looking at me obliquely.

"People are stabbing one another, Your Eminence, to prove that Brother Johannes is a saint and a worker of miracles. I witnessed a murder an hour ago."

"That is excellent, Padre!" he said, rubbing his soft hands, noiselessly, as if they had been in a basin of water.

"Is everything ready for the election of Leo's successor, Your Eminence?"

"Everything is ready, Padre," he sighed, "but we lack funds."

"What! Why, I have given you enough ducats to buy a kingdom."

"What is a kingdom compared to the Papacy, Padre? Does not a crown weigh less than three? The Pope rules half of the Earth. He rules not only lands, but souls. Think of that, Father! Dozens of princes and bishops and cardinals are ready to take the Vatican by storm to snatch the triple crown for themselves."

"The Vatican is in your fist, Your Eminence — everybody knows that."

"Everybody may know it, but not everybody is willing to allow it to stay in my fist!"

"Very well, Your Eminence. How much more is necessary?"

He calculated, his lips moving.

"Five hundred thousand ducats more, Padre."

"What! Why, there isn't as much gold in all Europe, Your Eminence!"

He placed his palm upon my shoulder, like a Hebrew merchant, and smiled sanctimoniously. "In Europe — no, but in your treasures, Father ——"

He was right. A fistful of jewels — the ones I received from my Arabian husbands, for example — would suffice, but I did not wish to make him feel how easily I could supply the necessary funds.

"Your Eminence exaggerates my treasures. Even the sea has a bottom."

"There are still three cardinals who absolutely refuse to vote for Brother Johannes, who even consider the death of His Holiness — premature."

He spoke with quiet emphasis articulating every syllable.

"They can be sent to prison, or on long and divine errands."

The Cardinal smiled, his lips drawn.

"What a king or what a pope you would make, Padre!"

"I am not ambitious."

Marianus laughed.

"The cardinals can be appeased, Padre."

I was certain that they had already been appeased and that the money he demanded was to increase the store in his subterranean vault.

"Three hundred thousand ducats, Your Eminence, will appease them."

He shook his head.

"I cannot afford more, Your Eminence, and I hardly believe the tiara is worth it."

"Ah, you do not know the value of the tiara, Padre," he said, a little afraid that I would withdraw the bargain.

"Are three hundred thousand ducats, added to what I have already given you, Your Eminence, of less value?"

"Well, that is exactly what I am saying. You have already given me a fortune, I do not deny it. But then remember, Padre, the Pope was still alive," he said significantly. "You are willing to add three hundred thousand now. The whole question is a matter of two hundred thousand more. That is all."

"That is all? Has the Papacy in its coffers — two hundred thousand ducats, Your Eminence?"

"The coffers of the Papacy have open bottoms, Padre.

They never fill," he said, smiling, "but much gold flows through them."

"The keys of St. Peter, Your Eminence, seem to weigh more than the gates of Heaven."

He laughed, his yellow face creasing like a sheet of paper in the hands of a nervous man.

"Your Eminence," I said after some moments of reflection, "I shall give you four hundred thousand ducats one hour after the election, and the new Pope shall retain you as his Secretary of State."

He played with his cross, his eyes squinting.

"So be it, Padre!" he added piously. "It is the will of the Lord!"

CHAPTER THIRTY-EIGHT

POPE JOAN — JOAN CAPITULATES TO THE MOON — ROMANO CRAVES AN AUDIENCE — I AM THE PONTIFF'S PROCURESS — A BLUSHING PONTIFF — JOAN POWDERS HER NOSE — THE VATICAN CACKLES — THE NEW LEPROSY — A QUESTION OF SYNTAX — THE RAGE OF THE CARDINALS — A NUN CONDEMNED — THE JUDGMENT OF POPE JOAN — HERESY OR A NEW GOSPEL — WAR.

I PREFERRED to wear neither the purple mantle of a cardinal nor the humble cassock of a friar. As a prelate of indefinite status and the Pope's physician I lived at the Vatican amid my herbs and my phials, planning the conquest of the Moon, while ruling the world through Joan, now Pope John VIII.

Despite the tiara and the pontifical robes, despite the triumph of her pen and tongue, despite the obeisance of princes and cardinals, Joan was disconsolate.

I tried in vain to cheer her. My words, my friendship, my love — all inadequate, all futile. In my arms she sighed. Often she turned her face, her eyes swollen with tears.

Had my power over Joan been transitory? Had the subsoil of her masculine nature raised into life fallen into slumber again? Joan was less and less Johannes the Youth of the North and more and more Joan d'Anglois, the lovely maiden who danced on the shores of the river Fulda. Gradually the contours of her body assumed a more definite feminine rotundity. Her face lost the slightly scholarly angularity. Joan was a charming woman dressed in the gorgeous habiliments of the Pontiff of the Christian World.

What power had triumphed over mine? What stimulated the woman and stunted the man in Joan, what new or ancient wind stirred the embers into flames?

I broached the question on various occasions. With feminine subtlety, she evaded answers, crawled out of the loopholes like a feline.

Finally, I determined, whatever the consequences, to bring the issue to a head.

"Joan," I said, "have you not conquered the Earth — and Heaven? Have you not demonstrated that woman is not only man's equal, but his superior, in a position preëmpted by him? You are greater than all your predecessors, and more honored. Emperors and princes willingly bend their knee before you. You have given a new life to the Church, and for once in generations, there are no antipopes. No one dares to entertain the hope to supersede you. You are more famous than Cleopatra, mightier than Zenobia, wiser than Aspasia. Joan, why are you sad?"

Joan embraced me.

"Salome, you have given me wisdom and knowledge. Monarchs are my vassals. You have afforded me joys mortals never experience, and yet I am sad. I am sad because I am still a woman."

"The day is rapidly approaching, thanks to our labors, when to be a woman will mean to rejoice. I created a female Pope. I shall fashion a feminine God!"

"I am sad not because I am a woman, Salome, but because I cannot be a woman to the full. My feminine nature clamors in me like a storm. My womb yearns to teem with new life. The tree bears fruit. The mare is heavy with foal. The bird sits over her egg. The fish spawns. Every female in Nature clamors to reproduce herself. Salome, you received immortality in lieu of motherhood, so great must be the compensation. No transitory throne, no earthly glory, however resplendent, not even a triple crown, can be an adequate consolation, if I am to forfeit my destiny — motherhood. I yearn to be a mother," she added, the catch in her voice a sob.

Was this a conscious or unconscious subterfuge? Did her feminine modesty conceal under the veil of motherhood an imperious sex impulse? Did the woman in Joan yearn for the embrace of the male? Was she in love with any particular man, or was it merely the chaotic urge within her, as yet unshaped?

I passed in mental review cardinals, bishops, officers, scholars, grooms. I could not recall any one in whom Joan seemed preëminently interested. Was it fear of arousing my jealousy which prompted her secretiveness?

The magnificent structure I had raised with infinite pains was crumbling before my very eyes. Once more I saw woman defeated by her nature. The Moon conquered Zenobia, Queen of the East. Would the Moon conquer the female Pontiff of the Christian World shattering spiritual as well as terrestrial thrones?

"No! No!" I exclaimed. "This time it shall not be!"

Joan looked at me with humid eyes.

I took her hands in mine and caressed them.

"Forgive me, Joan. It was the sudden shock of your words. You have a right to your happiness."

"No, Salome, not if my happiness hurts our cause."

"I cannot demand of you to be the sacrificial lamb to an idea, perhaps to an illusion."

"Not an illusion, Salome. Woman is on the path of triumph! But if it is true that I am a great Pope, shall man, as usual, reap the glory? If I masquerade forever as man, Salome, how can my triumph benefit our sex? At most, History will say that Pope John VIII instituted some reforms which made the lot of woman less miserable."

"Or with masculine equanimity forget to mention that part of our program altogether," I added, sighing.

The Pontiff's passion lent fire to her arguments.

"When the time is propitious, the world shall know, Joan, that Pope John VIII, who ruled the Earth with unequaled wisdom and understanding, was a woman."

"Perhaps," she said sadly. "Perhaps. But the world, if

generous at all, will think that I was neither man nor woman — but a strange hybrid! Salome, I want to be a full-blooded woman — not a hermaphrodite or an Amazon! Let woman triumph!"

"Fear not, Joan, posterity will know the truth!"

The Pontiff placed the cross that hung upon her chest to her lips, and closed her eyes gently in meditation or prayer.

I weighed matters. Should I allow Joan's arguments to sway me? Did she, inspired by the ancient instinct, speak prophetically?

"Joan," I said, "you shall be a mother!"

Was it modesty or happiness that flushed her face?

"It is still time. You are young. Even Papal vestments cannot conceal your loveliness."

"Your words, Salome, are sweeter than fresh honey fragrant with the perfume of flowers. I am still a woman," she added coquettishly, thrilled by my compliments.

"You will have a child — a girl as beautiful as Idun, goddess of Spring."

"She will resemble you, Salome. Your image is graven in my heart."

Our flame of enthusiasm, however, soon dwindled into a tiny flicker.

"It is not possible, Salome, I know. I must not allow my selfishness to overrule my good sense. I cannot jeopardize your gigantic venture. I am Pope John VIII."

"Popes have been fathers, Joan. Why cannot a Pope be a mother?"

Joan shook her head. "It is merely a whim, Salome. I must not indulge in personal pleasures. Your love will console me," she sighed.

She placed her chin upon her palm and gazed sadly into the distance.

"No, my child, my love no longer suffices, no longer fills every corner of your heart."

Joan made a feeble gesture of dissent.

"Do not fear to hurt me, Joan. You have a right to your own life and your own emotions. Have I not been baptized in the Jordan of the senses? Have I not drunk the overbrimming Cup of Passion? Shall I withhold from you one draft, or one sip?"

Joan made no reply. She did not try to deny that it was not the overpowering mother instinct, but her unsatiated sex that prompted her words, that saddened her. My magic, my friendship, my love, could not outweigh the masculine attribute which I lacked.

Should I allow my wounded pride to master me or jealousy to frustrate the life of my friend?

"Joan," I said, "for years you have been pulse of my pulse and breath of my breath."

"Yes, Salome," she whispered.

"Into all eternity I shall carry your image in my heart, proudly, as a soldier carries the flag he has snatched from his enemy."

"Yes, Salome."

"Whatever you do, whatever you say, you are mine forever."

"And you are mine, Salome, until the last tremor of my life forsakes me. And if it is true that Heaven or Hell follows Earth, in Heaven or Hell I shall still cherish my love for you."

"Joan, my dear, he who tramples upon his passions tramples upon his soul. If you forego your overpowering desire, I fear you will no longer be the great Pope, the inspired Pontiff. Something in you will be murdered."

Joan nodded imperceptibly.

"Besides, it is true. If your love results in a child, it will forward our cause, the cause of woman. We shall prove to the world that a woman can be both a great ruler and a great mother."

"I am afraid."

"Do not fear, Joan. I shall arrange everything. Neither the man you love nor any other living being shall dream that the Vicar of Christ has obeyed her nature until we are ready to proclaim the truth from the housetops."

Joan remained thoughtful.

"Joan," I asked in a whisper, "who shall be the father of — our child?"

A herald entered, making a genuflection.

"Holy Father, Master Romano, the Sculptor, craves your audience."

I was on the point of saying that His Holiness was too occupied to pose, when I observed an astounding change come over the face of Joan, as if a sudden flood of light had been shed upon it. Her eyes dazzled, her mouth parted slightly as in a kiss, her cheeks blossomed.

Ignoring my question, the Pope commanded: "Let Romano enter the studio. We shall receive him presently."

The herald knelt and left.

Joan rose, arranged the folds of her robe, and placed the tiara upon her head.

"Will posterity say that John the Eighth, Supreme Pontiff, was handsome?" she asked, her voice a trifle husky.

I flattered her. She pressed my hand in gratitude.

"You have not seen my statue, Salome. Won't you come with me to inspect the work of Romano?"

"Yes," I answered, suspecting vaguely the meaning that underlay her words.

Master Romano kissed the Fisherman's ring, lingering over the white hand of the Pope.

He was a youth of about twenty-four or five, tall, lithe. His hair was black, slightly curled, his eyes were blue. There was the pride of the Northerner in his bearing and the passion of the Mediterranean in his gestures. His voice had the mellowness of the ancient Greek, and his hands, as he molded the statue of the Pontiff, the precision of the Teuton. His full lips and his nose, a trifle aquiline, gave the impression of strength and sensitivity, while his chin, round and punctured by a vague dimple, bespoke hidden languors.

Romano arranged the Pope's robes, turned his face now to one side now to the other, until the perfect angle was achieved.

I sat in the corner, ostensibly engaged in reading my breviary but intent upon watching Joan and the artist whose hands were immortalizing her image.

The expression of Joan's face changed and wavered between that of the Pontiff ascetic and scholarly and of a woman coquettish and voluptuous. Romano, seeking to capture definitely the former changed his position, looked desperately at the light which streamed into the room, approached his model, withdrew and approached again.

Did the youth unconsciously feel the sex of Joan? Did the aura of her feminine nature envelop him, intoxicate him?

Romano was flustered. His hands trembled. His cheeks burned. His restless eyes were caught by the eyes of Joan as in a net. He turned his head. Joan sighed.

The sculptor, as if recalled to his duty, caressed the statue; the Pope, mindful of her mission on Earth, kissed her jeweled cross.

Had this youth awakened the slumbering female in Joan, or had he merely become the incarnation of a passion long smoldering? Had Joan dreamed of other and different loves? Something clutched at my heart. Anger, indignation, resentment tripped upon one another in my veins.

Joan, reading my thoughts, looked at me gently reproving. Mutely I begged her forgiveness. My emotions made a sudden volte-face. My hatred for the intruder changed to the vicarious love a fond mother experiences for her son-in-law. Joan realizing my new attitude threw me a glance of gratitude.

"Your Holiness," Romano said, his head lowered, "I cannot continue with my work to-day."

"What troubles you, Romano?" Joan asked, her face stretched forward, her lips pouting, as if consoling a sad child.

"I do not know, Holy Father!"

"Is it my fault, Romano?" The name lingered upon her lips like a song, like a kiss. "Shall I change my posture?"

Romano shook his head. "No, Holy Father. The fault lies with me. My eyes have misled me, and my hand has betrayed me. The expression of Your Holiness as I caught it in my statue is entirely inadequate," he said despondently.

"On the contrary, the statue pleases us enormously," Joan

said, rising and walking to Romano. "The work is excellent," she pursued, and looking at me, asked: "Are you not of my opinion, Monsignor?"

"Excellent," I said vaguely, surprised and amused at the typically feminine ways of the Pontiff.

Joan smoothed Romano's hand. "The Lord, my son," she said, "has blessed your hand and endowed it with the magic power of creation. Your eyes," she looked intently at him, "your eyes, Romano, are torches which illumine the wells of the soul."

"Holy Father," the youth murmured, breathing deeply.

"Monsignor," Joan addressed me, "am I not right? Is not this statue the work of genius? May we not expect Romano to rival the glory of Phidias and Praxiteles?"

"Yes," I answered, meditating on the risks Joan's amour might entail.

Flustered with joy, Romano grasped the Pontiff's hand, and kissed it rapturously.

Joan closed her eyes. Her bosom heaved. She loved the youth with a madder love than she had ever loved me. If I tried to frustrate her passion, Joan would relinquish even her triple crown for him. It was wiser for me, for my great work, to allow the infatuation its normal course, and become the Pontiff's procuress!

I removed Joan's wig which showed the tonsure. Her hair tumbled over her delicate white shoulders like a cataract of gold breaking over a dam. She shook her head joyously, as if to remove an invisible yoke. I combed her with a golden comb studded with jewels, which a Chinese emperor had given me.

I relieved her of the pontifical robes.

"How burdensome it is to be a man!" she breathed deeply.

"In spite of his inordinate vanity, man was not created for prolonged joy. He is painfully vulnerable."

"His masculinity seems almost an afterthought, doesn't it — as if there was no room left in his body for it?" Joan laughed.

"Man is an afterthought of creation. In the economy of

Nature he plays a minor part, but he extracts from it every possible value."

No longer accustomed to feminine attire, Joan was a trifle clumsy. She allowed me to dress her, moving her arms and legs and torso according to my instructions. She uttered little cries of joy at the sight of every new feminine garment. She ran her hands over the silk and velvet, caressed her body as if it had blossomed overnight. She postured before the tall silver mirror, the gift of the Caliph of Sevilla.

The Pope's bedchamber became a royal courtesan's boudoir. The rare Arabic and Hindu perfumes effaced the scent of incense. The dressing tables were strewn with jars of pomades and unguents and ointments.

"Salome, what a thrill to be a woman again!" Joan exclaimed, pushing the pontifical robes with the tips of her gold-embroidered slipper, and dipping her fingers in a golden bowl filled with a Hindu lacquer which made her nails glitter like rubies.

"Sit down, Joan," I scolded her. "You make me run from one corner of the room to the other trying to catch you."

She threw her arms about me. "I am so happy."

"Yes, but moderate yourself! The paint on your face is a smudge! You do not know how to apply it! Let me do it. I am as skillful as my maids who prepared me for the royal couch of the Arabian monarchs."

"Do you think I shall be delectable to my lover?"

"Let Romano see to it that he does not disappoint you, my dear. A man's passion is easily gratified," I said a little bitterly, suddenly remembering Cartaphilus and the boys bathing.

Like a bride who has not passed her period of adolescence, blushing and stammering, Joan asked one hundred and one questions.

"The eyebrows, my dear, are the curtains of the eyes, the casements of the soul. They must be trimmed with the utmost precision," I said, as Joan winced under the silver pincers.

"And the lips must have the freshness of roses at dawn, the sweetness of the honey still in its comb, the shape of the bow when the arrow of Eros pierces the heart of the lover," I continued as I molded her exquisite mouth.

Joan dipped the puff made of the feathers of fledgling white herons into the powder crushed from Hindu rice and perfumed with the scent of lilies, and tapped her nose, chiseled as a statue's. She laughed in glee.

Impatient, Joan placed over her firm, girlish throat the seven-rowed necklace of pearls which once adorned the imperious neck of Zenobia, Queen of the East. Her arms she encircled with the bracelets of the House of Herod. Her fingers flowed with the precious stones which the Roman Emperors paid in tribute to Teuton chieftains.

"Oh, the Fisherman's ring," Joan laughed. "I nearly forgot it on my hand."

She took it off, her face assuming for a fraction of a minute its pontifical severity.

"Keep it safely for me, Salome, until I am Pope again," she sighed.

Suddenly the enormity of the situation loomed before me. I had faced incredible predicaments, but this one seemed the maddest of them all. Was it really possible to leave the Vatican undetected, to return unmolested? Would Romano recognize the features of the Pope in the face of the young princess who came to his studio to offer him her virginity and her love? If Joan should become pregnant, could I really conceal the fact? There had been popes who committed fornication, who had several mistresses at one time, who indulged in strange vagaries. Their deeds were condoned or gossiped over gayly, but a pregnant pope ——!

I was about to say —"Joan, let us not imperil the rule of the world for the whim of tumescence!"

But as I watched Joan in her gorgeous feminine attire, I knew she would relinquish not only the triple crown, but Heaven and Earth for a kiss from Romano! She had completely forgotten her exalted rôle as Vicar of Christ. She was a woman, radiant, charming. The hourglass had been turned, and ten years had flowed back for her.

Joan walked slowly up and down the room, enchanted by

the frou-frou of her undergarments and the glimmer of the silks.

Suddenly lifting her skirts gently with the tips of her fingers, she began to dance. She was once again Joan d'Anglois, the loveliest maiden who danced on the shores of the river Fulda on Easter morning!

Her girlish exuberance made me relinquish my anxiety, and I exclaimed: "Idun, goddess of Spring!"

The die was cast. After all I had not lived in vain for nearly a millennium. I would triumph over this escapade, as I had triumphed over a thousand others!

"History will speak of the greatest of Popes, Joan — and Legend will sing of the most lovely of women!"

"Salome, I am so happy!"

I threw a monk's garb over Joan, and hid her face in the broad cowl. Once again I rehearsed with her the details of her return and the secret signals.

I accompanied Joan to the coach which awaited her outside of the Vatican.

As she raised her foot to enter the carriage, a misstep revealed her gold slipper and the dainty ankle under her cloak.

The guards tittered.

"Directly from the Pope's chamber," one whispered.

"His Holiness isn't such a saint, after all," another said, curving his lips into a whistle.

Joan crossed herself, and motioned to the coachman to go. I watched until the carriage was out of sight.

I entered the Pope's bedchamber, awaiting Joan's return. To while away the time, I read some quaint Arabian tales whose heroine was Salome, granddaughter of King Herod the Great. From time to time I munched cakes and sipped wine, and thought of my thousand years of love.

The Council gathered in the Palace adjoining the Lateran. Cardinals, archbishops, bishops walked up and down the hall propping against their tall staffs or clustered into groups. They gossiped about the latest amorous or political intrigues, boasting about their escapades and prowesses in the brothels and wineshops.

The jewels glittered and burned into the scarlet and purple mantles and soutanes, and at intervals the tip of a gold or silver scabbard clinked against the marble floor.

As scheming and unscrupulous as the Sanhedrin at the time of my grandfather Herod the Great, the members of the Council lacked both the subtlety and the culture of their prototypes in Judea.

Physically and spiritually infinitely better suited for the battlefield, the ducal antechambers, the common wineshops or the boudoirs, the Council, with few exceptions, was Christian only in name and garb. Of their religion they knew but the major dogmas, which they furiously defended in a barbarous and ungrammatical Latin.

"They say the Duke has a new mistress," a middle-aged bishop laughed, his mouth closed, his belly shaking like a mass of jelly in a platter.

"If he robbed the convent again," a bishop said threateningly, "he will have to pay a round Peter's Pence before I remit his sin."

"He will build another monastery!"

"I need a bell in my Chapel!"

"I need an altar!"

"Is it true, Doctor," a cardinal addressed me, "that hardly any wench is free from the New Disease?"

"So they say."

"What is the nature of the Disease?" two bishops asked overanxiously.

"It's a form of leprosy, I believe, that devours the nose, causes the hair and teeth to drop out, weakens the brain, and rots the limbs," I answered, purposely emphasizing the horrors, knowing that my words would strike terror in Episcopal loins.

"Is there any cure for it?"

"Only virtue and Mercury, Monsignor. It will have a great moral effect upon the world. Women will prize their virginity, and men will remain faithful to their wives."

The prelates laughed not too merrily. One of them slapped my back.

Bishop Felix, short, emaciated, myopic, dressed in woolen garments, stretched his neck toward Bishop Siegebert, a massive Teuton with eyes too watery to reveal any definite color.

"What are we coming to, brother?" Felix asked.

"We are on the road to perdition," Siegebert responded.

"Formerly, the Devil caught individual sinners with large hooks and delectable bait. Now he captures them in masses with large nets."

"What experienced deacons once hardly dreamed of, fifteen-year-old choristers practice nowadays."

"The Church should condemn to the stake all transgressors."

"I don't believe in punishing venial sins by a few Pater Nosters or alms. I'd give them brimstone."

"Make distinction between sin and sin, brother, and soon you can make no distinction between sin and virtue!"

The two zealots, excited by their own words, and blissful in each other's approbation, walked off arm in arm.

One cardinal looked after them, and laughed. He rubbed his hands, and said: "Sin? What is sin?"

"Sin, Your Eminence," a bishop answered, suavely, playing with the cross on his chest, "is that by virtue of which the Church prospers!"

François de Norman, a young cardinal, whose blue eyes gazed always into the distance, rubbed his long fingers as if they had been frozen, and smiled sadly.

"Monsignor," he said to me in excellent Greek, "between the zealots and the libertines, as between an anvil and a hammer, our Lord is beaten and crushed!"

As he moved his head, a few rays of the sun fell upon his face, and for a moment I had the impression that I saw Apollonius — Apollonius in his youth.

I had watched François on several occasions. He never mingled with the rest of the members. His attention was always riveted upon Joan, too timid or too disillusioned to speak. This was the first time he addressed me. I was about to speak to him, when the noise of the populace outside broke into the hall.

"Il papa! Il papa!"

"His Holiness! His Holiness!"

Trumpets, hoofbeats, shouts of triumph.

The prelates arranged their robes, and lined themselves against the walls.

The tall brass doors were thrown open. The heralds blew their long silver trumpets. Priests scattered incense from golden censers studded with sapphires. Guardsmen with immense spears whose reflection, like white tongues of fire, licked the silks and tapestries of the walls, marched to the steps of the throne, and separated into two phalanxes.

Borne aloft in the golden sedan, the Supreme Pontiff appeared. She was dressed in a scarlet robe embroidered with jewels. Upon her head she wore the triple crown. On her chest glowed a large crucifix embedded with diamonds.

The officers lowered the sedan in front of the throne, and lifted the Pope slowly, like a precious vase overbrimming. She turned toward the Council, and raising the fore and middle fingers, on which shone the Fisherman's ring, she austerely pronounced the blessing.

"In nomine, Patris, Filii et Spiritus Sancti!"

The Council responded "Amen!"

The Pope seated herself. Pages arranged her robe which fell like the tide of a red sea at her feet. Only the point of her brocaded slipper protruded.

The heralds marched out of the hall, followed by the rest of the attendants. The tall doors closed slowly.

One by one the prelates approached the throne, kissed the pontifical toe, and walked to their seats, wide armchairs upholstered with red plush, and surmounted by the keys of St. Peter.

Joan's face was pale and delicate. Her fine brow and beautiful eyes dazzled amid the coarse and bibacious faces of the ecclesiasts whose chief claim to rank was their gender. I thought of the numberless lies I had to invent and the petty trickeries to which I resorted to conceal Joan's sex — the corsages, the breastplates!

How easy to be man! What vainglorious posturings because he could flaunt to the world that which made him man!

More than ever I was determined to establish the equality of the sexes, and crush that distinction whose basis was man's temerity and woman's timidity.

"Sacred Council," the Vicar of Christ began, her voice caressing and mellow, indicative of her incipient gestation. "The Lord is about to bless our efforts in Spain. The Ambassadors of the Caliph have accepted our terms."

"What are they, Your Holiness?" one of the Cardinals asked.

"That the frontiers remain status quo, and that no violent means be employed to bring about conversion."

"Your Holiness," a burly Cardinal objected, "the word of Jesus must be carried forward forever! We bring not peace but a sword. Let there be war until the last of the dogs of the vile creed of the Camel-driver is dead or converted to the Truth!"

The Council applauded.

"Tut! Tut!" the Pope admonished like a mother. "It is not so easy to convert the infidels. The battlefields are gorged with the blood of our brothers, and to what avail? Not by the sword shall we conquer, but by wisdom and love!"

"He speaks like the sweet Lord Jesus Himself!" Cardinal François exclaimed, his eyes seeking the approbation of Joan.

"Your Holiness, did not our Lord Jesus say that he came to bring war, not peace?"

"Yes! Yes!"

"He also said that they who raised the sword shall perish by the sword!" the Pope answered.

"That was only to save the life of Peter, Your Holiness," the Cardinal quibbled.

"Did not our Lord proclaim peace on Earth?" Joan insisted.

"But not for God's enemies. It is visionary to permit the infidel to participate in his blessing."

The Council applauded.

"Very well, let us have war!"

The Council was taken aback.

"Where is our army, Holy Council? Straggling regiments half naked, and without munitions. Where is our gold? The coffers are empty. Name the great leaders! It is fortunate for us that the Mohammedans are deceived by our pomp and our high-sounding phrases! Is it we who offer peace, or they? Let us be practical, if we will not be Christian!"

And turning to the Secretary of State, who had grown still rounder and yellower, as if assuming the shape and hue of the coins he was enamored of, "Your Eminence, tomorrow the Ambassadors of the Caliph shall be escorted across the frontier to Rome with all the respect and honor due to guests of the Holy Church and the Holy Father!"

The Council grunted.

Joan spoke of other matters — the opening of colleges, the reform of monasteries and convents, the invitation of scholars to Rome.

Like angry steeds, the prelates stamped and fumed and clenched their teeth. Every innovation was considered a trick of the Devil. The Pontiff did not relinquish her program. Her small white hand was gloved in iron. Her will was unshakable. At intervals, she glanced at me, and found in my approbation the strength and courage to cope with a vain and ignorant rabble.

"When are the legates of our Brother, the Patriarch of Constantinople, due at the Vatican, Your Eminence?" she addressed the Secretary.

"Holy Father, the legates will be in Rome within two weeks, if the Lord permits and the winds are propitious."

"It is well," the Pope said, and turning to the rest, pursued: "We shall do all in our power to reconcile, at last, the two Sisters — the Church of the East and the Church of the West. We shall bring them together under the same roof — the Canopy of God!"

"How will the union be accomplished, Your Holiness?" a cardinal asked ironically.

"Like all unions, Your Eminence, by compromise."

"Compromise!" the prelates repeated, indignantly.

"Compromise on what matter, Your Holiness?"

"On that which has kept the two Churches apart and in enmity."

The prelates grumbled.

One cardinal, with a face flattened-in like a thing of one dimension, rose and exclaimed in a voice that seemed to come from nowhere, and tumbled in a heap, "Your Holiness, there can be no compromise on the filioque!"

"There shall be, if necessary!" the Vicar of Christ replied with assurance and dignity.

"It's a heresy that stinks to the nostrils of the Lord, Your Holiness. Filioque must remain forever the cornerstone of the Holy Edifice."

A bishop rose, and balanced himself like an acrobat on a wire. "Your Holiness, what becomes of the Holy Ghost if the Holy Ghost is torn in twain — if he no longer emanates from the Son as well as from the Father! Filioque!" He raised his bulging froglike eyes upwards in bovine beatitude. "Filioque — and the Son — and the Son, Your Holiness — Filioque — "

"Filioque," the others croaked like a pond of frogs.

The Pontiff interrupted. Her forehead gleamed with intelligence. Her face radiated gentleness and strength.

"We cannot allow a question of syntax, of elementary grammar, of a mere preposition, to cleave God's Church forever."

"Remove one stone, Your Holiness, and the Edifice tumbles and crumbles," a bishop with a predilection for puns and alliteration, said with delectation.

"If the Edifice be so frail that the removal of one stone cause it to tumble and crumble, then let it!" the Pope exclaimed, her face assuming martial severity.

The Council breathed heavily.

To conciliate them, however, Joan resumed, a benign expression flooding her face.

"Do not fear, brothers in Christ — our Edifice is rooted in the very pulses of the heart of man. Remove stone after stone, it shall still stand erect and unshakable! It will crumble only with the ultimate pulse of the last Christian heart!"

The prelates, unconvinced, were nevertheless overawed by the fervent words of the Pontiff.

The Pope pursued: "Think of the moral effect upon Christians and Heathens alike if the Branch which was torn from the Tree is grafted upon it once more! Let not our Church be a cracked vessel from which the honey and the perfume drip into the gutter!"

"No compromise on filioque," the prelates insisted.

"Filioque"— the others reiterated.

Joan looked at them in disdain, and without pressing the matter any further for the time being, turned to the Secretary of State.

"Your Eminence, is there any other matter to be brought before the Counsel of the Holy See?"

Cardinal Marianus handed the Pope a scroll.

"What is this?" Joan asked without reading it.

"The Ecclesiastical Tribunal begs Your Holiness to confirm the death sentence passed upon Maria del Val. They also beg that, because of the enormity of her crime, it be decided if she should be immured alive or consigned to the flames."

"What is her crime, Your Eminence?"

"For years Maria del Val lived in the disguise of a man. She studied canonical law, and was ordained priest. As such she performed mass and administered the holy sacraments."

"Sacrilege!" the prelates exclaimed, gasping with horror.

The Secretary of State droned on:

"Her sex was discovered during a painful attack to which women are prone. Stricken down by God, she fell unconscious at the altar, polluting the Holy Place, while she administered the eucharist."

"Abomination!" the Council roared. "Let her be immured!" cried some.

"No, to the flames with her," shouted others.

The Cardinal continued:

"The truth of her feminine nature has been attested to by three physicians, duly sworn."

Joan looked at me intently. My eye warned her to be

wary, but her pale and shivering nostrils indicated clearly that her anger and indignation were overruling her prudence.

Calmly, determined, the Pontiff tore the scroll and cast it to the floor.

"It is Our will to pardon Maria del Val."

The members of the Council caught their breaths. For a moment there was utter stillness — the stillness that precedes a hurricane.

"Your Holiness," several voices began suddenly, tumbling and stamping upon one another, like mad bulls.

"Your Holiness — this is almost blasphemy!"

"It is Our will!"

The prelates frothed at the mouth. Their faces turned pale.

"We shall be the laughing stock of Jew and Moslem! A woman — priest — defiling the flesh and blood of our Lord!"

"Is there anything in the Gospels which prohibits a woman from being a priest?" Joan asked, frowning. "Did our Lord resent the ministrations of women? What saint is greater than Mary Magdalene to whom Jesus appeared after he rose from the dead even before he manifested himself to his favorite disciple?"

The Council was too enraged for any coherent reply.

"The exclusion of woman is not a God-made law, but a simple Church ordinance, a custom. It is within the province of the Holy See to revoke it, whenever the Holy See so ordains."

"Your Holiness! Your Holiness!" the prelates stamped their swords and staffs, too indignant to condescend to denial or argument.

"Why should not a woman minister to the Lord? Is not our Church a good mother? Does she not, like a good mother, gather to her breasts all those who seek her love?"

The prelates looked at one another, astounded, offended, enraged.

"The time has come," the Pope pursued, her brows knit, her small hands tightened into fists, "to repudiate the infamous dictum of Gregory of Tours that it is impossible to think that woman possesses a soul. And I, John the Eighth, Supreme Pontiff, repudiate it, now and forever, as an offense to Heaven and a sacrilege to Mary, mother of Jesus, our Saviour!"

Joan rose and lifted her right arm.

"Heresy! Heresy!" the Council shouted.

"Silence!" the Pontiff commanded.

The first mighty blow against the slavery of Woman was delivered, and Man, vainglorious Cock of the World, crowed impotently against the rising Sun of Truth.

"The Son of Man issued forth from the womb of woman, and the world accepted Him. Shall not the world accept from the hand of woman, the wafer which is flesh of His flesh, and the wine which is blood of His blood!"

The prelates rose, and gathered about the throne, threateningly.

"No woman shall usurp the prerogative of Man!"

"No woman shall defile the sacred altars!"

"She is a carcass of corruption!"

"She has brought sin and death into the world!"

All the abominable epithets which Jokanaan hurled at me were hurled at woman. I almost expected to hear: "Too vile for the grave!"

Cardinal François de Norman approached the Pope, kissed the Fisherman's ring and the pontifical toe.

"Your Holiness," he pleaded, with tears in his eyes, "let the woman die!"

Joan cast a glance at the Cardinal, and turned her head away, fearing that the gentleness of his voice might shake her determination.

"It is Our will to pardon her!"

"The Church needs internal peace, Holy Father," the Cardinal continued. "Let us not create a new schism greater than the gulf that divides East and West. Let us be patient, even if it takes centuries to decide the question of woman's right to officiate at the altar. Holy Father, the Church, being eternal, can wait."

Joan stamped her foot. "Why wait? The Holy Spirit has

descended upon me. God, speaking through me, is infallible!"

"So be it!" François sighed, and walked away.

The Council became frantic. The cardinals waved their fists.

Joan's life was imperiled. A little longer, another impassioned remark, and murder would leap forth from the hearts of the cardinals.

I took the Secretary aside, and whispered something into his ear.

Cardinal Marianus, the Pope's Secretary of State, who had been wringing his hands disconsolately, seeing the end of his powers approach, beamed with joy.

Flashing his cross, studded with jewels, he called the Council to order.

"Holy Council," he shouted, "may the Grace of the Father and of the Son and of the Holy Ghost descend upon us!"

A few prelates responded mechanically — "Amen!"

"The Council has misunderstood the words of His Holiness."

They glared at him.

"His Holiness believes with the Holy Council that a woman should not be priest."

Joan opened her lips to shout an objection. She caught my warning eye, however, and remained silent.

"His Holiness merely offered a philosophical argument, not a practical measure."

The Council looked at the Pope. She remained impassive.

"What His Holiness desires is peace and harmony in the Church, and reverence among the worshipers."

The Council listened attentively.

"If the case of Maria del Val becomes known to the world, the Church will be condemned and ridiculed for its laxity and inability to differentiate between man and woman before she ordains a priest. For that reason, it is politic and prudent to hush the matter, and send Maria del Val to a convent on a vow of eternal silence! That is what His Holiness in his wisdom and love for the Church and the Council propounds!"

The prelates looked at the Pontiff.

"Have I had the honor, Holy Father, to understand the meaning of your words?" the Secretary asked.

Joan meditated for a while, then nodded.

Marianus looked at the Council triumphant.

"Is the Council willing to abide by the decision of His Holiness?"

"So be it!" a few answered.

The others grumbled.

"So be it!" the Secretary repeated. "The Council is adjourned! Pax vobiscum!"

The Council retired.

Cardinal Marianus remained.

"Your Holiness," the Secretary said, smiling ironically, "your idea of infallibility is most excellent. The Pope should be infallible. It would cure all the ills of the Church. It would end all schisms. But this age of popes and antipopes is not yet prepared for such a doctrine. It is, if I may say so, premature. But it shall remain in the secret archives of our Church. Perhaps some day a successor of Your Holiness may profit by your suggestion."

He kissed the Fisherman's ring, and departed, making the sign of the Cross.

I led Joan to her rooms.

She fell upon the couch, her face white and her hands shivering.

I unclasped her robes and loosened her garments. I rubbed her temples and wrists, and administered a soothing drug.

"Salome," she whispered, "Salome, we have lost!"

"We have won, Joan! The war is on! We shall triumph! Your words will reverberate through all Christendom, for all time!"

"They will plot to dethrone me and assassinate me. They will kill my child in my womb."

"Do not worry. We shall brave the storm!"

"I shall never be a mother, Salome!"

She smiled sadly. Her eyes had the strange and mystical look of King Onam, my last Arabian husband, before he was stabbed in the garden of the harem. Did she, like that lovely youth, catch a glimpse of Time and his scroll beyond the horizon of the Present?

"Come, Joan, you must rest."

"May I see Romano to-night, Salome?" she asked crumpling upon the couch like a hurt child.

"You shall see him to-night, Joan."

She placed her head upon my lap, and dozed.

CHAPTER THIRTY-NINE

DROUGHT — I CORSET HIS HOLINESS — NON PAPA SED MAMA — THE POPE HAS A BABY — A MIRACLE OF HELL — DEFEATED BY THE MOON.

For weeks the sun poured cataracts of flames upon Rome. The fields and vineyards lay prostrate, scorched. In vain the prayers and invocations to God and the Virgin, to the saints, and in secret, by many, to the ancient and pagan divinities. Famine, his wings outspread, hovered over the Capital, ready to swoop upon it, and devour it.

The people, desperate, stormed at the gates of the Vatican. The messengers protested futilely that His Holiness was too ill to bless the fields in person. In vain the assurance that he prayed in his chamber for the salvation of Rome. The populace scorned the cardinals and the bishops, and accepted, unconcerned, the spear thrusts of the guards.

The Vatican became a castle invested by lean and famished hordes, shouting and moaning by turns, like a mad refrain: "Save us, Your Holiness! Save us, Your Holiness! Save us, Your Holiness!"

"Salome," Joan implored, "let me go out, and pray for my people. It is the week of Rogation, and ever since the memory of man, at this time every Pontiff sprinkled the Earth with holy water, and implored God for rain."

"Prayers do not gather clouds. You cannot help your people, and you will harm yourself — and your child."

"My touch made the sick whole. My prayers may bring rain. Let me go, Salome!"

281

I looked at her intently.

"Is it too evident?" she asked, looking at herself.

"Motherhood is imprinted upon your face, Joan. Your breasts are ripe with sweet food. You are heavy like the Earth in Spring when the rain is abundant."

"I shall soon be a mother!" she exclaimed triumphantly. And immediately she sighed: "Alas, I am the Pope, destined to be the father of all, not the mother of one."

"You will be the mother of one who will bring us great joy, Joan. Whether a boy or a girl, your child will grow up in beauty and intelligence. It will inherit the genius of its father and the greatness of its mother. It will be the wonder child of the world — Jesus!"

My words consoled Joan a little. For a long time she had been fearing an impending doom. For hours she would pray to the Holy Virgin with whom she identified herself unconsciously. Exhausted, she would lay her head upon my chest and sob quietly. Knowing the vagaries of women in her condition, I would whisper words of tenderness and cheer. She would fall asleep murmuring sometimes my name, sometimes that of Romano.

"Save us, Your Holiness! Save us, Your Holiness! Save us, Your Holiness!"

The thick walls of the Palace were pierced by the ceaseless refrain.

"I must pray for my people, Salome. I am the Pope! I am Christ's vicar. Whatever fate befalls me, I cannot turn a deaf ear to their plea! If martyrdom is my fate, then let it be martyrdom! Perhaps it is the will of the Lord that I expiate for my sin!"

"Do not speak of expiation, or of sin, Joan," I said somewhat impatiently. "The fools and the wicked have branded motherhood with the stigma of sinfulness. You are as pure as Mary, the mother of Jesus."

"So be it, then, Salome!" she exclaimed, her eyes blazing with an unearthly fire. "Mary forfeited her Son to save Man. I shall forfeit myself, if necessary to save my flock from starvation!"

All my arguments proved futile. Seeing her firm resolution, I finally yielded.

"Very well, Joan, you shall go and bless their fields!"

"Will they suspect?" she asked, her fear for the treasured burden of her womb reasserting itself.

"I shall corset you with a very tight bodice and a swathe. You will look like a pale but corpulent friar."

She laughed a little, but again I detected the strange look in her eyes.

"But you must be very careful. If you are very mindful of your delicate condition, you will not be harmed."

She knelt before the statue of the Holy Virgin, and prayed for a long time.

The procession started from the Vatican to the Church of St. Clement. Joan rode upon a tall white horse. I rode at her side in case her condition should need my attention. We were preceded and followed by cardinals, bishops, friars, priests, carrying tall crosses and singing litanies, and the entire Roman population, exclaiming from time to time —
"Ora pro nobis! Ora pro nobis!"

The square of the Lateran near the Coliseum overlooked a vast amphitheater of fields and gardens. The procession stopped. The bells of the Cathedral pealed triumphantly.

Joan looked like a ghost. Her hand trembled as she sprinkled the holy water out of a silver basin to the four corners of the Earth. The psalms and the hymns rose like mighty trumpet calls.

"Ora pro nobis! Ora pro nobis! Ora pro nobis!"

The gray clouds which had wandered listlessly about the sky, changed to a deep black, driven swiftly toward the East by a wind which bent the dry branches of the trees and raised mountains of dust.

The people shouted hoarsely — "Ora pro nobis! Ora pro nobis!"

Joan raised the fore and middle fingers of her right hand.

"Omnipotens et misericors Deus, respice propitius nos famulos tuos —"

Her voice broke. She closed her eyes, and clenched her teeth.

"Are you ill?" I asked anxiously.

She shook her head wearily, and continued her prayer.

"Veni Creator Spiritus!"

"Joan," I whispered, bending toward her. "Do not strain yourself."

She looked at me, her eyes blurred, smiling drearily.

A few large drops of rain fell flatly.

The people shouted: "It's raining! It's raining! The Lord is listening to our Father's prayer!"

"Veni Sancte Spiritus —" Joan continued, her face crimson. Her lips trembled.

"It's raining! It's raining! Long live Papa Johannes! Vivat!"

"Veni, dator munerum." Joan uttered a shriek.

I jumped off my horse, and placed the tip of one boot in the stirrup of Joan's horse.

Joan moaned. Her head dropped upon my shoulder.

"His Holiness is ill!" I called to the bishops. My voice was drowned in the jubilation of the populace and the rumbling of the thunder.

"His Holiness has fainted," I repeated. "Help me!" I shouted desperately.

Two bishops rushed to my aid.

"Help me lift His Holiness off the horse," I ordered.

We raised her. It was no longer possible to conceal the truth.

Bishop Felix sneered. The pitiful cry of new life did not disarm his malice.

Placing his palm against his mouth, he shouted triumphantly, the shout of one who is at last avenged:

"Behold! Behold! The Pope is a woman! Pope John VIII is a woman!"

"Papa mulier est!" another bishop added.

"Non Papa sed Mama!" Felix corrected, laughing sardonically.

"The Pope is a woman! The Pope is a woman!" The words dashed through the crowd like mad bulls.

"The Pope has given birth to a baby! Il Papa is a mother!"

"Non Papa sed Mama!"

The people pressed about us.

They laughed. They mocked. They shouted obscene remarks.

"Non Papa sed Mama!"

"Kill the enchantress!"

"Kill the false Pope!"

"She caused the drought!"

"God punished us for her sin!"

"Torture the witch!"

"Burn her alive!"

I unsheathed my sword, and exclaimed:

"Stand aside, wretches. The first who lays hands on His Holiness dies."

"Her Holiness," some one corrected me, and a thousand voices laughed: "Her Holiness! Her Holiness!"

I snatched a crucifix out of the hand of one of the bishops and raised it aloft.

"It was a miracle!" I exclaimed. "The Lord has performed a miracle!"

A sudden flash of lightning awed and silenced the populace.

"A miracle of Hell!" Felix fumed.

One bystander laughed uproariously. "Papa pater patrem peperit, papissa papellam," he punned. His laughter provoked the risibility of the people.

An endless roar like a ribald sea, churned by winds, beat against my ears.

"Papa pater patrem —"

"Papissa papellam —"

"Peperit —"

"Ungrateful creatures!" I shouted. "Only yesterday your fields and your gardens were burning. To-morrow they will blossom again. Who has saved your property and your lives? Whose prayers were blessed? Whose words brought you rain?"

Another thunderclap crashed like the snapping of a Titan's whip.

The laughter ceased.

The people crossed themselves and muttered prayers.

Seizing the psychological moment, I grasped Joan and the infant in my arm, and mounted the horse.

"Make room there!" I ordered. "Stand aside."

The crowd separated into two banks.

I galloped at top speed toward the Vatican.

I dismounted and rushed into Joan's bedchamber. I deposited the two bodies soaked in water and blood upon the bed and severed the umbilical cord.

Desperately I tried to revive Joan. I used all the arts I had learned in Egypt and Arabia and India.

Joan opened her glazed eyes and muttered, "My baby."

Her head fell like a mass of lead. The infant, a girl, turned blue.

There was no time to lose. Already I heard the hoofbeats of horses and the shouts of the populace at the gate.

"Kill the impostor! Burn the wizard! To the stake with both of them!"

A demure nun, I made my escape by a rear door, and mingled with the crowd. At the Amphitheater, I saw two soldiers carrying a limp body, from which blood streamed copiously. I looked at the ashen face of the moribund.

"Who is he?" I asked anxiously.

"It's Romano, the sculptor," one of the soldiers answered. "He stabbed himself."

The other soldier raised a dagger, scarlet to the hilt.

I made the sign of the cross over the body and continued on my way.

The death of Joan crushed my spirits for a long time. I had never felt so lonesome, so disillusioned.

I wandered disconsolate — monk, nun, merchant, widow, princess, baron, wealthy, poor, in golden robes, in rags. I knew nearly all the languages of the Earth, yet there was no one to whom I could speak. The old were pathetically infantile, the young blustering and foolish. I dared not disprove historians who mutilated the truth. I dared not expose the lies for which men died.

I longed to hear the voice of a contemporary — even the grumbling of Kotikokura. I longed to touch something ancient, if only the head of Lakshmi. Was she still alive? Was she crossing rivers and deserts to find me again? Or had she long ago flavored the soup of some royal gourmet?

Cartaphilus — where was Cartaphilus, my lover?

CHAPTER FORTY

I AM THE RED KNIGHT OF THE CRUSADES — A SEPULCHER OR A CRADLE?

Once the East migrated to the West in search of food or adventure or impelled by an overpowering instinct for flight.

The pendulum of Time swung back.

The West returned East — towns, nations — a Continent uprooted. Murderers, poets, visionaries, peasants with the smell of the clod about them, fops with the scent of boudoirs, saints cadaverous from fasts.

Robes studded with jewels, tatters, shapeless beyond nomenclature, pedestrians with bleeding feet, knights mounted on steeds royally caparisoned, stubborn mules and patient oxen, chariots whose wheels tore sparks from cobblestones, carts that moaned like moribund women.

Knapsacks filled with moldy bread, caravans replete with delicacies, ropes tied around the waists to relieve the pang of hunger, belts heavy with ducats.

Heads streaming with ashes of repentance, heads crowned with helmets and coronets.

Trumpets and fifes and drums. Litanies, psalms, prayers, invocations, anathemas, halleluiahs. Pride, humility, anger, challenge, waving of fists, clenching of teeth....

Nightmare or a gorgeous dream? Insane cacophony or a magnificent orchestration? Death or chaos of Rebirth?

The West returned East to capture — a sepulcher!

Is man a hyena, I thought, in love with dead things?

May not the Holy Sepulcher be the Cradle of a New Civilization? Can Man know what secret forces impel him to action? Does the tiny spring that breaks through the rock dream of the immensity of the sea of which it will make part?

I must go along, I must witness the miracle — if miracle occur!

Besides, my fortune was depleted. My estates and vineyards were trampled under foot and hoof by the Crusaders. My castles in various parts of Europe lay in ruins. In Jerusalem, if the Holy City was captured I would unearth my caches, and remove a handful or two of jewels, sufficient now, because of their historical value, to buy Popes and Caliphs.

Had not the time come also to revisit the place where I first learned the meaning of love, of passion, of horror? And Cartaphilus — would he not be among the Crusaders? Would his boyish sense of adventure and his vanity, incurable through the ages, allow him to look upon this titanic pageantry without taking part in it, however carefully and subtly?

As a knight of the French army, armored in red gold, I marched to the City whose ruler a thousand years ago was Herod the Great, my grandfather!

CHAPTER FORTY-ONE

I MEET MY LOVER — OLD LOVE AND OLD MAGIC — THE APPARITION OF THE NAZARENE — THE WRAITH OF JOKANAAN — "WOULD YOU RELINQUISH LIFE?" — THE KISS OF TEN THOUSAND WOMEN — THE ANTICS OF KOTIKOKURA — THE MOON IS A FRIGHTENED BRIDE — THE EDUCATION OF LAKSHMI — CROSSROADS.

CARTAPHILUS, in the uniform of an officer but without armor, was sitting upon a rock, his head between his palms, staring at the ground.

I sent one of my attendants to summon him. Cartaphilus approached. I was on my horse in full armor.

"The Red Knight!" he exclaimed, saluting. "Your exploits, Monsieur, are the glory of France and Christendom!"

"Your valor, Monsieur le Comte de Cartaphile, is carved in golden letters upon the tablets of history."

I made a sign to my attendants to help me descend from the horse, and leave us alone.

I raised my helmet.

"Salome!"

He tried to embrace me, but the chill of the gold of my armor repelled him.

"Order your men to relieve you of this unkind fortress, my love! Grant me the bliss of pressing you to my heart."

"Don't you like my armor, Count?" I asked coquettishly.

"It is magnificent. No monarch is half so resplendent as you. A hundred legends have already been sung of the Red

Knight of Christ who defeated the Heathen. But what queen or goddess has a lovelier body than Salome?"

"Cartaphilus has not forgotten that the Red Knight, whatever her exploits, is but a frail woman, and delighted by words of flattery."

"Cartaphilus has not forgotten above all that he loves Salome now and forever."

Arm in arm, Cartaphilus and I wandered through the intricate and desolate lanes of Jerusalem.

Lepers skulked by, their bells around their necks ringing sinisterly. Soldiers in rags, haggard, wild-eyed, begged for alms. Friars with wooden crucifixes rising above their heads, their faces flushed from devouring fevers, walked like somnambulists, muttering the names of Jesus and the Holy Virgin. Starved men and mangy dogs and cats sought vainly precious crumbs in the débris. At long intervals a peasant urged a famished donkey whose ribs pierced through the skin like the wooden frame of a hut, or a cow whose udders were empty bags of gnarled flesh.

"The sepulcher is a sepulcher indeed," I said, "a universal coffin."

"Thus does the Nazarene reward his soldiers!" Cartaphilus said with bitter irony. "I do not begrudge my ancient foe his victory!"

"Where is the Temple, Cartaphilus? Only this tottering wall is left of all its splendor, and of the gorgeousness of the worshipers only these few ragged people weeping beside it. Where is the palace of Pilate? Where are the beautiful villas, the gardens, the vineyards? Where are all our friends, our enemies? Where is proud Caiaphas and his sons? Where are the Romans? And the Jews, alas, where are they? It seems to me, Cartaphilus, that even the climate has changed, and the soil which was so fertile has become almost a desert."

"We are two owls hooting desolation, Salome."

"What strange power did Jesus have over you, and Jokanaan over me, Cartaphilus, that although nations turn into deserts, we continue to live — eternally young? In vain have I pondered over the matter. In vain have I consulted the wisest of the sages, and the rarest of books. No one, nothing, has quite explained the mystery!"

"Not even Apollonius, Salome, is entirely convincing."

"No, not even he."

Cartaphilus looked around furtively. He whispered: "I visited the Place of Skulls again — and again — the Earth whirled about me — just like that time — more than a thousand years ago. Again there was a storm and an earthquake. Again the words of Jesus struck against my face: 'Thou must tarry until I return! Thou must tarry until I return!' It was maddening, Salome! I rushed through the streets like a maniac, asking the soldiers whether they had heard thunderpeals and felt the Earth shake. They laughed. They thought I was drunk. There had never been finer weather, they said."

"And I visited the spot — where the head of Jokanaan — hurled his doom upon me. There it was again — the head — beautiful as the sun — upon the silver platter — and again the lips reiterated—slowly, deliberately: 'Too vile for the grave! Too vile for the grave!' I was with my attendants on horseback. They had heard nothing. I shouted: 'Go away! Go away!' My attendants thought I meant them, and galloped off.

"Some day, perhaps, we shall understand, Cartaphilus. We have not lived long enough."

"Perhaps understanding means — death?"

"Perhaps."

We remained silent for some time.

"Cartaphilus, what have we lost by having lived far beyond the mortal span of men? Were the words of Jesus and Jokanaan a curse or a blessing?"

"What have we gained?"

"We have seen life's comedy on a vaster scale. The amphitheater spreads to ever receding horizons."

"To what avail, Salome, since it is forever the same?"

I pressed his arm.

"Cartaphilus, if it were possible, would you relinquish life?"

He looked at me.

"Not so long as you are alive, Salome, although you torment me as no woman has ever tormented a man. Oh, Salome — let our roads join from now on! Let us not wait any longer. Would I could say —'Life is so short, Salome! Do not relinquish pleasure! Drink deeply, and quickly!' Alas — you always postpone the consummation of our joy for centuries. But my heart beats as slowly as the one which is doomed to seventy years. Time passes as slowly for us, Salome, as for the others."

I did not answer for some time.

"Cartaphilus," I said, facing him, "look well into your heart which beats as slowly as that of a mortal man's, and see whether you really desire me — already."

He uttered an exclamation of eternal adoration.

"Cartaphilus, beloved, be sincere! Do you not, too, like myself, feel that the time is not yet ripe? You look upon the rest of mankind, and envy how quickly their love is consummated. But their love grows like the mushroom overnight, and overnight it perishes. Our love, Cartaphilus, is an eternal oak. It needs —"

"Eternity to blossom," he said pathetically.

"No, Cartaphilus. It needs — Time — but it will remain fragrant and mighty throughout eternity."

Cartaphilus sighed.

"You always see within my heart, Salome, as I cannot see myself. My heart is a mirror into which I can look with difficulty, but it faces you, and you can see the images reflected there. The time has not yet come. You are right. We must wander alone, seeking, seeking that which, perhaps once found, may not be worth the seeking."

"Who knows, Cartaphilus? Man's days are too short. What he discovers at the end of his tiny journey is not worth the seeking. But we — Who knows?"

"Who knows?"

We seated ourselves in the shade of an olive tree whose trunk had the shape of two tigers in mortal combat.

Cartaphilus took my hand in his and pressed it until I cried out. He laughed.

"Salome, tell me some of your amorous experiences!"

"They are part and parcel of my quest of you, Cartaphilus."

"Salome, even though you lie, my heart rejoices."

"And you, Cartaphilus — were not your experiences a quest of me?"

"Always, beloved!"

An ironic retort rose to my lips, but as I looked at his face, I knew he told the truth. I pressed my head upon his chest. He buried his lips in my hair.

"Not all the gardens of the world waft half the sweetness of your head."

"Cartaphilus, I have loved no one save you."

"No one? Not one youth, not one maiden?"

I shook my head.

"Tell me about them, Salome," he whispered.

And in whispers I mentioned the names of those I cared to remember, recounting their peculiarities, their weaknesses, the comedy and tragedy of sex.

Cartaphilus asked innumerable details, trying to discover inconsistencies in my narration.

"Salome," he said, suddenly, pushing gently my head away. "You cannot tell the truth! You are still a woman!"

"Cartaphilus!" I exclaimed, indignant.

He pressed my head back against his chest.

"How can I live without this dear weight upon me?"

"Many another dear weight shall press upon you, Cartaphilus!"

"They are all either too heavy or too light, my love. My heart is an apothecary's balance, and in vain do I place upon one platter beauty and glory and unendurable pleasure indefinitely prolonged, for upon the other platter is the love of Salome, outweighing everything."

My lips reached for his. He embraced me.

"You stifle me, Cartaphilus," I pleaded.

"In kissing you I kiss ten thousand women, my love."

He raised my head and looked into my eyes.

"Is my kiss the kiss of ten thousand men for you?" he asked.

I smiled enigmatically.

"I shall never know the truth!" he muttered, pressing his fists against my temples.

In the distance I saw Kotikokura's eyes glitter.

"Kotikokura!" I called. "Kotikokura!"

In a second he was at our side, like an animal who jumps from one branch of a tree to another.

I embraced him.

"Kotikokura, my ape, my monster, my enemy, my friend!"

He grunted. His face flushed.

Bowing stiffly like a courtier, he offered me a daisy.

I made a regal curtsy, and placed the flower in my hair.

"Is Ca-Ta-Pha still God, Kotikokura?"

"Ca-Ta-Pha God always."

"And Salome — always woman?"

"Salome woman always."

We laughed heartily. Kotikokura danced, uttering cries of joy.

"Cartaphilus, shall I dance for you?" I asked.

"Dance, Salome! Dance!" he exclaimed.

"Dance!" Kotikokura repeated, squatting at his master's feet.

The Moon, like a frightened bride, appeared haughtily upon the top of the hill.

I danced to the love of Cartaphilus and in defiance of my ancient foe.

Suddenly I stopped.

"I am getting old, Cartaphilus. I am out of breath."

The men laughed. Cartaphilus caught me in his arms and led me to my place on the rock.

Kotikokura began sniffing and looking around, his brows knit.

"What's the trouble, Kotikokura?" I asked. "Are there snakes in the neighborhood, or a wild lion?"

He did not answer immediately, but continued to stare.

A little uneasy, Cartaphilus asked: "Kotikokura, what's the matter?"

"Lakshmi! Lakshmi! Where is Lakshmi?"

"She is thousands of miles away from here, Kotikokura. She, no doubt, thinks of you and misses you, but I could not very well take her along with me on the Crusades, could I?"

Kotikokura was crestfallen.

"But you ought to be proud of her, Kotikokura. She isn't that simple tortoise you knew in Persia and in Africa. She has become civilized. Lakshmi has learned how to speak and count!"

"What!" Cartaphilus exclaimed.

"For a century or so, I made experiments on animals. Some of my discoveries will astound scientists, when I am ready to present them. The difference between man and his humbler brothers is by no means as great as man believes, and it may be that we have a common ancestry."

Kotikokura screwed up his nose.

"Man is man!" he exclaimed, vainglorious of his newly acquired dignity.

"At any rate, Kotikokura, you ought to see your Lakshmi."

He shrugged his shoulders disdainfully, but I knew he was anxious to hear more about her.

"Lakshmi can say not only 'yes' and 'no,' by nodding and shaking her head, she can also say 'perhaps.' She raises her eyes upward, and closes them slowly, as in reverie. And she can count — to twenty."

"That's more than Kotikokura could do some hundred years ago," Cartaphilus remarked laughingly.

Kotikokura again screwed up his nose until it was but a large yellow wart in the middle of his face. His eyes darted to and fro like young goats.

Seeing his affected disdain, I continued my eulogy of the tortoise.

"Lakshmi eats at royal banquets. I have constructed a sort of a ladder which she climbs, and a tall throne into which she drops like a dignitary of the Church. On these occasions she wears a crown, and a necklace of pearls that once adorned the throat of a princess."

Kotikokura pretended to be interested in his sandals.

"You ought to see with what grace she dips her paws in the golden bowl with perfumed water, and wipes her lips!"

Cartaphilus held his sides from laughter.

Kotikokura caught a fly and flicked its corpse away.

"She understands me thoroughly, my words and my moods."

"I suppose you tell her the truth, Salome," Cartaphilus said ironically.

"She knows how to keep a secret, and isn't jealous."

"She ought to make any man happy!" Cartaphilus grinned.

"Too clever — for a wife!" Kotikokura snarled.

"Times have changed, my friend," I said. "Many wives are cleverer than their husbands nowadays."

"Woman!" Kotikokura growled.

"And where is that marvelous creature now, Salome?"

"She is on my estate in the Palatinate, where her six attendants, on the penalty of forfeiting their lives, protect her from every inconvenience. She knows how to call them individually, by ringing a different bell for each!"

"She is indeed a marvel, Salome," Cartaphilus bantered.

Kotikokura rubbed his nose.

"But I haven't told you half of her achievements."

"I suppose she plays the harp and sings lullabies."

Kotikokura, following his master's sarcasm, began playing an invisible harp, and uttered sentimental sounds that must have terrified every mother for leagues around.

"Lakshmi knows how to draw magic circles with her paws — circles which would satisfy the most exacting of necromancers."

"Are you still interested in witchcraft, Salome?" Cartaphilus asked, somewhat superciliously. "You've bewitched me. Do you want to bewitch the whole world now?"

"You are fighting the Christian church with Logic, Cartaphilus. You will never win. I am fighting it with the primordial religions which are buried deep in the soul."

"I have seen a Witches' Sabbath, Salome. It was like the orgy in the Temple of the Goddess of the Triple Gate."

"No!" I said a little angrily. "That was only a dilettante's quest for unendurable pleasure indefinitely prolonged — a pedant's study of intricate patterns and gestures — the grammar and rhetoric of love without its poetry. Witchcraft is elemental and beautiful. It is the symbol of creation which Christianity considers vile and ugly. It's the rebellion of body and soul against the sterile creed of the Nazarene."

"Superstition!" Cartaphilus exclaimed. "Mohammedanism, Judaism, Christianity, Witchcraft — all, all of them. What we must bring into the world is Reason, Salome! I shall combat the monster of ignorance with intelligence — always!"

Kotikokura nodded so violently and so frequently, that I feared his head would drop to the ground.

"Intelligence, certainly, Cartaphilus — but like a bitter drug coated with sugar that mankind may swallow it."

"Have you succeeded, Salome?"

"I first tried to rule the Church from the inside by making a woman Pope."

Cartaphilus laughed. Kotikokura held his stomach.

"And what happened, Salome?"

"You are in a facetious mood. I cannot speak to you, Cartaphilus. And as for Kotikokura, he is no better than you."

Cartaphilus kissed my hand, and begged forgiveness. Kotikokura kissed the hem of my cloak, and assumed the severe and pompous expression of a watch-dog.

"Poor Joan!" I murmured.

"Who is Joan?" Cartaphilus asked.

"Pope John the Eighth — the greatest, the wisest, the purest of all Christian Pontiffs."

Cartaphilus knit his brow.

"Was there a John the Eighth who ruled the Church? I thought it was a mere legend. I suspected it was some more of your wizardry, like that in Persia, or you yourself sitting upon the throne of St. Peter's, a triple crown upon your lovely head!"

"You know that, like yourself, I never sit upon thrones, but rule the world from behind them."

"Our skin is worth a hundred popedoms and monarchies. By the way, why did you take the risk of joining the Crusades? It's dangerous! Are you susceptible to wounds?"

"One of my husbands — I forget which or in what country — in a fit of jealousy stabbed me in the throat with his hunting knife. He fell dead, whether conscience-stricken or poisoned by my blood which entered his body through a scratch I inflicted upon him, I can't tell. At any rate, I was ill for several days, and had an ugly scar for a few generations. It disappeared entirely, as you can see."

I raised my head. Cartaphilus kissed my throat.

"I had a similar experience. One of my wives bit off part of my small finger in a fit of love or hate. She, too, died on the spot. The finger grew back — look!"

I reciprocated his gallantry by kissing his finger, biting it with the tips of my teeth.

Kotikokura beat his chest.

"What's the matter, Kotikokura?" I asked. "This is not the Wailing Wall. What or whom are you mourning?"

Cartaphilus burst out laughing.

"Show Salome the spot where the robbers stabbed you, my friend, when you defended me against a dozen daggers."

Kotikokura blushed. With turned head, he exposed his powerful chest, once covered with hair sufficiently thick to protect him from the most inclement winter, but now cleanly shaven like a Roman Senator's.

A faint thread — like a cicatrice — was still visible. I bent to kiss it. He withdrew.

"Kotikokura!" Cartaphilus exclaimed. "Do you refuse the most beautiful, the most exquisite lips in creation? For shame!"

Kotikokura shrugged his shoulders.

"Tell me about John the Eighth, Salome," Cartaphilus asked.

I recounted the story of Joan.

"She loved you, Cartaphilus, and you, Kotikokura."

Kotikokura screwed his nose.

"You knew my whereabouts, Salome. You always know. Why didn't you send me a message to come to Rome?"

I did not satisfy his curiosity.

The Moon had climbed overhead like a giant spider creeping over the ceiling.

"The time has come, Cartaphilus. We must go our separate ways."

He tried once more to persuade me to remain, but I was obdurate. For a long while I remained in the delicious embrace of my lover. Finally, I tore myself away.

"Farewell until we meet again."

Kotikokura called to my attendants.

I mounted my horse and rode slowly over the top of the hill, swinging my sword like a silver kiss.

CHAPTER FORTY-TWO

I WALK ALONG THE SEINE — I MEET A BLACK CAT — THE MESSAGE OF THE BLACK SPANIEL — MASTER FULTON TAKES OFF HIS FINGER — DIANA, MISTRESS OF HELL — LE JUIF ERRANT QUI PASSE — THE WANDERING JEWESS? — MASTER BELLONIUS DRINKS WITH ME — I BUY A SOUL — THE WITCHES' COVENANT.

I WAS walking leisurely along the Seine, twirling my cane, and watching the tug-boats move insensibly across the water like things in a nightmare.

I had not been in France for a century, and nostalgia for the faces I had once known here passed over my heart like gray clouds. Marianne and Isabelle, lovely virgins who were my wives; Alphonse my husband; Marie, the orphan, whom I adopted and raised, and who disappeared one day with a young sailor; Bodin, the scholar, who knew all the languages of Europe, but who stammered so atrociously, that he finally conversed with his fingers; the poets who wrote sonnets to my beauty; the philosophers who stole my ideas; the courtesans who loved and hated me — all dead. Their very tombstones, if still existing, were thinner than leaves in autumn and tottering under the weight of birds which rocked themselves upon them a moment before taking flight.

Here, too, I had spent some time with Cartaphilus in delicious banter and in a dream of love. Kotikokura, like a resurrected Pan, played the flute, and danced about us while Lakshmi, the Wandering Tortoise, tapped my ankle, counted and drew magic circles, eyeing longingly her admirer, the High Priest of Ca-Ta-Pha.

I was aroused from my reverie by the sudden approach of a woman whose chin and nose were sharp arrows. She whispered in my ears: "Monsieur! Monsieur! Watch for the black cat that will cross your path!"

She jumped away like a kangaroo carrying her young.

I took a few steps, and encountered an enormous black cat which came majestically toward me, and rubbed her head against my legs. I caressed her. She purred like the snoring of a young lion.

Underneath her thick fur I discovered a bit of parchment on which something was written, too tiny for the naked eye. I placed the missive under the magnifying glass that adorned my Solomon's seal, and read:

"Monsieur, I am Yvonne your slave. Our Coven meets at Domremy, in the forest, near the lake, at the hour of the rat, the day after to-morrow. In the name of Diana, Mistress of Hell, Amen!"

The cat sneezed and climbed quickly to the top of a tree, from where her phosphorescent eyes, like two coals snatched from the fires of Hell, glared at me.

A little farther, an old beggar moaned —"Charity! Charity! in the name of Jesus, Charity!"

As I stretched my hand to place a coin in his cup, he opened wide his eyes, and straightened up like a young fir tree.

"Monsieur! Monsieur! Have you seen the black cat?"

"Yes."

"Watch for the black spaniel, Monsieur!"

And immediately he resumed his haggard air, and the darkness of night crossed over his face.

"Charity! Charity! In the name of Jesus!" he moaned.

I continued my way.

From one of the alleys, a dog came yelping toward me, as if some one had stepped upon his paws. He was jet black, except for a white circle around his rump. His ears swept the ground. His broad muzzle shivered like a blade of grass in the wind.

I whistled to him and snapped my fingers. He approached, crouched at my feet, and wagged his furry tail.

Under his leather collar, I discovered a note which read: "I am Suzanne, your slave! Is the Coven to be in the sign of the Bull or the Goat? In the name of Diana, Mistress of Hell! Amen!"

I scratched out the word "Bull," and replaced the note under the spaniel's collar. I clapped my hands. The dog dashed away, yelping desperately.

In the distance an old woman caught the spaniel, removed the collar, then beat him with a broom.

In the square, I noted a juggler surrounded by men and children, applauding and laughing at his tricks.

The keen black eyes of my friend, Master Fulton of London, twinkled under the enormous turban, and the heavy false mustache did not hide his shrewd mouth.

As soon as he caught sight of me, he proclaimed pompously: "Messieurs, I am now going to show you the greatest, the strangest, the most magnificent spectacle ever performed in any part of the world. Look at my left hand, Messieurs! Look well, gentlemen! How many fingers have I, Messieurs?"

"Five!" several voices answered.

"Count them, mon ami," he said to a boy.

The boy took Master Fulton's hand in his, and counted — "Un, deux, trois, quatre, cinq!"

"Splendid, mon enfant!" He pinched the boy's cheek. The boy screamed. The spectators laughed

"Because you are so clever, mon enfant," Master Fulton said, "you shall get my little finger as a souvenir to show your grandchildren that you have witnessed the greatest, the most astounding, the most marvelous spectacle ever presented in the four corners of the Earth."

Master Fulton made many gestures, uttered many fantastic words whose references and hidden meanings I understood, and finally began the process of removing his long sensitive fingers.

The tricks seemed so real that the spectators shuddered. Master Fulton offered generously his severed limbs —

long bits of pastry — to the children — and finally turned to me.

"Monsieur," he bowed to the ground, "may I offer you my thumb?"

He removed gravely his thumb, and placed it in my palm.

"Merci, Monsieur. And may I offer you in exchange a sow's ear?"

The people laughed. I placed a purse in the juggler's palm. It disappeared instantly in his sleeve.

"Monsieur," Master Fulton said pathetically, "has a man's thumb no greater value than a sow's ear?"

As usual, he was never satisfied with the money I gave him, although his belt was well-lined with my ducats. But he was too valuable to me as an organizer, to quarrel with him about his price.

"Very well, Monsieur," I said, "I shall add a pig's knuckle to the sow's ear, but not one fur of cat, nor a tail of spaniel more.'

I placed another purse in his hand, which followed the other in the wide sleeves of his black robe.

He bowed and thanked me profusely, while the spectators laughed, slapping one another's backs.

"Au revoir, Monsieur!"

"Until we meet again."

A little farther I bit into the thumb of Master Fulton, and found a piece of paper, rolled like a tube.

"Your slave Fulton, Monsieur! The names of Satan and Diana, King and Queen of Hell, be praised now and forever! I have converted Bishop Vandersee of the Netherlands. Thrice he has performed the holy black mass at a secret altar of the Cathedral. Three priests of Paris have sworn allegiance to you, Monsieur. Before long I shall bring to you, Monsieur, an entire nunnery. Heaven is melting in the flames of Hell!"

The success of Witchcraft seemed assured. The Christian religion which belittled woman was destined to disappear. The era of my sex was at hand.

Cheerful, I whistled to myself an old Roman song I heard in the days of Herod, my grandfather.

Suddenly the dust rose and whirled about me like an enormous top. A chilly wind blew angrily through the narrow alleys, beating furiously against the sails and the masts. Large drops of rain splashed upon the ground like the flat feet of ducks.

I entered quickly a wineshop.

The proprietor, pouting his lips and shaking his head, said: "C'est le Juif Errant qui passe, Monsieur."

I asked him what he meant.

"Monsieur must come from a far-off country not to know. For every one here knows that whenever there's a sudden storm like this one, it's the Wandering Jew who passes."

"The Wandering Jew?"

"The Accursed One, Monsieur, who blasphemed against our Lord Jesus! He must tarry until the Lord returns, and wander about always. The wind that you hear is his sighing, and the dust is due to the enormous shoes he wears. They say they are half-a-league long, and made of iron with long spikes inside."

He laughed. "You can imagine, Monsieur, what corns he must have. That alone would be enough to make him howl. They say that at midnight, if you listen closely, you can hear him groan — 'Jesus, forgive a miserable sinner!'"

I thought of the elegant Cartaphilus, driving in chariots or riding on Arabian steeds with saddles trimmed with gold and jewels, in search of unendurable pleasure indefinitely prolonged, and laughed in my beard which, like a triangle, adorned my face.

The proprietor placed my order upon my table and wiped his hands in his apron, the clean parts of which glistened like stars in a muddy sky.

"Tomorrow we'll hear of the boats wrecked and the sailors lost at sea — not to speak of the roofs torn off houses and the beasts killed."

"It is hardly conceivable, my friend, that this storm should cause such a universal disaster. It seems to me it has already abated somewhat."

He opened the door and looked out, sniffing like an animal.

"You may be right, Monsieur. The storm is abating. Perhaps it wasn't the Wandering Jew after all. Or maybe it was only his shadow."

"Or perhaps it was the Wandering Jewess," I laughed.

"The Wandering Jewess?"

"The Wandering Jewess, Monsieur, is a witch. She is Diana, Chief Devil of those miserable creatures who practice black magic," a tall man with a long white beard and white hair flowing over his shoulder, sitting at a table opposite mine, interrupted.

He raised his glass, and added pompously, "I drink the health of the honored guest!"

I returned the courtesy and begged him to sit at my table.

He seated himself opposite me.

"A bottle of your oldest vintage, Patron," he ordered.

"Yes, Monsieur."

A young man entered timidly. He cast a glance at us, and seated himself at a table in the corner. His large black eyes shone out of his pale sensitive face like glowing coals. His thin lips trembled. Who was he? Of whom did he remind me?

"Monsieur," the old man said, "I am Master Bellonius, pupil of Bertrand Trevisan, the world's greatest alchemist."

"I am Sebastiano, merchant from Genoa."

He rose and bowed, the tip of his beard swimming in his cup. Conscious that his cloak was threadbare in several places, he took it off, placed it over his knees, and wiped his forehead with an enormous red kerchief.

The innkeeper appeared, the bottle of wine high in the air.

"The finest in the world."

"The finest in the world, perhaps, Patron," I said, looking at the young man, "but not the oldest or the finest in your cellar."

The innkeeper protested.

"Tut! Tut! Bring us one of the bottles of Lachrymæ Christi which you are reserving for Bishop Renaud. They are hidden in the corner near the two barrels."

The man looked at me bewildered. Master Bellonius smiled. "Monsieur has been here before."

I made no remark. The innkeeper walked away sheepishly. The young man closed his eyes and breathed deeply. Who was he? Where had I seen him these many centuries past? Whom of my lovers did he resemble?

The innkeeper brought the new bottle of wine, and placed it on our table.

Curious to know what strange stories circulated among the people about Cartaphilus, I said: "Master Bellonius, the Wandering Jew is merely a legend, n'est-ce pas?"

"No, Monsieur!" he exclaimed. "The Wandering Jew is as alive as you and I!"

"Who is he really?"

Master Bellonius placed his elbows upon the table, while his beard, like a white napkin, here and there spotted by the yellow drippings of the yolk of a soft-boiled egg, spread in front of him.

"When our Lord Jesus—" He crossed himself. I did likewise. The innkeeper followed suit.

"When our Lord Jesus," he repeated, as if the first time had been merely an invocation, "walked His last walk to the Place of Skulls, where he was to be crucified by the damned Jews—" He stopped a moment to spit. The innkeeper did likewise. Unwilling to appear unsociable, I imitated the men, remembering with much amusement that what these people considered the symbol of utter disgrace, was a mark of reverence and worship among the tribe in Africa where once I was goddess. I could see them again invoking the blessings of the Sun, and puncturing every prayer with streams of saliva. The spittle contained fragments of their souls, which they sacrificed to Heaven.

Master Bellonius continued:

—"Isaac, a cobbler's son followed our Lord on His way to Calvary. When the Master asked him to carry His cross, he taunted Him, crying: 'Go on, go to your self-chosen doom!' The Lord, fastening His eyes upon him, said: 'I shall go, but Thou must tarry until I return!'"

The innkeeper, who had probably heard the story numberless times, seemed nevertheless very much interested in the words of the alchemist. He bent over the counter, his hands in his apron, nodding ceaselessly.

"Ever since that time, more than fourteen hundred years ago, Monsieur," the old man continued, "Isaac wanders from one corner of the Earth to the other, praying to the Lord to relieve him of his accursed burden."

I laughed. "He must be as ancient-looking as the olive trees in my country, and his beard must drag in the mud like the skirts of monks," I said, my words really addressed to the youth, who watched me with utter admiration.

Master Bellonius roared with laughter. The innkeeper threw his head back and shook in silent merriment.

Master Bellonius filled the glasses again, and toasted my health.

"The Wandering Jew," the alchemist resumed, "does not become old, Monsieur. His body, like his soul, neither lives nor dies."

"If he is always young, he ought not to be so miserable, then."

"Oh, if he were young because of the magic which is the Lord's essence, he would be happy indeed! But his body and soul rot always. He is like an embalmed carcass. Night and day he howls in pain and sorrow."

"They say there's so terrible a stench of corruption about him, Monsieur," the innkeeper added, "that he who comes near him, faints."

"But, Master," I pursued, "does the Wandering Jew do nothing but bewail his fate?"

Master Bellonius flared, indignant.

"He gives gold to the damned Jews!" He stopped again to spit, which seemed to be a sort of ritual whenever he mentioned my people. "That they may continue in their heresy and hate toward the Christians. That's why the dogs are so wealthy, Monsieur."

"That's true, Monsieur," the innkeeper nodded.

"Where does the Wandering Jew get all his money, Master?"

"He is in league with the Devil," he answered sanctimoniously, "who accompanies him in the shape of a gorilla. It isn't real gold but bits of iron painted yellow, whose falseness no human eye could detect, but which turn black in the alembics of the alchemist."

I was astounded at the accurate knowledge of the main details of the life of Cartaphilus my beloved. He was a cobbler's son and a converted Jew. He taunted Jesus who pronounced the judgment of endless life upon him. He wandered, always young, over the face of the Earth, so wealthy that he was supposed to be in league with the Devil — Kotikokura evidently. Poor, delightful Kotikokura — Devil and gorilla! He stirred the people against Christianity and helped the Jews.

That he was the power behind many thrones, that queens and empresses had been his mistresses, that he was the hero of many glorious legends — that Cartaphilus had been able to conceal.

Master Bellonius wiped the dripping wine from his mustache.

"Master," I asked, "is the Wandering Jewess the sister of the Wandering Jew or his mother?"

He laughed. "The Wandering Jewess is not really a Jewess. She is a vampire who battens on the blood of men. She is Lilith, the first wife of Adam, who afterwards assumed the shape of the wicked queen Herodias, and later that of her shameless and lascivious daughter Salome, who sold the head of John for a dance. Now she lives in the Moon and rules the bodies of women. Her blood is cold like the blood of crocodiles and tortoises and the seed of devils."

"They say she takes the shape of a tortoise, as big as an elephant," the innkeeper added, as he returned from serving the youth.

Who was he? I looked at him again. His eyes met mine yearningly.

"Does the Wandering Jewess ever take the shape of man?" I asked.

"Monsieur," Bellonius answered proudly, "it is easier for

a camel to pass through a needle's eye than for woman to take the shape of man."

The innkeeper threw his head back, and laughed boisterously.

The alchemist pursued: "She may tighten her breasts and squeeze in her buttocks, and even paste a false beard on her face, you can always tell her sex."

"How?"

"By her smell, Monsieur."

He wrinkled his nose.

"My dog can tell a bitch ten leagues away," the innkeeper said. "He begins howling and moaning like the Wandering Jew!"

"Besides, Monsieur, you and I know that a woman can't utter a sentence without showing her irrationality."

To overcome my impulse to slap his face, I struck the table a vigorous blow.

"Another bottle, Patron," Master Bellonius commanded.

"Yes, Monsieur!"

The innkeeper dashed into the cellar, in spite of his protruding stomach and short legs.

He returned quickly, out of breath.

"Tell the Bishop, Patron, that twenty-two bottles of the tears of our Lord should suffice him."

The innkeeper opened wide his mouth. The bottle hung by the neck precariously in his fist. His limbs turned outward, as if he had suddenly become bow-legged.

Master Bellonius laughed.

"Open the bottle, Patron! Don't look so dismayed at Monsieur's jest. Monsieur is the Bishop's friend, who told him of his little treasure in your cellar. N'est-ce pas, Monsieur?"

I smiled. "Master Bellonius could never be suspected for a woman in man's disguise. His logic is unimpeachable."

The alchemist, overcome by my mock compliment, grasped my hand. The innkeeper pulled the cork with a great flourish. The youth in the corner, pleased with my mind reading, smiled to me.

"As long as there is wine like this in France," the Patron

said, rubbing his hands in his apron, "why worry about the English?"

"Is it true that the French armies have been defeated again?" I asked.

The alchemist nodded. "We are a nation of women, Monsieur. We cannot wield arms any more. As for our military leaders —"

"They say that Gilles, Lord of Retz, is a genius — that he could save France if —"

The Master spat, and whispered in my ear:

"Monsieur, the Lord of Retz is a witch! He has sold his soul to the Devil."

"Is he not a white magician?" I whispered.

"He was, Monsieur, while under the influence of my great Master — but now he prefers the tail of the Devil to the cross of the Saviour!"

Was it possible? Had Gilles finally become one of my followers? Master Fulton would have informed me about it. His nose was sharp and his ears cocked to all rumors.

Master Bellonius raised his arm, and spoke, as if he addressed a multitude of people.

"What we need is gold. Gold is mightier than armies. Gold — pure gold — Christian gold — gold which blossoms in the retort of God-fearing alchemists!"

The word "gold" rang in his mouth like a long succession of chimes.

"Is it true, Master, that alchemy really transmutes base metals?"

He struck the table. The cups tottered.

"Parbleu! Is there a man, Monsieur, who still doubts it?"

"I profess my ignorance, Master. I have never had the privilege of witnessing such a marvel."

"You are fortunate indeed to meet me, then — for I shall show you not alone the transmutation of base metals into fine, but also"— he looked around the shop, and whispered into my ear, his beard tickling me like a sheaf of straws — "I have just filtered the final draft of the elixir that gives eternal youth —"

I looked at his long white locks and beard and his forehead creased like a sheet of yellow parchment. He placed his emaciated hand upon my shoulder, and smiled.

"In a few days you will not recognize me, Monsieur. I shall be younger than you."

"That may be, Master."

"Will you accompany me, Monsieur, to the laboratory?"

I should have wished to see how this charlatan tried to rob me of some gold coins, but I was anxious to reach Domremy, where the Coven was to be held.

"You honor me greatly, Master, but I must postpone the visit. I have important business to transact."

He was crestfallen.

"Tomorrow, however, at this time, should you wish it, I shall be here again."

"Good!" The innkeeper rubbed his hands.

"Very well, Monsieur. Tomorrow," Master Bellonius said pompously.

We rose. Master Bellonius made believe much embarrassment in adjusting his cloak. Meanwhile I paid the bill.

The innkeeper thanked me profusely. I shook hands with the alchemist, looked at the youth again, and left.

As I turned a corner, I felt some one pull my cloak gently. I turned around.

The youth I had seen in the wineshop grasped my hands.

"Monsieur! Monsieur!" he whispered, "I renounce God and Jesus! I am your slave now and forever!"

The tone of his voice brought back like a sudden wind the image of the one he resembled so strikingly. It was Daniel, my lover of Jerusalem, fourteen hundred years dead now! I could see him again, his dazzling white skin, his lips burning with passion, seeking my body. I could hear him shriek vile epithets at me. I could see him lie still in a pool of blood, the knife shivering over his chest. A great pity and tenderness for this youth, Daniel reborn, overwhelmed me.

"Who are you?" I asked.

"I am Robert de Vosges, your slave now and forever! I have been following you, Monsieur, the whole day. I was sure from the moment I saw you that you were not a man."

What! Had this youth's eyes pierced through my disguise

when for generations no one suspected my femininity? Was his nose keener than the alchemist's?

"Who am I, Robert?" I asked, hoping dimly he would say —"You are Salome, my love!"

He kissed my hand, and said: "You are he who is more powerful than Jesus! You are he whom I have worshiped in secret for a long time. You are Lucifer!"

I smiled. Daniel thought I was a witch. This youth, true to his prototype, considered me the Devil.

I watched him in silence for some time, trying to recapture the ancient thrill.

"I have sought the truth in white magic and alchemy. They are mere words and sham, Monsieur. Master Bellonius who was speaking to you is an old scoundrel robbing strangers of gold coins and beating apprentices. I am willing to forsake everything and every one, to follow you, Monsieur!"

There was something in the tremor and slight huskiness of his voice which indicated that it was not solely the love of witchcraft, but an unconscious love of me, which prompted his determination.

I longed to press him to my breast and whisper to him: "Love me, Daniel — Robert, love me!" I had been a man for too long a time, and weary of women's caresses. But my beard and my exalted diabolic rôle restrained me.

Besides, pity for the youth overflowed my heart. My love could only end in tragedy for him.

"Robert," I said, pressing his arm, "leave both black and white magic alone. It is dangerous to dabble in them. Man cannot cope with the mysterious and mighty forces of Nature, and live."

"Monsieur —" he pleaded, "Monsieur —"

Determined to save the youth from the possible fate of the others who loved me, I offered him a purse with gold coins.

"Robert, here is enough money to start you on any enterprise. Go your way, my friend, and forget you ever met me."

"Oh, Monsieur, do not scorn me!"

"It is not scorn, Robert," I said tenderly, "but my compassion for you which prompts me."

He laughed a little ironically. There was something of Cartaphilus in the drawing of his breath.

"Enterprise, Monsieur? Business, perhaps? I am a poet!" he said proudly.

"Very well, Robert. Here is enough money to keep you in affluence for the rest of your life. You will create works which the world will prize forever."

He hid his hands behind his back.

I remained silent, considering what to do. Should I accept the love of this youth? Should I jeopardize his life and happiness? Should I refuse him?

Considering my silence an unfavorable reply, Robert drew a dagger from underneath his cloak, and bared his chest.

I grasped his wrist.

"What is the meaning of this, Robert?" I exclaimed.

He let the dagger drop to the ground.

"Let me sign the covenant, Monsieur, with my blood!"

"Very well," I said at last, "since you will it!"

I kissed his shoulder, grazing the skin with my teeth, the symbol of the covenant.

CHAPTER FORTY-THREE

MONSIEUR PIERRE DE BOURLEMONT RETURNS TO DOMREMY — THE POET WITHOUT A SWEETHEART — ROBERT IN LOVE WITH MY SHADOW — I DISAPPOINT MY CHEF — ONE HUNDRED AND SIXTY DISHES.

We rode through the forest, cool as the patio of a Moorish house. Our horses trotted lazily on, unguided.

Robert delighted me by his intelligence. He had something of Cartaphilus, of Daniel, of Onam and of Joan. Like mother-of-pearl, his mind and face reflected now one, now the other. Had he been a woman I would have dedicated him to an exalted position in Witchcraft. That he was a man, both irritated and rejoiced me.

"Robert, what is your opinion of woman?"

"Monsieur, I love and revere woman!" he exclaimed as a challenge to my question, in which he detected a shade of derision placed on purpose to test him.

"Woman is the light of the world, Monsieur! She is the touchstone by which a civilization can be judged. Tell me how you treat woman and I shall tell you how prosperous, how happy, your country is."

He waited a moment for my praise at the new twist of an ancient proverb. But I was too pleased to speak. My heart leaped at his words. I had not heard such eulogy since the time when Ulric gave me his heart on the shores of the Tiber.

"Why is France at the mercy of her enemies? Why have we no longer great artists and poets, Monsieur? Because we scorn woman, Monsieur! Because we do not worship at her shrine! Some day I shall write a new Roman de la Rose. I shall surpass Guillaume de Lorris and Jean de Meung in my praises of woman. I shall sing her beauty and her grace, her perspicacity and her intelligence. I shall sing her love and her tragedy!"

His black curls darted bluish rays. His lips trembled, his nostrils shivered like a thoroughbred's.

Was it Joan who spoke in this youth? Was it an unconscious feeling that I was a woman?

"Is it your sweetheart, Robert, that you are praising in terms of womankind?" I asked, laughing.

"No, Monsieur, I have no sweetheart."

"What! No sweetheart — a poet, handsome, clever and nineteen?"

I pressed his hand and looked into his eyes. He turned his face away, unwilling to show how deeply he blushed.

After a long silence, he said: "Monsieur, I am in love!"

"So I thought!" I laughed heartily. "What princess, what queen, has captured your heart?" I asked banteringly.

"She is a Queen, indeed, Monsieur!"

"On what throne does she sit, Robert?"

"You will laugh at me, Monsieur, if I tell you who she is!"

"No, Robert," I said tenderly, "I shall not laugh. On the contrary, I shall help you obtain her graces — if she happens to be a little reluctant."

He sighed.

"She shall sleep in your arms, Robert, I promise you, even if she has dedicated herself body and soul to the Holy Virgin or if I must convoke her from the kingdom of the dead."

He looked into my eyes, but, dazzled by the light in them, his eyelids drooped.

"Alas, Monsieur, it will not be so easy!" he muttered.

"Is she dead?" I asked solicitously.

"Who knows whether Salome is dead or alive?" he sighed.

"Salome?" I whispered, my voice a falsetto, which happened whenever unconsciously I wavered between my male and my female rôle.

"Salome, whom fools call a vampire, and cowards fear. Salome, symbol of beauty, of joy, of love!"

"Where did you see Salome, Robert?" I asked.

"As a child I saw a picture of her in a book. I fell in love with her. Since, I have read every story about her and listened to every legend. I worshiped her image in marble and in color. I have vowed eternal love to her. Moved by my passion, she visits me in my dreams, Monsieur."

"How does she look in your dreams, Robert?"

"Her body is a white flame. She dances before me, Monsieur, as she danced before the King of Judea. But when I try to embrace her, she laughs and disappears. Her laughter is the song of a cage of nightingales. How fortunate was Jokanaan, Monsieur! I would gladly relinquish my head for a kiss of Salome! I seek her mouth as a swift-running river seeks the sea!"

His eyes blazed. He breathed heavily.

"Salome!" he whispered, gazing into the distance.

"I can see her now, Monsieur!" he exclaimed suddenly. "She dances among the branches of that tree yonder, Monsieur!"

"That is my shadow, Robert," I said, smiling.

He looked intently.

He sighed. "It's madness, Monsieur, I know. Salome is an illusion, a will-o'-the-wisp. She is Fata Morgana haunting the minds of men. Alas, Monsieur, having seen Salome, how can mortal women entice me? Their wiles are ridiculous. Their kisses chill. They are angry at me for scorning them. In their indignation they even call me shameful names. I am dying for the love of Salome, Monsieur!"

He covered his face with his hands.

I placed my arms around him.

"Robert," I whispered into his ear, "Salome shall be yours!"

He grasped my hands.

"Monsieur, give me Salome for a day, and keep my soul and my body forever!"

"Salome shall be yours, Robert," I repeated.

"Monsieur, shall I be able to endure the joy of her

touch? Shall I be able to kiss her lips and not die of the bliss?"

"Salome is yours," I sighed, "but whether she shall bring you happiness or sorrow, Robert, I do not know."

"I do not seek happiness, Monsieur. I seek Salome and, if need be, death. For this I relinquish God and Heaven and Parnassus. For this I am your slave, Monsieur, unto the end!"

The sun, a golden platter, crashed against the trees and broke into a myriad fragments which glowed between the hoofs of our horses.

In the distance Domremy nestled timidly among its hills. On the top of one of them lay the Château de Bourlemont, drowsy like an aged woman. I had bought it during the Crusades, and from time to time I lived in it, experimenting on animals and educating Lakshmi in the grand manner of the salons.

Several months previously I ordered my agents to have the castle renovated and made habitable again. As Pierre de Bourlemont, sole heir to the ancient house of Bourlemont, I was returning to my paternal estates.

When we reached the foot of the hill, three men on donkeys came galloping to meet us. They jumped off the animals and made obeisance.

"Seigneur, I am Richard, your steward, and these are François, your chef, and Joseph, your groom. The rest of your servants, Seigneur, are in the castle awaiting you and your guests."

"I have only one guest to-night, Richard. My retinue will arrive later."

"One guest?" he asked, astonished, his side beards, like an Assyrian monarch's, shivering on his heavy red cheeks.

"I prepared a banquet for one hundred," François said, his hands in the air.

"For one hundred?"

"Your ancestors, Seigneur, never entertained less. And my grandfather, who knew your grandfather, Seigneur, used to tell my father when he was a boy that the lords of the

Château de Bourlemont were the envy of the King, Seigneur."

"Those heroic times are gone, Richard. People are not what they used to be."

"That's what my grandfather says," he sighed.

He pulled at his beards until I thought they would remain in his hands like wisps of dry hay.

"Seigneur, I have invented forty new dishes for to-night's banquet," François said pathetically, his eyes creeping out until they hung on the rims of their sockets like desperate people wavering on the edges of precipices.

"I have prepared patties of beef à la Lucullus, pies of leveret seasoned with twelve Arabian spices, tongues of herons, swans, cranes, and buzzards. I have roast of stork à la Charlemagne, and venison of bear à la Nero. I have salads of bryony and mallow sprinkled with mace, caraway, poppy, rosemary, hyssop and ginger, I have ———"

Fearing that he would never end, I interrupted him — "How many dishes, François, have you all in all, since forty are of your own invention?"

He meditated for a few minutes. "One hundred and sixty, Seigneur!"

I burst out laughing.

"François, things have changed. Only in Africa people still consider enormous paunches the symbol of nobility and beauty. Slimness is all the rage at the civilized courts nowadays."

François was scandalized.

"Seigneur, the nobility will not look any different from the starved peasants who live on onion soup and black bread."

"We shall have to find other signs of blue blood, François."

Seeing his desperation, I placed my hand upon his shoulder and said: "My friend and I will honor your dishes."

"Thank you, Seigneur, thank you, Monsieur," he added, addressing Robert.

The three men mounted their donkeys and trotted behind us.

CHAPTER FORTY-FOUR

THE WITCHES' SABBATH — THE MASK OF THE GOAT — THE VICEROY OF HELL — HOLY DUALITY — PHALLIC PÆANS — SWOLLEN EARTH — HELL'S SACRIFICE — A BANQUET OF CORRUPTION — AN ANCIENT FRIEND RETURNS.

"This wall of vapor will allow us to witness the Coven, Robert, without being observed ourselves. I prefer not to mingle with my worshipers this night."

The youth was strangely pale. In his eyes trembled a dream.

"Robert," I whispered, my lips touching his ear, "tonight, after the Coven, Salome shall be yours."

His shivering hand gripped my arm as if to steady himself.

"I shall conjure her from the bosom of Time and make her your bride, Robert, for a night — or forever."

"Salome," Robert murmured, pressing nearer to my side.

Whose voice was it? Who pronounced my name? Who was this youth whose heart fluttered like a bird startled in its nest?

"Will you recognize Salome, Robert?" I asked timidly.

"I have known her for centuries, Monsieur," he answered, his eyes half-shut. "Since the time when she was the most beautiful Princess of Judea and saints and monarchs offered their lives and their thrones for a kiss of her lips."

"And who were you then, Robert?"

"I was a poet singing the beauty and the love of Salome. Like a moon-struck prophet I wandered the streets of Jerusalem invoking the name of Salome."

"Did she love you then, Robert?"

"Once she deigned to look at me. The rim of the shadow of her robe touched my feet. I swooned. I died."

Robert stared at me bewildered, as if suddenly awakened from a profound sleep.

"Monsieur, have I raved again?"

"You have told the truth, Robert. You have known Salome for centuries, and she loved you. You were Poet and Prophet and King. Alas, you always died for her love. To-night, however, she will be yours, my friend."

"I feel her presence already. It is as if her perfumed breath were playing upon my face, as if I heard the echo of her voice, as if she caressed me with phantom fingers."

"That is true, Robert. Salome is beside you. Her love envelops you. When the Moon which tips the hills yonder disappears to the West, and the Sun is a thin silver line mingling with the blue of the horizon, Salome shall lie in your arms!"

Robert knelt and kissed my hands.

"Monsieur, my soul is your slave forever!"

I pressed my lips against his forehead burning with fever.

"Rise, Robert. My worshipers are coming. To-night I have appointed my Viceroy to be among them. He will tell them of the truth of Heaven and Hell and Earth."

The witches came singly and in groups, flying on broomsticks, crawling like snakes, hopping like birds, wabbling like bears, galloping like horses, barking, meowing, howling, hooting, braying, neighing, crowing, bellowing, cackling, whistling.

Some carried torches, others candles, which cast fantastic shadows in the reflection of the full moon.

Each one stopped and knelt backward to the altar, a large rock from the center of which rose an obelisk, the form of a priapic cross.

Suddenly they remained silent, crouching against one another in awe. The Grand Master approached, hopping. He wore the mask of a goat. Two black horns rose from his temples, and between them a tall black candle flickered.

A white skin surrounded his loins and buttocks, and a red tail trailed on the ground. His feet were shod in boots cloven in two like hoofs. An ivory phallus, black and spiral-shaped like a screw, preceded him, casting an enormous shadow.

The worshipers marched in a long single file, and one by one kissed the symbol of the Grand Master's sovereignty, his buttocks and the rump of the tail.

He made a sign and all squatted about him, their hands underneath their knees.

"In the name of Diana, Mistress of Hell!" he exclaimed.

"In the name of Diana, Mistress of Hell!" they repeated.

"And of Satanas, Master of Hell!"

"And of Satanas, Master of Hell!"

"And of Evil, Daughter of Hell!"

"And of Evil, Daughter of Hell!"

"Amen!"

"Amen!"

"Speak! How have you honored the Kingdom of Hell since our last Coven?"

One by one, the worshipers recounted their deeds:

"I have rid a man's bed of a too faithful wife, Master."

"I have twisted the tongue of a woman who took the name of Satan in vain."

"My neighbor's cow will remain barren even if mounted by a dozen bulls, Master. She made the sign of the cross when the name of our Lord of Hell was mentioned."

"There is death in the family of a churchgoer who blasphemed Lucifer."

"The lean, hungry dog which Françoise chases out of her kitchen is her own husband. She is seeking him everywhere, while he is at her door yelping. He betrayed one of your worshipers and married a churchgoer. Let him bark at her door, until she poisons him, Master."

"Yvonne is no longer a virgin, Master. Her offspring belongs to our Mistress, Diana."

"The three gray mice I gave Marie are sucking her soul

out of her. She will come to the Coven at the next full Moon, Master."

"I have gathered the aconite, Master."
"I have gathered the poplar leaves."
"I have gathered the soot."
"I have gathered the baby's fat."
"I have gathered the cinquefoil."
"I have gathered the deadly nightshade."
"I have gathered the sweet flag."
"I have gathered the bat's blood."

The Grand Master praised, admonished, warned the idle ones, threatened all with severe beating, death, plague, mutilation, sterility, impotence, if they did not work zealously for Diana and Satan.

Suddenly he called out: "Jeanne Darc — Jeanne Darc!"

A profound silence fell upon the worshipers.

He rose and stamped his hoofs.

"Is she not with us?" he bellowed more like a bull than a goat.

The witches moaned, groaned, neighed, crowed.

"Marie, Isabel, Helen, come forward!" he commanded.

A hen, a cat, and a fox approached the Grand Master, making noises according to their nature.

"Silence, Daughters of Hell!"

They formed a circle, holding hands.

"You were appointed to bring Jeanne Darc. Where is she?"

"She would not come!"

Their voices sounded like cracked iron bells.

"Silence!"

They made three circles.

"She is ours. Her grandmother was a fairy. She sold Jeanne's soul to the Infernal. Jeanne is not a woman, although she is seventeen years old. Her blood does not belong to the Moon, but to our Mistress Diana. Jeanne is predestined to be a witch! Bring her hither!"

He stamped his hoof furiously.

"Mix Jeanne's food with aconite," the Grand Master commanded.

The three witches answered: "Yes, Master."
"Mix it with the deadly nightshade!"
"Yes, Master."
"Coax her, threaten her, praise her, scare her. Bring her to us, or you shall roast at a small fire in Hell forever!"
"We shall bring her, Master!"
The Grand Master hopped to the altar. All the witches hopped after him.
He sprinkled the altar, exclaiming:
"Lord Satan, visit us!"
The congregation repeated: "Lord Satan, visit us!"
"Aquerra Goity!"
"Aquerra Beyta!"
"Cabron Arriba!"
"Cabron Abaro!"
The Grand Master turned to the worshipers and sprinkled their heads.
"Sanguis eius super nos et filios nostros!"
"Sanctus, Sanctus, Sanctus, Satanas, Satanas, Satanas!"
"Pleni sunt infernus et terra gloria tua!"
"Per omnia sæcula sæculorum!"
"Amen!"
From the orifice of the obelisk in which before the arrival of the witches I had placed a chemical, a stream of black smoke rose and a smell of sulphur pervaded the air.
The witches jubilated.
"Satan is with us! Satan is with us!"
The Grand Master jumped upon the rock. The others made a wide circle about him, and holding hands began to dance.
Seven times they turned around, then broke loose.
The Grand Master jumped off the rock, and exclaimed:
"Har! Har! Satanas! Satanas!"
Suddenly there was a great whir in the air as if a large flock of eagles flapped their wings, and a black steed descended amidst the witches, too awestruck, too terrified to utter a sound. Upon the steed rode the lordly Viceroy of Hell. He was dressed in a scarlet velvet robe. Two golden

horns rose from his temples. His face glowed with phosphorus. From the nostrils of the steed curled blue smoke. From the tips of the Viceroy's fingers, as he blessed the prostrate worshipers, issued cloven flames like the long nervous tongues of vipers seeking prey.

"In the name of his Majesty Satanas, Lord of Hell, and of her Majesty Diana, Lady of Hell — the Holy Duality!" the Viceroy pronounced.

"Amen," the witches muttered, pressing their faces to the ground.

"And to the endless glory of Her who rules the Moon — whose perfect name is too sacred to be uttered save in the Holy Precincts of the Lower Kingdom!"

"Amen!"

"Hearken, Children of Hell! The throne of Jahveh, the jealous father devouring the happiness of his children, is tottering. His kingdom is coming to an end!"

"Praised be Satan!" the witches howled.

"His priests are forsaking him and his heaven for the glory of Hell!"

The worshipers uttered a roar of triumph.

"No longer shall the Usurper of Heaven throttle souls and bodies! What are his laws but denials of pleasure? What is his virtue, save a eunuch's consolation? Is not Sin the quest for self-expression? Is not Sin the urge to partake of the feast of Nature? Is not Sin the passion which impregnates the Earth with the seed of Beauty?"

The Viceroy cracked his whip, and the air split with flashes of lightning.

"Hail, Messenger of Satanas and Diana," the witches exclaimed, their arms flung in the air.

"Jahveh and his bishops have spread the lie of the Trinity! Father, Son and Holy Ghost! And where is the Holy Mother? Does not the Mother precede the Father? Does not the Earth antedate the seed? Jahveh and His Trinity are routed, pursued by the truth of Satan and Diana, the Holy Twain, Man and Woman!"

"Hail, Satan and Diana! Hail, Man and Woman!"

"The Tyrant of the Sky has terrorized the Earth with

names. He has called Satanas the Evil One, the Archfiend, the Father of Lies, the Archenemy! He has invented the fable of the hatred of Ahriman and Ormazd! But Ahriman and Ormazd, Light and Darkness, are one, even as Day and Night are one, the two faces of Truth! Good and Evil are one! Man and Woman are one! Satan and Diana are one!"

The witches, as if prodded by irons, rose, and began to dance wildly about the Viceroy.

Robert muttered like a man in sleep: "Monsieur! I worship you!"

The Viceroy cracked his whip. The witches fell upon their faces.

"Athwart the horizon the Gods of Life are returning to Earth — Odin and Eros and Persephone and Athena and Priapus and Aphrodite and Apollo and Freya — male and female, harbingers of Beauty and Joy and Power and Freedom! Satan and Diana and She the Perfect One are leading them to victory! Rejoice, for yours is the kingdom of Earth and of Hell!"

"Amen!" the witches thundered.

"In the name and to the glory of the Holy Twain!"

"In the name and to the glory of the Holy Twain," the witches responded.

Out of the horns of the Viceroy burst forth flames, followed by a cloud of black smoke which enveloped the horse and the rider.

"Avaunt!" the Viceroy commanded.

In the air a whir, as if a large flock of eagles flapped their wings — and a sudden blaze, as if a meteor flew through space.

The Grand Master stamped his hoofs.

"Dance here!" he ordered.

"Dance there!"

"Saute ici!"

"Saute là!"

"Play here!"

"Play there!"

Violins — trumpets — tambourines ——

Wild, mad dancing — back against back — belly rubbing belly — bodies clinching like wrestlers — legs and arms and heads shaking convulsively — whipping of buttocks, tearing at breasts — shouting, screaming, howling!

Bodies thrown into the air — bodies rolling upon the ground — bodies falling upon bodies — indiscriminate. Flesh and wood and ivory pressing into flesh, tearing, bleeding, clawing. Pain and torture and joy!

Man turned to bull and stallion and frog and goat and hog — Man turned to Earth — Earth fecundating — Earth swollen with life — Earth pregnant — Earth bursting with Spring — Earth united again to Earth by the umbilical cord — Dung and blood — and flesh — Genesis!

Robert, maddened by the orgy, danced about me, pressed against the trees, moaned.

Suddenly he shouted, "Salome! Salome!" pointing to my shadow which broke through the vapor and stretched among the witches.

"That is but the shadow of Salome, Robert."

Robert, his bloodshot eyes glaring at me, did not hear.

"Salome will be yours at dawn!" I whispered.

"Salome!" he repeated, rushing among the witches.

There was a sudden lull among the monads of Hell followed by shouts of triumphant jubilation.

What happened? Had the witches heard Robert pronounce my name — my name which could be uttered only in the Holy Precincts of Hell? Would they assail him for the profanation? Would they hail him as another messenger of Satan? I dared not leave my place of concealment. I had not provided for this emergency.

In the insane convulsion of bodies I could not distinguish Robert.

Suddenly in the distance a cock crowed. Another answered him. A third chimed in like an echo.

The Grand Master tottered to the altar and blew a ram's horn. The shadow of his ivory priapus, and the shadow of the horn formed a grotesque cross in the distance.

The witches dragged themselves to their feet like somnambulists awakened upon the edges of roofs. They mounted their brooms and vanished.

I rushed out.

"Robert! Robert!" I called, the echo of my voice breaking the early dawn like glass.

In the slimy and nauseous remains of the Witches' Sabbath Robert lay, blood oozing from every orifice of his naked body, like black wine out of a jug cracked in numberless places.

"Robert!" I whispered, bending over him. "Robert!"

It seemed to me that he made a vague movement.

"Robert, Salome calls you."

His lips moved as if to call my name.

"Robert," I sobbed quietly, "you have been sacrificed on the altar of Salome! It is thus my worshipers worship me!" I added bitterly.

A sudden tremor convulsed the body of the youth for a moment, then his limbs stretched and stiffened.

A great misery overwhelmed me.

I propped against the obelisk from which a thin thread of smoke rose upward like a sword balancing itself upon the nose of an acrobat.

A flock of noisy crows turned in circles. An owl hooted in one of the trees. In the distance several dogs barked to one another disconsolately. The Moon was a thin colorless sheet of paper which children cut to make toys. The first rays of the sun touched warily the rim of the hill as if still uncertain whether to proclaim the conquest of Day over Night.

Something pricked my ankle. I thought it was a bramble, and bent to pull it out, when my hand touched a pulsing, scrawny thing.

"Lakshmi! Lakshmi!" I called out overjoyed.

I placed my arms around her neck, and smoothed her carapace.

The Turtle pecked at my ankle, shook her head, nodded, looked upward, tapped the ground twenty times, made magic circles. Was it to show that after an absence of a century she still remembered what I had taught her, or bewildered by her joy in finding me, her mute and imprisoned body sought means of expressing itself?

"Is it really you or one of the witches enchanted into a giant chelonian?"

Lakshmi stretched her neck forward. Vishnu and the Moon shone upon her plastron like eyes.

"Lakshmi," I said, my voice a sob, "they have killed my lover! I cannot leave his beautiful body to rot or be devoured by these birds of prey which anxiously await my departure. Salome was a flame of beauty to him. Let the flames embrace him!"

I built a funeral pyre and placed gently upon it the mutilated body of him who possessed me in his dreams. . . .

CHAPTER FORTY-FIVE

THE TABLE MANNERS OF LAKSHMI — I SEARCH FOR A REDEEMER — REVERIE.

I was balancing on my Chinese chopsticks the tender bones of a young squab which François, my chef, had roasted and prepared with two dozen spices. My only guest was Lakshmi, who sat opposite me at her table, eating cabbage with the punctiliousness of a princess of Cathay.

"What a generation, Lakshmi! They find it inconceivable that a person should bathe daily. One of my servants crosses herself every time I come out of the pool. And yet, they find it a most natural phenomenon for the Devil to accost them on the road and bid them sign their souls away with their blood. They would not at all be astonished to encounter Jesus and the saints. Every virgin has visions of Paradise."

Lakshmi sneezed.

Our tables were set on one of the balconies of the Castle, which afforded an excellent view of the village of Domremy.

I could not tell which delighted me more — the mingling of the perfumes which rose to my nostrils or the delicate aroma of the spices which invaded my palate.

I raised my cup filled with a wine that dazzled like molten gold.

"A votre santé, Madame!"

Lakshmi flourished a leaf in the air.

"Lakshmi, life is not an evil after all. Of course, we never can tell whether it is a good or an evil, since we have nothing to compare it with, and things have meaning and value only in relation with one another."

I replaced my glass on the table.

"Nevertheless, as long as the body functions properly and the senses are satisfied, we may say that life is not an evil. Do you agree with me, Lakshmi?"

Lakshmi struck her beak against the bowl.

I sighed. "No, it is not quite so, Lakshmi. There are things that gnaw at the soul more painfully than the canker which devours the body."

Lakshmi appeared untouched.

"To see one's work misinterpreted, misapplied, misjudged, O Lakshmi — how can a turtle understand the torments of the spirit?"

Lakshmi looked at me, one eye shut.

"I cannot forget the horrible Witches' Sabbath when my poor Robert was mangled and mauled. How did my worshipers understand the words of my Viceroy? For the freedom of the soul they substituted the lust of the body. They turned the Kingdom of Hell into a cesspool of bestiality. Who are my followers, Lakshmi, but frustrated souls, frustrated bodies, seeking in the tortuous bypaths of sex the adjustment and stability which life denies them."

I filled another glass.

"The broomstick cannot supplant the cross, Lakshmi. Diana cannot conquer Jahveh!"

The bell of a neighboring church rang drearily like a hammer striking nails into a coffin. The monotonous dingdong of Christ cast a gloom about us. I replaced the morsel I held in my hand upon the platter, and Lakshmi turned her eyes upward as if in disconsolate meditation.

"Man, Lakshmi, considers himself the Martyr of Creation. Pompous tragedian, he chooses torture as the symbol of his soul. He would rather strut about, protagonist of sorrow, than dance joyously, buffoon of pleasure. Clown of Fate, he pierces his own heart that he may seem dignified to the indifferent stars."

Lakshmi, entirely unconcerned with the Destiny of man, once more resumed her air of imperturbability.

I struck my glass against the table.

"Lakshmi, that is why Christianity succeeded and neither my Witchcraft nor the Logic of Cartaphilus shall ever destroy Christianity! In the shadow of the cross, man worships with greater delectation than in the glow of the sun! Jesus was the most astute of actors. Had he relied upon his teachings his name would have long been forgotten. Other poets, other prophets before him, said what he said, preached what he preached. But the Cross, Lakshmi, the Cross!"

Lakshmi dipped her paw in the bowl of rosewater.

I stood up.

"Lakshmi, woman will never be saved until she immolates one of her sex on the cross!"

Lakshmi looked at me.

"No, Lakshmi, Salome cannot accept apotheosis with all its attendant dangers. Salome will be the first and the last of the Holy Trinity — Mother and Holy Ghost — invisible, inscrutable, unexplainable. But who will be the Daughter of the new Godhead, the Middle Figure — flesh and blood, and pain?"

Lakshmi wiped her beak.

"Where can I discover a suitable sacrifice, Lakshmi? Who is great enough for the Cross?"

I looked at her intently.

"Alas, my ancient friend, why are you not a human? What a magnificent sacrifice you would make!"

Her eyelids drooped in disdain.

"I understand. You prefer a cabbage-leaf to martyrdom. That's what distinguishes your race from ours — not your clumsy legs or carapace glittering with the image of your husband and the symbol of my enemy, the Moon."

She began to descend her ladder.

"Oh, Lakshmi, if you only knew the magnificence of illusion! If you only guessed what beauty lies beyond reality, what gorgeous vessels sail beyond the horizon!"

As if to spite my efforts to civilize her, Lakshmi began to drink noisily out of her trough, shaking her head like a bird.

A few straggling soldiers marched by, beating a drum

drearily. It was one of the decimated companies, leaderless, disheartened, that lost contact with the main French army. Wandering from village to village, looting, robbing, drinking, they shouted imprecations against the Dauphin.

"Look at the flower of manhood, Lakshmi! See the meaning of valor, my friend! If woman showed as little courage and prowess, man would roar with laughter, cover her with ridicule, and pull the remnants of her weapons out of her hands! Why don't we treat man with equal scorn? Why does woman, her hands upon her lap, helpless, wait at the mercy of man's vagaries?"

Lakshmi made a magic circle with her beak.

"Are you invoking the spirits, Lakshmi?"

Lakshmi looked up, then closed her eyes slowly.

"Not the spirits, Lakshmi, but a real woman, flesh and blood, who could show mankind that her sex lacks neither strength nor courage! A woman who could lead these bedraggled soldiers to victory!"

Lakshmi nodded.

"Not that it matters in the least whether the English or the French own the land they are disputing. What matters is that woman show herself glamorously heroic! Man is a child. He does not recognize valor and prowess save theatrically, Lakshmi. It must be so among tortoises also. The male of the species is attracted by surfaces only."

Lakshmi, for no reason that I could see, began to count, tapping the floor with her forepaw.

"Sorcery, money, ammunition, everything is at her service — but where is the woman, Lakshmi?"

I walked up and down the balcony, my hands upon my back, passing in review all the women that I knew in various parts of the world, intelligent, beautiful, crowned. No, not one was suitable!

Suddenly the name of Jeanne Darc rang in my ears. Was it the spirit of one of the witches, captured by the magic circle of Lakshmi, that whispered the name? Who was this girl, granddaughter of a fairy, whose soul was pledged to Satan, but who refused to join my worshipers? Who was this girl, who, at seventeen, had not yet become woman —

whose blood belonged to Diana, not to the Moon? Why was the Grand Master so anxious to make her a witch?

The attendants of Lakshmi came to take her out for a walk. Other servants cleared the tables. Richard, the steward, brought me my Chinese pipe and liqueur.

I reclined upon a divan, and smoked. The smoke took the shape of Cartaphilus, of Ulric, Herod, and my Arabian husbands, one by one in a long file. For the time being, I forgot my mission, woman, the Moon. My pipe dropped out of my hand, and I fell asleep.

CHAPTER FORTY-SIX

MAID, BOY OR FAIRY? — THE HIDE AND SEEK OF LIFE — "I AM JEANNE DARC, SEIGNEUR"— JEANNE'S FREEDOM FROM THE MOON — I PLAN A CAMPAIGN.

I was walking in the garden, Lakshmi at my heels. The sun began to set, and the leaves of the trees merged slowly into one another.

Suddenly, from the direction of the spring which in forgotten times had cured fevers and agues, a voice as clear as the running water, singing a patriotic martial air, arrested my attention.

Was it a youth or a girl? There was a gentle quiver in her throat which reminded me of another voice I had heard — was it only yesterday or hundreds of years ago?

Who was it? Was it a fairy — one of the fairies reputed to dance and sing around the great Charmed Tree, the Arbor Fatalium, from which every twelvemonth May the Bride of Spring was born?

I whispered to Lakshmi to return to the Castle, while I walked on tiptoes in the direction of the mysterious singer.

Underneath the Arbor Fatalium, unaware of my presence, a shepherdess continued to sing, while a little away a half-dozen sheep were grazing and bleating.

Her hair, her profile, her voice, Joan — Joan d'Anglois, Pope John the Eighth, my unforgettable companion! Was it possible? Did people come to life again after the lapse of centuries? Was death merely a game of hide and seek?

Was life a colossal merry-go-round, in which the same figures turned and turned forever?

"Joan," I whispered softly.

The girl stopped short in her singing, and looked around. Her full face was even more startlingly akin to my friend's — the same nose, the same eyes, the same lips, the same chin!

She did not see me, and resumed her song.

"Joan," I whispered again, a little more loudly.

She rose, frightened.

"Who is calling me?" she asked, in a voice not soft enough to be a woman's, not deep enough to be a man's.

"Seigneur!" she caught her breath.

"Your singing pleases me greatly. I am sorry I interrupted you, Demoiselle."

She blushed, but regained her poise. Her body was lithe and tall. Dressed in manly garb, her feminine attributes could hardly be discernible.

"Forgive me, Seigneur. My sheep strayed into your grounds. I should have driven them out, but instead, I took a rest, and sang."

"Forgive you, my child? Why, I am delighted. I am sorry your sheep did not stray into my garden before ——"

"They did, Seigneur, for, in truth, I drive them here myself from time to time. I love to sit under this tree and watch the spring yonder. I used to dance around it with my friends when I was a child."

Her frankness delighted me. There was little of the shepherdess about her. She might have been a lady — or a youth — brought up in a Lord's manor.

"I often dream of the fairies that once dwelt in this tree, Seigneur. My grandmother used to tell me about them."

"Do they not dwell here any more, Demoiselle?"

"I do not know, Seigneur," she sighed.

I looked at her, studying every trait and comparing them to my ancient friend's, now, alas, less than the echo of the breeze that ruffled the leaves, less than the last trembling ray of the sun.

"What is your name, Demoiselle?"

"I am Jeanne — Jeanne Darc, Seigneur."

I started. I could not tell whether it was because the name reminded me of Joan, or because this child was the one mentioned at the Witches' Sabbath.

The sheep, scared by a crow that dashed by, ran off, huddling together.

"I guess I had better go, Seigneur."

"Where do you live, Jeanne?"

"Yonder, in that gray house, opposite the Church. You can see it from here, Seigneur."

She made a motion to go.

"Do not go yet, Jeanne. Don't worry about the sheep. They'll turn back. Won't you sit down again, as before, and sing me a song?"

She looked at me, her eyelids lowered like a bashful boy.

"If Seigneur desires ———"

I nodded.

Again she sang, the quiver more pronounced, like the catch in Pope John's voice, a patriotic ditty. Meanwhile I broke the branch of a tree and made a garland which I placed gently upon her head.

She looked up and smiled. "Merci, Seigneur. I shall hang the garland on the blessed Mary of Domremy."

"No, Jeanne. Keep it. It will bring you good luck."

"I shall keep it, Seigneur."

"Why do you always sing martial songs, Jeanne?"

Her face changed. She was positively a youth.

"Because," she answered, her voice thoroughly masculine, "I love France and her King. If I were a man, I would be a soldier and fight to the death for my country's deliverance from the English yoke. Our men are cowards!" she added disdainfully.

"Women have been warriors, Jeanne. Many a queen was mightier than the kings of her day."

"Our women, Seigneur, do not dare. If I could don a soldier's uniform, I would march to the front, my sword unsheathed. Alas, a woman must wear skirts and stay at home leading sheep!" she said bitterly.

Was it the desire to wear man's clothing that prompted her patriotic outburst?

The sheep were bleating pathetically.

Jeanne rose.

"I must go home. It is getting dark."

"Will you come again and sing for me, Jeanne?"

"If Seigneur desires."

"Tomorrow and every day, Jeanne. The grass is excellent here."

"Merci, Seigneur!"

She kissed my hand and called to her animals.

I watched her fine boyish body swing until it disappeared from view.

Could she lead and inspire an army? Would man obey her, and through her glorify womanhood? Would the strangeness of her sex, which set her apart from other women, impel her to heroic deeds and sacrifices? Was it essential for woman to differ from her sex in order to wield power? Zenobia, Cleopatra, Pope John the Eighth, all women and yet not women! This shepherdess also — a woman but free from the dominance of woman's archenemy — the Moon! Was Jeanne the Woman of Destiny? Would she have the courage, the endurance, the will-to-power to outgeneral Man? A woman became the wisest of popes. Could a woman become the mightiest of soldiers?

I deliberated for a long while.

Lakshmi approached with an air of dignity, as became the wife of Vishnu.

"Lakshmi, is Jeanne the Woman of Destiny?"

Lakshmi placed her paw upon my foot.

"So be it!" I exclaimed at last. "The die is cast!"

How should I go about it? Merely giving the girl a soldier's uniform would mean nothing. I must inspire her with an indomitable will! I must awaken in her a martyr's or a prophet's passion!

Satan she would not accept. The witches could neither frighten her nor persuade her to join their ranks. Not the Devil, but the Saints must visit her. What black magic could not accomplish, white magic must. Jeanne was too sensitive, too much the child of her generation, not to believe in mysterious forces. Besides, was she not the granddaughter of a fairy? Did she not come to the Arbor Fatalium in hope of hearing once again the voices that she heard in her childhood?

"Come, Lakshmi, I must plan my campaign in the solitude of my closet, and put in working order my magic lamps and other such trifles."

CHAPTER FORTY-SEVEN

I AM ST. MICHAEL—JEANNE DOFFS HER CLOTHES—THE REAL MIRACLE—GILLES, LORD OF RETZ, WRITES A PLAY—BLUEBEARD'S LIBRARY—BLUEBEARD'S MINION—WHITE MAGIC AND BLACK—GILLES DE RETZ DREAMS A DREAM—THE BOY-GIRL OF DOMREMY.

"Jeanne! Jeanne! Jeanne!"

I threw my voice from various parts of the garden as if I had been approaching her from different directions at the same time.

Jeanne rose startled.

"Jeanne! Jeanne! Jeanne!"

My voice approached the spring slowly. Jeanne made a motion to go in that direction. I changed swiftly the sound, so that my voice reached the Arbor Fatalium, under which she was standing.

"Jeanne! Jeanne! Jeanne!"

My voice touched her body.

She knelt.

"Who calls me?" she asked, trembling.

My voice spoke directly over her head, as if I had been standing there.

"St. Michael, in the name of the Father and the Son and the Holy Ghost!"

The reflection of the lights which I manipulated from my hiding-place flooded the tree and Jeanne with white flames.

Jeanne made the sign of the cross.

My voice mingled with the flames as if coming out of them.

"Thrice has St. Catherine visited you, Jeanne, that your soul may be purified and your heart obedient. I come now in the name of Jesus, Lord of the World, to order you to save your country, Jeanne! You shall lead the King's army to victory!"

"The Lord be praised!" she whispered, her face uplifted.

"Come forth at dawn, and you shall find at this tree a horse and a soldier's uniform. Don it, and ride at the head of the army, in triumph."

"I shall come at dawn, as you command."

I changed the flames from white to red, which lapped like great tongues the body of Jeanne.

Jeanne gasped and fell in a trance.

I approached quickly, and put a ring upon her finger, as a sign that what she had heard had not been merely a dream.

The sun grasped with his myriad fingers the crest of the mountains. The stars, aware of the presence of the God of Earth, took flight one by one. The moon, too proud to acknowledge defeat, still lingered, her train threadbare and lusterless hanging among the branches of the trees.

Jeanne came to the Arbor Fatalium with a firm step. A white horse was pawing the ground impatiently. Over its saddle hung the complete uniform of a French soldier.

Jeanne knelt and prayed in silence. A beatitude like that of the saints of the Italian painters flooded her face. Suddenly, however, the features tightened, her mouth set. She unsheathed her sword, and raised it above her head.

"Vive la France et son Roi!" she exclaimed.

She threw off her shepherd clothes and her wooden sabots. Her body was as delicate, as firm and as luminous as the sun which crowned the mountain. Save for the slight efflorescence of her chest, where two tiny moles glowed like rubies, she might have been a youth. Her limbs were straight and her arms well molded and muscular.

Jeanne struggled with the martial clothing as a child who tries on her mother's gown.

She twisted her braids around her head, and placed the helmet upon it, a trifle at an angle like a vain warrior in search of romance.

She walked to the spring, and mirrored herself within it — a soldier, but still a woman!

Like a young god riding Pegasus, Jeanne contemplated the landscape, made the sign of the cross, and waving her sword like a flag, galloped away.

My heart was heavy, whether with great joy or great sorrow I could not tell.

"Lakshmi, to what divinity shall I pray that our venture prove successful? The gods will doubtlessly hinder us, and the goddesses have been slumbering too long to be much concerned."

Lakshmi raised her head, and stretched her neck.

"We shall pray to no god, Lakshmi. Let us proclaim the end of the age of the gods, and the beginning of the age of Woman!"

I raised my arm upward, Lakshmi raised one of her paws, and nearly fell upon her back, crushing the image of her husband and breaking the moon into stars.

A watchman of the castle informed me that a soldier, on horseback, was at the gate asking an audience.

"Let him enter!"

From the window I could see Jeanne tie the reins around the trunk of one of the trees, and follow my servant. Her carriage was proud, her step confident, and her face had the seriousness and assurance of a person long accustomed to command.

Jeanne entered, and saluted. I noticed that the helmet had descended lower over her head, and understood that during her absence she had sacrificed her braids to the profession of arms.

"Seigneur," she said, when we were alone, "I am Jeanne Darc, soldier in the King's army."

I pretended great astonishment mingled with a little irony.

"What! Does the King engage women to combat his enemies?"

"I am charged by one greater than the King, Seigneur, to free my country from the English yoke!"

"Who is greater than the King, Jeanne?"

"St. Michael, Seigneur. He came to me in a vision and commanded me to lead the King's armies. He brought me a horse and a soldier's uniform."

"St. Michael? How do you know it was St. Michael, Jeanne?" I asked sternly.

Jeanne looked into the distance, her eyes transfixed.

"He came riding naked upon white flames, and his voice rolled about me like thunderclaps."

Where was that gentle, unsophisticated shepherdess of a day ago? Overnight she had acquired an uncanny power which for the moment bewildered me.

"Seigneur," she said, "I have come to ask you to take me to the King."

"To the King, Jeanne?" I feigned astonishment.

She paid no attention to my intonation.

"Yes, Seigneur, that he may allow me to lead his armies against the English, in the name of France and St. Michael."

I smiled vaguely.

"The King, Jeanne, may not be so easily persuaded to allow a woman to command his men, even if you could convince him that St. Michael himself came riding naked upon white flames to visit you."

She looked at me proudly.

"St. Michael will dictate the words required to convince the King."

A strange light illumined Jeanne's face. She who some hours previously had been the dupe of a ventriloquistic trick and the play of magic lanterns, had acquired a new and transcending personality. She was no longer my creature. The tiny spark I ignited had blossomed into a flame. I was as surprised as Jahveh must have been when His words incarnate became a universe.

Jeanne waited, calm and unperturbed, her hands gripping the hilt of her sword.

I rose.

"Very well, Jeanne. I shall help you gain admittance to the King."

"Merci, Seigneur," she said simply, as one thanks a passer-by for the information as to the whereabouts of a neighboring town.

"Before we can approach the King, however, we must win the confidence of Gilles de Retz, the richest man of France and the most valiant champion of the crown. He can persuade the King more easily than St. Michael."

"Order your men to get ready, Seigneur, we must start at once."

A little amused a little startled by her dictatorial air, I obeyed.

Gilles, Lord of Retz, was in excellent spirits. His wife, whose attentions had long annoyed him, had retired to one of his castles on the Loire; his military exploits were crowned with success; but chiefly, his play, a vast pageantry based upon the life of the saints, had stirred to wonderment the entire nation.

From all parts of his enormous patrimony, whose boundaries were the Loire, the Atlantic, and the frontiers of Poitou, his vassals had come to do homage to his histrionic and dramaturgical abilities. Dignitaries of Church and Army applauded vociferously. Only the Dauphin had stayed away, ostensibly because of illness, but as every one knew, from duke to peasant, because jealousy of the young lord gnawed at his entrails. And only his former guardian and uncle raged and fumed impotently to see the richest Barony of France dwindle to satisfy an insatiable vanity for display and pomp.

Gilles had just changed his actor's garb for his golden armor encrusted with gems.

His tall lithe body concealed great physical strength and his black hair and eyes uncontrollable passion.

He smoothed his soft downy beard which darted short

rays of blue with his long white hand sparkling with jewels.

The guests stared in awe at the regal luxury of the Castle. The walls were covered with cloth of gold. The ceilings glowed with magnificent frescoes. The floors were tiled with white unveined marble from the rarest Italian quarries and jade which pirates had stolen from the sacred temples of Cathay.

Every bedchamber had ewers of gold embossed with Greek and Egyptian designs, filled with rarest perfumes of Araby and India — myrrh, attar, heliotrope, rose, jasmine, wild clove, cinnamon, olibanum.

The library, the largest in France, contained manuscripts of great antiquity, including some which had been saved from the flames at Constantinople and Alexandria. Bindings of velvet and crocodile and ivory. Pages illumined by the great masters of Italy and Spain and the Orient.

People whispered of the labyrinthine secret rooms with subterranean passages and laboratories where alchemists who never saw the light of day solemnized with mystical rites the wedding of rare metals.

The ladies, melancholy, sighed, for they had already discovered that neither their beauty nor their coquetry could captivate the most charming, the most cultured, the most spectacular Lord of France. Young officers in quest of commissions and prelates of fine bearing in quest of a bishopric, strutted about like cocks to attract the attention and, perhaps, the fickle affection of Gilles.

For the time being, however, they were doomed to disappointment. For the Lord's eyes and ears and tongue, sweetened with the honey of poetry, were all for the new choir boy, whose arm he held tightly locked in his, as they walked up and down the halls.

The youth's eyes, a little moist from emotion, were riveted upon Gilles. His blond curls grazed from time to time the cheeks of the Lord, as the latter inclined to hear more distinctly what the youth whispered.

"Rossignol, no nightingale in the Palace of the Son of Heaven in Cathay has ever sung half as sweetly as you sang today."

The boy blushed deeply.

"No nightingale, my Lord, has ever sung for so munificent and magnificent a Master."

"I am not your master, Rossignol. And henceforth call me Gilles."

The youth hesitated.

"Call me Gilles, Rossignol!"

The boy whispered in his ear: "Gilles!"

The Lord of Retz pressed the boy's arm, until the latter caught his breath.

Gilles looked at him, his eyes darting a strange flame, his lips twitching.

The youth started.

Gilles de Retz smiled.

"Do you fear me, Rossignol?" he asked, his teeth gleaming like a young wolf's.

The boy shuddered, and shook his head.

The secretary, who knew the Lord's moods, considered this a propitious moment to inform Gilles that Baron Pierre de Bourlemont had brought him "The Book of the Dead," the sacred bible of the Egyptians, an extremely rare manuscript, illumined and bound in the skin of the crocodile of the Nile, studded with the pearls which once adorned the throat of a Pharaoh.

Gilles unclasped his arm from the arm of Rossignol, and looked at the precious gift. His eyes blazed a new lust, and his face shone with intelligence. He was no longer the actor, the sensation-monger, but the scholar, the philosopher, the voracious seeker of knowledge.

Gilles ordered his secretary to take the book to the library, and approached me. He thanked me effusively, and discoursed on the religion of Egypt with a precision and insight which astonished me.

Gradually I switched the conversation to politics, and, imperceptibly, reached the military situation of France. By that time we had left the halls, and were walking in the garden, whose splendor and exotic nature were in consonance with the rest of the palace and the character of the owner.

Gilles raged against the Dauphin and Georges La Trémoille, the power behind the throne. He could not forgive the imprisonment of the Duke of Brittany in the Castle of Choison.

"France!" he said contemptuously. "Is there a France? King? Is there a king? King of Bourges!" he said, laughing ironically, "that's all — King of Bourges!"

I praised his own military exploits and spoke of certain Roman tactics which might be used to excellent advantage. The Lord became enthusiastic. He was neither the dandy nor the scholar now, but the soldier.

This man, I thought, had the capacity of becoming the most ruthless despoiler of his generation or its mightiest genius. And I recalled that all men of consequence wavered between good and evil, between Ormazd and Ahriman. The slightest turn in the scales made the god or the demon.

At an appropriate moment in the conversation, I introduced the subject of Jeanne Darc. I recounted her life and her origin, her visions, and her sudden change of character — all except my share in the miracle. I emphasized the fact that the Moon had never subdued her body.

Immediately the Lord of Retz became interested.

"Where is this prodigy?" he asked.

"She is awaiting us yonder, my Lord," I answered, pointing to where Jeanne, riding proudly upon her horse, her sword piercing the reflection of the Moon, looked like a statue of silver carved in a block of marble. The rays which played around her helmet surrounded her head with a halo.

Gilles caught his breath.

"She is not a woman, Baron! She is the spirit of Youth! She is Apollo! She is Mars, when Mars was young, and marched to divine victories!"

In vain I sought the features of the former shepherdess. Was it my words or the armor which had transformed her and strengthened and molded every feature? What strange alchemy, what alembic, had transmuted the base rustic metal into gold?

Rossignol approached timidly the Lord of Retz and tapped at his sleeve as a nightingale taps with its beak.

Gilles glared at the youth. His eyes darted once more the flames from the strange fire which was his soul. His tall brow knit making a deep valley terminating at the ridge of his nose. His nostrils opened wide and shivered. His beard suddenly glowed with a blue light like an amethyst in the dark. I realized why his enemies had nicknamed him Bluebeard.

The youth stammered, "Pardon, my Lord!" and skulked away.

"Jeanne Darc shall lead the armies of France," Gilles spoke, his arm outstretched like a man foretelling a prophecy. "She shall ride like a dream incarnate at the head of the troops. Her presence shall stir the breasts of men to valorous and heroic deeds! I swear it! I, Gilles, Lord of Retz!"

"When do we take Jeanne to the Dauphin, my Lord?" I asked when he had ended his apostrophe.

"At once, Baron! I shall order my men prepare for the journey!"

From a thicket a voice as gentle, as melodious as a nightingale's reached us as if flying upon timorous wings. For a moment Gilles stopped and listened enraptured, his lips opening slightly, and his eyelids drooping. How many men was this man? What demons, what angels strummed upon the lyre of his soul? What melodies, what cacophonies, were they destined to produce?

My thoughts provoking his, he said: "Baron, who am I? What am I?"

"You are the greatest genius of France, my Lord."

"Genius?" he said deprecatingly. "What is genius, if he still be man? I am beyond Man, beyond love, beyond hate, beyond good, beyond evil." He sighed. "Alas, Baron, I am not beyond death! Neither white magic nor black magic, Baron, gives eternal youth or eternal life. Neither Jesus nor Lucifer has power enough to change the Adamic curse."

"Neither Jesus nor Lucifer, my Lord, but man himself."

"How?"

"Some day he will discover a subtler way of creation. Not out of his loins, but out of his brain shall he have offspring. That offspring will be perfect. It will know neither the pang of birth nor the pain of death, and its every nerve will be attuned to joy, as every nerve now responds to pain."

He grasped my arm, and looked into my eyes.

"I shall be the Creator of a new race!" he exclaimed. "I, Gilles de Retz, shall be a greater Jahveh, who will need no Son to redeem his world, nor a Devil to tempt it!"

Into what flower of good or evil was the seed I had cast destined to blossom!

Suddenly, as if wrenching himself away from the new idea, he said: "Come, Baron, let us discuss our plan of attack with the boy-girl from Domremy."

CHAPTER FORTY-EIGHT

THE APPREHENSIONS OF LAKSHMI — THE ARSENAL OF AN IMMORTAL — JEANNE IS WOUNDED — JEANNE'S TANTRUMS — THE MOON WAXES OVER JEANNE — GILLES DE RETZ CRAVES AN AUDIENCE — I DISCUSS WHITE AND BLACK MAGIC WITH BLUEBEARD — WHY I NEVER LOVED GILLES — THE MARTYR'S CROWN FOR JEANNE — A CRUCIFIX OF FIRE — I GET ME TO A NUNNERY.

THE snow fell dismally like thoughts from a divinity suffering with the headache, and turned to mud as it reached the ground. The sky was a ceiling of dull steel, and so low, one bent instinctively not to strike one's head against it.

Our outpost, a rectangular wooden structure like a box constructed by a clumsy boy, lay in the middle of the road, ready to be kicked by the boot of a nervous giant passing by.

The battle had been on for three days, a dreary hand-to-hand skirmish. I dissuaded Jeanne from engaging in it, and Gilles considered the entire maneuver a tactical error. But the Maid was obdurate, and the Lord de Retz finally acquiesced, and joined her.

Our staff was on a reconnoitering tour, and only Lakshmi, the mascot of the regiment, and I remained, warming ourselves at the little stove which was more generous with smoke than with heat.

"Lakshmi, adorable tortoise," I said in the tongue of the poets who wrote the Rig-Vedas, for she understood me in whatever language the mood prompted me to use.

She tapped my foot with her paw.

"You are more precious to me than the sacred goat which the priests sacrifice to Agni, the Purohita, goddess of bounty."

Lakshmi tried in vain to utter a sound.

"Do not attempt to speak, Lakshmi. Let not the tortoise imitate man and parrot. Enough falsehood has already been uttered. One more straw may break the back of the Camel of Life."

Lakshmi tapped my ankle.

I stirred the fire, and wrapped myself in my cloak of a Captain in the French army, upon which shone a row of medals.

"Lakshmi, woman can no longer be ridiculed for lack of courage or military prowess. Jeanne has outgeneraled the best and the most seasoned in the manly profession of arms."

Lakshmi stretched out her forepaws like a dog.

"How did she accomplish it? It was not merely sorcery and the superior artillery which I had purchased, nor the excellent generalship of Gilles de Retz. Why did the soldiers, whose mockery of woman is proverbial, obey Jeanne, who did not even disguise her sex? Why did they willingly die for her? She is not the most beautiful woman in France, nor does she have the glamour of royal blood — a simple shepherdess, who can neither write nor read, dressed in the simple uniform of a private."

Lakshmi raised her head upward in sign of incomprehensibility.

"My words have tapped the World Reservoir in her soul, Lakshmi. They have awakened from its deep slumber the primeval Will of Woman. A hand buries a tiny seed in the ground, and moisture and the sun call to it in a mystical tongue. The seed breaks through rocks, and rises a giant oak, one hundred feet high.

"I was the moisture and the sun that stirred the seed in the soul of Jeanne. I never dreamed the tree would be so luxuriant, that its branches would touch the clouds. I thought I fashioned a creature, a Golem, obedient to my plans. Instead, an individuality has emerged which transcends my ideas, which transcends even me, Princess Salome, with the wisdom of fifteen centuries."

Lakshmi yawned, drowsy from the heat.

"Like a somnambulist, unerring, Jeanne led armies, defeated an enemy whose power was in vain disputed for nearly a century, crowned a king and fashioned a nation. Unless History persists in being gossip, scandal and falsehood, Jeanne Darc will be hailed forever as a greater general than Cæsar and Hannibal and my grandfather, Herod the Great."

Lakshmi looked at me, her circular eyes blurred.

"But why is Jeanne so irritable recently against her friends and aides-de-camp? Why did she undertake this campaign so patently wrong from every military point of view? Why did she scorn so petulantly my advice and that of Gilles de Retz? And what did she gain by marching against Paris, disobeying the King and incurring the enmity of the nobles? Even the soldiers who followed her blindly, commence to grumble. I have heard some sing a ribald song about Jeanne. What has happened, Lakshmi?"

Suddenly I remembered Zenobia and her irrational deeds.

"Is it possible, Lakshmi?" I asked, rising, and stamping my sword. "Is it possible that the Maid is becoming a woman?"

Lakshmi stood up suddenly. Her head moved in all directions at the same time. She crept into a corner, and looked at me wildly.

"What is the matter, Lakshmi?" I asked.

She crawled into her carapace as a child crawls underneath its quilt at the sight of a strange face which scares it. Only her beak stuck out grotesquely.

"What is it?" I asked, uneasy. "Are you ill?"

The question sounded ludicrous. Lakshmi ill! I had known her for a thousand years, and always her appetite was enviable and her mien cheerful. Could Lakshmi become ill? Could she ever die? Did she not possess, even more than I, the power of recuperation and renewal, being more elemental, nearer to the primeval fountain of Life?

I listened attentively. Vaguely I could hear now the echo

of hoofbeats. It was this that had frightened the tortoise.

"Do not fear, Lakshmi. No evil shall befall you or your mistress."

I pulled my sword out of the scabbard.

"One touch with the point of this and the enemy falls dead instantly. No snake's fang is half so sharp or half so deadly."

Out of an invisible pocket of my armor I produced a small gold box. I snapped it open.

"Look, Lakshmi. This tiny syringe which lies so snugly, so innocently here, contains a liquid more efficacious than a regiment of men. One spray of it and for a quarter of a league around, all living beings are paralyzed. They do not die, but for hours, for days even, they balance themselves like rope-dancers upon the thin line that separates being from non-being."

Lakshmi looked at me quizzically.

"Some day when human ingenuity will equal human cruelty man will consider arrows and swords and catapults mere toys. He will discover that tiny syringes concealed in golden boxes contain a vaster and swifter death than all the plagues of the Hebrews. I, at least, shall not speed that day, Lakshmi. I have come to build, not to destroy."

Lakshmi tapped my ankle.

"But do you think man will exterminate man from the Earth? I doubt it. He will invent counter-drugs and counter-poisons, and will continue to spawn on forever — perhaps."

Lakshmi cocked her head to the door.

"And if it should become necessary for us to vanish instantly, Lakshmi — this cross when released by a secret spring belches fumes which envelop us with a dark wall that no eye can pierce. We can gallop away to freedom. There are always steeds pawing the ground in my vicinity. Our enemies bewildered would seek us in vain. Then do not forget, Lakshmi, I can summon to my aid hypnotism and incantation, and sorcery and herbs and ointments — and beyond it all, the Life force which for some inscrutable purpose wills it that Lakshmi and Salome and Cartaphilus and Kotikokura be immortal! Still I shall take no risks."

Lakshmi, a little more confident, raised herself lazily upon her legs, and looked more like a bull than the wife of Vishnu.

"I do not know what battles you had to wage in my absence, Lakshmi. It may be comparatively easy for a tortoise to continue living for centuries without being molested. The life of man is an incessant warfare. My ancient friends, the Romans, used to say, *Homo homini lupus* — man is a wolf to men. If in order to live a generation or two, he must arm himself with spears and cuirasses and knives and drawbridges, and artillery, and locks and bars and poisons and codes of laws and religions — think how intricate, how elaborate, how deadly must be the weapons of one whose life is measured in terms of centuries, perhaps æons!"

From the distance a bugle-call sounded.

"No, it is not necessary, Lakshmi, to use any of our weapons or masks against the fumes. It's our own men returning."

I opened the door and listened attentively.

"There is something in the hoofbeats that bespeaks defeat, Lakshmi — or — has something happened — perhaps — to our Jeanne?" I muttered anxiously.

I lit a torch and waved it in the air.

A torch answered my signal.

"I was right, Lakshmi, it is a signal of distress. If our Jeanne is killed, Lakshmi, what a tragedy! But perhaps it's only Gilles de Retz, or some other general — " I said a little more hopeful.

"At any rate, let us prepare my herbs and ointments."

Gilles dashed into the room.

"Baron, where is the physician?" he asked.

"What's happened, my Lord?"

"Jeanne is wounded, Baron. Where is the leech?"

"He went with the other officers reconnoitering."

"I shall have him court-martialed, the fool!"

"Where is Jeanne, my Lord? I know enough of medicine to treat a wound in his absence."

Before he had time to answer, two soldiers brought the Maid into the room.

"Place her on the cot," I ordered the men. "Don't move her. That's right."

Jeanne's face was chalky white. Blood trickled to the floor in a thin long stream. Her armor was streaked with red and black.

Gilles paced up and down, swearing vengeance against the Burgundians, and the English, and vowing that he would have the physician's head.

I ordered the soldiers to undo Jeanne's armor, and leave.

Alone with Gilles, I stripped the Maid naked. The wound was superficial, and would be, I was certain, easily amenable to my treatment. In a few weeks, or even less, Jeanne could lead once more her embattled legions.

Gilles cast a long glance at the body of Jeanne, then turned his face, half in disdain, half in disillusion. He had recognized, as I did, that the Maid was no longer that strange creature hovering between boy and girl, but a woman. Her breasts were full, as if yearning for the lips of a new generation. Her hips had become rounder and plumper. Her legs had acquired the feminine contour. Her arms had a rotundity which obliterated their muscular power. Delicate curves accentuated her femininity.

The strange love Gilles bore the Maid suffered a shock. She was no longer the boy-girl of Domremy, a halo about her head. The male in Jeanne, in her body at least, had disappeared. But mine was a far greater disillusion. I knew that before long the Maid of Orleans would like the rest of womankind follow, shackled, the Argent Chariot of the Divinity who rules alike the blood in our veins and the waves in the sea,— who had not relinquished her dominion over my body for fifteen hundred years.

What I had sensed and feared was taking place. Jeanne was no longer the transcendent personality of a few months ago. She no longer tapped the Universal Brain. She was not instinct — the accumulated wisdom and power of ten thousand generations. The Womb of Life had cast her forth. Weaned from the Breast of the Primordial Will, henceforth she was a separate entity, guided by her own intelligence and logic, and therefore capable of error and fallibility. The conflagration I had ignited, had turned to ashes, where Jeanne must painfully seek for the embers.

From now on the blood that nourished her brain would be drawn to nurture her womb. Her unerring judgment would be the tribute exacted by the Moon. Even if her genius were as great as that of a Zenobia, she, too, like Zenobia, would be caught in the travail of potential maternity.

Lakshmi huddled in a corner of the room. I sat upon the divan, my legs underneath me, my head upon my chest.

"We have lost, Lakshmi. Jeanne is in prison. The King and the army are against her, and the priests have forced her to recant. Woman is doomed to failure, Lakshmi. Before the Maid paid her toll to the Moon she vanquished all obstacles. Her plans were infallible, her mind moved with the precision of the stars.

"She is woman now, a remarkable woman, a woman of genius — but a woman nevertheless. Her soul no longer transcends Earth's three dimensions beyond space and time. She has learned the meaning of fear and doubt and apology."

My steward entered to announce a masked officer of the King.

Fearing the sly intrusion of a spy of the Church, I leaned over the ramparts of the castle where a tall soldier was standing with three companions. His face was concealed by a silk mask. But something in his bearing was familiar to me. I recognized Gilles de Retz. Upon a sign from me the drawbridge was lowered and the Maréchal entered.

"Maréchal," I said, laughing a little, "the mask cannot hide the man."

Gilles removed the mask.

"Baron," he replied, "I did not wish to be recognized by the secret agents of Burgundy. I want to discuss with you the fate of Jeanne Darc. The boy-girl of Domremy will be consigned to the flames by Bishop Cauchon. The King is too cowardly to draw his sword for his benefactress. My army and my treasury are momentarily depleted. My estate is mortgaged to the hilt. I have come to you for assistance. You alone can save the savior of France."

For a long time I remained silent, watching the Maréchal stalking up and down the room. Time had played havoc with him. His face bespoke strange rites and stranger debauches. His eyes darted with a curious diabolic light and his beard seemed to glow a deep, uncanny blue. Two parallel lines made a cicatrice across his tall forehead.

The Maréchal, suddenly realizing that I had not answered him, stopped short and, propping his long nervous hands upon his heavy curved sword, looked at me intensely.

"Baron, time passes. Another week and we may no longer be able to snatch Jeanne from the pyre."

I maintained my silence.

"If you come to my assistance," Gilles said, somewhat angrily, "I can gather a force in three days strong enough to surround the enemy and snatch the victim out of their very jaws."

I knew that the Maréchal spoke the truth. I had followed every step of her trial. I knew of her confession. A surprise attack would probably enable us to secure her freedom. Jeanne's life was in my hands. Should I save her? Should I allow sentiment to dominate reason?

I had lost one bout in my game with Destiny by yielding weakly to the maternal cravings of a female Pope. Should I lose the world once more to spare the greatest woman soldier of all time?

Womankind needed a martyr. If I rescued Jeanne now from the flames, her life would end in an anticlimax. Would Christianity ever have conquered the world if Peter's sword had saved Jesus from crucifixion?

"Maréchal," I said, "Jeanne is as a daughter to me. I stirred the clot in her peasant soul and planted the soul of greatness. Out of the depths of her being, burst the flames of genius. You and I assisted, but it was she who saved France."

Gilles' face brightened with hope.

"It is for this reason, Baron, that we must not leave her in the hands of the executioner."

"Maréchal," I said, "is Jeanne the girl you once knew, clad in armor like a young god, whom you beheld for the first time in your garden?"

Gilles tightened his lips.

"Is Jeanne the strange being wavering like a resplendent twilight between the two sexes?"

The Maréchal did not answer. His face was clouded. The flame in his eyes dimmed to an uncertain flicker.

"That Jeanne is dead. The Jeanne in the hands of the Bishop is merely a woman. Her reverses, her vagaries, her confession are the consequence of her transformation. She has submitted to the yoke of the Moon."

Gilles' strong, sensitive nostrils quivered like a thoroughbred stallion's.

"If we save Jeanne," I pursued, "we shall rob her of her greatness. The female in her will clamor for expression. She will bear children to some rustic lad. The heroine will disappear in the housewife. Men will cease to believe the legend of her greatness. They will refuse to admit that France was saved by a woman. If she makes her exit from the stage through the flames of the faggot she will forever remain a martyr. If you save her now you destroy her fame and your vision."

Gilles made no reply. His face under his blue beard changed from red to white. Was he moved by anxiety for the Maid or by the secret jealousy that another man might possess her?

"The Maid has given birth to France, but France is still at the mercy of internal and external foes. To become a mighty nation she needs ——"

"Needs what, Baron?" Gilles asked, his fine body bent forward like an animal on watch.

I placed my hands upon his, which gripped the hilt of his sword.

"She needs a national saint whose very name shall be a standard borne aloft by a conquering army, a song that stirs the blood of her men like wine."

The Maréchal's lips trembled with unuttered words. His beard darted rays like a blue sun.

Why had I never loved this man, the most extraordinary, the most brilliant, the handsomest, of his generation? How had he, who was so sensitive to the nuances of sex, never penetrated my disguise? Had our attraction for each other been unconsciously transferred and incarnated in the love we bore the Maid? Was Jeanne the mystical consummation of our mutual passion?

I continued my argument. Was it to silence my own conscience, or to persuade Gilles?

"The fortunes of war are unpredictable. Even if we raise a force strong enough to release Jeanne from prison and the stake, how long before the Burgundians, the English and the King, forgetful of their mutual grievances, and fearful of our power, will unite to destroy us? Your head will be the target of every arrow."

"I am not afraid of death," he exclaimed proudly. "I love life, but it is so brief that I sometimes am tempted to hurl the paltry gift back into the lap of the stingy gods."

Gilles sighed. The soldier became the scholar bending over multicolored phials and faded parchments.

"Life is not worth living," he said meditatively, "unless it can be stretched beyond Nature's niggardly allowance, hardly more than a dog's or a horse's, less than that of a parrot or of a turtle. Man is the jest of an ill-humored god."

He looked at me with curious and steady insistence.

"Baron, you are versed in occult lore. Tell me, have you discovered anywhere a fountain of youth? Can man lengthen his life to parallel his ambition?"

As a man whose barns are bursting with grain forgets his neighbor's famine, so had I forgotten the pathetic destiny of humankind. Man's brain transcends time and catches a glimpse of eternity, but the Fates that spin his life have not added one inch to the thread.

"Maréchal," I replied, "if the gods make sport of man, let man conquer the gods. Let him create out of his own brain a new Adam or a new Eve whose life will be measured in æons. Jahveh created man in His image but man has outgrown his creator intellectually as the butterfly outgrows the caterpillar."

The eyes of Gilles were two torches.

Looking at me curiously, he asked: "Is the Other One, the Dark One who challenged Jahveh, more generous to his worshipers? Can the alembic distill from black magic what it cannot extract from white magic and from prayer?"

"White magic is the infantile acceptance of ancestral illusions. Black magic is the battering ram that opens the gate of Heaven and Hell. Sorcery is the fiery furnace within which man may forge a new cosmos."

Gilles' mind was an apothecary's balance weighing my words.

A few months before this I would have pursued my argument until Gilles had joined my black army of witchcraft, but the last Witches' Sabbath had destroyed my faith in the possibility of defeating Jahveh and of placing a woman upon the throne of God. I no longer considered that it was desirable to ascend Heaven on a ladder with rungs of broomsticks.

Jeanne Darc, martyred, was the embodiment of my hopes for womankind.

It was not sufficient to refuse aid. Gilles might plead for help elsewhere. Perhaps even his decimated army was sufficient to snatch Jeanne from her tormentors and forestall the mystic consummation of the Maid's mission.

"Maréchal," I said, "your life is a vase filled with precious essence. Don't spill it for the sake of a gallant gesture."

Gilles walked up and down the room, his hands behind his back.

"What is man? What is woman? What is a whole generation? A wave, a tide in the Sea of Time. He who seeks Truth must be hard, must be merciless, Maréchal."

"Maréchal," I explained, "let Jeanne die as bravely as she has lived."

Gilles stopped in his peripatetics and scrutinized me. Did he ever suspect my strange destiny?

"It is better," he said at last, deliberately, "to love the vision of the Maid than the flesh of the woman. If the flames consume her body, I shall possess her spirit forever."

He waited anxiously for my reply.

"If," I said pontifically, "her body perishes in the flames of the stake you can snatch her spirit from the flames of Hell."

"So be it."

He began to make the sign of the cross, but did not complete it.

He turned upon his heels.

"Farewell, Baron."

"Farewell, Maréchal."

Lakshmi had listened, unemotional and motionless, to our dialogue.

"Lakshmi," I called, "the die is cast! Jeanne is the female Christ that shall save womankind!"

Lakshmi approached slowly.

"Oh, Lakshmi, something in me sobs and mourns. I abhor the part of Judas. Yet without Judas the fate of Jesus can not be fulfilled. If I could but save the Maid and burn an effigy in her stead! And yet, what right have I to snatch away from Jeanne her crucifix of fire?"

Doubts assailed me. Love gnawed at my heart. A violent impulse to run after Gilles de Retz shook my legs. It was still time. I could still convince him that I was wrong. I could still rescue the Maid from the devouring flames.

I gritted my teeth.

"She must die!" I exclaimed.

I dropped upon the sofa, my head between my hands. Lakshmi huddled against my feet.

I rose slowly and looked in the tall Egyptian mirror which hung in the angle of the room. I felt a great disgust for my masculine attire. My pasted beard nauseated me.

"Lakshmi," I sighed, "I long to be a woman once more. Pierre de Bourlemont is a handsome man, but Princess Salome is the most beautiful woman of her generation, of every generation. I am weary of the caresses of women and the jealous glances of sweethearts and husbands. I shall be a woman again!"

Lakshmi tapped my ankle.

"Ah, you agree with me, Lakshmi! Besides, I wish to forget."

Lakshmi continued her chelonian caresses.

"But whither shall I go? What shall I be — princess, courtesan, adventuress?"

I meditated for a long time.

"I have it, Lakshmi! For the time being, until I find myself once more, I shall retire to a convent. I need a century to wind upon a spool the entangled threads of my life. A nunnery, Lakshmi! The Church is still a good mother, gathering strange children in her ample lap!"

CHAPTER FORTY-NINE

FESTIVE CORDOBA — I AM BURNED AT THE STAKE — THE UNREPENTANT TORTOISE — THE INQUISITION SINGES THE DEVIL'S TAIL — I DESTROY MY GOLEMS — THE MOON IS UNCONQUERED — LAKSHMI YAWNS.

Cordoba was in a festive mood. The sun had hardly dipped his silver feet into the Guadalquivir when the people began to crowd the narrow tortuous streets, decorated with wreaths and ribbons of all colors. The former capital of the Ommiads resumed, at least for the day, her ancient gayety.

The City had witnessed many an auto-da-fé, but never had one so stirred their imagination. It was not only that Salome, Jewess, heretic, witch, was to be consigned to the flames, but also her familiar, Lakshmi, a giant turtle who understood all human tongues and within whose carapace, studded with precious stones, lodged not flesh and blood but the infernal spirit of Beelzebub imprisoned by the seal of Solomon.

The bells of the Mezquita tolled dismally, incessantly. The solemn procession started. The Dominican fathers preceded carrying the flag of their order and the flag of the Holy Inquisition. Behind them, separated by a tall cross, the culprit followed stretched upon a black coffin and strapped to the back of a donkey. She was dressed in a yellow sanbenito, on which was written the endless list of her crimes. A long conical cap covered her head. Tied to her feet, a large turtle upon whose shell were painted the grotesque tortures of hell.

Behind the victim walked pompously the alcalde corregidor, the dignitaries of the Church and State, in gala dress, and at a respectable distance, the populace, jesting, jeering, or solemn.

The Conversos had once more grown wealthy. The Church took this opportunity to warn the former Jews of the fate which awaited each and all of them if they deviated in the least from the tenets of the true faith, or if, under the cloak of their new names, they pretended to belong to the sangre pura.

At every crossroad the monks stopped to preach and read the accusations against the witch whose destiny here and hereafter was foreshadowed by the black coffin and the two unlit black candles on either side of her head. Never in all eternity, such was the meaning of the symbol, would the Lord of Creation have mercy upon her, and light her path from hell into purgatory.

In the distance beyond the Sierra Morena, the Sun, like a heretic divinity, was expiring in flames.

The Square in front of the Mezquita was crowded with impatient people — pedestrians and riders on burros and horses. They grumbled against the monks and the slow procedure of justice. They had grown weary of the sermons and the litanies. Besides it would soon be too dark to enjoy to the full the sacred spectacle.

In the center of the Plaza the stake had already been planted. At its base the wood and the faggots, sprinkled with tar, invoked the spark of life.

Suddenly the bells of the Cathedral clanked toneless, like things of lead. The guards with pointed spears pressed the spectators into a semicircle.

The culprit barely moved her feet. Two officers of the Holy Inquisition dragged her after them. Her eyes were wide open, and her lids motionless. Her face was bruised and swollen from the torture.

Behind them came the Verdugo, a powerful man, pockmarked and dark-skinned, the inheritance of Moorish ancestry. He was dressed in scarlet. In one hand he carried a rope and a lighted torch; with the other he pulled a chain attached to the neck of the reluctant turtle.

On seeing the animal, the populace uttered a cry of exultation mingled with horror.

The Verdugo bound the woman to the pole, and around her feet he chained the tortoise.

The Officer of the Holy Inquisition held a crucifix in front of the victim.

"Salome, recant! Kiss the holy cross! If not, in another hour your soul weighted with sin will be cast into the lowest pit of hell. While you are still upon Earth, recant!"

The victim shook her head. Her eyelids fell and rose quickly.

"The Holy Mother will be merciful to you, Salome. If you recant, you will be strangled to death before you are consumed by the flames."

The victim shook her head. A hideous smile twisted her lips.

The Officer grew furious.

"For the third and final time, according to the merciful usage of the Holy Church and the Holy Inquisition — Salome, will you recant?"

A tremor passed through the body of the victim. Her lips shivered, but there was no sound.

The Officer held the cross above his head.

"In the name of the Father and the Son and the Holy Ghost and by the order of the Holy Inquisition, after due and just trial was given you, and a due opportunity to recant was offered to you and refused, Salome, accused and found guilty of sorcery, perjury, heresy and secret worship of the Jewish religion which your ancestors had abjured, you shall burn at a slow fire, and your ashes be cast to the four winds!"

The people uttered a cry of joy!

"Burn the witch!"

"Burn la judía!"

The Officer turned to the turtle.

"Lakshmi, relinquish the spirit of the Evil One which is

lodged in your body, and with whom Salome held converse!"

The turtle pulled at its chain.

"Lakshmi, return to the fold of turtles, an innocent beast! Relinquish the Evil Spirit — and you shall continue to live!"

The turtle made no sign of understanding.

Once more the Officer repeated his exhortation; then, turning to the Verdugo, he said:

"Let this vile creature burn at the same fire with her whose familiar it was. Let their infernal ashes mingle together, and together be cast to the four winds! So be it!"

He stepped aside. The people shouted jubilantly.

The Verdugo applied the torch to the faggots, which crackled like joyous laughter.

The tortoise moved its neck in all directions, opened wide its eyes, pulled at the chain.

The flames rose. The body of the victim was encircled as with a scarlet veil. The sparks danced like mad fireflies.

Suddenly a stench of sulphur pervaded the air.

A heavy smoke choked the spectators.

"Satan is burning!"

"The Devil has his tail singed!"

"La judía stinks of her race!"

An unearthly roar issued from the mouth of the victim, followed by a jet of flames like a giant tongue.

The people pressed back. The animals stamped their hoofs neighing and braying. The Officer of the Holy Inquisition raised the cross in the air.

A terrific noise like a thunderclap tore the body of the victim. The fire was a volcano in action. Molten nameless débris flew in all directions.

The Verdugo and the Officers rushed into the Mezquita. The people, maddened with fear, ran in all directions, shouting:

"Hell is loose!"

"Hell is loose!"

The Plaza was empty.

I lingered until the last flame subsided, and saw that

nothing remained of the victims of the auto-da-fé save a hillock of ashes.

I struck my burro lightly with my stick, and urged him forward. He moved slowly, rocking like a camel, under the weight of the trunk which contained Lakshmi, wife of Vishnu.

We reached the Guadalquivir, whose waters stroked lazily the flanks of my boat.

Night had nearly set in. The place was deserted. I judged it safe to open the trunk and release my prisoner, since the burden, while very precious, was a trifle beyond my strength.

Lakshmi blinked in utter insouciance.

"Come, Lakshmi, get into the boat."

She walked slowly behind me, measuring her steps like a duck.

The boat almost capsized under her weight.

I steadied it, boarded, the empty trunk upon my back, and before taking the oars, I transformed myself from an aged muleteer into a young and prosperous merchant.

"You may breathe the fresh nocturnal air, Lakshmi. At dawn you will once more enter the trunk, and become mere merchandise."

Lakshmi gazed at the moon placidly.

The burro on the shore brayed sadly, his head thrown back like a tenor's.

I rowed, humming an ancient song.

Lakshmi listened, her head cocked.

"Do you remember this song, Lakshmi? Who sang it to you, centuries ago as you crossed the Ganges or the Nile?"

Lakshmi looked at me sentimentally like a young calf.

I stroked her gnarled neck.

"Ah, Lakshmi, what tortures we have been spared! How powerful is hypnotism, reinforced by gold! Were our judges and the Verdugo automatons obeying the commands I uttered at the trial, or clever charlatans, glad to be enriched and strike terror into the hearts of the people, particularly those of my race? Could they not distinguish between the reality and the eidolon? I created the doll in my image, as every god and every artist must create, but although I clothed her in flesh, the breath of life was not within her. Had I created so much better than I knew?"

Lakshmi placed her head upon my foot like a contented dog.

I laughed.

"They got more than they bargained for, Lakshmi! They did not know that I would conceal an explosive in the body of my creature. In the annals of the Church there will be written forever that upon this day the Holy Fathers had consigned to the flames Satan indeed! The descendants of these cruel and ignorant witnesses shall utter with awe the name of Salome!"

I sighed.

"Alas, Lakshmi, the Jews will pay heavily for this! The Jew is the paymaster of the world in more than one sense, my ancient friend! Is there a race among the tortoises also against whom hatred never ceases, and prejudice blossoms eternally?"

Lakshmi blinked.

"At midnight, Cordoba, city of Ibn Roshd Averrhoës, and Moses Maimonides, the Aristotle and the Plato of the Middle Ages, shall witness another and more magnificent auto-da-fé! They will hear a mightier thunderstorm than Jove has ever hurled against them and the flames will delude them into the belief that the Sun has risen long before his appointed hour! My laboratory, hidden in the vault of my villa and crowded with my creations, will turn into ashes! I am a jealous god, Lakshmi! No one shall defile my work, or bungle it by trying to imitate it!"

Lakshmi yawned.

"No, for the time being, I have not succeeded. The suggestions I received from the precious manuscripts of Maimonides have been of value, but I must follow different paths if my dream of creating a new and finer race than that of Adam and Eve shall ever materialize. I do not regret the century I have spent in this city. I have learned much. If you had not been hidden in the trunk, Lakshmi, you, too, might have been deluded by the doll which I had to sacrifice to the superstition of these Christian barbarians. Not yet flesh and blood — but very nearly. Not alive — but containing the spark of life."

Lakshmi rose on her feet for a moment, then resumed her former posture.

"Had I desired to take revenge upon these people, I could have crumbled their Cathedral and all their judges and the Verdugo, like things of glass. But I have come to build, Lakshmi, not to destroy. I have come to heal, not to wound. Even the conflagration which will follow the explosion at midnight will be limited to my laboratory. No one, nothing, will be harmed beyond its boundaries."

I sighed.

"I regret greatly that I had to use a living scapegoat for you, Lakshmi. I tried to create a being supremely beautiful and supremely intelligent. I cannot, with all due respect to you, think of a turtle as the embodiment of perfection."

A sneer crossed Lakshmi's reptilian face. Her red eyes glowed with a weird intensity.

"It is true, of course, that each living being considers his kind the image of divinity. Still, judging impersonally, Lakshmi, can you compare a turtle to man? Does your magnificent carapace, O wife of Vishnu, equal the mind of man, which is *his* shield against the elements?"

Lakshmi made a sound which more nearly approximated laughter than any she had hitherto uttered.

Piqued, I pursued:

"Lakshmi, nothing in Nature compares with man. The firmament itself is but the projection of his imagination. The gods are his puppets. In his eye he carries the Cosmos. In his hand lies the Destiny of Life!"

Lakshmi blinked, as if a fly had disturbed her. About her circular eyes there was a look of condescending boredom, such as a grandmother might bestow upon her prattling and arrogant descendant.

For the first time she irritated me.

"Lakshmi!" I exclaimed, rowing vigorously. "How dare you dispute the supremacy of man? What other being walks erect, speaks, thinks, and even challenges the gods that fashioned him? What other being dares conceive a race greater than himself, made by his own imagination and his own hands?"

Lakshmi continued her bored attitude.

"Oh, I know you judge man by his cruelty and his superstitions. You judge man by his autos-da-fé, by his wars, by his lies, by his tyranny, by his slavery. All that is true, Lakshmi. Man is cruel, and superstitious, and false. He is a comedian, a clown — but what a clown, what a comedian, Lakshmi! And what a comedy he invents for himself — forever varied, forever glamorous!"

Lakshmi yawned. She raised her paw politely half-way to her mouth, as I had taught her. The grotesqueness of the gesture reconciled me to her impudence.

"Oh, well," I said, "how should a turtle understand man?"

Lakshmi closed one eye and looked whimsically at me with the other.

"At any rate, your scapegoat did not suffer as much as the stupid bystanders imagined. I injected her with a drug which deadened all sensations."

Lakshmi tapped my ankle approvingly.

"I understand, Lakshmi. We can never overcome our racial prejudices, even though we live as long as the stars. You and I shall agree upon everything save the relative ranks of man and the turtle in the hierarchy of Nature."

Lakshmi smiled the half-malicious smile of the very ancient.

The Moon cut into the clouds like a white scimitar.

"And still she is unconquered. Still she rules the sea — and woman!" I said, pointing upward with one of the oars from which the water dripped into the river noiselessly. "Still, I, too, Salome must pay her tribute, although I can delay my payments if my will or my needs demand it."

Gloom hung over Spain like a black panoply. Never had she suffered so shameful, so tragic a blow. The bells of the churches rang dolefully like Oriental women bewailing the dead.

In vain the officials expostulated with the people. In vain did they try to convince them that the Invincible Armada was destroyed not by the valor of Spain's enemies, but by the gales.

The people gathered on the plazas and in the wineshops arguing, condemning, prognosticating.

"How many boats, did you say?"

"One hundred."

"What! More than two hundred. All of them."

"All of them save those in which the brave officers fled."

"How can a queen — a woman, ruler of an island, not larger than a fist, conquer the pride of the seas?"

"She is not a woman. They say she is a witch, a heretic, the spawn of Satan!"

"I thought England was one of our possessions — an heirloom of — God bless him — our King."

"What difference does it make what she was? She has become the Mistress of the Seas. Before long she'll conquer the Earth."

"No one will conquer Spain, fools! We shall build another fleet — a greater Armada!"

"And who will supply the money? The judíos took all the gold with them when they were driven out."

"They did not. The Holy Inquisition has a million eyes which pierce walls. She has a million noses which smell hidden vaults. She has a million claws which unearth treasures."

Nothing consoled. No balsam healed the bruised pride.

"Lakshmi," I said, as I clasped my belt around my naked waist. "The God of Israel has avenged his chosen race! Spain is dying!"

Lakshmi scratched the bottom of the trunk.

"We do not linger another day here. I shall arrange my finances later — perhaps in a century or so. Meanwhile I have been able to hide from the million eyes, noses and claws of the Holy Inquisition enough jewels, packed in this belt, to build another Armada. Let any one try to undo this belt, Lakshmi," I laughed. "In a fraction of a second his hands will turn to ashes! Besides I have enough wealth under a hundred names in all parts of Europe and Asia to buy a dozen thrones and a dozen armies."

Lakshmi continued to scratch lazily the trunk.

"Something infinitely more interesting than money, however, is attracting my attention just now — even more than the new race I am planning to create. It is the Queen of the English! Her navy rides the seas, unconquered steeds! Who is she? What is she? Is she a greater Zenobia, a more magnificent Cleopatra? I must see her!"

Lakshmi was unconcerned.

"At dawn we leave, Lakshmi! As soon as we are out of Spain, you are no longer the prisoner of the trunk. You will be my free companion again!"

Lakshmi showed no sign of interest.

"What, does not this news please you, Lakshmi! Apollonius come to Earth again!" I exclaimed ironically, "considering the bottom of a trunk the equal of the free Earth, finding the difference between liberty and slavery a mere matter of words!"

Lakshmi yawned, and stretched out.

CHAPTER FIFTY

DAMN QUEEN ELIZABETH! — SLAVE OF THE MOON? — HUNTING WITH THE QUEEN — THE QUEEN'S FAVORITE — LINGERING PRELUDES — ELIZABETH IS NOT A WOMAN — ELIZABETH IS NOT A MAN — I SOLVE THE SECRET OF ELIZABETH.

LAKSHMI sat upon the cushions like a voluptuous houri awaiting her master.

I entered quickly into the room followed by one of the maids whom I dismissed peremptorily.

I threw my fan and cloak upon the couch.

Lakshmi's head trembled in quick waves like a pendulum which is suddenly shaken by a heavy wagon dashing over cobblestones.

"This damned Queen Elizabeth is exasperating, Lakshmi! She ignores me or smartly twists every one of my remarks into a pun or an epigram like her favorite poet, Will Shakespeare, who has made it impossible any longer for an Englishman to speak simple prose."

Lakshmi stretched her neck forward amorously.

"In vain did I marry Van Ruyter in Amsterdam, Count of Holland, Duke of England, Baron of Germany, and what not. He died of sheer love after six months, poor man! The titles I have inherited avail me not at all. I have even become a Protestant, Lakshmi!" I laughed, "but it's all love's labor lost, my friend. Her Majesty snubs me! Why? Am I no longer charming? no longer interesting? no longer beautiful? no longer the Aspasia of the West? Am I getting old?"

Lakshmi crawled toward me, and tapped my ankle.

I patted her knotted head.

"My faithful one!"

I summoned one of my attendants.

"Ale and my pipe," I ordered.

"Yes, my lady!"

"I have become more English than the English," I said as I blew the smoke into the air, and took a long draft of the beer. "They are a strange people, the English, Lakshmi. You have to cultivate a taste for them as for olives — or their ale. At first you hate them, then you respect them, then you love them, and finally you discover that you do not know them at all!"

Lakshmi watched the circles of smoke, amused.

"Would I could teach you to smoke, Lakshmi! You would look so lovely with a long pipe sticking out of your beak! I would buy one for you incrusted with precious jewels like your carapace. Alas, you turtles never feel the need of new sensations throughout eternity! In that lies your inferiority to man, who invents for himself new joys, new passions, new pains!"

Lakshmi yawned, like a bored, sophisticated débutante.

"Is Elizabeth a great queen, Lakshmi? Her courtiers fawn upon her and write the most extravagant verse that was ever penned or sung. Even the poets of Araby when I was queen to — let me see — how many brother kings — sixteen, or eighteen — in all the luxuriance of their tongue were a little more modest in their praises of me! And you know that in my youth I was — rather delectable!"

Lakshmi sneezed.

"Elizabeth's ministers, however, are often enraged against her. She always vacillates. Even the victory over Spain was the result of her indecision to act. The elements favored her. Only a week before the great disaster of the Invincible Armada she was ready to capitulate. Is this weakness or strength? Is it folly or wisdom? Should a monarch, like the Fates, spin upon the loom of events dispassionately?"

Lakshmi crawled back to her cushions.

"Does not Elizabeth suffer, like the rest of the daughters of Eve, periodic madness? Is she not the slave of the Moon any longer? Was she never under her yoke like Jeanne

Darc in her first flush of youth? They call her a virgin, Lakshmi — she whose court is a harem of young boys! Did she never, like the rest of royalty, desire progeny, a son or daughter who would sway her scepter, whose shadow begins to loom over the Earth?"

I tapped my feet in nervous anger.

"How shall I approach this woman, Lakshmi? What must I do to gain her favor? I must know her. She intrigues as no other of her sex intrigued me. The rest were obvious. Their greatness, their pettiness, their tragedies and comedies were easily decipherable. They were daughters of the Moon. Perhaps Elizabeth withholds the secret I have been seeking for centuries, Lakshmi! Perhaps if I discovered it, I would not have to create a new race. Perchance the human race is still amenable to perfection."

Lakshmi followed the circles of smoke with her eyes, as a dog follows the movements of birds or insects.

"Next week I shall have the occasion of seeing Her Majesty at the estates of her favorite lord. They say those visits invariably end in orgies. *In vino veritas* still holds true, I hope. It is good of her she does not ignore me entirely, but how can she without causing ill feeling with the Dutch, her recent allies? I am still the Duchess Van Ruyter!" I said proudly, emptying my cup.

The royal hunt was over. In the distance the fanfares announced the return of Her Majesty and her party. The castle buzzed like a beehive suddenly disturbed by the blow of a stick. The servants rushed to and fro rolling barrels, carrying enormous platters with victuals, jostling against one another, shouting orders, swearing.

The deer, from whose large open wounds the hot blood streamed to the ground, were carried on poles over the shoulders of attendants. Behind them the dogs barked drearily, stopping at intervals to lap the small pools of black and red which gathered in the muddy grooves formed by the boots of the men.

The horses, whitened with foam and breathing heavily through their open mouths, were led by the grooms to the stables. The party on foot entered the garden, laughing and lauding the valor of their sovereign, the sexagenarian Diana of the Chase.

Elizabeth reclining on the arm of her host, was flushed. Her features, sunken somewhat in the fat pouches characteristic of old age which was fast approaching, still showed sensitiveness and intelligence. Her eyes, changing quickly from gray to gold, had lost nothing of their sharpness. Over her small lips, a little parched, played an ironic smile. A lock of hair, dyed a brilliant red, stole coquettishly from underneath her plumed hat and curled over her tall brow. Her small flat hips did not make the voluptuous circular movement characteristic of woman and the perennial delight of the male. Her bosom, however, was full-blown and matronly, as though she had nursed several children. Her hands were long and energetic, but her feet, encased in golden-tipped boots which reached half-way to her knees, were tiny and she gave the impression of mincing her steps.

She stopped suddenly, as if she decided to remain in the middle of the garden. The entourage halted. The Queen changed her mind, and continued her walk, moving with an imperceptible waddle as if uncertain whether to walk or stop. She compromised and pursued her way in a lateral direction.

Suddenly she said to her host: "My Lord, we will feast in the garden."

"Yes, Your Majesty!"

The Duke lingered awhile before issuing his orders to his attendants. A sharp glance from his sovereign convinced him of her final decision.

In a few minutes, like a thing of magic, the garden was lined with tables. The foods steamed. The wines sparkled. The smoke of the pipes rose like clouds. The taciturn nobles of the foggy Island of the North became loquacious. Their laughter broke the air. Epigrams and ribald jests, and flowery verse pressed and tripped upon one another like flocks of sheep on hearing the call of the shepherd and the barking of the dogs.

The smell of the roasted venison delighted the nostrils of

the lords and ladies. They tore the meat hungrily with their fingers and devoured it like starved peasants. They cast aside the wines, and shouted:

"Ale! Ale! Damn ye all!"

The foam of the beer whitened the beards of the cavaliers and tinctured the dainty mouths of the noblewomen. The cups overbrimmed, and long dark streams flowed under the tables in all directions.

The Queen, surrounded always by several of her young favorites, recounted anecdotes which made them roar with laughter and slap their thighs.

Once in a long while, she cast me a glance whose meaning I could not decipher.

Again I had found it impossible to approach her. She smiled vaguely at my words, and continued flirting with her youths.

"We will have music, my Lord," she addressed the host.

The host clapped his hands, and ordered the musicians to enter.

Her Majesty rose. The others followed suit.

"Dance!" she commanded.

We danced in circles, holding hands, or in pairs. Elizabeth made tiny, dainty steps, her finger-tips in the open palm of her partner.

The dancing became more and more elemental and at times resembled the disjointed and frantic movements of my African tribe.

Each number was followed by loud guzzling of ale and shouting of obscene toasts.

The Queen, finding it difficult to keep pace with her courtiers, or remembering suddenly her royal dignity, ordered the music to stop and the musicians to disband. She fell into a chair. One of the young men fanned her. Another put a cup of ale to her lips. A third one straightened her robe. And all in a jargon of Latin and English verse and prose, false iambics and unfinished sonnets, praised her beauty and her terpsichorean talents.

Elizabeth, smothered with compliments, was radiant. She rose, and beckoning to one of the young men, reclined upon his arm, and entered the Castle. The others scattered in pairs, holding one another amorously, and walking more or less unsteadily toward the numberless little bowers thoughtfully provided with couches and benches.

Only the Earl of Worcester, a young man of about nineteen or twenty, tall, blond, and delicately featured, remained. He dropped into a chair, placed his elbows upon the table, and his beardless chin upon his palms. For a long time he looked intently at the door of the castle through which Elizabeth had disappeared. He struck the table a powerful blow, which made the cups shake and totter.

"By my faith," he growled, "I shall pierce him through!"

He stood up, and placed his hand upon the hilt of his sword.

"Thou shalt pay dearly, or I am not the true son of my father!"

Suddenly he turned his face in my direction. He squinted his sea-blue eyes, blurred from drink. Smiling lasciviously, he came swaggering toward me.

He kissed my hand.

"Forgive my choler, Duchess. It is not becoming the Earl of Worcester, who, by your permission, considers himself something of a philosopher and stoic," he hiccoughed.

"Even a philosopher and stoic has the right to become angry when the cause warrants it, my Lord."

"True, by my faith, my Lady, and you are a philosopher yourself. I have often heard you utter words that our Will Shakespeare would gladly call his own."

"You honor me greatly, my Lord," I said, intrigued and pleased by the youth's arrogance and self-assurance.

"Shall we drink a toast, my Lady, to — to —" He looked at me. "I shall drink a toast to your beauty, which"— he lowered his voice — "as far surpasses that of Her Majesty as the noon-sun surpasses the light of a star!"

We clinked.

The Earl emptied his cup at one gulp and turned it bottom up.

"Nay, my Lord, do not put your cup away. Shall we not toast — to — to our friendship?"

"We shall!" he exclaimed, casting an angry look once more in the direction of the castle.

The Earl placed his arm around my waist, and we walked slowly up and down the main pathway of the garden, bordered by gigantic oak trees, the shadows of whose leaves made a silver arabesque under the light of the Moon.

"And the cause, my Lord?" I asked.

"What cause?" he asked, frowning a little.

"The cause of my Lord's choler?"

"Hahaha," he laughed drunkenly. "The cause, my Lady? The cause has vanished! I shall never more pierce his treacherous heart — for has not his treachery made it possible for me to walk at your side, my"— he looked at me, uncertain whether to dare say the words —"my red-headed Star!"

His strange compliment delighted me.

"What care I for the Queen of the English, when I am with the Queen of Beauty?"

I thanked him, and returned an appropriate compliment.

We reached the table once more, and drank again to — to our love.

"And, be it for only a night, my love — for a night of love — with you — I would give my life!" he said, pressing his lips upon mine.

The young man's audacity thrilled me, or was it the perfume of the flowers that rose daintily on the wings of the breeze, or the wine, or the sudden shrill cries of satisfied love that issued at intervals from the bowers?

"I know the secret spot," he whispered, placing his forefinger to his lips, "which Elizabeth frequents when she is my Lord's guest, although to spite me to-night she preferred the Castle." He laughed. "Haha! Who is the loser, my love? Not I! Not I!" He placed his hands upon his hips and shook himself proudly.

"Not we!" I added.

My affection for the youth was not entirely disinterested. It was common gossip that the Earl had been the Queen's paramour for several months. Perhaps in this half-intoxicated, half-vengeful mood I could draw out of him the information I desired.

The bower was a royal architecture of flowers. The couch was carpeted with petals of many colors and many shapes.

We dallied for a long while. The hands and the mouth of the youth pressed into my face, my throat, my breasts. Overcome by my feminine instinct, I stretched out upon the couch, awaiting the consummation of the most ancient of rites.

The youth sat beside me, his face flushed with passion. His hands tipped with flames, caressed me. The prelude continued but the song remained unsung. I drew him nearer to me. He whispered words of adoration. His lips trembled. His body was aglow.

It was not the wine that restrained him, nor his modesty. I plied him, I urged him. His body was rigid with desire, but like a knight who touches the breastplate of his adversary, yet never plunges into him, the Earl pursued his endless preliminaries.

"You are as Elizabeth must have been in her youth, my love — as beautiful and as desirable, as the poets sing of her."

His words were rapture, his challenge was impassioned, but his touch remained sterile.

I tantalized him. I urged him. My hands made him drunken. He vacillated, but he never succumbed.

"Elizabeth was my first love," he whispered, "Elizabeth and now it is you — you as she was in her glory."

"Love me," I whispered, pressing my mouth against his.

He buried his head in my bosom. He pressed me to his chest like a vise. I closed my eyes and waited. I grew weary and restless under his kisses, that played forever upon the surface, exquisite, but not piercing.

He had never had another love save that of Elizabeth. Was it she who had taught him the tantalization of passion without its consummation? the caress without the glorious warfare of the sexes? the game sans the victory?

"Do you also wear a girdle of chastity like Elizabeth?" he asked, blushing.

"Is it the girdle that protects her virginity? Or is her virginity the invention of her poets?"

"She is a virgin!" he exclaimed.

"A virgin with so many lovers?" I laughed. "With you as her sweetheart?" I tried to awaken his manly pride.

He looked around suspiciously for a moment, then, bending to my ear, he whispered.

"Elizabeth is not a woman."

I stood up.

"Then it is true what they say about her — that she is a man!"

"No, Elizabeth is not a man."

"Then what is she?"

The Earl was reluctant.

My kisses, reinforced by frequent drafts from the cup, urged him.

"Once I saw her naked," he whispered. "Nobody else has ever seen her naked."

He remained silent for a while.

"We were in her bedchamber. I was exhausted from love and wine. My eyes were closed. She thought I was asleep. She undressed. Her breasts, white as marble, white like yours, with fine delicate blue veins ——"

"Yes," I said, piqued at the comparison between my breasts and hers.

"She stood before the mirror. I opened wide my eyes, but she did not see me. She took off her girdle which covered her nakedness. I caught my breath. She looked around. My eyes were tightly shut again. I snored like a trooper at the end of the battle. She would have sent me to the Tower instantly or ordered my head chopped off had she ever guessed that I discovered her secret."

"What is her secret?" I asked anxiously.

The youth looked carefully about him, but despite our solitude, refused to answer.

"I know," I said, "she is incapable of being a wife.

Membranam habet," I added, dropping into Latin. "Everybody gossips about it."

Desirous to prove that he knew more than I, more than any one else, he mumbled:

"Non membrana sed membrum," as if the Latin absolved him from the guilt of confession.

The youth, now completely drunk, laughed uproariously between his hiccoughs. His mood changing suddenly, he burst into tears. Sobbingly, he buried his head in my lap. His rhythmic breath came like a baby's, but his hands were not asleep. I left the couch, fearing that when the morning brought him new strength, he would recommence his caresses à la reine vierge!

Weary, the Earl stretched himself out upon the couch and promptly snored, this time in earnest.

"Lakshmi," I said in Arabic, fearing that the walls might have ears, "I discovered the secret of the Virgin Queen!"

Lakshmi awakened with a start, blinked.

"What it is will not interest you at all, I know. I understand now why she so obstinately refused an intimate acquaintance with me. She feared me. She knew that somehow I would extract her secret which she guards with the jealousy of a god. I have discovered it nevertheless. And even if the young Earl in his intoxication saw things larger than they were, as some see double, his words contain, no doubt, a good deal of truth. Elizabeth no longers interests me, Lakshmi."

Lakshmi out of sheer courtesy, closed only one eye.

"She does not help me solve the problem of womanhood, — for she is not a true woman. I shall continue my researches and my wanderings. What one will not reveal, perhaps the other will."

Lakshmi yawned.

"Sleep on, Lakshmi, while I shall think over a new itinerary. In the dawn of Day, in the profound silence of the Earth, I shall hold communion with my soul and the Universe."

Lakshmi fell asleep immediately.

CHAPTER FIFTY-ONE

I AM MADAME DE LA ROCHOUART — I START A LETTER TO CARTAPHILUS — A NOTE FROM COUNT LEOPOLD —"HE LOVES ME, HE LOVES ME NOT"— LOVE ON THE DANUBE — FERDINAND SNEERS — I MARRY LEOPOLD — I HAVE A RIVAL — LEOPOLD'S ASSIGNATION — METAMORPHOSES — I TRANSFORM MYSELF INTO A BOY — EROS MELTS INTO APHRODITE — LAKSHMI'S NECK POINTS EAST.

LAKSHMI, my footstool, did not mind my weight, or the fact that one of my feet crushed the Moon and the other Vishnu, her husband. She raised her head from time to time, and her eyes blinked, as I read to her parts from the letter of Cartaphilus, my perennial, predestined, and eternal lover.

I laughed.

"Nothing will change him, Lakshmi. He is a child at sixteen hundred, and will no doubt be a child at sixteen thousand. He is now the Dalai Lama of Tibet, seeking the Ultimate Truth of the Celestial Circle, which he hopes to find by contemplating his navel. But he certainly is right. I have neglected him too long. A letter a century ought not to be too much of a strain."

I dipped my plume into the inkhorn and bent over the parchment.

"How can I crowd life and ideas and emotions in a few symbols? How shall I begin, Lakshmi?"

Lakshmi blinked in utter unconcern.

"Shall I begin by telling him that I am now Madame de La Rochouart, descendant of Pierre de Bourlemont, and widow of Baron de La Rochouart, killed in a duel? Shall I describe my castle, which once was a monastery, and Vienna, whose sophistication is more mature and gayer than that of Paris? Shall I also tell him that Salome is famous, not for her escapades, but for her virtue? that even the Emperor himself, admonishing his mistresses, cites me as a model to follow? Shall I tell him that I have introduced a new style of bustle and headgear which are the rage both here and at Paris?"

I bit the tip of the pen.

"Now, let me see, Lakshmi — where did I see Cartaphilus last, and when?"

I scratched Lakshmi's head with my pen, as an aid to memory.

"Yes, I remember now. It was at the Convent of the Sacred Flame in Rome where I was a demure Mother Superior. Do you remember the beautiful little nun, Beatrice, who was immured next to my cell, because she had sinned with a young lieutenant, who expiated by becoming a Trappist monk?

"Poor child, I saved her from a horrible death. I sent the nuns and the keepers on a holy trip for the day and like a mason, I broke through the wall that would have stifled her to death."

I tried to recall her face, but could not.

"How did she look, Lakshmi? I know she was lovely and beautiful, but I can only remember that she had a tiny nose, pertly turned up, as if always ready to laugh.

"For five years she was my secret next-door neighbor. No one ever suspected that behind that calcimined partition, Beatrice, whose soul should have been purging in the flames of Hell or the more gentle waters of Purgatory, still clung to her delicate body."

I placed my pen upon the table, and sighed deeply.

"Now I remember, Lakshmi. Beatrice had almond-shaped eyes like a Japanese girl, an adorable dimple on her right cheek and another in a place more delicious still. No wonder the lieutenant had fallen in love with her, and for the loss of her became a Trappist.

"Beside Joan d'Anglois, Pontiff of the Christian World, whom I loved with a passion equaled almost by my love for Cartaphilus and you, dear Sacred Tortoise, Symbol of Silence, Beatrice was the only human being who ever heard the story of my life. It was as though I spoke to a sepulcher. Only a dead woman can be entrusted safely with a secret. I'll never tell this to Cartaphilus. It would enhance his conceit. He would dance like a dervish!"

Lakshmi uttered a little cry, which might have been a sneeze, a laugh, a cough, or a growl of indignation against my indictment of our gender.

"Oh, it isn't possible, Lakshmi, to do good to a human being. I saved the poor girl from suffocation. One more day and she would have been free from all pain. Indeed, she was barely conscious when I broke down the wall. I gave her life. I was a benefactress, a goddess. For months before she died, however, she was in agony, and no drugs could alleviate her pain.

"You remember, Lakshmi, the day she died. It was the day after I saved Cartaphilus from the Inquisition at the hands of Pope Alexander the Sixth, the subtlest, the most implacable, the most corrupt of the Borgias.

"On her chest I placed a cross and the manuscript containing the story of my life, which she wrote, in her intricate and lovely handwriting, day by day. Always at the beginning of each page was a little orison that the Lord help her tell the exact truth, and always at the end of the page, a prayer that the Lord be merciful to her, a sinner, and to me the best of mothers. Who knows who will find the dust of her body and the dust of my life?"

Lakshmi rolled her eyes.

"Is it this that I should write to Cartaphilus? A little episode, a trifling incident? A hundred years have passed. What have I done? 'A century!' people utter in awe. Dynasties are born, and Empires die, and only a few legends remain, to testify that the memory of man is a large-holed sieve, which Time shakes forever.

"What have I done in a hundred years? Is it not enough that I have lived? Must the sea take count of the boats which crossed it, or the winds which howled their eternal lamentation? Must the mountain remember the myriad silver dawns or the suns which died in their own blood? And you, Lakshmi, is it not enough that you have breathed, that you have chewed your cabbage-leaf? Why must only man discover a reason, other than life itself, for living?

"Still, I must tell Cartaphilus what advances I have made toward the liberation of our sex, Lakshmi — both because my vanity prompts me, and because he will be glad to see that I am hastening the moment when two free beings, two equals, will unite in eternal marriage.

"Well, what shall I write to him, Lakshmi? Shall I recount my experiments in the nunnery and monastery? Shall I tell him of the strange discovery I made about eunuchs? How little sultans know about them, or else they would never entrust their precious wives into their hands! It is true that they may not engender progeny, but they can achieve subtle pleasure. Ah, many a royal consort, displeased with the weary caresses of her lord and master, who dutiful to the Koran visits in regular rotation each of his numerous flock, invites the Sphinx-like guardian to her couch!

"What wrong notions people have about sex, Lakshmi! They divide men and women into two distinct entities. They never see how the two merge, how they interchange. Not the outer organs but the inner ones make the male or the female — the inner organs, so concealed that one can only guess at their existence, and which pour into the blood fluids and vapors determining the direction in which Cupid aims his arrows.

"Do you remember, Lakshmi, my experiments with animals? Do you remember how I turned a cackling hen into a vainglorious cock, and a demure kitten into a pugnacious tom-cat? If only some day I could fashion for myself tools sufficiently delicate to pierce through the walls which guard with infinitely greater jealousy the secret of life than the wall of China guard her ancient civilization!"

Lakshmi's head shivered.

I laughed.

"Do not fear. I shall not experiment with you, my old comrade! You will remain forever the lawful wife of Vishnu. I shall not transform you into an Amazon."

Lakshmi was placated.

"The Church, like an unabashed mother, has seen her children naked, and discovered that not all are the true sons of Adam or the true daughters of Eve. She has seen that there are many who waver between the father and mother, or who partake of both, undecided which to be. Does not the Church demand from the daughters-sons of Hermes and Aphrodite a solemn oath how he-she will approach the conjugal bed — whether as he or she?

"But you are not at all interested, Lakshmi, and I have not yet started the letter to Cartaphilus."

I dipped my plume into the ink and began writing.

"Cartaphilus, Much-Beloved, Dalai Lama, Greetings!"

Some one knocked at the door.

"Entrez!"

A page, bowing deeply, delivered a note, and waited for a reply. My hands trembled as I opened it. I felt the blood rush to my face; I thought I saw a smile flit across the mouth of the page, and I blushed more deeply. I wrote a short note, and gave it to the youth, who departed.

"Lakshmi! Lakshmi!"

The Turtle turned about as quickly as she could.

"Lakshmi! Graf Leopold von Mansfeld invites me to go skating with him to-night on the Danube! Ah, but that does not mean anything to you, does it, Lakshmi? You are not interested in the fact that he is related to the Emperor, that he is one of the most charming men of Vienna, soldier, poet, philosopher! You do not even care that he is handsome, that he is — you might say — a Teutonic Cartaphilus — tall, blond, blue-eyed. He resembles Ulric, too. You don't know who Ulric was, Lakshmi. No matter!"

I walked up and down the room, looked into every mirror.

"Am I really beautiful, Lakshmi?"

Lakshmi looked at me wearily, as a grandmother might look at her descendant, who has received an invitation to her first ball.

"He loves me, Lakshmi! He loves me! Let me see if he really loves me!"

I plucked the petals of a daisy of silk.

"He loves me — he loves me not — he loves me — he loves me not — he loves me — he loves me not!"

Angrily, I threw the stem away.

"You lie, Miss Daisy! He loves me! I can tell by his note, simple as it was. I can tell by his handwriting. He loves me!"

What had come over me? Princess Salome, mistress of a thousand loves, blushing like a school-girl, tearing the petals of daisies, dancing about because a man invited her to skate in the moonlight on the Danube!

I did not wish to analyze, to question, to reason. I was happy — that was sufficient.

I rang for my maids. Three of them dashed into the room.

"Get my things ready, quick! I am going skating to-night! Quick! I shall be in the boudoir in a few minutes. I shall wear my ermine coat to-night!"

They smiled to one another, made curtsies and left.

Lakshmi tapped my ankle.

"I am sorry, Lakshmi. I cannot take you along. If you were a lap-dog, I might find room for you in the sleigh, but you need a sleigh all to yourself. Besides, I want to be alone with the Count."

I laughed.

"Perhaps some day I shall teach you to skate, my friend. It will be greater news than a scandal at Court. A tortoise skating in the moonlight on the Danube! What a sensation!"

I glanced at the table.

"Oh, the letter to Cartaphilus! I forgot all about it! Forgive me, my Much-Beloved, my eternal fiancé! You can easily wait a generation or so for a reply to your letter. Mortals must be served first. Listen, Lakshmi, do you hear the jingle-bells of the Count's sleigh? He is already at the gate. I am losing time. Au revoir, Lakshmi. Adiós, Cartaphilus!"

Leopold encircled my waist more firmly, and led me gently forward.

Was it the Moon which flooded the Danube or the Danube which cast its reflection against the sky?

We glided along in silence like silver-shod dreams. From time to time, the skaters uttered shrill cries of pleasure or mock terror, and snatches of songs whisked by us and disappeared like birds.

The pressure of Leopold's arm became greater and greater, until I barely had space enough to move my legs.

Suddenly he turned and whispered into my ear: "I love you!"

My head reeled. It seemed as if the Moon, and river and stars and the air — had suddenly burst into a triumphant jubilee! "I love you! I love you!"

The world had become an immense belfry and innumerable silver bells chimed one by one —"I love you! I love you!"

Leopold stopped suddenly, and looked into my eyes.

"You are more dazzling than the Moon. I love you!" He pressed his lips against mine in a rapturous kiss.

My heart was a sea which rose and swelled and overflowed. I closed my eyes and buried my face in his shoulder.

"I love you," I murmured.

When I raised my head I saw Lieutenant Ferdinand von Hanau, Leopold's aide-de-camp, his arms akimbo, his arched lips slightly open in an ironic smile, saluting Leopold. He was dressed in his uniform, a red tunic trimmed with gold and white leather trousers tightly drawn over his legs, molding his lithe young body, whose iron muscles shivered and played. On his head he wore a fur cap trimmed with a long aigrette which waved in the air like the triumphant standard of youth.

He looked at the Count, his black eyes blazing, then slowly closing, under their long dark lashes, slightly curved outward. A blue flame seemed to leap from the eyes of one to the eyes of the other.

Leopold turned his face for a moment. Something chilled me. A heavy gray cloud suddenly floated between the Count and me. My heart shrank as if a hand had crumpled it. I shivered.

"Are you chilly?" the Count whispered, his lips grazing my ear.

"Non, non, ce n'est rien," I smiled drearily.

"Bon soir, madame," the Lieutenant said, as if he suddenly noticed me. He bowed with exaggerated deference, his arm upon his chest.

"What a wonderful night for skating!" Ferdinand addressed Leopold.

His voice, a trifle high-pitched, irritated me.

Leopold was apologetic.

"Have you ever seen the Danube — more —" The Count sought for an adjective.

Ferdinand's mouth twisted into an insolent sneer, as he finished the sentence ——

"More slippery."

The Lieutenant was about twenty-one or two, proud with the pride of youthful virility. There was about him an evanescent charm of a wild thing, the insouciance of a young faun. He was a Greek god in the uniform of an Austrian officer.

As he looked from me to Leopold his face changed its expression from disdain to dreaminess and sensuality.

A few skaters pressed us closer together.

The Count muttered something. Ferdinand laughed heartily. His voice rang in the cold air — a challenge and a victory.

Once more the two men looked into each other's eyes, and the flame of their glance was as a rapier with a blue glint piercing my heart.

I pressed Leopold's arm.

"Shall we continue our skating?" I whispered.

"Yes, yes, of course. Will you accompany us, Lieutenant?"

Ferdinand grinned slowly, and shaking his head, said: "Merci, non. I prefer to skate alone — on such — a night, Leopold — alone — with the Moon!"

He bowed.

"Au revoir, Madame. Auf Wiedersehen, Leopold!"

With a swagger, he made a semicircle and disappeared, whistling a tune.

I took Leopold's arm, and we skated for a long time in silence.

"He is a fine chap," Leopold said, a trifle guiltily. "I have known him since he was a boy. He comes of one of the best families in Austria. He was my page, and now he is my aide-de-camp."

"Yes," I said indifferently.

"He is a man of courage and a faithful friend!"

"Yes."

Why the vague unrest in Leopold's voice? Why did he consider it necessary to explain his friend? What secret was there between the two? Why my instant and instinctive antipathy for the young man?

The Count stopped suddenly, looked into my eyes for a long while, then embraced me passionately.

"I love you, I love you," he repeated again and again, kissing my mouth, my eyes, my cheeks, my throat.

The cloud between us vanished. Even the Moon, my ancient enemy, assumed an air of friendliness.

"Leopold," I whispered, "Leopold! I am so happy!" My voice broke, and something gripped me at the throat.

"Salome, my beloved Salome."

"Salome?" I asked astonished.

He smiled. "No other name fits you half as well, beloved. Salome, the most beautiful, the most seductive, the most alluring of women!"

Every word he uttered was a song. His lips were honey and his breath perfume.

"What makes you call me Salome, Leopold?" I asked, intrigued.

"It was you yourself, dearest, who signed the note Salome."

I laughed a little, but I was uneasy. I must not let my emotions overpower me too much. Who knows — I might — inadvertently — betray my age even!

"Salome!"

I was about to exclaim, "Cartaphilus, I love you!"

"Leopold, Leopold!" I repeated several times, as if to

forget the other name, as if to repent for having thought of another, even unconsciously.

"I love you. I shall love you always — and always, Leopold!"

"Salome — your name is a dance — a mad dance of joy!"

"Leopold, I shall dance for you!"

"Dance, my beloved!"

I danced for Leopold's heart on the frozen Danube with greater abandon than I danced for John's head. The Moon wound herself about me like a white scarf. At my feet, the river, like a silver mirror, reflected my movements. I was as a flame breaking through the winter night!

Leopold watched, as a man entranced. His eyes glowed. His hands were pressed together in unconscious adoration.

"Your heart, Leopold, give me your heart!" I whispered.

"Salome, my love!"

Ferdinand passed by. He stopped a moment, watched me scornfully, then applauded dully, with the tips of his fingers.

"Brava! Brava!" he hissed, a lascivious sneer about his lips. The Count was not aware of his presence. His eyes were riveted upon me.

Ferdinand skated on.

I fell into Leopold's arms, who pressed me to his chest until I was breathless.

"Salome, I adore you! Salome!"

My marriage to Graf Leopold von Mansfeld created a sensation in the Capital.

He resigned his commission in the army, and we retired to one of his ancestral castles on the banks of the Danube.

We lived in almost complete seclusion. Weeks, months passed, as migratory birds pass over the surface of rivers, barely ruffling the waters with their wings.

"Lakshmi," I said one day, "forgive me for my neglect of you. I am so happy, my ancient friend! Happy people are cruel!"

Leopold entered.

"In conclave with Frau Lakshmi again, dearest?" he asked, laughing.

"We women understand each other so well, you see, my love."

He seated himself upon the sofa. I jumped upon his knees.

"Leopold, tell me, dear, are you satisfied with your wife?"

He did not answer, but smoothed my hair with the tips of his fingers. A delicious sensation of happiness invaded my body, such as I had not experienced since I was a little girl on the lap of my grandfather.

"Why don't you tell me about your campaigns, dear? Everybody says that you are a great strategist."

He smiled. "What a child! Always stories!"

"When I am with you, I feel like a child. All the centuries roll off ——"

He laughed heartily. "The centuries — again!"

I laughed, and promised to myself to be more careful of what I said. It was strange how my husband's proximity broke the dykes of my consciousness, and the sea of my life overflowed at will.

"What a strange and sensitive child you are, Salome! You speak of centuries, of kings and emperors a thousand years dead, as if you had actually seen and known them."

"Perhaps I did know them ——"

"That's true; after all, who can tell what ancestors are still alive in us? Speaking through us, they make us poets and heroes!"

If only I could tell him the truth! Oh, no, no, never! To him I would remain a mortal woman destined to age and decrepitude and death. A woman who must snatch like all the other women the sweetness of the moment.

I looked at Leopold closely. He was thirty-five. Already tiny wrinkles gathered about his eyes, and a few gray hairs strayed among the blond ones, unwelcome prophets proclaiming destruction. Leopold would get old, and die! I could not endure the thought of it.

"Beloved," I said, "if only you and I could live on forever — if only our love could remain young and fresh as it is now!"

He shook his head.

"No, my dearest, that would be disastrous. It is the constant realization that everything passes, like a river, that gives love a meaning and a sting."

"You don't love me any more, Leopold," I exclaimed.

"I do. I love you, Salome, but I have lived enough," he said wearily.

"Enough? What do you mean?"

"Have I not lived enough, my child, since I have already achieved what every human being hopes, and generally in vain, to achieve — a supreme love?"

There was something in his voice which rang false. I looked into his eyes. He lowered his.

"Leopold — there is a dream in your eyes — a dream of other women — women whom you loved once — women you long to possess. Tell me the truth! I shall understand."

"You are a child," he answered, caressing my throat.

"I may be a child, Leopold, but I have lived too — and read ——"

"Love?" he smiled sadly, not listening to my words, "Love? I have never loved another woman, Salome."

"What!" I laughed dryly. "Leopold — why, you ——"

"Never!" he exclaimed disdainfully, placing me on the sofa and rising.

He walked up and down the room, his hands upon his back. He stopped in front of me.

"You are the only woman I shall ever love, Salome."

"But am I your first love?" I asked.

He nodded.

"The last?" I asked timidly.

"My last."

He seated himself next to me.

"Darling, why do you think it's necessary to lie to me about your past? Don't you trust me? The other women ——"

He interrupted, a trifle angry.

"There were no other women!"

What did he mean? No other women? He was thirty-four at his marriage, famous for arms and gallantry — and yet a virgin! No, that was too ridiculous! What did he mean?

Was there a secret in his life which not even I could discover?

He took my hand in his and fondled it.

"By the way, Salome, to-night is the première at the Opera. His Majesty, the Emperor, has placed his Imperial box at our disposal. Will you go? You haven't been anywhere for a long while. You must be bored a little."

Was he bored with me? Had my love become a trifle irksome? What was there in the ring of his voice which hurt me? I made a vague gesture of refusal.

"But, my dear, the invitation of the Emperor is really a command," he said somewhat irritably.

Still hurt, but unwilling to show it, I rose, and clapped my hands, joyously:

"Yes, let us go, dearest! I'll put my new gown on — you know, the silver taffeta with pearl trimmings — and the coronet which your aunt, the Duchess of Anhalt, gave me as a wedding gift!"

"Yes, do that!" he said, absent-mindedly.

"Do you think I shall look beautiful, Leopold?"

"You are always the most beautiful of women, Salome!"

I threw my arms around him, and kissed him.

Our entrance at the Opera caused a great flutter among the spectators. The silks of the ladies rustled furiously. The sabers and spurs of the officers clinked and rang like jingle bells. The capes of the civilians rose like billows of a sea or beat nervously like wings. Bowing and smiling, and striking of heels against heels.

Two officers of the Imperial Guard led us to our loge which was surmounted by the Crown of the Holy Roman Empire.

It seemed to me I was once again Princess Salome and at my side walked my husband, a tetrarch or a king. But as I looked at Leopold as handsome in his civilian clothes, velvet and rare laces as in his uniform, my heart swelled with joy. Of all my husbands I loved him most. At that moment, not even the proximity of Cartaphilus would have delighted me more.

Whispers, whether intended for my ears or not, I could not tell, spoke of my beauty, of my royal carriage, of my exquisite dress.

The theater was a sea over which sparkled a myriad-colored sun.

Leopold was restless. The music seemed to irritate him.

"Dearest, don't you like the singing?"

"Yes."

"The soprano is marvelous. And she is beautiful, too. Look, dear!"

Leopold clenched his teeth.

What preoccupied his mind?

I placed my hand upon his. He withdrew it gently, but firmly.

The first act was over. The public applauded enthusiastically.

"Bravo! Bravo! Bravissimo!"

The curtain drew together. The people rose to greet one another, or focused their opera-glasses. Our box was bombarded by dozens of tiny cannons.

A little flushed, I pressed Leopold's arm.

"Darling, look. They are all admiring us!"

He shrugged his shoulders.

"Aren't you proud that your wife is the center of admiration, dear?"

He did not hear me.

"What is it, dear?" I asked, anxiously.

His lips twitched.

Suddenly, as if he had flown in, Lieutenant Ferdinand von Hanau appeared in our box, radiant, dazzling in his tight-fitting uniform of a Hussar.

Leopold's face flushed. He jumped from his seat, and grasped the young man's hand.

Their eyes blazed with that same flame as on the night when we skated together on the Danube. Once more a cloud gathered between Leopold and me.

And again, as an afterthought, as if I never mattered,

the Lieutenant bowed before me with an exaggerated courtesy that was almost an insult.

"Bon soir, Madame." Across his impudent lips flitted the sneer that had chilled me at our previous encounter.

Who was this youngster who dared to treat me, Princess Salome, with that cold disdain? I regretted that I was not at the Court of Antipas, Tetrarch of Galilee. I would have ordered his head severed from his impudent neck.

Leopold was oblivious of my presence. I had not seen him so vivacious for weeks.

I bent over the balustrade. All eyes in the audience were riveted upon the two men. There was a general whispering like the hissing of numberless snakes, and grinning and tiny mock gestures.

I clenched my fists. My face flushed. I tried to calm myself. After all, what reason had I to be so indignant? The two friends had not seen each other for months, since our wedding. Had they not the right to be overjoyed? Had not my husband the privilege to forget me for a few minutes? Should I demand not only a man's love but his exclusive companionship, and glare and growl Cerberus-like against his friends?

Was this the sum total of my struggles to liberate woman from her bondage? Was I the inspiration of this tyrannical attitude of the new generation? There had emerged not a new and proud being, but a petty monitor, a schoolma'am, a ferule in her hand and venom on her tongue.

The gavel struck the floor of the stage thrice. The intermission was ended.

Slowly, reluctantly, the buzzing, the rustling, the clanking, subsided, stopped. The leader's baton rose and fell. The orchestra played a few bars. The curtains drew apart slowly.

Leopold and Ferdinand seated themselves next to each other, while I occupied the throne destined for Her Majesty the Empress.

The two men were in complete oblivion of what was transpiring about them. There was an aura of ecstasy about their faces.

It was a friendship greater than friendship. And I who was the many-stringed lyre on which Love had played every cadence of its gamut, I, who had drunk of the ichor of the gods — I was racked with jealousy.

My hand itched to pierce the young Lieutenant's heart. On my lips trembled a hundred imprecations.

Gradually, however, my anger subsided. I had a rival — so be it! I, who conquered the centuries, would conquer a mortal, whose existence ended with a few rotations of the Earth about the Sun! I would be to him I loved — everything — every one — and in the blaze of my greater passion, the minor one would melt and turn to ashes!

As I placed one foot upon the step of our carriage, I heard Leopold whisper to Ferdinand.

"To-morrow at ten."

"Where?"

"At the Hunting Manor."

The two friends parted.

We drove in silence for a while, then, as if nothing had happened. I discussed the music and the singers. Leopold was very affable, but in his ears there rang, I knew, a much more exquisite music than that which had floated across the stage. There rang — the word — the promise — "to-morrow!"

Like Jupiter on that miraculous night when Hercules was conceived, I, too, would stop the sun from rising on the morrow. This night I would merge into another night! "That impudent and handsome youth," I thought, "shall wait in vain at the Hunting Manor. I shall obliterate his very memory."

I laughed a laugh of triumph. Leopold looked at me uneasily.

My boudoir was a temple of Love. The sofas and chairs were like hands caressing, and the silver mirrors replied with their reflection to every gesture of passion. The essences of the rarest flowers, like an exquisite melody, pervaded, imperceptibly, the room. A lamp, like the rays of the sun filtering through silk, fashioned a chiaroscuro which soothed, while the frescoes and paintings by the great Italian masters stirred the imagination to dreams and desires.

Leopold in his dressing-gown of black velvet came to bid me good-night.

I filled two glasses whose crystal dazzled like diamond.

"A l'amour!" I toasted.

"A l'amour," he replied, with a "double entendre," blushing guiltily at his duplicity.

I smiled indulgently. "Wait, beloved," I thought, "I shall soon bind you to me as Venus bound Tannhäuser to herself. I shall bind you with a double chain — to Venus and — to her son!"

I pressed my glass to his lips.

"Drink, beloved! The night is young, and to-morrow is on the knees of Jove!"

There was a twitch about his lips, like the tiny ripple a pebble makes on the surface of the water.

I laughed.

"Leopold, will you excuse me for a moment?"

I retired behind a screen made of the tusks of giant elephants and upon which were carved the amours of the Goddess of the Triple Gate.

I emerged — a boy — a page in blue velvet.

The rotundity of my womanhood hardened into the severity of masculine lines. Aphrodite stiffened into Eros.

My breasts vanished in the metamorphosis, and unlike other women, whose femininity is emphasized in masculine habiliments, every contour of my body partook of that epicene charm which delighted the blue-bearded lover of Rossignol and Jeanne Darc.

I walked about the room. My gait had the sauciness of youth. I threw a glance at the mirror. My face was a boy's face!

I stopped in front of Leopold, who, bewildered and entranced, had watched every gesture and movement I made.

I smiled the insolent smile of youth conscious of his masculine power and prowess.

Leopold exclaimed in uttermost delight: "Eros!"

His face was illumined as with a torch.

His hands, trembling, caressed and searched every part of my body, and they were not disappointed. Had not I explored the secrets of the African Aphrodite in the love temples of India?

"You are Eros," he exclaimed triumphantly, "and your body is his body!"

He carried me to the sofa, and bending over me kissed me with a rapture he had never kissed before....

The reflection of the Moon through the window shivered and broke under us like a white sea in a storm. The storm changed to the various parts of the compass. Passion took numberless shapes and forms. Not in vain had I been a priestess in the Temple of the Goddess of the Triple Gate!

Leopold swooned in ecstasy.

My eyes swimming with passion, I leaped off the sofa, and wound about my body a Spanish mantilla embroidered with gold and studded with jewels.

The austerity of my lines disappeared.

The stiffness of Eros melted into the softness of Aphrodite. I was the Astarte of the Triple Gate. My breasts blossomed again. The enticing mystery of the epicene vanished into the voluptuousness of all-comprehending womanhood, all-encompassing, all-enclosing.

I took a few steps into the room. My gait was the gait of Egyptian dancers.

Leopold reclining, his eyes heavy with desire, murmured words of love.

He rose, approached me, and took the mantilla off my body. He breathed deeply the scent of my body and the scent of the boudoir. Slowly, carefully, deliberately, he placed the cloak around the lamp....

"Salome — Eros — Aphrodite," he whispered.

Our mouths drank of each other deeply, incessantly. All Passion's secrets were distilled into our kisses. The double flower of pleasure blossomed for us out of the bosom of Night. We were neither man nor woman — but a dual rapture, a gust of passion.

Weary at length of my tantalizing caresses, Leopold fell

asleep as a child between my breasts, incarnadined by his kisses.

"There will be no to-morrow," I smiled.

"Leopold," I whispered.

He did not answer.

"Still asleep, my darling?"

I tapped the pillow, then suddenly uneasy, I opened my eyes wide.

"Leopold!"

The sun flooded the room, and outside the rays filtered through the snow-flakes, as through a silver sieve.

Suddenly I heard the tinkling of bells. I looked out of the window, my heart sinking with premonition.

In the distance, I caught a glimpse of two figures reclining in a sleigh. I strained my eyes. It was Leopold. His hand rested upon Ferdinand's shoulder.

An insolent metallic laughter broke the stillness of the morning. I watched the sleigh become smaller and smaller, until it was a blue spot in the white of the snow.

Lakshmi tapped at the door.

I opened it.

"Lakshmi!" I said sadly.

I waited for her to enter, but she did not budge.

"Come in, Lakshmi, my ancient and faithful friend. Come in, my adorable footstool."

Lakshmi did not stir. She stretched her head forward, and remained like a statue of mother-of-pearl.

I walked into the room. She did not follow me.

"What troubles you, Lakshmi?"

Her neck was an arrow pointing East.

I watched her for a long while, trying to discover the meaning of her gesture.

Finally I understood.

"You are right, Lakshmi. Like a weathercock, you point in the right direction. The Wind of Destiny has shown the way. East! East! To Tibet and Cartaphilus! To the ancient gods and the immortals!"

Lakshmi approached me, and tapped my ankle....

CHAPTER FIFTY-TWO

I SEEK THE LAMA, CARTAPHILUS — I ENTER TIBET — CARTAPHILUS WORSHIPS HIS NAVEL — THE INSOLENCE OF KOTIKOKURA — I AM A NUN OF BUDDHA — THE BAD TASTE OF THE GODS — THE PARALYTIC EAST AND THE BLATANT WEST.

PERCHED upon the mountain like a stork on one foot the Temple of Buddha the Conqueror seemed the symbol of the insecurity and transitoriness of all things terrestrial.

Descending from the yak, whose immense horns and long silky hair glistened from the morning dew, I walked alongside of the animal, leisurely, in the direction of the holy house whose avatar of Buddha was Lama Cartaphilus. At my heels, like a faithful dog, Lakshmi followed, with the uttermost confidence that all things are best in the best of all possible worlds.

I turned around.

"Lakshmi, before long we shall be in the presence of our equals — the two immortals, Cartaphilus and Kotikokura."

Lakshmi lowered slowly her horny eyelids.

"How can you be so unsentimental? When I am as old as you, shall I, too, gaze drearily ahead of me, Lakshmi?"

The yak mooed sadly. The echo of her melancholy voice tore the mist whose shreds clung to the mountains like cobwebs.

"Our beast is hungry, Lakshmi. Let us stop awhile, and feed her."

I placed a hillock of hay in front of the yak. Her enormous mouth, whitened with foam, moved like a pair of scissors, and made a noise like the applause of professional claqueurs.

The sun appeared suddenly on the peak of the Himalayas, like a tiara of molten rubies upon the head of a Pontiff garbed in a mantle of white silk. Poppies red and blue pierced the snow and looked about like mysterious eyes.

"Let us utter a prayer to the Immortal Gautama Sakyamuni who guided our steps to his sacred precincts."

Lakshmi lowered her head.

"What a trip, Lakshmi! If I count the years rightly, it took us nearly a generation from Vienna to Tibet — sufficient time for my husband, Count Leopold von Mansfeld to be gathered to his forefathers, or sit, doddering at his fireside, dreaming of Salome, who one marvelous night, long, long ago was for him both Eros and Aphrodite!"

I laughed drearily.

"Or, perhaps, he gazes with impotent senile lasciviousness at the pages whose youthful bodies are firmly molded in their tight-fitting uniforms."

I sighed.

"I loved him, Lakshmi — but it is folly to love a mortal. Mortals are too restless, too avid of the moment. They must snatch their pleasures quickly, sipping at a dozen cups at the same time, like mad bees on spring days."

A monk approached. He was still young, but his face was a wrinkled parchment drawn across a skull, out of which flickered vaguely two eyes, like a pair of fireflies at dawn. He was naked with the exception of a girdle around his loins, and a pair of sandals whose strings dangled and impeded his walking. His skin was covered with sores and bites and vermin which the holy man in order to achieve redemption allowed to torment him. His few black teeth chattered in the chilly morning air.

I opened one of the sacks which hung over the back of the yak, and offered him a bowl of rice. He ate drearily, as if merely to be polite to the Universe, thanked me in the name of Buddha, and resumed his aimless itinerary.

"Lakshmi, is it possible that God prefers pain and ugliness to joy and beauty?"

Lakshmi held a blade of grass in her mouth, horizontally like a green mustache.

"In my day in Jerusalem, if a man lived the martyr life of this monk, he was at least a prophet who thundered in magnificent dithyrambs anathemas against sin and iniquity! It was not his own precious soul that he yearned to save, but the souls of his brethren!"

A flock of crows flew past us with a piercing, triumphant cry.

"Some dead monk, no doubt, Lakshmi, whose carcass invites the birds."

Lakshmi looked unperturbed.

My yak finished eating, and licked her mouth with her great red tongue.

I rubbed her nose and smoothed her curly fur, which hung like fringes of a cape.

"Now, good mother, you shall give us of your milk."

I placed a bowl on the ground and pressed gently a heavy udder like an enormous ripe grape. The milk flowed into the bowl to the brim, and spilled generously, making a large white puddle which Lakshmi lapped greedily.

I drank the warm essence of life.

"Lakshmi, look at this kindly and humble creature! Her back is loaded with the goods of the world; her womb is heavy with progeny; her udder feeds us. How like a woman, Lakshmi! And how like a woman the scorn accorded her! Is it she or her vain mate, the bull, who is the symbol of divinity?"

Lakshmi, her head hoary with the milk, looked at me sadly. The she-yak mooed pathetically. I sighed.

The sun spread a roseate glow over the Himalayas which rose in tiers like the colossal rungs of the ladder on which gods descend to Earth, and the perfect spirits of men ascend to Heaven.

In the distance a caravan of yaks meandered like a file of gigantic ants. From time to time a bear raised his head over the cliffs, sniffed the air and vanished.

I took the small silver mirror out of my belt, and arranged coquettishly my one hundred and eight plaits in honor of the one hundred and eight Chapters of the Kondjur. I reddened my lips and my cheeks and printed a tiny spot the shape of a heart upon my chin.

"At any rate, Lakshmi, I am a real Tibetan woman. No one suspects the hoax. Oh, if the holy monks at the gates of Tibet had guessed what whiteness lies under this yellow paint, who knows in what dungeons our bones would rot now! As for you, Lakshmi, you are positively a Mandarin of the First Order with that proud green mustache of yours!"

Lakshmi looked disdainful, as if being less than the Emperor or the Empress of Cathay was too insignificant an honor.

"If you could press your paw upon my heart, Lakshmi, you would feel how it beats, now that the Temple over which my beloved is Buddha, looks at us like a dreamy eye!"

Lakshmi admired the patient yak which ruminated beatifically.

"You do not know why, do you, Lakshmi? I have come as the bride of Cartaphilus," I said demurely, my face reddening a little.

The blade of grass dropped out of her mouth.

"We shall marry at once! After all, aren't seventeen centuries of betrothal sufficient, Lakshmi? What if I haven't achieved what I set out to do, what if the Moon still tyrannizes over woman, and man still postures, the Peacock of the Universe? Has Cartaphilus achieved perfection? Is he not still seeking what he sought when the incomparable Apollonius, handsome as an Olympian, gauged with his wisdom Heaven and Earth? Can we not continue our work together? Must I seek the embraces of unfaithful mortals? I am lonesome, Lakshmi, and so is Cartaphilus. What we really seek is each other!"

Lakshmi bent to raise the blade.

"Lakshmi," I asked, laughing, "for how many thousands of years were you betrothed to Vishnu, God of the Universe, before you married him? How many tortoises did you embrace before you became worthy of the supreme love? Or were you a virgin? Were you the first tortoise that inhabited the Earth? Are all the billions of tortoises that crowd the lakes and seas or wander silently on the surface of the Earth spawn of your spawn, unworthy progeny of Lakshmi and Vishnu?"

I looked at her intently. Something that resembled vaguely a smile, or a sneer crossed her beak.

"Ah, my chelonian friend, if only I could decipher the wrinkles upon your head or the light that plays upon the magnificent lacquer of your carapace! What hieroglyphics carved upon the most ancient pyramids or drawn upon the most sacred parchments of the Hindus or the Egyptians could unfold half as marvelous a tale?"

Lakshmi yawned.

"But we had better continue our journey. We are still about a half-hour away from the Temple."

I mounted the yak. Lakshmi kept in step with the dreary hoofbeats of my beast.

"What bride, Lakshmi, would undergo perils such as I have undergone in order to meet her groom — deserts, mountains, seas, marauders, pirates, irate monks, soldiers with drawn swords, wild animals, wars, pestilences! I spent a fortune sufficient to buy the whole of Tibet to bribe the guardians of this land! What male or tortoise, or god, Lakshmi, is worth it?"

I stopped a moment, then added, "— save Cartaphilus!"

Lakshmi closed one eye.

"Do you think he will recognize me, Lakshmi, in the guise of a Chinese peasant woman? How funny I look — yellow as a lemon, my eyes squinting as if I gazed at the noon-day sun, my hair blacker than the wings of the crows that flew past us a while ago?"

Lakshmi lengthened her steps.

"Oh, yes, he will recognize me. His heart is trembling with joy — a secret joy which he cannot name. He feels I am near him. Do I not always know when he is in my vicinity? Are not our souls and our bodies branches of the same tree? Do we not draw life from the selfsame root?"

I entered the Temple, Lakshmi at my side.

A heavy column supported the room like an umbrella. Around the walls were statues of wood and bronze of the gods — Varuna and Ushas, and the avatars of Vishnu — Matsya the fish, Varah the boar, Vaman the dwarf, Yama the implacable judge of the dead, Karma the turtle.

In the corners, the worshipers squatted or stood motionless like ecstatic spiders, their eyes riveted upon themselves or in vacuity, hoping to capture in their spiritual nets, Nirvana, the priceless Fly! From time to time they turned their prayer-wheels, repeating with the monotony of the bee buzzing over a flower the eternal invocation — "Om mani padme hum! Om mani padme hum! Om mani padme hum!"

In the center of the Temple upon a pedestal of jade, his legs underneath him, his hands upon his lap, Cartaphilus sat — the Avatar of Gautama the Buddha. Over his shoulders was thrown a robe of yellow and red silk. Upon his head he wore a miter the shape of a turban. His yellow lacquered body was stripped to the waist. His eyes elongated like a drowsy cat's gazed at his navel around which glowed like a halo — the symbol of eternity — a phosphorescent circle.

To the right of him, Kotikokura, whose natural color required no paint, endeavored to concentrate his restless eyes upon his navel, which protruded from his body as if still bound to the umbilical cord of his maternal ancestor.

By the sudden flush of his face, and tremor of his lips I knew that Cartaphilus was fully aware of my presence, but like the god he embodied upon earth, he remained motionless and unperturbed. Kotikokura watched his master with the corner of his eye, and imitated his immobility.

Lakshmi wandered about the statues, remained standing in front of Vishnu for a while, then approached Karma, the turtle, and tapped the base with her beak. Ecstatically, like a person recently anointed with holy water, she returned to my side.

I approached the ear of the Lama, and whispered: "Cartaphilus."

Lakshmi approached Kotikokura and struck him with her paw.

For a time neither the erstwhile god of Africa nor his High Priest deigned to budge.

Slowly, Cartaphilus raised his head, looked at me, his eyes blurred with the months, the years perhaps, of concentration.

"Sholom Alechim," I said, bowing.

In a voice which seemed to emerge from the depths of the Universe, he said in Greek:

"Salome, seek thy soul in contemplation, for only in contemplation shalt thou find thy soul."

This Biblical alliterative manner of speech amused me.

I laughed a little.

Kotikokura raised his head, looked at Lakshmi with an air of supreme disdain, and growled something which sounded like a grotesque echo of his master.

Lakshmi, scared or amused, withdrew her head quickly.

"Is the navel the new habitation of the soul, Cartaphilus?" I asked.

"The soul is at the core of the Universe, even as the navel is at the core of the body. Contemplate the core which bindeth us to Life even as the umbilical cord bindeth us to the womb of our mothers. Sever the chain from Life with thy contemplation even as the midwife severeth the umbilical cord with her scissors."

I looked at him, bewildered. Was he jesting? Was he in one of his theatrical moods?

"Free thy body from the dross of the Earth, and thy soul from the dross of Life! Enter Nirvana!"

"What is the meaning of this gibberish, Cartaphilus?" I asked playfully.

A supercilious glance reminded me of the youthful Cartaphilus, who although the son of a cobbler had the impudence to ridicule royalty.

"Won't Cartaphilus ever change?" I asked. He understood the ironic undercurrent of my words.

"What are queens and princesses? Their bodies are sepulchers wherein worms feast and make merry," he replied, his lips lengthening into a sarcastic sneer.

What had come over him? Why, when I loved him most, when I came to offer myself to him, did he treat me with superhuman disdain?

Too angry, too hurt to answer him, I stamped my foot, and muttered under breath — "Isaac!"

Kotikokura, less philosophic than his master, kicked Lakshmi with the tip of his sandal.

Lakshmi looked at me pathetically.

A monk entered, knelt before Cartaphilus, then joined the rest of the worshipers in silent contemplation and in turning the prayer wheels. "Om mani padme hum! Om mani padme hum!"

"Gautama taught humility, but disciples notoriously misinterpret their masters!"

"I am not a disciple. I am the Lama. I am Gautama incarnate!" Cartaphilus exclaimed.

Kotikokura bowed until his head touched the ground.

"And Kotikokura is Gautama's High Priest!" I laughed.

"Go, woman, seek thy soul!" Cartaphilus pointed his forefinger to the door.

Kotikokura pointed his foot to Lakshmi.

A multitude of emotions gripped me — to wring the neck of the two men, to shout ugly epithets, to cry, to laugh, to throw my arms around my ancient companion, and say — "Cartaphilus, my beloved, my husband — stop playing the pious and divine comedian! Let us be happy at last!"

Cartaphilus lowered his eyes, and began once again the endless contemplation of his navel.

Kotikokura imitated his master.

I waited a long while, undecided what to do. Finally, recalling that I was Salome, princess and queen, maker of popes and heroines and martyrs, I turned my back upon an impudent upstart divinity, and motioning to Lakshmi, left the Temple.

I sat at the open door of the Temple dedicated to the World Mother. My garb of a Buddhist nun hung heavily on me in the hot sun, and I fanned myself with a dry bamboo leaf. Lakshmi at my side chewed gloomily the withered heart of a cabbage.

The wooden pillars supporting the Temple were rotted and covered with dull-colored lichen on which crawled long-tailed lizards. The Eastern wall was a large painting of the Goddess in whose womb the Universe lived for æons before it was born. The snakes in her hair had lost their contours. Her fine delicate face was nearly obliterated and the golden dragon which had originally upheld her had turned to a smudge. In the wide crevices nameless vermin laid their cocoons.

On the floor filthy with ancient footprints three women, ageless and sexless, sat in tatters, grumbling and praying from time to time — the last of the worshipers of her who created the cosmos.

At intervals a peasant passed by, emaciated and dreary-eyed.

"I followed the advice of Cartaphilus. I became a nun of Buddha. I sought my soul and the final meaning of Life in the hollow of my navel. Contemplation without action, Lakshmi, leads not to Nirvana but to vacuity."

Lakshmi tore at the cabbage angrily.

"Look about you, Lakshmi, see the ignorance, the filth, the superstition, the hopelessness rampant among these Tibetans, who in their insuperable vanity consider themselves the chosen ones of Buddha! My people too consider themselves the chosen children of Jahveh, although they are the slaves and scapegoats of all the nations."

I laughed bitterly.

"What odd taste the gods display in their choice! How shabbily they treat their favorite progenies!"

A horse so lean that his ribs had already torn through his skin in places, and covered with wounds over which large flies buzzed ominously, tottered wearily by.

"What strange and cruel kindness, Lakshmi! They starve

these poor beasts tortured with disease, when they are no longer useful and their skins are valueless, but if one in compassion should put an end to their misery, Tibet would be scandalized. The priests in their divine wrath would stone the offender to death!"

Lakshmi crushed a worm with her paw.

"Lakshmi!" I exclaimed, "you have killed a child of God! Your soul must wander from leprous body to leprous body in numberless incarnations before you expiate your sin! Do you not see with what infinite care and tenderness these people remove from their bodies the lice which devour them?"

Against the background of the mountain, a man whose gray beard nearly touched the ground stood in ecstasy, his right arm, withered, raised above his head.

"This is the symbol of the East, Lakshmi — a paralyzed arm. In paralysis and death it seeks life. But life is action, Lakshmi!"

Lakshmi continued her murderous career. Her paw followed mercilessly the surprised vermin which infested the cabbage.

"There is muscle in thought as there is in the leg. To gaze in ecstasy at the navel or the sky is merely to hypnotize oneself. Even Cartaphilus discovered this. He is no longer a Lama. He has left the Temple of Buddha the Conqueror, and he is seeking me. Ah, but he shall not find me so easily! I must punish him for his arrogance. In my heart, of course, I have already forgiven him. He is only a male-child, absorbed in new toys."

Lakshmi, disgusted with the cabbage, approached me and tapped my ankle.

"Perhaps it was Providence, after all. The time is not yet ripe for our union."

Lakshmi lowered her horny eyelids.

"And you have forgiven Kotikokura, have you not, Lakshmi? He is hardly out of his swaddling-clothes!"

I rose.

Lakshmi uttered a sound which approximated laughter.

"To-morrow we return to the West, Lakshmi — to the

blatant, the noisy, the coarse, but living West! The East is no longer our home, Lakshmi — although we both had our birth here! We have outgrown our race and our ancestry! Come, Lakshmi, let the dead bury the dead!"

CHAPTER FIFTY-THREE

THE COURT OF CATHERINE — PLATONIC FRIENDSHIP — THIRTEEN LOVERS — CATHERINE BARES HER HEART — THE STALLIONS OF THE EMPRESS — THE MALICE OF THE WANING MOON — VILLAGES OF POTEMKIN — WANDERING JEWESS AND WANDERING TURTLE.

The imperial garden was illuminated with hundreds of Japanese lanterns hanging from the branches of the trees like many-colored moons caught in a net.

The élite of the Russian nobility walked up and down the pathways which formed a colossal star about the base of the great stairway of the palace.

The jewels dimmed the lights of the lamps and the perfumes obscured the scents of the flower-beds. The enormous hoops of the ladies rubbed and creaked against one another like boats in a regatta, while the long silver spurs on the boots of the officers rang like bells.

Count Nicolai Nicolaievitch Vorontsov, rotund, red-faced, long-whiskered, who was designated by Her Majesty as my escort, because of his knowledge of French, approached me, as much as my hoop allowed, and whispered into my ear the newest scandals. He laughed and coughed at the same time, and his face swelled like a turkey's crest. As if to console himself that he must forever remain a spectator in this delightful comedy, he uttered "Nitchevo! Nitchevo!" at the end of each salacious episode.

"Her Majesty," he whispered, "does not discard her lovers as she discards her gloves. Whoever she has deigned to notice even once, is forever remembered. Generalship, governorship and even a crown is the reward of those who have tasted of one hour of Imperial favor!"

He caught his breath, and sighed.

Did he sigh because his grotesque homeliness had always precluded so distinguished an honor?

I looked into his eyes whose original color may have been blue, but which like an imperfect dye had nearly entirely disappeared in the strong acid of time.

The Count placed his arm about my waist, as if absent-mindedly, but finding it too difficult an undertaking because of the rheumatism which tormented him, dropped it, and laughed ironically.

"Nitchevo!"

I smiled.

He kissed my hand. "Ah, Madame, vous êtes exquise!"

"Merci, Monsieur!"

He looked at me, his ironically inflamed eyes half closed, his bulbous nose creased like a ruffled lake.

"Ma chère, I am old enough to be your father — will you allow me to give you a good counsel?"

"Fathers always have that privilege," I answered.

"And daughters the privilege of disobeying, n'est-ce pas?"

He tried to laugh, but his face became scarlet. He decided to be serious.

"What is the advice you would give me, Monsieur le Comte?"

"Beware of Gregory Alexandrovitch!" he exclaimed, his forefinger, as stubby as a sausage, raised in the air.

"Is Prince Potemkin so dangerous?" I asked.

"Dorogaya," he pressed my hand, "Gregory Alexandrovitch is not a man — he is ——"

"Not — le Diable?" I interrupted in mock terror.

"He is a stallion!" he exclaimed. And in his voice there was that melancholy envy the ox bears his unexpurgated brother.

"Have you not heard about his amours?" he asked.

"In the week that I have been on Russian soil, I have heard so much that I have decided to relegate many things to sheer gossip, Count."

"That is so. There is a great deal of gossip in Russia, alas! We are mighty talkers and boasters. But what they say of the Prince is truth, I swear it, Madame!"

"What do they say, Count?"

"What they say, dushenka? What don't they say? And what is the difference what they say? What I have seen with my own eyes, Madame — what I have heard with my own ears —" He raised his short arms to indicate that he would need eternity to recount everything.

"Look about you, Madame — there is hardly a beautiful woman holding the arm of her sweetheart or her consort who has not been bruised by his caresses!"

"Aren't the Russians jealous, Count?"

"The Russian loves his head a trifle more than his woman!"

"Is the Prince really so powerful?"

"Even the moujik knows that the Batushka of all Russia is Gregory Alexandrovitch Potemkin, Governor General of all the Southern Provinces, Grand Admiral of the Black Sea, Prince of the German Empire, official occupant of the apartment adjoining Her Majesty's boudoir! And to think, lubushka, that his father was a mere major — not even a baron! Ah, what a great heart beats in the chest of our Czarina! Whom she loves — prospers! He is like a plant blessed by the rain and the sun!"

He pulled at his beards, and sighed —"Nitchevo!"

"And does Her Majesty allow the Prince to indulge in his extramural escapades?"

"She watches him as a cat watches a mouse. She has a hundred spies, but you just tell her what happens, and you are a lucky dog if you are not dispatched to Siberia! What, her little Gregory Alexandrovitch is unfaithful to her! We are all jealous of him. That's what it is!"

He laughed suddenly, closing his eyes.

"They say, however, that his day is nearing twilight."

"Has he been ordered to vacate the Imperial apartment?"

"Not that, not that — but even stallions are human, you know. Even a river runs dry if there is a drought, if the winds don't allow the clouds to gather!"

The gates of the palaces were thrown open, and a company of trumpeters played the Imperial march.

"You will soon see, dorogaya!" the Count whispered.

The nobility aligned itself in two files.

Under a golden canopy, carried by eight officers, Her Majesty, Catherine II, Empress of all the Russias, leaning upon the arm of Gregory Alexandrovitch Potemkin, descended the marble stairs into the garden.

The officers lifted the canopy and carried it away. The visitors bowed and made curtsies as Her Majesty or the Prince addressed them or shook hands with them.

Catherine was in a joyous mood. Her face had lost some of the podginess which I had noticed in our first encounter. Her sea-blue eyes had a girlish mischievousness in them. Her small mouth was puckered into a constant smile. Underneath the voluminous hoop of brocaded silver, her body vibrated and danced.

Potemkin in his uniform of Admiral of the Black Sea, loaded with decorations, towered over the rest like a colossus. His face indicated his common ancestry — two small keen black eyes, high cheekbones, a heavy mouth, a square chin. He was a stallion — but not a stallion de race. If he pulled the chariot of state, he would pull it as a mighty draft-horse, tearing over cobblestones, noisily, impetuously, crushing under his powerful hoofs whatever was in the way.

Potemkin took out of his pocket a snuffbox encrusted with diamonds, opened it and offered it to Her Majesty, who placed the tips of her fingers in it, rubbed the tobacco delicately, then drew it into her nostrils. She closed her eyes and sneezed daintily into her lace handkerchief. This was the signal for a dozen snuffboxes to be tapped and opened, and a general sneezing among the ladies and gentlemen.

Tiny grains of tobacco dotted the nostrils of the visitors or spotted the mustache. I thought of the strange habits of people and how much lovelier was the smoking of pipes in China.

Servants brought platters of sweets and flagons of wine. The guests raised their glasses and toasted to the Empress and to one another. The silence which had fallen over the people at the appearance of Catherine gradually gave way to laughter and bantering.

Her Majesty whispered something into Potemkin's ear. He turned around, scrutinized me, then smiled, his large white teeth dazzling.

There was an animal magnetism about the man which was undeniable. Count Vorontsov grunted and scraped his feet. Her Majesty made a sign to me to approach. She looked at me and then at the Count, and a wicked little smile crossed her lips and eyes.

Gregory Alexandrovitch laughed noisily.

"Well, Count," he said, his voice rumbling like the beating of a huge drum, "you are a fortunate dog to have so beautiful a companion!"

"Yes, Your Highness."

"How is your asthma?"

"The same, thank you."

"And your rheumatism?"

"The same."

"And your digestion?"

"Thank you."

"Hahahaha!" the Prince roared.

Catherine struck his arm.

"Gregory Alexandrovitch, will you let my good friend Nicolai Nicolaievitch alone?"

"Surely, Your Majesty. Shake hands, Nicolai Nicolaievitch."

The Prince tightened his fist over the Count's hand. Vorontsov bent in pain, breathed through his open mouth, danced.

Her Majesty laughed. The guests applauded.

"It's enough, Gregory Alexandrovitch," Her Majesty commanded.

The Prince unclasped his hand. The Count shook it violently, and, to conceal his embarrassment, laughed.

"Now, Gregory Alexandrovitch, entertain our guests. As soon as they see me, all merriment goes out of them. I am like the head of Medusa among them. Besides, I desire to speak to the Baroness."

Potemkin kissed Catherine's hand, bowed to me, and mingled with the crowd. Vorontsov was undecided whether to stay or go. Her Majesty whispered into his ear: "Watch him, Nicolai Nicolaievitch."

"Yes, Your Majesty."

Catherine took my arm, and we walked slowly away from the rest.

"We Russians are primitive in our humor."

I looked at her. She had really become a Russian — her face, her speech, her manners.

Guessing my thoughts, she pursued: "A sovereign must understand her people. She must make herself in their image. She must be their prototype, body and soul. I have forgotten I was ever a German."

"All Europe envies Russia. My friend, Voltaire, speaks of it as the one place in which liberty and intelligence rule, Your Majesty."

"When I came to Russia I made the following resolutions: to please the Grand Duke, to please the Empress, to please the Nation." She sighed. "I was not successful in my first resolution. The Grand Duke was more fit for a clown than for an emperor, and he had even less talent for a husband. He was far more interested in his dogs and cats and maidservants than in me. It is history now."

Did she try thus to excuse whatever share she had in Peter's assassination?

Catherine kissed the small cross which hung around her neck and said piously, "May Jesus and the saints forgive him!

"In my second resolution I was often successful, although it was not an easy matter to please the sainted Empress. In my third resolution, the world is my judge. Russia was a nation of barbarians and illiterates.

"I have built academies, I have created a great navy and a great army. I have abolished flogging. I shall free the serfs and introduce a code of laws based on the philosophy of Montesquieu. I am putting into practice the new humanity of the Encyclopedists. I have enlarged my country's territory, that liberty may have wider frontiers."

She struck the ground with her tall ebony cane encrusted with sapphires.

"By the help of God I shall drive the Turk out of Europe and make Constantinople a Russian seaport!"

Her face glowed with intelligence and magnanimity. I was in the presence of a greater Zenobia. Had I discovered at last the Messiah who would free woman?

"Ah, if I were a man!" she exclaimed.

"Your Majesty," I said, "what male monarch in all the world can compare with you? The era of woman is here!"

She smiled sadly.

"To govern one must have eyes and hands. A woman, alas, has only ears!"

She turned abruptly about, and looked intently in the direction of her guests.

Her face had lost her majesty and her beauty. She was a middle-aged woman worrying about the escapades of her young lover.

"Your letter of introduction from Voltaire was a jewel," the Empress said absent-mindedly. "That man is the greatest genius the world has even seen. He understands human nature as no other man. Ever since I was a little girl I have read every line he wrote, and every line is perfect."

Once again, she turned around.

"Ma chère," she said anxiously, "I believe I have neglected my guests too long. Let us go among them."

I caught a glimpse of Potemkin bending over the shoulder of a woman.

"In a few days I shall send for you, Baroness. We shall talk of many things at our leisure."

I thanked her for her gracious invitation, and we walked in silence, rather rapidly, toward the others.

The last echoes of the great chimes vanished in the air, like eagles in flight. The cupolas and the turrets of the Kremlin were pools of gold in which the sky mirrored itself. A barge floated on the canal lazily like a reverie. In the distance a regiment of cavalry galloped to the barracks.

For a long time I bent out of the window, and numberless thoughts, like fireflies, lit in my brain and vanished. A nostalgia for my childhood and my native city invaded my heart. I longed to sit once more on my grandfather's lap, and hear him recount tales. I longed for my nurse, for my cousin, for the hills that overlooked Jerusalem. I longed for my pristine hopes and illusions.

What was this world in which I moved as a dream? Who were these strangers that surrounded me? What had I in common with them? Why dance attendance to this middle-aged queen who was a slave to the biological functions of her sex? A few more years, and Her Majesty Catherine, Empress of all the Russias, and her lover, Prince Potemkin, Admiral of the Black Sea, and all the ladies and gentlemen of the court and all the millions of people that inhabited the vast Empire, would be as the dust under the hoofs of her steeds. A few more centuries and all these mighty fortresses, and palaces and churches would be less than the snuff which made the Empress sneeze.

Were it not wiser to gaze upon the comedy like a god, and like a god laugh? Were it not better to let these children play out their lives like toys whose springs are wound? Should I not shrug my shoulders and say, "Nitchevo"?

No, no! If the gods merely laughed, I would be greater than the gods! I would mingle my destiny with the destiny of these mortals! I would not be like a tree thousands of years old, rooted to the same spot forever and forever bearing and shedding its leaves!

I was Woman — and my children were the children of the Universe! Had I been a mother, would not my blood run by now through the veins of all the inhabitants of the Earth?

Scraping of the feet and several coughs interrupted my meditation. I looked around. Count Nicolai Nicolaievitch Vorontsov, dressed in a colonel's uniform, saluted, clicking his heels. His face was more scarlet than ever, and his eyes more colorless.

"I have been looking high and low for you, Madame," he said, tearing at his mustache, stained from the snuff.

"I am sorry, Count."

"I was standing with you near the gate. I turned around for a moment to watch the guards change, and as I turned back — you had disappeared."

I laughed.

" 'Where is that child?' I said to myself, squinting my eyes in all directions. 'Where is she? How did she disappear? Did the gypsies steal her?' "

"Or maybe — Gregory Alexandrovitch Potemkin?" I added, in mock terror.

"He, of course, is capable of everything. But I trust you."

"Merci, Monsieur," I curtsied.

"Well, for a half-hour now, I have been rushing up and down, entering into all the rooms, opening doors that I should not have opened. What strange things one sees, nenogladnaya, when one opens a door unexpectedly!"

He wiped his forehead with a large colored handkerchief.

"But the Lord be praised. I have found you at last."

"And I am glad you have found me, Count."

"Is it true, dorogaya?" he asked, pressing my hand and looking tenderly into my eyes.

"Yes."

He kissed my hand several times.

"Je vous aime, ma chère!" he exclaimed suddenly, pressing both hands upon his chest.

He looked at me, his lips trembling, expecting no doubt that I should either be scandalized or burst into laughter.

"Je vous aime aussi," I said in all sincerity, for I had grown to like this grotesque man more than any one else in Russia save Catherine.

"Ma chère, ma petite, cara, querida, Liebchen," he stammered through a half-dozen languages, rubbed his hands, stood upon one foot, then upon the other. Had he been a dog his tail would have wagged itself out of its socket.

Suddenly he stiffened up.

"It's he!" he said, breathing through his mouth.

"Who?"

"Gregory Alexandrovitch. I can recognize his footsteps. When he walks not only the floor shakes, but the ceiling."

"You exaggerate, mon cher. He is not quite so big."

"No? Don't you think so?" he asked delightedly.

"I have seen taller and more powerful men than he. And he is not particularly handsome."

"Isn't he? You are an angel!" He kissed my hand.

"He is inspecting his stallions," he whispered into my ear.

"His stallions?" I asked.

"Not his precisely. The human stallions of our Little Mother," he smiled bitterly. "Gregory Alexandrovitch chooses them and trains them."

"What do you mean?"

He motioned to me with his forefinger. We walked on tiptoes. He pointed to the keyhole.

"Regardez," he whispered.

About a dozen young men, gigantic in every respect, dressed in officers' snug-fitting uniforms, were prancing up and down the hall, their muscles taut. Potemkin, his snuff-box in his half-closed palm, watched them intently. Now and then he complimented one, or scolded another for not standing more erect.

Vorontsov pulled gently at my sleeve, and led me away.

"That man is a true animal, ma chère. He not only sees through wood, he can smell spies a mile away.

"I must give the Prince credit for his ability to choose — that I must. Our Little Mother can depend upon him." He rubbed his hands with malicious glee. "Many of them are privates or corporals, but after they pass through Her Majesty's bedchamber, they will all be generals." He sighed. "And look at me — at fifty-five I am still a colonel — I, a Count. I fought in two wars, I have been as faithful to Matushka as a dog. Still a colonel," he repeated pathetically.

A lady-in-waiting of the Empress approached us.

"Madame, Her Majesty commands your presence."

The Count lingered for a long time over my hand. Across his heavy blue-veined nose ran a tiny stream of tears.

Suddenly he turned upon his heels and rushed out.

I knew he was the best friend I had in Russia, who would sacrifice his life to defend me.

Her Majesty reclined upon the low sofa reading a book. I was welcomed by a salvo of barks of great variety. There was the proud growl of a bulldog, the melancholy whine of a greyhound, the staccato of a dachshund, the petulant tirade of a spaniel, the yelp of a Japanese poodle. In the corner, running up and down a pole, a monkey clanked his chain muttering endless imprecations.

"Silence!" the Empress commanded, and immediately the animals obeyed. Only the vague echo of a growl persisted for a moment.

Her Majesty laughed.

"The Imperial guard is well trained, n'est-ce pas?"

I curtsied deeply, and remained standing.

"Ma chère, I beg you not to be formal. I long to be treated like a human being, not like a goddess. I am bored with worshipers. Please seat yourself next to me. There is a stool."

The Empress burst into laughter.

"I am rereading for the tenth time 'Candide.' How civilized a country must be to produce a genius like Voltaire, Baroness! If a Russian created such a masterpiece, I would raise a statue to him at every crossroad."

She sighed.

"We are too young. The blood of the wild hordes of Attila still courses in our veins. But the future is ours! A monarch must sow. He cannot hope to reap."

She stood up and looked at me intently, then drawing my head to her lips kissed me on both cheeks.

"You are so beautiful, lubushka! The poets of Russia are writing sonnets by the hundreds to you. They say that never since Helen of Troy or Cleopatra or Salome has there been such a beautiful woman."

The mention of my name made me blush.

The Empress pressed my hand. "Ah, to be so young that one can still blush! All Russia is in love with you — even Count Vorontsov!"

She slapped my arm and laughed.

"He is a very good man and as faithful to Your Majesty as a dog," I said.

"That is true. And he is more cultured than all of my courtiers."

"He is very sad that at his age he is only a colonel, Your Majesty."

"I shall make him a general to-morrow, the poor capon! It's curious how insignificant all things are, save sex. If a man with Nicolai Nicolaievitch Vorontsov's brain appealed to me as a man he would be viceroy of the Caucasus by this time!"

The monkey chattered.

The Empress walked over to him and placed her finger in his mouth.

"You agree with me, don't you? Sex rules the world. The gods have not stinted you," she laughed.

Catherine returned to the sofa, opened her snuffbox, and offered me the tobacco. We sneezed and wiped our noses.

"My monkey understands me sometimes better than a human being," Catherine said, as if to excuse herself for indulging in conversation with the animal.

"My tortoise understands me perfectly."

We remained silent. Catherine played with her cross. From time to time she tapped the back of her snuffbox meditatively.

"My spies are reporting strange goings-on in your laboratory, Baroness, curious animal noises, smells and vapors of rare chemicals, extraordinary tinctures and essences in fantastic flasks, and"— she looked at me slyly —"secret formulæ in the hidden cabinet in the wall of your boudoir."

"Spies, Your Majesty?" I asked banteringly, trying to disguise my alarm. I now understood the mysterious warnings of my friend, Count Vorontsov.

Catherine laughed. "Of course. I have a million watchful eyes. I know what my people do. I know what my people think — or I would not be Catherine!"

I promised to myself greater secretiveness.

"Until now," Catherine continued, "man preëmpted the

laboratory. Women have been but rarely students of Science."

"Woman is awakening, Your Majesty. When she realizes at last that she is neither a toy nor a breeding machine, she will equal man!"

"In my new code I shall give woman perfect equality before the law. She will be able to hold property in her own name. Schools and universities will throw their doors open to her."

"Your Majesty will go into History not alone as a great monarch but as the feminine Moses who delivered woman out of her Egypt."

The Empress seemed absent-minded.

"What shall it profit me to rule fifty million men, if I get old and wrinkled and undesirable — if I must buy love? Yes, buy and cajole and command?"

I recited a catalogue of her allurements.

"I have scrutinized myself in many mirrors. They all tell me the same tale. They shout at me my age. Besides, I need no mirror to tell me that youth is gone."

She took my head between her hands, and looked into my eyes.

"Dushenka, what do your secret formulæ hide? My scientists could not decipher your code."

"Your scientists?"

"I convened the whole Academy!" She laughed. "And I shall not fathom what is hidden behind those magnificent eyes of yours. Even Voltaire found it impossible. He wrote me that his mind was like glass trying to cut into yours which was adamantine."

"Voltaire is an old flatterer."

Catherine shook her head. She sighed. "I am no longer young. The Moon has nearly ceased to stir my blood. The ocean of womanhood is turning dry. The frequent flushes, my migraines, my sleeplessness — all these are the muffled drums announcing the death of my youth. Is there no way, mein Schatz, to restore or prolong the tides of sex?" She patted my cheeks.

I was startled. In my effort to liberate woman from the

yoke of the White Tyrant of the Skies, I had not considered that her freedom might be a curse! I had seen the tragedy of woman in the throes of her slavery. Now I was confronted with the tragedy of her liberty.

"Is there no way, dushenka?" the Empress pleaded, kissing my cheeks.

"Your Majesty," I answered, "I have learned how to arrest the tides of the Moon temporarily or for a length of time, but how to prolong them or restore them, I do not yet know."

The Empress sighed. Her hands fell limply upon her lap.

"In time, however, we may snatch that secret also from Nature's jealous fists."

"In time? In my time?" she asked eagerly.

"Perhaps."

"If you can repurchase an hour of my youth, you shall have all the gold of my treasury, all the herbs which grow in any part of the Earth, all the instruments, all the laboratories! Work, ma chère, investigate, hasten, before it is too late! Remain with me, be my guest, my friend, my sister!"

I knew that my experiments would require generations, but I grasped the opportunity to remain with Catherine. Perhaps I might help to shape the destinies of a new nation and bring the first dawn of freedom and happiness to my sex.

"How short-lived is the blossom of love, Baroness! And how foolishly we let the spring pass us by! When I married my husband — may the saints forgive him — I knew nothing, nothing at all of sex. I had a hazy notion of the difference between man and woman. I shall never forget what happened after the wedding ceremony. I entered the nuptial chamber, trembling with fear. I walked up and down the room until, weary and miserable, I threw myself upon the bed, dressed as I was. In my despondency, I rang for the lady-in-waiting, and asked her to undress me. I begged her to tell me my duties. She smiled ironically, but I could not extract a word from her.

"An hour or so later, Peter entered. For a long time he babbled about his dogs. He had court-martialed one that day because he allowed an officer to pass him by without barking. He was the sentinel dog, he said, and supposing the officer had been a spy, the fortress might have been stormed and taken by the enemy. Law was law and neither man nor beast could break it with impunity.

"When he got tired speaking, he undressed and stretched out beside me. I crawled in a corner, scared to death. What was he going to do to me? What would happen?"

The Empress took a long snuff.

"Nothing happened. It was very warm and I was tortured by fleas. And that was my nuptial night. Peter dallied with chambermaids and gypsies, but in our conjugal bed, he snored. I remained a virgin almost until he died — and for him always."

She nodded, her lips tightened.

"Ah, had I only known then what I know now! Had I only guessed how fugitive are the moments of pleasure!"

"Have not the other men, Your Majesty, atoned for the failure of Peter?" I asked jestingly.

"I have not had more than thirteen lovers. Is that much for an Empress? Sex is the only thing that makes me feel that I am a human being. Sex levels all. Sex eliminates all distinctions. It is the lowest common denominator."

I turned my head, and noticed through the open window, the company of "stallions" which Potemkin was training for the pleasure of the Empress, marching in the courtyard.

I could not suppress a smile.

Guessing my thoughts, Catherine said, pointing her thumb in the direction of the window: "That is no more important than a cup of wine which graces the banquet. I do not count them. They do not count."

She pulled the ear of the yelping poodle.

"I said I had thirteen lovers, thirteen men who stirred my heart, but I really never understood the meaning of love until I learned it from Gregory Alexandrovitch Potemkin. What a man he was! Prodigious in every respect! Every muscle steel!" Her eyes clouded with memories. Suddenly she laughed.

"They say he is betraying me. Fools! They do not know.

it's the giant tree that is blasted by lightning. My Gregory Alexandrovitch can no longer betray me!"

I did not care to undeceive her. Potemkin's capacity, though largely diminished, was not yet obliterated, according to very authentic reports from Catherine's own ladies-in-waiting.

"Gregory Alexandrovitch still loves me. He chooses my youths with the eye of a connoisseur. Vicariously he gives me through them that which he lacks. When their sturdy arms close around me, I am embraced by Gregory Alexandrovitch. In my moments of ecstasy I stammer his name."

Potemkin entered the room. He seemed even taller and more powerful. His enormous shoes reminded me of the seven-league boots. The dogs rushed into a corner and huddled together. The monkey crouched belligerently. The ikons and the candelabras shook and shivered.

Catherine stood on her tiptoes and kissed her lover's cheeks.

Potemkin kissed my hand. He coughed a little and his small shrewd eyes winked at the Empress.

"You may speak openly, Gregory Alexandrovitch."

Across his heavy mouth a sneer passed which Catherine did not discern.

"I have scoured the Empire to find suitable toys for the Little Mother," Potemkin said, smacking his lips.

The Empress rubbed her hands. She looked like an old cocotte into whose ears a man whispers an obscene jest.

"Are they well groomed, Gregory Alexandrovitch?"

"Out of the bandbox, Your Majesty," he answered, tapping his mighty leg with the end of his whip.

My eyes met the eyes of the imperial procurer. Uneasy, he opened his heavy snuffbox, took a deep breath of tobacco, and sneezed so noisily I made a gesture of fear.

The Empress laughed.

"No one equals my Gregory Alexandrovitch," she said, pulling him down on the sofa.

"You are a dear," she whispered, and kissed his cheek.

"I am unhappy, Your Majesty," he sighed.

"Unhappy?" she asked, worried.

He nodded.

"What is the trouble? Tell me, Gregory Alexandrovitch!" she asked in a motherly tone.

He sighed, and shook his head.

"Tell me," she pleaded.

"I am ruined, Matushka!"

"Ruined?"

He nodded pathetically.

"Nitchevo," he added. "As long as the Little Mother is happy! You ought to see the boys." He smacked his lips. "They are as tall as I!"

Catherine's face beamed.

"But tell me, darling, what is the trouble?"

"I am ruined. My estates are rotting. I need a thousand serfs, Little Mother!"

"You shall have them, Gregory Alexandrovitch. Of course, you shall have them."

He kissed her hands several times.

"My angel! My angel!" he whispered. "May you live forever!"

"Did you say they are as tall as you?" she asked, her eyes dazzling.

"One of them has legs like the marble statue of the gladiator in your antechamber."

She rubbed her hands.

He sighed deeply, like the pulling of a bucket out of a well.

"You are an angel to give me a thousand serfs, Little Mother — but what is the use of serfs if you can't flog them when they disobey? Since your ukase, the stinking boors consider themselves our equals. They are lazy and our harvests are rotting."

Catherine remained pensive.

"What calves that Lithuanian has, Matushka! I wager he could have crushed under his feet the largest lion in the arena."

Catherine's nostrils trembled like a mare's who hears in the distance the snorting of her approaching mate.

"One of my young men has the voice of a thrush. He

sings more beautifully than all the archimandrites in the cathedral."

"Good!" the Empress exclaimed. "I love music, though I have never been able to master the scales," she addressed me.

"And there is one —" The Prince whispered something which I could not hear. He laughed and slapped his thighs. Her face flushed and her fist clenched.

Potemkin beat his leg with his whip.

"Why don't you flog your slaves if they disobey you, Gregory Alexandrovitch?" the Empress said.

"Thank you, Little Mother, thank you!" Potemkin exclaimed triumphantly.

Suddenly Potemkin rose and clapped his hands. He nodded significantly to the Empress, who returned the signal. He kissed her hand and mine and walked to the door.

"Oh, Gregory Alexandrovitch, come here!"

He rushed back.

The Empress giggled.

"Nicolai Nicolaievitch Vorontsov is only a colonel, Little Father. To-morrow I make him a general. Bring me the patent to sign."

"The Capon a general, Little Mother! Hahahahaha!"

His laughter shook the furniture. The animals huddled together in terror. He walked out roaring, "General Capon! General Capon!"

Nicolai Nicolaievitch Vorontsov lay stretched out upon the couch in his uniform of a Russian General. His face was drawn and white. His features, no longer puffed, were not homely, and his nose had lost its grotesqueness.

He pressed his lips to my hand.

"It is so good of you to visit a dying man."

I tried to console him.

He smiled wearily.

"I have another day or another hour, dorogaya, and I am satisfied. Life was not particularly kind to me. Maybe death will prove more amiable."

He breathed deeply many times.

"No, I am unjust to life, ma chère; she was very good. She sent you to me."

I smoothed his hair.

He closed his eyes. A beatific smile played about his lips.

"If you had been sovereign of Russia," he murmured, "our country would have prospered like Paradise."

"Catherine is a great ruler, Nicolai Nicolaievitch."

"Ruler? The Procurator of Crimea and his stallions are the rulers of Russia! I am dying, I may speak the truth — even in Russia."

"Impaled upon the phallus, Catherine struggles helplessly," I said bitterly.

"She has spent one hundred million rubles on her lovers. Gregory Alexandrovitch binds his banknotes in volumes. He is wealthier than any monarch in Europe, the miser! He has involved Russia in useless wars. He prevents Catherine from making Russia a civilized nation."

He stopped to catch his breath.

"But his day is over. He is devoured by disease. Alas, Catherine is getting old herself. Death will come too late to save Catherine's greatness."

Tears trickled down his cheeks.

"Nitchevo! Nitchevo!" he muttered.

His face became more and more drawn. His body stiffened. He opened his eyes with great difficulty.

"Adieu, mon amour," he whispered. "Let me see your glorious face once more. Come nearer — nearer. I cannot see."

I placed my face upon his.

"You are more luminous than the sun. You give sight to the blind."

There was a gurgle in his throat.

"Let the priest come in," he whispered, his voice far away.

I made a motion to the priest in the anteroom, who was walking up and down, pulling at his beard impatiently.

Nicolai Nicolaievitch moved his lips, and his eyelids stirred vaguely. His body convulsed. The priest administered extreme unction to the unconscious man.

Several minutes later, the priest reëntered the anteroom.

"May Jesus Christ and the saints receive the soul of Nicolai Nicolaievitch Vorontsov!" he said, making the sign of the cross.

An old servant shrieked.

"Sh! woman!" the priest admonished. "You will scare the angels away with your noise. Bring me a glass of vodka, I am dying of thirst."

I hid my face in my handkerchief and wept. I had lost a friend.

The Imperial coach, lacquered with heavy gold, seemed ablaze. As we entered, the white satin which covered the seats rustled like a queen's petticoat. The wheels rolled swiftly over the cobblestones, leaving behind them tiny furrows of sparks. The driver cracked his long whip over the mighty backs of the six black steeds, the favorites of the stable of the Empress of all the Russias.

The perfume of thousands of wild flowers floated in the morning air, and over the valley the hills glittered like a silver laurel.

"This is Paradise, ma chère," Catherine said, breathing deeply. "If I had the courage I would make one of these towns in Crimea the seat of my government."

I made no comment. I wondered if my ruse of exposing Gregory Alexandrovitch Potemkin would prove successful. I wondered if the courage of the driver, a young officer in disguise. would falter at the critical moment.

Catherine pressed her breasts.

"They are as firm, ma chère, as they were when I was a girl," she said joyfully. "After my death, you may disclose the secret of your art to the rest of womankind."

I cast a glance at her. Her face had the sallowness of age. Her eyes had lost their luster. The red lids were almost hairless. Her mouth drooped. There was an odor of senility about her. She who had worshiped at the altar of sex, who had sacrificed an Empire to her passion, had lost every trace of seductiveness. Nothing remained save the ravages of lust.

She caught the meaning of my look. A sneer of bitterness flitted across her lips as she drew out of her purse a silver mirror, on which fell the reflection of her face and mine.

"How have you succeeded in remaining so young, Baroness, so beautiful? Time has not added one wrinkle. The years have passed you by unmolested."

Her words were spiked with envy.

"Your Majesty flatters me. Why should time spare me?"

She pointed her gnarled finger to the mirror.

"The sun this morning is unusually favorable to my complexion," I remarked lightly, careful not to excite her jealousy.

"The sun makes no distinctions, dushenka."

"Your Majesty's face is truly regal this morning."

Catherine laughed. Her yellow teeth protruded precariously from her shriveled gums.

"Regal? I understand. I must not forget that I am the Empress. I have a divine duty to my people. I must keep the rabble in check. I must aggrandize my territory. I must watch over the felicity of millions. Who can deny that I do all that a ruler must do?" she said arrogantly. "But I am also human. I am a woman. Regal!" she growled.

She placed her hand upon mine. There was something of the coolness of the snake in her skin.

"Darling, why do you keep your secret from me? Why do you not tell me how to replenish the spring of my life?" Her eyes assumed the melancholy of a dog's.

How could I appreciate to the full the tragedy of one whose life was measured by a few rotations of the Earth around the Sun, whose youth could only last between one dream and another? Does the oak within whose stem the centuries inscribe their passage understand the sorrow of the rose?

"My experiments will bear fruit shortly, Your Majesty."

"You speak of time, Baroness, as the immortals speak. Shortly?" she sighed, removing her hand.

I began to fear the jealousy of this old woman.

"I know," she muttered to herself, "I am old, and should lay aside the toys of youth. I cannot. All ages have the same joy — but we are either too young to understand it or too old to grasp it. He who tells you differently lies.

"Nitchevo!" she exclaimed, stamping her cane. "I am the Empress, and while I wear the crown, I can commandeer all Russia to my bed!"

Would it be possible for me to continue my influence over this woman, since she had lost all hope that I might restore her youth? She was the female of the species, bound to the Earth and to her womb. Would she relinquish the men who ruined her and her empire, but also supplied her with that which gave her the illusion of youth?

We rode in silence. The Empress scratched with the tip of her cane the belly of the hound which lay outstretched at our feet.

Suddenly she pointed outside of the carriage.

"Look!"

On one of the tall milestones were carved in large letters: "This way to Constantinople!"

"My grandson will be Emperor of Byzantium. I swear it by the holy saints!"

Against the background of the hills the houses glistened, harmonizing with the landscape.

"Gregory Alexandrovitch Potemkin is a great governor. Not one of my villages in Russia looks as prosperous and beautiful as these over which he rules. Look at those houses, with gardens and vineyards. Look at the flock of sheep grazing happily. The shepherds have the air of great seigneurs. O fortunate people! O fortunate Crimea!"

This fulsome praise of a man whose rascality was the byword of Russia, this blindness to reality in so perspicacious a ruler, revolted me beyond endurance.

"Your Majesty," I said irritably, but instantly changed my tone, remembering that I had a much subtler way of discrediting the Prince. "Your Majesty," I repeated suavely.

Catherine did not heed my interruption. She pursued the eulogy of her former paramour and present procurer.

"I shall order the rest of my governors to visit Crimea. Gregory Alexandrovitch will teach them how to rule! I shall make him Viceroy of all my possessions!"

The moment had come. I gave the agreed signal. The driver made a sudden detour. We rode toward the hills.

Catherine was unaware of the change in our direction. She murmured to herself the physical prowesses of Potemkin and his successors, tittering with senile delectation.

We reached a magnificent villa. The turrets rose triumphantly, challenging elements and foes.

The horses galloped toward it.

The building shivered at our approach. Under the spur of the whip which cracked across their bellies the horses pressed forward. Suddenly their heads struck one of the walls, which tottered.

Catherine stopped short in her mumbling and looked out of the window. Her face changed from white to red. She rose from her seat, but the new impact of the steeds made her fall back.

"Scoundrel!" she shouted, addressing no one in particular.

The animals, maddened by the unexpected barrier, stamped their hoofs wildly, foam streaming from their great mouths.

The house swung, collapsed, tore under the iron of the beasts. The Imperial coach rolled over the cardboard ruins.

The driver pulled the reins with all his might, raising the powerful necks of the horses. The bits were spattered with blood. The animals stopped, their huge bellies blowing like Gargantuan bellows.

The Empress jumped out of the carriage.

"What is the meaning of this?" she demanded.

The driver, awed by the threatening attitude of the Monarch, fell to his knees.

"Your Majesty," I answered, pointing to the shreds that once were houses and vineyards and peasants, "this was one of the villas of Gregory Alexandrovitch Potemkin, paper and paint. Thus did he deceive Your Majesty and the world with mimic pomp. The real villages of Crimea are over the hills yonder where disease and squalor and starvation hold sway. Gregory Alexandrovitch never invites Your Majesty to see them. There you would hear the peasant and the landlord alike curse the name of Potemkin."

The Empress closed her eyes. I thought I was making a deep impression upon her.

I pursued: "For the sake of Russia and civilization, Your Majesty, let the reign of Potemkin come to an end! Let him no longer throttle all your efforts to bring justice and light to the world! Woman has her arms outstretched to you, Your Majesty! Emancipate her!"

Catherine, her eyes blazing, glared at me.

"Your Majesty —" I said, a little more wary.

She raised her cane and struck the kneeling driver a violent blow over his face. A long streak of blood ran across his cheek and neck.

"Your bones shall rot in the snows of Siberia, you impudent lout!" she shouted.

I caught my breath. The blood rushed to my face. I knew the blow was meant for me. The sentence, too, was mine.

"But, Your Majesty," I said with all the tranquillity I could muster, "this man is a patriot. He risked his life for the love of his country and his sovereign. He has shown Your Majesty the truth!"

Catherine propped upon her cane. Her head shook, her lips had the wryness which comes from swallowing something bitter. Her anger added two decades to her years.

"How dare you assume," she addressed me, her voice choking her, "that I did not *know!*"

The Empress took short, tottering steps toward the coach, striking the ground with her cane like an aged beggar.

Lakshmi was standing on the top of her ladder, her neck stretched to its limit, like an astronomer observing the stars.

"Be my compass, Lakshmi, in my eternal wanderings, for Russia is no longer safe or profitable. Her ruler is plunging her headlong into the abyss of reaction."

The tortoise made no motion.

"I am weary of Jahveh's spawn. Would I were another Samson crushing the entire edifice, rotten with falsehood and stupidity and vanity and superstition and hate and injustice! The pillars are too mighty. The race of man cannot be destroyed. So be it, let it continue to live, slave of the Moon and the Phallus! I shall create a race of gods in a new Garden of Eden!"

The tortoise looked at me quizzically.

"Yes, it is possible, Lakshmi. At least I can try it. Jahveh created man out of mud. I have subtler and more noble ingredients. It may take centuries. I can wait."

Did Lakshmi smile?

"Europe is old and rotten. Let us flee to a new continent, whose climate is balsam, whose solitude will allow me to work undisturbed by lovesick empresses and red-eyed rebels."

Lakshmi descended the ladder slowly.

"We are going to South America, Lakshmi, to establish a Super-Race!"

The turtle approached me, and tapped my ankle.

"Come, Lakshmi, let us leave behind us our Lares and Penates, let the Wandering Jewess and the Wandering Turtle resume their march through Time and Space!"

CHAPTER FIFTY-FOUR

I CREATE A NEW EDEN — I DREAM OF HOMUNCULA — I AM THE NEW MOTHER — MY SECRET LABORATORY — MECHANICAL GOLEMS — HOMUNCULA SLEEPS — THE CARRIER PIGEON.

THE pampas stretched flatly like an open palm, and merged with the horizon. The sands blew gently from the North, shaking the leaves of the ombú and bending gracefully the tall, luxuriant grass. At intervals large flocks of sheep huddled together, their restless bodies glittering in the sun like churned milk. Vizcachas, scared by my presence, fled in every direction, seeking refuge. Flamingos flapped their wings of fire, and overhead wild ducks screeched defiantly.

Lakshmi bit the tender tips of the grass like an aged and toothless gourmet.

"Lakshmi, this is the site which I have bought for the New Paradise. Here I shall give birth to Homuncula, the Super-Being. From this spot shall proceed the new life which will replace the chosen creation of Jahveh. Homuncula shall eat of every fruit of every Tree of Knowledge, unafraid and unashamed. Her flesh shall be more delicious than manna and more fragrant than flowers. Her mind will transcend the intelligence of man, as the mind of man transcends the intelligence of turtles."

Lakshmi looked at me, one eyelid raised.

"Her voice will be more melodious than the song of nightingales, and her words more harmonious than the chiseled sonnets of great poets. She will not be born in the travail of another, and if she dies, she will die in splendor as a star in flames. Every cell of her body will be a universe of joy. Beyond man, beyond woman, beyond god — the incarnation of the cosmic dream!"

Lakshmi pulled at an obstinate blade.

"I have learned much since my experiments in Cordoba, Lakshmi. Life and death and immortality have acquired different meanings. The homuncula I sacrificed to the hoguera was a crude and distorted caricature of the new and glorious being. She was as the sketch of a clumsy child compared to Leonardo da Vinci."

Lakshmi looked at me quizzically.

I sighed. "Of course, I may not succeed. My creation may prove a sorry abortion. She may be the marvelous song that visits the dream of a musician, but vanishes when the heavy hoofbeats of day break upon his sleep, and he seeks — seeks in vain to recapture it on his keyboard."

I raised my arm defiantly.

"No matter! I shall never relinquish! A more obstinate Lucifer I shall plant roses in the sands of the desert! And no one — neither King nor Inquisition — shall hinder me."

I made a motion which encircled my vast territory.

"I shall surround my lands with a mightier wall than that of China, an immense belt and canopy of clouds and vapors pregnant with lightning and fire, which will destroy any enemy, however numerous, however powerful. No cannon shall pierce this intangible mighty fortress. For miles beyond the New Eden, the air will be unbreathable save to those I shall care to welcome. I shall construct pestilential marshes whose microscopic inhabitants shall be more deadly to my enemies than the most subtle of poisons."

Lakshmi's head shook as in fear, but in her eyes I detected a smile of half-malicious irony.

"My dominion will be the enchanted land which lurks in the dim subconsciousness of man, the fabric of the songs of poets and the metaphysics of philosophers."

My body was taut as that of a Messiah in the throes of his prophecy.

"My laboratory shall be more difficult of penetration, save

to myself, than the mysterious bowels of volcanoes. The exquisite texture of the body of the Homuncula until stirring with life shall not mingle with the noise and dust of the Earth."

I became ecstatic.

"I shall create a New Heaven and a New Earth for the New Eve. The old and monotonous face of the Earth will become radiant and young again. I shall mingle the fauna with the flora in infinitely varied forms. Trees will march majestically like conquering monarchs. Roses will give birth to animals whose velvety furs will spread exquisite perfumes to the breezes. Tortoises with shells of mother-of-pearl and necks as smooth as the breasts of doves will fly like eagles."

Lakshmi frowned. Her red circular eyes glowed like coals.

"I am weary of the Earth, Lakshmi. The Earth is beautiful only to those whose lives are numbered by a few of her mad dances about the Sun. The Earth is a senile mother, who mumbles the same prayers forever, and forever knits an unvarying pattern. I am the New Mother! I am the Mother eternally young, eternally seeking, eternally changing. The old must die that the new may prosper!"

I adjusted my field glasses.

"Lakshmi! Lakshmi!" I exclaimed jubilantly. "They are coming! They are coming!"

Lakshmi stretched her neck in the direction which I indicated.

"Look at the hundreds of wagons which obliterate the entire horizon! They are bringing my belongings and the material for the building of my castle. See the great army of architects and builders and servants riding on horses and donkeys! Look, there is the new Ark, Lakshmi!"

Lakshmi's neck nearly tore itself away from the rest of her body. In her eyes there was a look of wistfulness. Was it the memory of Noah and the strange companions of those forty days?

"There it is — a whole fleet of iron and steel, containing ten thousand species of animals and birds and insects and creatures unnamed and unknown by the scientists of the world. They will reveal to me the essence of life from which I shall fashion Homuncula, the dream of the poets, the hope of the philosophers! The essence, Lakshmi, purged of all impurities — the causa causarum, the urge, the passion, the rapture, which is Life. Eternity cleansed of Time!"

Intoxicated by my vision and my words, I danced — the Dance of Life!

Lakshmi, overwhelmed by the rhythm, raised now one leg, now another, and turned in circles about my feet.

I descended the steep stairway covered with a thick velvet which drowned the noise of my footsteps. Lakshmi followed, tumbling from one rung to another.

A thin line of light, like the silver thread of Ariadne, guided my path through the intricate labyrinth of corridors until I reached a tall portal, watched by two steel giants.

I breathed upon the gate. The eyes of the giants lit like four red stars. Their mighty arms stretched as if in salutation, and the portal opened noiselessly like a stream of oil.

I entered, Lakshmi at my heels. The portal closed again, as noiselessly. The immense hall was flooded by a mellow light as a full moon bathing the solitary house of a hermit.

Tables with instruments more sensitive than the plants which at the touch of the wing of a butterfly shiver and shut their petals. Tubes through which fell at long intervals an infinitesimal drop of the essence of existence. Scales which measured the pulse of hearts long withdrawn from the bodies of animals. Crystals through which the eye, made sharper than the ray when it leaves the core of the sun, penetrated the universe of the atom. Alembics which distilled the elements into their quintessences.

"Lakshmi," I said, "this is my laboratory — more subtle, more intricate than the complex mechanism which binds the billion cells of man and woman to the billion universes."

Lakshmi seemed unusually interested.

"You are the only creature, human or chelonian, to have seen it. No other footstep, no other voice, has ever penetrated it. No hand can force its portal. The arms of the steel Golems would lock themselves upon any one giving the false signal — lock fatally, irrevocably."

I approached an alcove. With my finger-tips I made the sign of the inverted eight lying on its belly — symbol of infinity — upon the brass curtain. The curtain rose slowly and vanished into the ceiling.

Upon a golden bed, like a Princess of Fantasy, Homuncula slept.

Her skin was whiter than the marble which sculptors seek in the hearts of quarries. Her face was resplendent as the sun at noon. Every cell, every atom, was created for ecstasy, and immune from pain. To her or him who possessed her, she would give unendurable pleasure indefinitely prolonged.

"Alive, and yet not alive, Lakshmi — how shall I breathe into her the breath of life? What Logos, what mystic word did Jahveh utter which awakened the clod into consciousness?"

Lakshmi crouched in a corner, her body hidden, the tip of her beak hardly visible.

"What do you fear, Lakshmi? Do you fear the new, like man?"

Lakshmi withdrew her head entirely.

"Ah, Lakshmi, if only I could discover the magic formula, the last drop of the ingredient which changes the simulacrum of existence into life? Is not life part and parcel of the cell? Does not life lodge in the invisible secretion of the gland? What is life, Lakshmi?"

Lakshmi was the shell of a tortoise, motionless.

"Is there something beyond mechanics, beyond histology?"

I passed my hand over the breasts of Homuncula.

"No texture of a flower's petal is half so smooth, Lakshmi, nor half as delicious to the senses."

I walked about the laboratory, testing the various instruments, watching the progress of each experiment.

"Come, Lakshmi, to-day I am not in a mood for work. I am restless, I do not know why. I am assailed by memories. Let us go back to Earth."

I made the symbol of eternity in the air. The brass curtain fell silently, concealing the New Creation. I repeated the signal, the portal opened to let me out, then closed again.

Lakshmi preceded me, taking greater strides than I had ever known her to take.

I smiled. "Lakshmi, you are jealous of the ingenuity of man! You are awed by the unknown."

When we reached the top of the stairs, I said: "Before we return to Earth, Lakshmi, let us glance at the New Garden of Eden."

I turned to the left and ascended a few steps. We reached a tall stone wall. A Golem stopped us with drawn sword. I gave the password. The Golem lowered his sword. The wall opened like a drawbridge, and we entered, Lakshmi clinging to my heels.

Out of the chalices of roses issued songs — more delicate and more harmonious than ever issued from the throats of nightingales. From the beaks of storks trailed vines, whose grapes were fluttering butterflies. Many colored lizards grew tip on tip into trees that hung like weeping willows. The leaves of the arbutus were the plumes of swans gliding silently as dreams upon the pond, breast on breast upon their shadows.

Lakshmi stopped to chew at a cabbage-leaf. The leaf spread its wings and disappeared.

Lakshmi, bewildered, looked in all directions.

I laughed heartily.

"You are too greedy, Lakshmi. Eve lost Paradise by chewing at an apple. You might lose your precious neck by chewing at a cabbage-leaf!"

Lakshmi walked warily, on the edges of her paws.

"Even Eden bores me to-day, Lakshmi. Come away."

The steel sentinel opened and shut the wall. I breathed deeply the air of the ancient Earth.

"There is something oppressive about new things, however beautiful they may be. These humble trees, these monkeys that whistle to us, these common birds and dogs and fowls, these ignorant servants rushing to do my bidding —

all the vulgar things of life soothe me to-day, while my Eden and my Homuncula and my giant Golems grip my heart in melancholy. After all, life is quotidian — a matter of habit. We long to see again that which we once saw, to hear the same tune, to walk the same paths. It is difficult to get accustomed to a new rhythm, Lakshmi."

Lakshmi chewed in comfort a real cabbage-leaf.

"You do not fear that it will fly away, or peck at your beak, Lakshmi." I laughed. "The prose of life must run parallel with her poetry. We cannot endure beauty for too long a time. But Homuncula will be different. She will not know the meaning of nostalgia. She will not remember. She will not fear the future. She will live in the Present only — the Present which man never recognizes, which passes him by like shadows of birds in flight!"

I looked up. A white dot moved overhead, breaking through the gases and thin clouds.

"What is this, Lakshmi?"

Lakshmi looked up, one eye closed.

"That is right, Lakshmi. To see better one must close one eye. One eye for reality, the other for imagination. Thus truth is discovered."

The dot became larger and larger and moved obliquely in my direction.

"It's one of my carrier-pigeons, Lakshmi!" I exclaimed joyously.

I held out my hand. The pigeon descended upon it, lightly as a snowflake. Around its neck hung from a thin gold chain a letter. I unclasped the chain. The pigeon flew upon my head and cooed.

I tore the envelope, my hands shaking.

"From Cartaphilus, my immortal lover, Lakshmi!"

Lakshmi tapped my ankle joyously.

"This is why I felt a strange uneasiness at my heart. This is why neither Homuncula nor the Garden of Eden could console me. It was the premonition that my beloved would be with me to-day."

I read intently.

It was a message pregnant with tidings.

"Yes, I shall leave again for the Old World! According to Cartaphilus, Lakshmi, things of great moment are taking place there. Countless new discoveries, which may help me in my work. A mighty Queen who rules the world. Woman arisen from slavery. And above all, Cartaphilus himself. I yearn to see him, to embrace him. I am lonesome, Lakshmi! And he misses me so! Yes, I am going. I shall leave you here, that the spirit of Vishnu, your immortal and eternal husband, may protect my household!"

Lakshmi tapped vigorously at my ankle.

"Thank you, Lakshmi. I know that nothing will go amiss, while you, Immortal Tortoise, Upholder of the Universe and Protector of Home, rule my dominions."

Lakshmi's eyes glowed with pride.

"Come, fly upon my hand, sweet bird!"

The pigeon flew upon my open palm. I pressed my mouth against its beak.

"You are the symbol of love, the words of my lover made incarnate!"

The pigeon cooed, its chest swollen.

CHAPTER FIFTY-FIVE

I ARRIVE IN LONDON — CENTURY-BLOSSOMS — MY VICTORIAN LOVER — THE METAMORPHOSIS OF KOTIKOKURA — MY BIRTHDAY CAKE — CARTAPHILUS RULES THE BRITISH EMPIRE — I HAVE A TIFF WITH DIZZY — THE MYSTERY OF LORD BEACONSFIELD — I AM RECEIVED AT BUCKINGHAM PALACE — QUEEN VICTORIA IS NOT AMUSED — I MAKE A PROMISE — I EMBARK FOR BUENOS AYRES.

THE train puffed like a thousand dromedaries in flight. The Colossus shivered, rocked, groaned — a beast in the throes of death.

"London! London!" the conductors shouted.

The handle of the coach turned, the door swung wide open.

"Salome!"

"Cartaphilus!"

We embraced. We separated. We looked at each other. We embraced again. We smiled. We laughed. Tears flooded our eyes. We uttered incomprehensible words of endearment in all possible languages.

"These young lovers," some one whispered, a little acridly.

Cartaphilus presented me with a bouquet of golden flowers.

"To the Immortal One," he said, "the flower that blossoms once in a century. A hundred springs kiss its roots in vain before it deigns to greet the sun. I have raised them with my own hands, tenderly, anxiously, since they were nothing but thin threads of roots."

I pressed the flowers against my heart.

Cartaphilus crushed them in his embrace.

"You do not know what significance I attach to the flowers, Salome," he said, raising his forefinger.

"What?" I asked naïvely.

"The day you accept them, you are my wife."

I made a mock gesture of returning them.

Cartaphilus caught his breath.

"I would not part with them, my dearest, for all the crowns of Great Britain and India. But why precipitate our conjugal felicity?" I asked coyly.

Cartaphilus looked at me, his eyes twinkling diabolically.

"I promise you, my love," I said, "that long before the thin threads of another plant blossom into a new secular flower, we shall celebrate the wedding of Cartaphilus and Salome."

When I finally extricated myself from his embrace, I espied, behind him, a gentleman dressed almost exactly like Cartaphilus — a gray cutaway, tall silk hat, white gloves. One eye twinkled maliciously through his monocle, and a large sunflower glowed upon his lapel. He bowed and grinned incessantly.

"Your Englishman, Cartaphilus," I whispered, "is maligned. He is not half as prim as they say."

"What do you mean?"

"You have a rival behind your back, Cartaphilus. He has been flirting with me for the last ten minutes."

Cartaphilus turned around, and burst out into an interminable laughter.

The gentleman was very indignant.

"Kotikokura!" Cartaphilus exclaimed.

I looked intently.

"My dear Kot!" I called out.

We laughed uproariously. The people looked at us, shocked by our boisterousness.

No longer the bashful youth, Kotikokura allowed himself to be embraced, and even deigned to reciprocate faintly the pressure.

I looked at him at arm's length.

"I would never have recognized you, Kotikokura. You look positively Nordic!"

Kotikokura beamed. He kissed my hand several times, and pulling the sunflower from his lapel, presented it to me with a great flourish.

I placed the flower among those of Cartaphilus and pressed them to my lips.

"Have I changed, Salome? Do I, too, look Nordic?" Cartaphilus asked.

"You are as vain — and as handsome — and as young — and as lovable — and as provocative — as you were — oh, about eighteen or nineteen centuries ago — at the Court of Pilate."

"And you, my love — you are a thousandfold more exquisite than all the legends poets have created about you."

On the arms of the two English lords I walked out of the station through a sea of curious oblique looks of eyes too well-trained, too prudish, too dishonest to stare.

The gilded wheels of the landau shone like Phaeton's chariot, and the proud horses pawed the ground impatiently.

The lackey, in the uniform of an admiral, jumped off his seat, opened the door of the carriage, and immediately resumed his place, stiff and solemn as a statue of Pontifical Infallibility.

Was this the London I had known three centuries previously? The Thames still pursued its melancholy course, and the fog rose from the tops of houses like fantastic horns. But where was the braggadocio, the broad gesticulation, the uncontrolled merriment and challenge of the people? Where were the multicolored uniforms of the civilians? Where the clanking of swords, the waving of plumes?

After a silence, Cartaphilus asked somewhat banteringly, "How is your daughter Homuncula, Salome?"

I ignored his tone, and answered:

"Homuncula is still unborn, Cartaphilus I seek the final ingredient, the ultimate formula which will awaken her."

"The kiss of the Prince that awakens the Sleeping Beauty," he continued, in his jocular manner.

"Precisely. Who knows what the meaning of that tale really is? Perhaps it was originated with my first Homuncula. Ah, if I could only discover the spark that lights the flame of life! Then, Cartaphilus, our own immortality will be invested with a new meaning."

"Have you created her in your own glorious image?"

"She is as I would have been had I been conceived, not in a womb (though a regal womb)—not from the loins of man (though the seed was royal)—but from the very essence of the World Spirit. She will see what no mortal has ever beheld. Her eyes will pierce through every wall which surrounds us. Her tympanum will vibrate in unison with the Cosmic Rhythm. Her body, infinitely more sensitive than the tentacles of sightless beings, will feel the tremor of the waves of light. Her mind attuned to the Cosmic Intelligence will not plod through logic or jump more or less accurately over the springboard of intuition."

Cartaphilus smiled skeptically. Kotikokura adjusted his monocle and smoothed his gloves.

"A very homely proverb, 'The proof of the pudding is in the eating,'" I said sadly, "but, nevertheless, true, I know."

"How strong the mother instinct must be in you, Salome —that it impels you to create in a phial ectogenetically, the progeny Nature refuses to fashion in your womb!' Cartaphilus said very seriously. "I believe in your ultimate achievement, Salome. Life changes, evolves, and perchance advances. Mankind is casting off its swaddling clothes— the infantile mythologies of Moses and Saint Paul. It is seeking fearlessly Truth!"

I stood up a little in the carriage.

"I proclaim Man's independence from Nature! I place my yoke upon her mighty neck!" I exclaimed.

"No, no, Cartaphilus," I added, sighing. "It is not quite true. I have discovered much of the technique and mechanism of Life. But Life itself escapes me. Nature is not a steed that can be yoked. Nature is a vast and turbulent ocean. At most, we can span a bridge across her stormy bosom. I have stretched the first cables."

"Salome," Cartaphilus said, taking my flushed face in his hands, "Salome, I pray you, do not wait until the bridge is fully constructed, and pedestrians can walk across it, their hands upon their backs, in perfect safety. Do not postpone the consummation of our love until you harness the tides of existence!"

I closed my eyes and whispered, "I love you, Cartaphilus, and yearn for your embrace."

He pressed his lips upon mine.

The pedestrians looked at us, frowning, shocked.

"Are the English so jealous of another's happiness?"

"Not that precisely, Salome. They all endeavor to become models."

"Models?"

"Yes, tiny replicas of the Great Model, their sovereign."

Kotikokura coughed as if to draw my attention. I felt a trifle guilty for having neglected him.

"Lakshmi, in her own chelonian, cold-blooded fashion, is sending her best love to you, Kotikokura," I said, smiling.

Kotikokura made believe he did not hear. The features of his face were drawn in righteous indignation.

"Is there a Lady Kotikokura, my noble friend?" I asked. "Are you married?"

His face changed. There was the ancient grotesquery about it. "Woman," he growled as of yore. Then, like a nouveau riche who makes an atavistic error of conduct, he turned his monocle slowly around his eye, and said in most fastidious English, "Lady."

Cartaphilus could not control his laughter. Kotikokura was as motionless, as rigid as the lackey in front of us.

"We shall drive first to your mansion, Salome," Cartaphilus said after a silence.

"Not to yours?" I asked demurely.

"Oh, no!" he exclaimed. "What, harbor my fiancée under my roof? Why, Her Majesty would be scandalized. Dizzy, her prime minister and my factotum, would declaim in Ciceronian manner against the evil times that have befallen his beloved England. English society would feel the tremor of a moral earthquake. The sympathetic nerve of the common people would throb with indignation."

"Really?" I clicked my tongue.

"Victoria," he continued, "is a model wife, a model

mother, a model grandmother, a model queen. Nobody in England utters a word or makes a gesture without consulting, consciously or unconsciously, the Supreme Image. What would she say, what would she do, under the circumstances? Would she approve? Would she scowl? Would she reply disdainfully? Would she smile? Never since you were goddess and queen of Africa, Salome, was there a matriarchy so perfectly, so subtly organized! Your heart ought to rejoice, my love!" he said mockingly.

"Matriarchy is no longer my objective, Cartaphilus. I wish to liberate woman from the yoke of the Moon and of convention. But that is only an incident in the evolution of a new world."

Cartaphilus looked at me strangely.

"Have I changed, Cartaphilus?" I asked.

"Greatly."

"Perhaps. Nineteen centuries have mellowed me. Once I sought revenge against the gods who made woman in the image of Pain and Sorrow, revenge against you."

"I know," he interrupted, "I never could distinguish between your love and your hate."

"Who can tell the deathless twins apart?"

The horses trotted slowly through the crowded streets. From time to time the coachman's cracking whip made spirals in the air.

"Yes, it was you, Cartaphilus," I said meditatively, "you who first stirred in me my anger against man. It began with the day when you flaunted your manliness in the sun and ridiculed me. It was then that I became a woman, and as a woman envious of that which woman lacks, and enraged at him who possesses it! But now I know that every possession makes us its slave. To be the slave of the White Goddess is no more irksome than to be the slave to the God whose image is the Obelisk and the Cross!"

"That is true, Salome. Woman in her envy does not realize that the Earth, Mistress of Man no less tyrannical than the Moon, forces upon him a Rhythm akin to that of woman. In the Rhetoric of Life there is Earth Rhythm as well as Moon Rhythm. You wrote me, Salome. of your disappointment and disillusion with woman. Zenobia, and Pope Joan, and Jeanne Darc, and Christina of Sweden, and Catherine of Russia, all at the last slaves of the womb! But what of the kings and geniuses among men, Salome? Invariably all great careers end in tragedy and frustration. Why? Because we are slaves of the Earth and slaves of the phallus. Between the Earth and the Moon, between phallus and womb, what respite is there for mankind?"

"There shall be a new covenant between Man and the Gods when Homuncula and her progeny replace the Adamic brood!"

"So be it, Salome! Meanwhile, let me drink the honey of your lips. Let us not discuss the Universe, even if the professors can prove that it really exists. Whisper into my ear, that you love me, Salome. There are universes beyond the Universe. I am willing to sacrifice every one of them for your kisses."

Our hands clasped, our eyes riveted upon each other, we uttered eternally ancient, eternally fresh, words of passion.

Flags waving from every window as if the entire city in a clandestine mood signaled to a million lovers. Cannons booming ceaselessly like a boy beating upon a newly gotten drum. Companies of soldiers and sailors marching gayly through the streets to the latest military tunes. Churches offering hallelujahs. Vendors offering rattles, confetti, balloons.

The Queen's birthday!

"When is your birthday, Salome, my love?" Cartaphilus asked as we looked out of our balcony.

"You ought to know! I am a month younger than you."

"What! A month and a year older," he said in mock indignation. "Will you never overcome your feminine propensity for fibbing about your age?"

Kotikokura grinned. His chest dazzled with Russian decorations conferred upon him more than a century ago by Peter the Great. His monocle slipped from his eye in elegant boredom.

"I shall order a cake as large as the floor of the royal ballroom, my love. I shall engage the chefs of the kings and emperors of Europe. All the four corners of the Earth will be plundered of their choicest fruits and nuts and spices. Over the glazed surface the finest calligraphers of China shall indite for me a poem of changeless love. And around the great circumference, like an army of diamonds marching in ceaseless circles, nineteen centuries of candles will blaze!"

"Cartaphilus!" I exclaimed. "Why traduce me! You make me older than my years."

"Old, Salome? You are as old as the first dawn that greeted the Earth, as the first vision of beauty that leaped in the breast of man, as the first kiss that bewildered and enraptured! You are as old — and as young!"

I pressed his hands, and whispered, my voice choked: "I love you!"

Kotikokura coughed a little.

"Do you know who will carve the birthday cake, Salome?"

"Disraeli, of course."

"How can I conceal my thoughts from you? Your mind is a flame that pierces the asbestos that surrounds the brain while your calm eyes watch the circus of ideas. Yes, Dizzy, Lord Beaconsfield, whom I trained to carve the map of the world, will carve and distribute the cake of eternal love. His manner will be so gracious that he who receives but a crumb will not look with envy upon his neighbor."

"Is Cartaphilus a tamer of lions?"

"It is easier to tame a lion than to win the heart of Salome."

"Ah, but the whip of Cartaphilus! How it stings and how it soothes!"

"How can one be certain of taming that heart?" he asked, pressing his hand against my breast.

"It is yours, Cartaphilus. Put the whip away."

"Never," he exclaimed. " 'When thou goest to women,' my friend Nietzsche says, 'forget not the whip!' "

"Incorrigible Cartaphilus!"

We laughed. Kotikokura grinned.

"How do you like my friend Dizzy?" he asked, after a silence. "He is enamored of you."

"Dizzy is an elderly Cartaphilus at the court of Victoria."

"Which means — ?" he asked, lifting his brow.

"He is vain, sad, brilliant, conceited and charming, an accomplished flatterer, yet faithful. Inordinately proud of his acquired position, yet laughing into his fashionable scraggy goatee at empires and at thrones. Lascivious, but an impeccable husband; timid at heart yet audacious; blatant and dignified, charlatan and philosopher, more visionary than a poet, more practical than an usurer! A tragic comedian, the symbol of our race, the perfect minister of your invisible government, as Kotikokura was the perfect High Priest to your godhood!"

"Bravissima!" Cartaphilus applauded.

Kotikokura's face endeavored to lengthen like an Englishman's. His eyes were motionless.

Noting his irritation, I asked with uttermost dignity: "Is Ca-Ta-Pha still God of the Universe?"

"Ca-Ta-Pha — God in sæcula sæculorum," he answered, clasping his hands piously, like the Archbishop of Canterbury.

I could not refrain from uttering: "Amen!"

"At any rate," Cartaphilus said, "I have added India and the Suez Canal to the realm of Victoria. It amuses me that the greatest Empire of the modern world owes its predominance to a Jew."

I smiled.

"Your predilection for the Chosen People seems irrational after nearly two thousand years, Cartaphilus."

"Call it poetic justice, or a game. Jewish brains possess a maturity and a mobility too often lacking in Nordics. It pleases me for the time being, to govern the world through my compatriots. We irritate and cajole and rule though the lassoed steeds stamp the ground in rage."

Cartaphilus rubbed his hands gleefully.

"Incorrigible child!"

"Incomparable Queen!"

"Is it not futile for us, Cartaphilus, to concern ourselves with statesmen who feverishly rule for a day and scientists who discover truths that do not survive their generation? Poor ants, painfully rolling bits of mud into their cells — to no purpose. What have we in common with them?"

"Nothing and everything, Salome. We have lived nearly two thousand years, but we are still — thirty or"— he smiled —"thereabouts. Our glands, holding in some mysterious way the key to our immortality, keep us young. We are young, but the Earth is old."

"May not our immortality be merely a normal life indefinitely prolonged? Can we escape the eternal rhythm? Even the mountain flows, and eventually melts away. Everything moves, vibrates, dissolves. Our life is the life of the mountain. The life of the others is like that of the rose and butterfly. Jesus and John disturbed, accelerated or altered some biochemical process. What their secret was we already guess, but cannot yet state in definite terms. Such temporary variations cannot nullify the implacable laws of the Universe."

Cartaphilus said nothing. He seemed more interested in the sound of my voice than in my words.

"Two thousand years, Cartaphilus, what is that? It takes longer for a single ray of a star to reach our tiny Earth. Two thousand years — was that enough for you to discover the meaning of Truth? Was it sufficient for me to unyoke woman from her bondage to the Moon? I have learned, it is true, how to control the lunar tribute through chemicals, through the hidden rays of metals, through hypnotism. But not permanently and not with absolute safety. Two thousand years — what does it mean? We remember some of the secrets that the others harbor only vaguely in the subcellars of consciousness. We can envisage the future a little more clearly because we can decipher more accurately the tapestry of the Past. But that is all. We are not even entirely immune from accident and disease."

"I am glad of it, Salome!" Cartaphilus exclaimed suddenly. "We are of the Earth! The Earth is our Mother! We vibrate to her rhythm. We are not too far beyond humanity to feel its tragedy — its comedy! We are children of Adam and Eve. I am glad our brains are prisoners of the cranium that holds them. I am glad our nerves and our glands will never allow us to transcend the planet which gave us birth, which, like the guardian of the bridge, may some day demand from us the toll of death! We sail with each new generation the boat that tosses upon the endless Sea of Time. Our eyes are sharper, Salome, and we catch glimpses of the worlds that glimmer beyond the horizon, but we cannot reach them except in the company of mankind. We may steer the Boat, but ——"

I interrupted the pæan of joy. "No, beloved, we can fashion a boat of our own. I am weary of the noisy crew, weary of the monotonous tossing. Don't you see that the boat is caught in a monstrous eddy that turns forever in the selfsame spot? We can make a dash across the horizon!"

"Whither Salome goeth, I go!"

The butler announced: "Lord Beaconsfield!"

The Prime Minister, in his gala uniform almost as burdened with medals as Kotikokura, entered quickly, his bony body bent forward, his mouth open in an ingratiating smile.

He kissed my hand with a flourish, bowed deeply to Cartaphilus, his hand upon his chest, and nodded to Kotikokura, as one nods out of a carriage window.

"Her Majesty was simply superb," he fluttered. "I really thought she was going to embrace me."

"How the Earl of Beaconsfield must have flattered his Queen!" Cartaphilus laughed.

"Flattered, my dear Graf?" He made a gesture first of indignation, then replacing his monocle over his shrewd, sharp eyes, he said, smiling, "How can mankind live without flattery? Did not Jahveh flatter the mud that was Adam, calling it Man?"

"And one single rib painlessly withdrawn from his sleeping body calling it Woman?" I added ironically.

"Ah, Señora," he kissed the tips of my fingers reverentially like an ikon, "it was not the rib. The scribes misquoted the angels who dictated the Book of God. It was the heart."

Turning to Cartaphilus, he said, "Flattery, my dear Count

— who does not like flattery? And when you come to royalty, you must lay it on with a trowel!"

"The fox," reverberated through my mind. For a moment Disraeli assumed the features of my stepfather Antipas with his sharp nose, sharp chin, sharp hands — an Antipas whose tongue was the wily Snake's tongue that cost humanity its paradise.

"Was the Queen in a mood to listen to my proposal — my Lord?" Cartaphilus asked.

Disraeli drew a silk handkerchief out of his sleeve, like a prestidigitator, and crushed it slowly between his palms, but in lieu of rabbits and doves and goldfish, there issued out of his mouth speech — speech mellifluous, honeyed, modulated.

"I have not broached the question of Egypt, Graf. On my Queen's birthday, there must be no mention of state affairs."

"The French, my Lord," Cartaphilus said somewhat irritably, "are not celebrating the Queen's birthday. They are working feverishly against us."

Disraeli smiled, his eyes half-shut, like a Chinese divinity. He replaced his handkerchief in his sleeve. "My Lord, I have paved the way, smoothed the path to her Imperial mind."

He waited a moment, then stretching his neck forward, continued: "This is what I said to Victoria, Queen of the United Kingdom of Great Britain and Ireland and Empress of India:

" 'To-day Lord Beaconsfield ought fitly, perhaps, to congratulate a powerful Sovereign on her Imperial sway, the vastness of her Empire, and the success and strength of her fleets and armies. But he cannot, his mind is in another mood. He can only think of the strangeness of his destiny that it has come to pass that he should be the servant of one so great, and whose infinite kindness, the brightness of whose intelligence and the firmness of whose will, have enabled him to undertake labors to which he otherwise would be quite unequal, and supported him in all things by a condescending sympathy, which in the hour of difficulty alike charms and inspires. Upon the Sovereign of many lands and many hearts may an omnipotent Providence shed every blessing that the wise can desire and the virtuous deserve!'"

Disraeli stopped, breathed deeply, bowed, like an operatic star.

Cartaphilus applauded. "Bravo! Bravo!"

Kotikokura struck the finger-tips of one hand against the other and repeated with a guttural French accent: "Bravo! Bravo."

"Thank you, Count," Dizzy bowed to Cartaphilus. "Je vous remercie, Monsieur le Baron de Kotikokura," he added, turning to the High Priest of Ca-Ta-Pha.

"The Faery was enchanted. Her cheeks flushed like a little girl's. The visitors were green with envy. The Prince of Baden hissed into his consort's ear: 'Der alte Jude!'"

The Prime Minister rubbed his thin hands gleefully.

"Lady Beaconsfield beamed upon me like a fond mother whose boy recites a poem, for which he gets a medal."

The Earl shrank to the size of a spindle-legged schoolboy, his mother's pet.

"And Her Majesty," I added, half maliciously, my voice a trifle thinner as if addressing a child, "beamed upon her Prime Minister — like a — fond grandmother?"

Disraeli looked at me quizzically, frowning, as if my words had suddenly illumined a hidden angle of his brain, as if he had suddenly become aware of a truth long struggling for recognition. Still unwilling to admit it, he exclaimed, "Oh, let them say what they will! Let them say that I flatter my Queen, that I am a consummate actor, that I am a Jew, ambitious and avaricious. In life one must have for one's thoughts a sacred depository, and Lord Beaconsfield," he struck his chest like a worshiper before the Wailing Wall, "ever presumes to seek that in his Sovereign Mistress."

The Earl stopped, to allow his words to take root. Then, still protagonist, author, director of a romantic drama, he declaimed: "He lives only for Her, and works only for Her, and without Her all is lost!"

His arm outstretched, he addressed Cartaphilus:

"Graf, whatever the impugned motives of jealous and incompetent rivals, you and I have served England as none of her boastful sons. Was it not your gold — four million sterling — that bought the Suez Canal? Did we not create an Empire and an Empress?"

Cartaphilus placed his forefinger to his lips. "It was not I——"

The Prime Minister stopped like an obedient secretary, and bowed.

"The Rothschilds, Graf, since it pleases you to remain incognito. History, however, will some day divulge the secret."

The butler served champagne. We drank to the long life of the Queen and Empress. Then the Prime Minister toasted, "To the Reina de las Pampas, Victoria of the New World."

Disraeli laughed heartily like a boy, his goatee shivering upon his ironic chin, as he described the guests at the Buckingham Palace.

I mentioned the names of the most significant artists and thinkers of England. None of them had been invited.

Disraeli made a gesture of vague distress.

"Her Majesty, Señora, does not regard her Court as an Academy where titleless professors, however proficient in the arts and sciences, may hobnob with her country's nobility."

The aplomb of this upstart whose title still pinched his soul like a pair of new boots, irritated me as much as centuries ago the impudence of a cobbler's son mocking royalty. Only he within whose veins blue blood had coursed for many generations knows the true meaning of democracy, only he applauds wherever the royalty of genius manifests itself.

Cartaphilus read my thoughts and laughed. Kotikokura, sensitive to his master's reactions, grinned, revealing his teeth like an Englishman.

"My Lord, other Monarchs were patrons of the arts. They did not consider their Courts halls where the roster of sonorous titles may be called out like the names of cities in a railroad station."

The Prime Minister straightened up indignant, but immeditately, bowing low with Oriental suavity, he said, "The rebellious youth of the New World reverberates in the words of Señora."

He opened his snuffbox, the gift of Victoria, and offered us its contents. He barely dipped the tips of his nails, and delicately touched his nostrils.

Cartaphilus seemed much amused.

"Was Lady Granville considered worthy of an invitation, my Lord?" I asked.

"Lady Granville, Señora, comes of an illustrious family. Alas, she is divorced."

"And Lady Hawerton, my Lord?"

"Lady Hawerton, Señora, married a second time." Across Dizzy's lips a smile alighted for a moment like a bewildered bee, and vanished.

"My Lord, Victoria is a great Queen, but she cannot forget that she is above all wife and mother and grandmother. The scent of the nursery is about her. She has corseted the body of woman, and the iron bars are cutting into her soul. My Lord, the false propriety of the modern Anglo-Saxons, unfortunately induced by Her Majesty, will be an incubus for generations — on all mankind."

The Prime Minister, accustomed to the tirades against him and his government, smiled, twirling the ribbon of his monocle around his finger, a conscious or unconscious gesture denoting the manner in which he twirled the destiny of those who opposed him.

"The corset, my Lord, is the symbol of the Victorian age. It misshapes and deforms and shifts from its natural position the anatomy of the body and the mind. Have you not noticed how pathetically ignorant of themselves are even the men and women of culture and education? They know the roots of Latin verbs, but not the roots of their beings."

Dizzy nodded, but said nothing.

"Victoria is honest in her purity. She is naturally, instinctively, what the others are because she has set the style. Purity has changed to prudery and hypocrisy."

"Have not the great and the virtuous always been misinterpreted, Señora?" Lord Beaconsfield deigned to answer.

Beyond this he would not commit himself. The rest of the conversation became a monologue, a tirade against a typical feminine régime, which amused Cartaphilus and his High Priest and seemed not at all to perturb the Prime Minister.

"My Lord," I said at last, "I should like to present some suggestions for the improvement of the condition of my sex. Her Majesty would grant me an audience?"

Dizzy became once more the actor. He spoke of the great pleasure his Faery Queen would have in conversing with the Reina de las Pampas, whose eloquence was equal to her beauty. The true Oriental, he invoked the phenomena of Nature, colors and perfumes and zephyrs and heavenly bodies.

"This very day, Señora, I shall write to my Queen of the delight that awaits her."

He drew his watch out of his pocket. His face lit. He was again a child.

"Lady Beaconsfield is awaiting me in the garden to tell me again how well her Dizzy performed to-day," he giggled.

Was I wrong? Was this mother-child attitude between man and woman, perhaps, the only adequate relationship of the sexes?

Cartaphilus discussed for a while the Egyptian question, and instructed the Prime Minister in his maneuvers. Dizzy listened abstractedly. He was no longer the statesman, the actor — he was the tired boy longing for the lap of his mother.

He bade us adieu and left hurriedly.

"Dizzy is growing dizzier and dizzier," Cartaphilus laughed.

Kotikokura raised his eyebrows, and wiped his monocle.

Victoria, Queen and Empress, sat upon her throne, her hands clasped upon her lap. Her cheeks a little puffed and her lips drooping gave the impression of a royal hen hiding underneath her voluminous skirts her numerous progeny.

Neither Zenobia nor Elizabeth nor Catherine seemed so typically the mother of the race. None so truly the obedient and respectful wife. I could remember no salon or palace where I had encountered her prototype. Perhaps only in some far-flung cottage or ancient patriarch's abode.

I was not elated. Rather I felt a dull indignation throbbing in me against the elemental female.

The Queen began a long eulogy of her Prime Minister. The grandmotherly attitude towards her infant prodigy became more startlingly evident.

"Lord Beaconsfield is the only person who appreciates the Prince," she said. "To him, as to me, Albert was absolute perfection."

Mindful of the fact that I was not permitted to proffer questions, but only to answer Her Majesty's queries, I tried, nevertheless, to lift the conversation out of the bog of sentimentalism, to withdraw her attention from the worship of a wraith.

"Madam," I interposed somewhat timorously, "in some South American states woman has almost achieved emancipation."

"Emancipation?" Victoria exclaimed, her eyes wide open, her hands unclasped, as if startled in her sleep.

"Yes, Ma'am. And we look toward Your Majesty for moral support and encouragement."

The Ruler awakened in her. Her eyes blazed.

"Señora, my country, by the Grace of God, shall never harbor this canker!"

"What canker, Ma'am?"

She did not answer my question, but pursued as if addressing the Parliament, her forefinger in the air.

"I shall never allow this folly of Women's Rights to take root in England! I shall enlist every one who can speak or write to join in checking this mad, wicked folly with all its attendant horrors, on which the poor feeble sex seems bent, forgetting every sense of womanly propriety."

Victoria stood up. I looked unconsciously upon the floor, half expecting a flock of chicks to rush in all directions.

"This is a subject that makes me so furious I cannot contain myself. God created men and women different — let them remain different, each in their own position. Woman is the wife and the mother of the race. She would become the most hateful, heartless and disgusting of human beings were she allowed to unsex herself; and where would be the protection which man was intended to give the weaker sex?"

She reseated herself.

"I shall write a letter to the leaders. I shall ask Disraeli to assist me to stamp underfoot this immoral Crusade. Every woman who propounds it deserves to get a good whipping!"

I did not know where to begin my argument against this incredibly narrow-minded view of so important a question. To silence my indignation, I said acridly, "Ma'am, is woman to remain forever the slave of her gender?"

Victoria stared at me scandalized.

"Madame," she replied, her head raised in uttermost contempt, "pas de plaisanteries! We are not amused!"

She nodded, her head turned peremptorily toward the door. . . .

Furious, I entered the landau and drove home. Cartaphilus awaited me, smoking long Russian cigarettes, the recent gift of the Czar.

"Ah, my love, my Reina de las Pampas!" he exclaimed, and rushed to embrace me.

"Don't touch me, Cartaphilus! I bristle like a porcupine!"

I threw my hat and gloves on the table. I turned my ring upon my finger a dozen times. I stamped my foot.

"Give me a cigarette, Cartaphilus."

He lit a cigarette, and placed it between my lips.

"What's happened, my dear?"

He finally succeeded in holding my hand, and kissing it. The touch of his lips was like a balm that soothed. I flung my arms around him and kissed him.

"I love you, dearest. I love you," I exclaimed.

Bewildered, delighted, Cartaphilus seated me upon his lap. We embraced in silence for a long time.

I rose and arranged my hair.

"Victoria showed me the door, Cartaphilus."

Cartaphilus watched me, uncertain what attitude to take.

"Oh, it's perfectly all right, Cartaphilus. You may laugh now."

Cartaphilus burst into laughter.

"What a relief — my love — laughter was in me like a dynamite — but I did not dare — you looked like a Juno furious against her faithless Jove."

"Perhaps when Victoria overcomes all sexual memories, forgets her perfect Albert, she may become a great monarch. Just now she still quakes in her royal boots. In the substrata of her mind, stirring nervously under her crown, still lurks the age-long feeling of inferiority. She quivers before the wraith of Albert."

"Have you not achieved what you have striven for, Salome? Victoria represents the era of woman. Does it not delight you?" Cartaphilus asked, somewhat banteringly.

"Man — Woman — What are they but the product of mud inspirited by a tribal primitive divinity ——"

Cartaphilus interrupted me.

"Mankind is so young, Salome. It takes millions of light years for a ray of a star to travel across the universe. What can we expect of a creature whose life can be counted in days!"

"It is not true, Cartaphilus! Man is young compared to the universe — but aged and dying, nevertheless. Shall we say that a fly one summer old is in its infancy, comparing its longevity to that of the turtle? The fly is only one summer old, but already its body is stiffening on the window pane. Mankind has nearly completed its cycle of existence. The time has come for a Super-Race, for my Homuncula to be born into the world ——"

"Damn your Homuncula!" he exclaimed, throwing his cigarette away.

I placed my hands upon his shoulders, and looked into his eyes.

"Cartaphilus, you have not yet wearied of ruling your dear England and the rest of Europe. Your banks have not yet gathered into their strongboxes all the gold of the world. When you desire to cast away your invisible crown ——"

"I cast it away this very moment for your kiss, Salome!" he interrupted, dramatically.

I smiled. "You talk like Dizzy. But the Queen of the

Pampas, unlike the Faery Queen, can read men's thoughts."

He did not answer. Like a guilty boy, he feigned indignation.

"We shall be married for centuries, my love," I said, "let us not hasten foolishly — before the supreme moment ——"

"Set the date," he said half angrily. "I am willing to wait, but I must know when my torture ends."

"Torture? Tut, tut!"

"You do not understand," he said whimperingly. "Your heart is ——"

"What?"

"A precious stone."

"It is adamantine in its love for you."

We bantered and courted and vowed endless affection.

"May I at least sail with you to Buenos Ayres?" he pleaded.

I nodded.

"Kotikokura! Kotikokura!" Cartaphilus shouted.

Kotikokura entered solemnly.

"Come, get things ready, my ancient friend. We are going to Buenos Ayres to conduct the Queen of the Super-Race to the New Eden."

Kotikokura bowed stiffly.

CHAPTER FIFTY-SIX

MY WEDDING FEAST — THE EPITHALAMIUM OF NATURE — FINDING AND SEEKING — LAKSHMI LAYS AN EGG — NUPTIAL CONFIDENCES — I TELL THE TRUTH — MY FIRST TWO THOUSAND YEARS OF LOVE — HOMUNCULA SMILES — THE TYRANT OF THE SKIES — THE FOOD OF HOMUNCULA — HOMUNCULA, OUR DAUGHTER.

"Hymen himself, Salome, officiated at our wedding! His chant has stirred Earth and Heaven. Look, beloved, the sun is a tilted chalice overbrimming, and every one, everything, partakes of the wine and is drunken with rapture."

I wound my arms slowly about him. We gazed into each other's eyes, until our sight became one, and our dreams merged as waters of rivers merge.

"Cartaphilus, I am your wife now and forevermore. Mountains may tear themselves away from their roots, stars may alter their flaming paths, oceans, forgetting, may inundate the deserts, the Moon, rebellious, may refuse the light of the Sun, but you and I, forever and forever, are one and inseparable."

Cartaphilus whispered, "Forever and forever."

Our mouths pressed against each other, deeper and deeper, and our breaths and our pulses and our nerves and our thoughts rushed together and were welded as steel is welded in white flames.

We resumed our walking, our arms clasped about each other's waists, talking at random about many things and many people.

The branches of the ombú trees rocked under the weight of the birds, while underneath feathers and plumes of all hues — sacrificial offerings to the god of passion — turned in fantastic dances.

Insects, shimmering with the gold of pollen, lay drowsy on the wide-open petals of flowers.

"Why is it," Cartaphilus asked, "that you left France so suddenly at the time of the Revolution, my love?"

"Because," I answered, "the Revolution could teach me nothing. Of revolutions one can safely quote always: 'Nihil sub sole novi.'"

"It seems strange you were never interested in the mistresses of Roi Soleil and le Bien-Aimé."

"Louis XIV and Louis XV were not extraordinary men. People mistook the luxury that surrounded them for the glory they shed. They were the slaves to the Phallus even as Catherine was a slave to the Womb. Their favorites merely ruled because they knew instinctively the laws that govern the carnal appetites. They influenced not through their brains or personalities, but through their organs of generation. They never met men on an equal plane, and never sought the emancipation of woman. On several occasions I tried to enlist the help of Mme. de Montespan and Mme. de Maintenon, the mistresses of Louis XIV, and Marquise de Pompadour, the favorite of Louis XV. They thought I wanted to supplant them, and tried to poison or incarcerate me."

Cartaphilus laughed heartily like a boy.

On the lake whose waters were a molten diamond swans clustered together, their beaks buried in their breasts. About the rim of the shore as a necklace of crushed pearls glimmered the spawn of fish. Like the gurgling of wine running through a narrow-throated bottle the bullfrogs reiterated their hymeneal vow.

"Once a thousand women, the most beautiful, the most voluptuous, stormed my body with their flesh and laved it with the tide of their kisses ——"

"Yes, I know, Cartaphilus. The Bath of Beauty has become the leitmotif of poets and artists and the distress of moralists and eunuchs——"

"But my soul," he continued, "my soul remained dead within me. Last night, Salome, for the first time since the dream of love awoke in me, for the first time in two thousand years, my soul and my body vibrated in unison. Thus the clay that was Adam was startled into life."

"Thus my Homuncula, dearest, will thrill the Earth when she arises — some months from now."

"Nine months?" he asked quizzically.

"Perhaps," I answered, trembling with ecstasy at the memory of our nuptial joys. "She is your child, Cartaphilus."

"My child? It is true indeed that a father never knoweth——"

"Your child, my love, for always your soul was bound with mine, and I have created my ectogenetic daughter in the image of both of us."

"Strange, Salome! Until this moment Homuncula was a creature that amused me, that interested me vaguely, philosophically. I suddenly feel a tenderness for her. I am a father!"

"We are all mothers and fathers, Cartaphilus. Do we not unconsciously seek always to be those mighty giants, those all-powerful gods who watch over us in our cradles? Why does every cell yearn to create itself?"

Kotikokura emerged suddenly from the forest, his eyes blurred, his step a trifle unsteady, his face flushed. He averted our look and passed us by hurriedly.

In the distance a flock of sheep bleated sentimentally.

Cartaphilus laughed. "Our friend is no longer the Nordic nobleman with the Oxford accent. He is Pan again — the eternal denizen of the wilds."

For a long while we were silent.

"Cartaphilus," I asked, "have the two parallel lines really met?"

"There never were two parallel lines, Salome. There was only one straight line, but our sight was blurred, and we saw it wavering and separating. We have been one since the birth of Time, and we shall continue to be one until Time, too weary to pursue Infinity, shall merge with it, and be no more."

"It was I, Cartaphilus, that broke the line into two. Perhaps at bottom it was my feminine vanity to make you pursue me, or at least, to create that illusion. Did the prize equal the effort, my beloved, or like Apollonius, do you believe that that which is found is not worth the seeking?"

"Apollonius lived too little to know the true meaning of finding and seeking. In the short lives of mortals whatever they discover is too insignificant. Who, what man, what God, having found Salome, could consider a million years too long a pursuit? Besides, have I really found her?"

He took my head in his palms and looked into my eyes.

"What do you see, Cartaphilus?"

"What can one see when one looks into the blazing sun? He knows that life begins and ends there — but he must shut his eyes or go blind."

Cartaphilus closed his eyes. I kissed them.

"As long as my husband remembers to flatter me, I shall be happy."

Something rolled and struck the tip of my shoe.

"What is this, Cartaphilus?" I asked, a little scared.

He raised the object.

"An egg, Salome — a golden egg!"

"It is not a fowl's egg, nor a peacock's — nor a ———"

Lakshmi approached quickly, her legs spread wide apart.

"It's a testudinal egg — a divine chelonian!" I exclaimed.

"It is the first time in all the centuries I have known Lakshmi that she has given forth potential offspring."

"Lakshmi," I said scandalized, "is it possible? At your venerable age — indulging in such youthful sports?"

"Our wedding, Salome, has seduced the whole world," Cartaphilus laughed.

Lakshmi looked away guiltily.

I kept the egg in my palm.

"It is worthy of the wife of Vishnu, God of the Universe. Have you ever seen so smooth, so dazzling, so perfectly fashioned an egg, Cartaphilus?"

"Never," he answered, and turning to Lakshmi, "My compliments, Our Lady of Turtles!"

"Who knows what greater Vishnu sleeps within this golden sphere?"

"A greater Vishnu?" Cartaphilus said. "I should rather think a smaller Kotikokura!"

"How dare you accuse my ancient friend of adultery?"

"What is a little adultery — once every thousand years or so — among immortals?"

I looked at my husband reprovingly.

He raised his hand, "Never, Salome! I swear it!"

Lakshmi tapped my ankle, unawares. The egg rolled to the ground, breaking into a pool the shape of a star.

"Lakshmi, forgive me!" I exclaimed.

Lakshmi looked meditatively at the wreckage, then lapped it slowly.

"Perhaps it is better so, Lakshmi," I said. "Who knows what hybrid universe you would have hatched!"

"Besides, Vishnu would never brook bastard progeny," Cartaphilus added.

"Sh!" I warned Cartaphilus, placing my forefinger to his lips. "Do not say disparaging things about my dear Lakshmi. She understands everything," I whispered.

Cartaphilus smiled.

"Oh, yes, my love, she does, and in any language. How often her look or her tap suggested what I should do or whither to go! How lonesome I should have been without her!"

Lakshmi cast a side-glance at us.

"If only some day some one could decipher the meaning of her tapping, who knows what marvelous things we might discover! Do not forget that we are children compared to her, Cartaphilus. She may be a hundred thousand years old."

Lakshmi raised one horny eyelid in mockery or disdain, then licked her forepaws and followed us.

"Cartaphilus, tell me, do you not remember with regret the caresses of your other loves? Last night, when our bodies melted into one another, when our kisses enraptured the world, did you not recall the eyes of one, the skin of another, the smile of a third, the lips, the breasts, the whispers, the laughter, the promises, the stifled cries, the grateful sighs?"

"At night a flickering candle guides one's footsteps. When the sun is overhead a thousand torches stare blankly like the blind eyes of owls. I remembered nothing, no one last night — save you."

"The men and women I knew, Cartaphilus, were like tiny streams which suddenly plunge into the sea, lose their form and their identity in the mighty waters, becoming undecipherable waves and tides."

Cartaphilus looked at me, smiling ironically. "What of your wives . . ."

"Cartaphilus, you forget that I am well-versed in the secret of the African Aphrodite. Psychology is superior to physiology, and mind rules always."

Cartaphilus raised an eyebrow.

"Salome, beloved wife, tell me the truth at last!"

Lakshmi looked at me, one eye closed, the corners of her mouth lowered.

"That is the truth!"

Lakshmi stepped in front of me. I nearly tripped.

Cartaphilus laughed.

"Lakshmi, who understands everything and knows all your deeds and all your thoughts, warns you or laughs in her inimitable chelonian fashion."

"I have told you the truth, Cartaphilus, the truth as much as any woman can tell any man, her husband in particular. And you, my incomparable consort, have you told me the truth?"

"I swear, Salome, I have never told you a lie!"

"I loved," I said, "as I understood love at the various stages of my development. At the beginning, because of the hate I bore you and the masculine envy you stirred in my heart, I sought to crush man. It was the struggle between the male and the female, the elemental warfare of the sexes. Despite my conquests, I considered myself defeated. I loved Jokanaan because I believed he made no distinction between the sexes. I regarded his prophecies of Heaven as a parable, meaning that the day would come, if his words were heeded, when woman would be the equal of man. Alas, he hated woman - - he hated me, symbol of femininity — with an unquenchable hatred."

Cartaphilus caressed my hand.

"We owe our love to the hatred of two men, Jesus and Jokanaan. Their curse was our blessing."

"In order to forget, I wandered into many strange spheres. I unraveled the entangled threads of the Spool of Passion. China, Africa, Arabia, India, each country offered a new experience or a new variant of the ancient rite.

"Gradually, however, my anger against man waned. I was baptized in the waters of experience. I sought not merely the carnal thrill, but love.

"I loved the child in Onam. I loved David for his youth. I loved Robert because he stirred the memory of the others. I loved Ulric because he was the new man, the man who revered woman, physically and spiritually. I loved Ferdinand because his manhood was made delicate and tender by his feminine nature. I loved Joan with a love that most nearly approached my love for you, Cartaphilus."

I continued the catalogue of my amours, endeavoring to discover the nuances that differentiated one from another.

"Do you remember Herma?" Cartaphilus asked. "Herma, the child of the French Revolution?"

I nodded.

"We both loved her, Salome."

"Yes. She was the symbol of the period in which she lived. She was a true descendant of the son of Hermes and Aphrodite who bathing became united in one body with the nymph Salmacis."

"She loved you more, Salome. Was it because her masculinity predominated?"

"Perhaps."

After a silence, I said, "But all the time, Cartaphilus, I was fully aware that I was wandering in an intricate maze, seeking the outlet, where you, my beloved, awaited me. My two thousand years of love were but the corridor that led to our nuptial chamber."

Cartaphilus drew my head upon his chest.

"If the maze had been more intricate than the mad dance of these butterflies pursuing one another, and your emergence had required more æons than for the sun to turn into a pallid moon, I should still have waited for you — not patiently perhaps," he added, "not without grumbling, not without cursing feminine perversity, but waiting."

I pressed my head deeper into his chest, and whispered his name many times, like an incantation.

In the trees opposite the monkeys pursued one another from branch to branch, until the males uttered cries of triumph and the females groans of pleasure. Only Abelard, curtailed by one of the flowers of the New Eden, like the famous monk of the Middle Ages, whose name he bore, jumped to the ground, weary of the calisthenics. Rotund and stately as a bishop, he unsheathed a banana and munched it delicately with his front teeth.

"Do you remember him, Cartaphilus?" I asked.

Cartaphilus looked at him attentively.

"I do not believe I ever had the honor ——"

"Oh, yes! You saved him from the maw of the carnivorous flower on your last visit — before you started the World War."

"He must be much older than he looks."

"The pruning rejuvenated him like an operation by Steinach."

"Probably."

The monkeys pelted Abelard with shells of nuts. He looked up disdainfully, and walked away with utmost dignity like a lady falsely accused of an impropriety.

Suddenly Lakshmi freed herself from our feet. She stretched her head in all directions as if in search of something, then withdrew it quickly, and disappeared entirely in her shell. The monkeys clambered to the top of the trees and chattered furiously. Not a bird sang. A flock of white peacocks dashed by, their wings tightly drawn against their backs, uttering shrill cries. The surface of the lake creased as if a colossus had blown over it.

"What is the meaning of this?" Cartaphilus asked.

I stood up with a start.

"Homuncula! Homuncula!" I cried, rushing in the direction of the New Eden. Cartaphilus followed.

The Earth rocked under our feet like a boat whose anchor is removed. A hot wind like the breath of an animal fanned our faces. Fearing Cartaphilus would lose his way, I kept his hand.

"I hope no evil has befallen our Homuncula," I whispered, out of breath, as we reached the portals.

Homuncula had her eyes wide open. . . .

"Cartaphilus," I exclaimed, pressing against him. "Our child is welcoming us, look! The Earth, aware of her sight, reeled with joy! Homuncula!" I called.

A smile like a thread of light piercing through a wall crossed her lips.

"The soul has stirred in her, Cartaphilus! Strange! I feel as once I felt when my baby was alive in me!" I said, pressing my hands against my body.

"The center of the Universe is still the womb, Salome."

"Until Homuncula becomes the mother of a new race!"

Cartaphilus watched Homuncula intently.

"Is she not beautiful, Cartaphilus? Have you ever seen such whiteness of skin, such perfection of form, such grace?"

"I saw — last night."

"No, never!" I answered with motherly pride.

"On what do you feed her that her cheeks are snow on which two petals of a red rose have fallen?"

"There is an invisible umbilical cord between her mind and mine, Cartaphilus. She lives in the womb of my brain, and is fed in the placenta of my thoughts."

A vague smile of incredulity flitted across the lips of Cartaphilus.

"While you were endeavoring to rule the world, Cartaphilus, and you have recently seen with what disastrous results ——"

"The World War may not have been as disastrous as it

seems, Salome. The air has been cleared of Victorian prudery and people are more amenable to new ideas."

"At any rate, while you were interested in power, I have discovered a few secrets of Nature, which, leaking out now and then and duplicated in the laboratories, startle man. Even if my new race does not populate the world, the world will be a much more exciting place to live in."

"Perhaps."

"Before long woman, though still a slave to the Pallid Tyrant of the Skies, will no longer pay the toll in pain and discomfiture, but with the ease with which she breathes, and she will pay it whenever most convenient. Nor like poor Catherine the Great will she sorrow that the Moon, removing the scarlet insignia of her rule, will leave her a tortured being, neither woman nor man. A tiny injection into her body will recharge the mysterious batteries of her being. And I have not neglected man. With what avidity he clings to the few years in which his manhood blossoms! How he fears the withering days! There will be no more winter in the garden of his sex!"

"How will you stave off the shriveling hand of age, Salome?"

"The hormones of the young introduced into declining bodies startle them into pristine vigor! Ah, if only the scientists in all parts of the world with whom I secretly communicate were not so short-lived! By the time an idea of mine becomes clear to them most of them are too old or too worn to pursue their researches. Nevertheless, now and then, by accident or divine intuition, a mortal stumbles upon a discovery."

Cartaphilus kissed my hand. "O Aspasia of the World! O Queen of Wisdom!"

"Look at this lamp, which sheds a brighter and more soothing light than the sun at the meridian. It is not merely light. It is food. It is delicious manna to our Homuncula. Her body will never be clogged with impurities. Her breath will be sweeter than the breeze at daybreak."

"I feel its influence myself. It is as if I walked upon the

peaks of the Alps, the perfume of far-off vineyards in my nostrils."

"And look, Cartaphilus, is not Homuncula made for sheer delight to herself and to her lover?"

"She is more perfect than Herma."

"Oh, Herma!" I exclaimed disparagingly.

"You loved her, Salome," he said, a tinge of jealousy in his voice. "Of those we once loved nil nisi bonum."

"I loved her, and she was exquisite — as you know — but he or she who enjoys the caresses of Homuncula will be drunken for the rest of his life — if indeed, unlike the bee in his hymeneal flight, he survives. If the gods of Olympus still lived, and still pursued their amorous careers, they would storm my gates now, and break through the invisible screens. They would barter their immortality for one embrace of Homuncula!"

"Is she immortal?"

"I do not know. I have eliminated all the rudimentary, the superfluous organs which cause so much misery in man. Her body does not begin at the period when the Earth was a sea of flames or a shoreless ocean, when animals as bulky as mountains uprooted for their sport giant oaks with the ease with which Lakshmi tears a leaf off the cabbage. Her body begins with the Present, with the Future, as far as I am able to peer through the narrow shadowy corridor of Time. I have reshaped and redistributed the internal organs. There will never be impingement or cramping. Her blood is schooled and trained to defeat every harmful organism that may find its way into the system. Her glands function with the perfection and precision of the stellar movements. If she is not immortal, Cartaphilus, she will partake of the longevity of the great trees within which the centuries inscribe their passage in the endless parade of time. And like ourselves she will be young always — or at least age will mean neither decrepitude nor impotence.

"She will change, slowly, harmoniously as the green leaf of summer turns to the russet of autumn. And if she dies, she will dissolve like a dream. She is not born in the pain of another. She will not die in the agony of her own."

"O most fortunate daughter of a most adorable mother!"
"And of a most delectable father!"

We embraced and swore for the myriadth time eternal affection. The lips of Homuncula parted vaguely.

"Our daughter blesses our union, Cartaphilus!"

CHAPTER FIFTY-SEVEN

NEWS FROM MME. CURIE — THE FAILURE OF MRS. EDDY — MISTRESSES AND KINGS — LAKSHMI'S ELEVATOR — KOTIKOKURA ROCKS HIMSELF — THE GIFT OF ADAM — A FORTUNATE DIVORCE — SUPERSEX —"I AM I AND YOU ARE YOU"— KOTIKOKURA GROWLS — THE DEAFNESS OF LAKSHMI — A THUNDERCLAP — HOMUNCULA WAKES — WILD OATS AND WILD BLOSSOMS — CARTAPHILUS DISCOVERS A FAN — THE FISHERMAN'S RING —"SALOME, I LOVE YOU"— THE ROAD TO TRUTH.

"Look, Salome, Madame Curie has discovered a simpler way of obtaining radium," Cartaphilus said, pointing to the screen on which the news of the world was hourly dispatched from our secret airport.

I shrugged my shoulders. "Six hundred years ago the Jewish alchemist, Gershom Mendez of Sevilla, made a similar discovery."

"Christian Science is taking root in South America. A woman divinity born in modern times!" Cartaphilus exclaimed as he continued to read the message.

"Mrs. Eddy stole her philosophy from Spinoza, her faith-healing methods from the Portland watchmaker Quimby, her methods of organization from the Mail Order Business which flourishes in North America. She was a Yankee yogi driving a good bargain with Christ and Man. She succeeded in convincing her followers, but never herself. Her divine knees trembled. She was the twin of fear. She was haunted her entire life with hallucinations of persecution. Her critics she considered witches and devils torturing her with their malicious animal magnetism. An unrelenting tyrant over others, she was the shivering slave of her own shadow."

"My adorable wife is not in a mood for applauding the achievements, terrestrial or divine, of her sex," Cartaphilus smiled.

Kotikokura refilled our glasses with the precision of an English butler. Lakshmi tapped the button of her elevator which lifted her like a weightless thing to her regal throne perched upon four golden legs.

"Lakshmi never seems to use the ladder. She prefers her ascenseur," Cartaphilus laughed.

"She uses her ladder in moments of great emotional disturbances only. In this manner by the time she reaches the ground or her lofty seat, she overcomes herself, so to say, and is once again the unperturbed divinity supporting the universe. It is for this reason that on one side of the throne I placed her ladder and on the other the elevator."

Kotikokura seated himself in his rocker, and twirled his thumbs, exquisitely manicured.

The sun sieved through the vines which roofed the bower, and stretched at our feet like a giant spider asleep. The robots waved their silver fans and cooled the air pregnant with the perfume of lilacs.

"I applaud the achievement, Cartaphilus, not the sex of him or her who achieves. We have lived long enough to know that it is childish to divide mankind into two sexes. The visible organs do not determine the sex of the individual. Sex is a question of nuances, not of white and black. We are the children of both Adam and Eve, and all partake of the double-blossomed flower."

"Woman, however, is the more fortunate of the two, Salome, for the gift of Adam to his daughters, although only a miniature replica of himself, is an added source of pleasure. Eve's bequest to her son is too niggardly for any purpose — two buds never destined to unfold upon his bosom."

"That is true. The male vestige in woman even when it is less accentuated than in Herma — our sweetheart of long ago — still pulsates with joy."

"In woman many are the promontories and vales of delight and long is her endurance. Man, alas, is limited both in time and space!" Cartaphilus sighed.

"Still," I said, "it is very difficult to determine what Eve's gift to the individual man really is — for when least evident in his physical propensities, it may be sublimated in his imagination, in his temperament, in his art, in all the delicacies of his soul. And Adam, too, did not relinquish merely flesh of his flesh to his daughter. He also gave her a spiritual dowry."

Cartaphilus lit a cigarette and placed it between my lips, then lit one for himself. Kotikokura filled his pipe, Lakshmi looked quizzically, her head cocked to one side, at the smoke which rose like the long poles of a panoply, united overhead, and emerged through the interstices of the vines.

"Once I sought perfection, Salome — the lithe body of John the beloved Disciple, and the sweet body of Mary of Magdala, merged into one. They were the first to awaken love in me, and I yearned to possess them both again, so tightly woven into each other that nothing could cleave them apart."

Cartaphilus laughed. "I found that the perfection I sought was achieved most successfully by the snail. A snail Cartaphilus needs but to cross the garden to discover his ideal love. Each individual is his John and his Mary in one."

"According to the legends of the East, man, too, was once upon a time a double being, but God or Evolution or mere Chance clove him in two, and whatever the pinion of snails may be, who can deny it was a most fortunate divorce?"

"A most fortunate divorce, Salome, which made our marriage possible. But even if Nature had fashioned me like the snail or like Adam before the creation of Eve, I should still have dreamt, and yearned for you."

"And I for you, Cartaphilus."

He embraced me. Kotikokura in a sudden Victorian mood, turned his face.

"Nature is too slow and too unreliable," I said after a long silence. "We must evolve consciously — a new race of beings — physically perfect men and women, but each partaking spiritually of the other sex. Thus shall we have once again that union we seek forever, and that forever eludes us. We must fashion a Supersex, Cartaphilus!" I exclaimed.

"There are already signs of this development, Salome. Freud and Einstein and Steinach have revealed the soul and the body and the relativity of all things terrestrial and heavenly, and in this revelation, the intelligent civilized man has caught a glimpse of his duality."

"Not man — not woman — not male — not female — but a composite of both — a conscious commingling of the two. Not a hermaphrodite — who is neither fully male nor fully female, who relinquishes part of the one for the possession of the other. The symbol of the hermaphrodite is a double minus sign. The symbol of the Supersex is the double plus. To physical perfection it adds the Psyche of the opposite sex. The love of the Supersex is not determined by the mere accident of molecular combination, localized in one specific zone, but by the entire biochemistry of its existence."

"Salome, is it because you are a woman and I am a man that we have attracted each other for two thousand years as planets attract each other through immeasurable spaces? If it were merely this, why did even the most passionate embraces of all others leave something unsatisfied in us, something to yearn for, to seek? Love draws life from the great common root — sex — but each blossom is distinct. Each has its own perfume and its own color. We have attracted each other not because I am a man and you are a woman — but because"— he looked into my eyes —"I am Cartaphilus and you are Salome."

"Because you are you and I am I," I whispered.

Lakshmi, suddenly perturbed, started in her throne. She turned her head in all directions, fixing her look upon Kotikokura. With alarming alacrity she descended the ladder.

Kotikokura's eyes dashed to and fro. He rose and grumbled something between his teeth.

"What is the matter, Kotikokura?" Cartaphilus asked.

Kotikokura growled. He puffed at his pipe with such vigor

that the innocent toy of peace turned into a malevolent war engine belching smoke.

Lakshmi walked out followed by Kotikokura.

"Where are you going, Kotikokura?" Cartaphilus demanded.

The ears of the High Priest of Ca-Ta-Pha tightened against his head in canine fashion. He pretended deafness.

"Lakshmi! Lakshmi!" I called. Lakshmi was even deafer than her companion. Angrily, indignantly her paws struck the ground.

"Can you imagine, Cartaphilus, two that you would substitute for my Lakshmi and your Kotikokura?"

"Not if we scoured the whole Universe!"

"But what ails them both recently? They mope, they hide in corners, they grumble and growl and glare."

"They are jealous of the attention you pay Homuncula, Salome!"

An ink-black cloud passed slowly over the roof of the bower, followed by the crash of thunder and the blazing whip of lightning. The robots stopped fanning. The table shivered, tilted. The glasses fell and broke into a thousand fragments.

"Is this another earthquake, Salome?" Cartaphilus asked, anxiously. "You have chosen a bad spot for your New Eden."

"On the contrary, I chose this place because according to its history it has always been singularly free from volcanic disturbances."

"Why these extraordinary manifestations then?"

"The Earth is impatient to witness the birth of Homuncula, Cartaphilus," I said jubilantly. "I am certain she has moved. I feel her in my womb!"

"Are you sure Nature is benign? May she not be rather angry — or jealous — because you usurped her prerogative of creation?"

A thunderclap interrupted our conversation.

"I must go and see what has happened to my child — to our child!"

"No, wait until the storm is over, Salome!" he warned.

I laughed. "The Wandernig Jew — symbol of storm — fears a little wind?"

"I am a coward for your sake, my love. I tremble to see you exposed even — to a cold."

"Come, dearest!" I insisted, pulling him gently after me.

The trees bent upon themselves like people suffering with the cramp. Crows flew in circles, cawing wildly. Animals crouched, trembling, or dashed into hiding places. The ground was a bed of torn leaves and petals.

The gates of the New Eden were ajar. The iron Golems made no gesture to defend the entrance.

"Cartaphilus," I whispered, "my heart is a hammer beating against my chest. I am afraid. Perhaps you are right. Nature may be in a malevolent mood. Homuncula —"

Cartaphilus smiled. "Nature may be entirely unconcerned about us. She may have an attack of hysterics for a reason all her own."

The light of the lamp shed its soft rays, caressing like the hand of a mother. Homuncula reclined upon her elbow. Her face beamed with intelligence.

"The Earth jubilates, Cartaphilus — even if a trifle too violently. Look at Homuncula! She has moved! She is nearly born! Have you ever seen a more rapturous vision?"

Homuncula smiled.

"She welcomes us, Cartaphilus!"

Addressing Homuncula, I said: "Creature of Beauty and Joy, awake! Let the rhythm of Life stir within you! The Earth, your lover, trembles with ecstasy! Awake!"

Homuncula stretched forth her arm.

I knelt and pressed her hand to my lips.

"Your skin is honey and wine. It soothes and it inebriates."

"Speak!" I pleaded.

Homuncula's lips parted and curved. An intangible something pervaded the place, like the memory of a forlorn song or the kiss of one who is no more.

Cartaphilus and I looked at each other, our hearts overbrimming.

Homuncula closed her eyes slowly, as if weary or dreaming.

On tiptoes we walked out of the Sanctuary of Birth.

Cartaphilus rummaged about the library, looking over my curiosities and mementos, reading a few lines of a manuscript, making annotations.

"Are you ambitious, my dearest?" I asked. "Are you working for your doctor's thesis?"

"I am seeking, Salome — seeking —"

"What?"

"The Truth."

"Why this mania for that ill-mannered boor? Is not Falsehood more charming, more seductive?"

"Ah, if I but knew the origin of these strange and magnificent trophies, Salome! If I were certain of their significance — what promises, what joys, what delights made their former possessors relinquish them to you!"

"Cartaphilus is jealous!" I clapped my hands.

"Who would not be of Salome?"

"Who should not be of Cartaphilus?"

"The wild oats a man sows are as ephemeral as the wind. The Earth refuses them. They pass over her face rootless and seedless."

"And the wild oats of woman, beloved?"

"They grow luxuriantly. Their greedy roots devour and destroy the others. They ——"

"My delightful Victorian!" I exclaimed, embracing him. "How the dear Queen would dote on you and your rhetoric!"

"But Salome, Queen of the Earth, mocks me!"

"She mocks you and she loves you!"

"Why do you not tell me the whole truth, Salome? Am I not old enough to hear — everything?"

I shook my head. "You are a child — forever. Besides, you have read my memoirs. You are holding a chapter in your hand now."

"Yes, of course. I have even appended some marginalia where you malign me in your own incomparable fashion ——"

"Where I malign, I tell the truth, Cartaphilus."

"Thank you. And what of the kitchen Latin of that nun to whom you dictated what seems the truth ——"

"A bride of Christ who had betrayed her bridegroom, but to me was faithful. She was the only woman I trusted, with the exception of Joan — the Pope. She was immured, Cartaphilus. I did not fear her."

"I understand. But why couldn't she write so that I might read with greater ease? Why didn't you teach her sufficient grammar to distinguish between the masculine and feminine endings? Half of the time I cannot tell the gender of your loves."

I laughed heartily.

"Perhaps it was done purposely — to intrigue my adorable husband."

"He is a living toy — to tease and to torment ——"

"And to love ——"

Cartaphilus hugged me so tightly that I screamed.

"Love and revenge at the same time?" I asked, breathing deeply.

"Love without end," he answered.

He opened a fan and read:

> *"Has Nature changed her way,*
> *That Noon comes dancing*
> *In the midst of Night?*
> *It is the luminous face of Salome*
> *Flooding the hall!"*

"Thus wrote the Son of Heaven to my Beloved," Cartaphilus smiled, a trifle sadly.

"There are no more Sons of Heaven," I sighed.

"But Salome is still Noon dancing in the midst of Night." Cartaphilus placed upon my finger the Fisherman's Ring.

"Your Holiness," he said, kissing the tip of my slipper, "bless me!"

"Cartaphilus, Isaac aforetime," I said with pontifical gravity, my forefinger raised, "be thou faithful and loving to Salome, thy wife, now and forever. Sin no more!"

Instead of making the sign of the cross, I kissed his lips.

"What Pope offered you the symbol of his power — and for what favors?" Cartaphilus asked, his brow knit in mock anger.

"This ring is poor Joan's, Cartaphilus. I took it off her finger when she died, after giving birth to her baby. Once upon a time she begged me to remember her and her love when you embrace me. Embrace me, Cartaphilus, that I may remember her."

Cartaphilus pressed me to his chest in a long and passionate embrace.

"Cartaphilus," I said, "I could not remember Joan. In your arms I remember no one, nothing. The Universe is annihilated."

"Salome, I love you," he said, and his heart flew into mine.

Cartaphilus unfolded parchments and opened books, deciphering through the magnifying lens the hieroglyphics of Egypt and Arabia.

"The road to Truth, my love," I teased him, "is a thorny one."

"But a most exciting and interesting trip, nevertheless. When pieced together these fragments, these stray memories, the bits of parchment and of silk woven into one continuous pattern would astound the world. Let mankind hear your story as it heard mine — more or less mutilated and misinterpreted — but generally true."

"I am not a writer, not ambitious to appear in print," I laughed.

"Of course not, my love. You and I live. Let those who fear life, write. And yet, is it not just that they to whom Nature distributes a few niggardly years upon Earth, should learn of the challenge of Princess Salome to the Moon and to Fate?"

Cartaphilus laughed a little.

"My friends, Professor Basserman and Doctor Lowell of Harvard, who still doubt my true existence, in spite of the fact that they published my autobiography, would spend their remaining days most delightfully, dovetailing the fragments of your tale, the Story of Womankind."

"How much more innocent is the life of man compared

to that of woman! In spite of the prattle of freedom and the overthrow of Victorian prudery, is the world able to endure the truth?"

"The truth — no — Salome, but the partial truth. Those who dare can guess the rest."

I laughed.

"Let me dispatch these precious documents to my incredulous friends. Or, rather, let us place them in a golden pouch sealed with the seal of Solomon, and upon our next trip to Europe, drop it from our airplane over their doorstep. Perhaps, too, your words will stir to quicker life the Superman and the Superwoman — the Supersex race!"

"Homuncula —"

"Even if Homuncula is born," he interrupted, "she cannot possibly populate the Earth in a day! Would it not be better for her, if the world dimly comprehended the audacity of your vision?"

CHAPTER FIFTY-EIGHT

VAGUE PREMONITIONS — HOMUNCULA MOVES — THE DISTURBANCE OF LAKSHMI — THE JEALOUSY OF KOTIKOKURA — HOMUNCULA RISES — EARTH PROTESTS — PARADISE LOST — LIFE WITHOUT END AND LOVE WITHOUT FLAW.

"CARTAPHILUS, I am uneasy. I have been uneasy for days."

"Dearest," he said, caressing my hand, "what do you fear?"

"I do not know. For two days I have not seen Homuncula. I dare not enter the New Eden. I have become superstitious. I count the number of steps I take to the Gate. Whether I walk slowly or fast, the number is always unpropitious, according to the Kabala."

Cartaphilus smiled sadly.

"If you and I cannot overcome our ancestors, is it surprising that even our present contemporaries, despite mechanical contrivances, and laboratory discoveries, are still the craven slaves of the totems and taboos that ruled the lives of their animistic brethren ten thousand years ago?"

"We are born in fear, Cartaphilus, and die in fear. Fear of joy and fear of sorrow. And the greatest of all fears is a mother's fear. When I saw Homuncula last, she was more beautiful than ever. She sat up and looked at me with her eyes that dazzle like jewels. I felt a slight pressure of her hand. She breathed gently like a zephyr that vaguely moves a leaf, now one way now another. And yet — I am disturbed!"

I started. "Do you not smell the sulphur in the air, Cartaphilus?"

Cartaphilus took a deep breath, and shook his head, laughing a little.

"After all, Diana, former Mistress of Hell, should not fear a little sulphur."

His effort to console me left my anxiety unassuaged.

"Last night the owls screeched ominously. The bed shivered."

"It may have been love's sweet memory."

"For a week now," I said, paying no attention to my husband's facetious remark, "the seismograph has behaved strangely. The barometer plays hide and seek."

"All of which proves nothing, except that at this season in this part of the world, the weather fluctuates rapidly, and that somewhere — maybe a thousand miles away — a volcanic eruption is shaking the Earth."

"The animals refuse to come out of their dens. The birds migrate."

Cartaphilus persisted in his endeavor to cheer me.

"It's in the nature of birds to change their abode."

"Those which do not discover the free passage — the secret air-lane, through the poisoned gas-screen, drop dead."

"There will always be enough birds to grace your paradise."

"The servants forget their errands, stop in the middle of the rooms, as if pulled by ropes. Things drop out of their lifeless hands. Suddenly, as if driven by an invisible power, they rush about aimlessly."

"Servants, my love, are reputed to do precisely what you say under very normal conditions."

"The Golems and the robots no longer act with absolute precision!"

"The dynamos need readjustment!"

"Lakshmi — did you see Lakshmi, Cartaphilus?"

"Certainly, I saw her, this morning."

"She is not the Lakshmi I have known for centuries! She has not touched a cabbage-leaf for weeks. Her throne is empty. She wades in pools like a common turtle. She does not tap my ankle or look at me quaintly. Last night she scared me. Her eyes glowed like red-hot coals in the dark."

"You are nervous, my love, and you see your own anxiety reflected in Nature."

"No, Cartaphilus. You yourself, are you not anxious about Kotikokura? He has been away for days!"

"The servants have seen him on several occasions. He is in the woods. Some atavistic impulse — an overpowering need to hold communion with the ghosts of his ancestors or trail the spirit of a simian inamorata ——"

The shadow which crossed the forehead of Cartaphilus belied his unconcern.

"He is jealous of Homuncula, Salome. That is quite natural. He fears that my affections will be transferred to another. He showed the same temper on other occasions. Once in England I remember distinctly, when I spent a night with W. H., the boy-girl of Shakespeare's sonnets, he growled for hours. He vowed he would strangle her."

"Do you think he is planning to harm Homuncula, Cartaphilus?" I asked, trembling.

"No. He strangles only wives — mortal wives — his and mine. That's his specialty. Come, my dear, you having braved life, and steered over the uncharted Ocean of Time, will you run your boat into a morass of fear?"

"Let me place my head upon your chest, Cartaphilus. Be my haven."

I was on the point of falling asleep, when a terrific crash made us both jump.

I rushed to the window, and threw it open.

"The sky is an ocean of blood!"

Cartaphilus could not conceal his anxiety. He vainly sought some meteorological explanation. His words were lost. A hurricane struck against the building like a catapult. It raised dust in spirals, overtopping the trees, and drove over the horizon mountains of clouds.

Riveted to the spot and unable to utter a sound, I pressed against Cartaphilus.

The ceiling cracked. The walls tottered. Paintings fell to the floor as if torn by angry hands.

"Cartaphilus," I whispered.

Servants rushed through the courtyard screaming, their faces livid. Horses and sheep and animals of all descriptions broke through their stables and cages, monkeys clambered up and down trees, howling and bellowing and roaring and chattering — an insane cacophony that froze the marrow — a wild stampede like a madman's nightmare. And above all circles of predatory birds —

The Earth shivered — a Colossus in fever. A thousand jets of flame rent the sky. Trees fell, their roots in the air. The ground cracked, and out of its parched mouth spouted long streams of boiling water mingled with steam and mud and débris, the vomit of a drunken world!

"Cartaphilus, let us flee! Let us hide from Chaos!"

We tried to move. Our feet were nailed to the floor. We could not budge.

"Is this the end? Are we doomed, my love?" I asked.

"Whatever our fate, it is well. We are together!"

The building rocked as if shaken by an invisible Samson.

"Cartaphilus!" I pressed his hand.

"Salome!"

The walls tore from their angles, like a body dismembered by the rack of the Inquisition. Mortar rained down slowly like blood.

"If we could only move, Cartaphilus! If we could only escape. What power holds us in its claws? Why are we paralyzed?"

A thousand thunderbolts merged into one! Our heads reeled. Our bodies swung.

"Cartaphilus!" I shouted.

The building lay about us, a mountain of shapeless stone. . . .

In the distance a silver vision, dawn breaking through a fearful night: Homuncula —— !

"Cartaphilus, look!"

Cartaphilus held his breath.

"She has arisen! She lives! Homuncula!" I called, "Goddess of Love, hail!"

Homuncula stretched her arms forward, more luminous

than the rays of the sun. She took a few steps toward us. Her body swayed like a young poplar in the summer breeze. Her bosom heaved with the rhythm of divine music.

The mad upheaval which preceded was a mere tarantella compared to the tumultuous cataclysm, to the wild uproar which followed the appearance of Homuncula. The elements were furious beasts tearing at the Earth, ripping its entrails. Flames gushed from its cloven body like water from a gigantic geyser. The abysmal wound, like a monstrous gaping mouth devoured the exquisite vision of Homuncula and my Garden of Eden.

A hill of molten débris obliterated the ghastly cicatrice....

"Cartaphilus," I sobbed, "she is dead. Nature, the jealous hag, has swallowed her up."

"Ca-Ta-Pha — Ca-Ta-Pha — Ca-Ta-Pha," Kotikokura's voice pierced the air.

Cartaphilus whistled a strangely modulated sound like the call of the African tribe. In one moment from nowhere Kotikokura appeared, and threw himself at his master's feet.

"Ca-Ta-Pha — Ca-Ta-Pha —" he murmured, kissing his hands.

"Kotikokura, my eternal friend," Cartaphilus patted his head.

An invisible hand unbound our legs. We were free!

"The strange mysterious Power that gave us life has shielded us once more from destruction," Cartaphilus said.

"Look," he continued, "the clouds are vanishing as if swept away by a broom. The hurricane is a feeble groan. The Sun, a golden cornucopia, pours its bounties upon the Earth once more."

"Everything will live again, save Homuncula," I said bitterly.

Kotikokura was radiant.

I scowled. He hid his face.

"My love, Nature will not allow man to interfere with her dominion. Longinus, you remember, always quoted the proverb —'Natura non facit saltum.' She prefers her slow and measured step to sudden flights. This is the meaning of the Tower of Babel and the flood, of Jahveh's disinheritance of man. We are recapitulating a chapter from the Book of Genesis," Cartaphilus continued; "we are driven from the new Eden perhaps for the same reason that expelled Eve from Paradise. In the beginning all creatures increased by division like the amœba. It is possible that Nature or the World Spirit was experimenting with a new way of reproduction in which love and sex played a part. But the experiment was not yet complete.

"The sin of Adam and Eve was not that they ate of the Tree of Knowledge, but that they ate too soon. Had they waited longer, Life would have evolved a procreative process combining efficiency with agonies of delight, not the messy and brutal method prevailing on earth that lacerates woman's body and makes her a slave to the Moon. Adam and Eve impatiently reached out for the new gift before the gods had perfected it. You and I and all mankind pay the penalty for their rashness."

"Homuncula was too beautiful, too perfect," I sighed.

"Exactly. But do not mourn her, Salome. A hundred thousand years, or a million years hence, the incarnate child of your dream will appear again. Nothing is lost in the universe. Then the Earth, no longer her stepmother, will welcome her. And, if we still live, Homuncula will recognize you, Salome. She will know she was conceived in your soul. She will know that she is your daughter."

"Your words, Cartaphilus, are more soothing than balm."

"What matters it, Salome, if the world perish, so long as our love blossoms forever?"

"Thus Adam must have spoken to Eve or Lucifer to Lilith. It is the language of all lovers, eternal or ephemeral."

"Look, Salome, the golden pouch we destined for our two professors lies resplendent like a crown on top of the ruins. Is it the seal of Solomon which protected it, or some magic of our own? Kotikokura, my friend, be the guardian of the priceless treasure!"

Kotikokura swung it upon his back.

"Lakshmi," I said suddenly, "where is Lakshmi?"

"Where is Lakshmi, Kotikokura?" Cartaphilus asked.

wrought upon us by Jesus and Jokanaan. If we weary of life, we can barter our immortality for descendants."

I did not answer.

"Or shall we continue to live within the limitations imposed upon us by the forces within us? Shall we accept the mold of the Potter?"

We continued in silence for a long time.

"Cartaphilus," I said, "have we really lived? Perhaps we are only the symbol of mankind, dreaming of life without end and love without flaw? Who are we?"

"We are reality which gives birth to dream. We are the dream in whose liquid eyes reality is mirrored. We are the horizon toward which humanity travels forever."

"— and which forever recedes."

THE END

Made in United States
Orlando, FL
20 July 2023